I0565576

PAUL GRIMSHAW

VOYAGERS
OF THE GRAY DAWN
Finding Henry

Travelers of the Gray Dawn: Part I

Paul Grimshaw is a freelance journalist, author, lover of history,
and working musician plying his trade along the
Grand Strand of South Carolina since 1998.

Voyagers of the Gray Dawn: Finding Henry, is his second novel.

VOYAGERS
OF THE GRAY DAWN
Finding Henry

Part I in the *Travelers* series

A NOVEL

BY

PAUL GRIMSHAW

CHART HOUSE PUBLISHING

SOUTH CAROLINA

CHART HOUSE PUBLISHING, OCTOBER 2015

Copyright © 2015 by Paul Grimshaw

All rights reserved under International and Pan-American Copyright Conventions. Published in the United States by Chart House Publishing, South Carolina.

Grimshaw, Paul 1960—

ISBN – 13: 978-0692394281
Library of Congress LCCN Pending

First Edition October, 2015   34567890

Chart House Publishing: www.charthousepublishing.com

Cover Illustration: Kimberly Dawn Clayton

Cover Design: William Craven

- for those who serve in the armed forces, and for the 70-million men, women and children who perished in World War II.

Acknowledgements

Special thanks go to my family, and also to my friends, who are not only *like* family, they *are* family. Since we all share common ancestry, we're stuck with one another.

Thanks, too, to those many readers who've encouraged this work, suggesting that my *Travelers* story go on.

Author's Note

Some of the characters featured in this book are historical figures—most are not. Some of the dialog attributions are factual, based on historical record—most are not. Some of the incidents portrayed actually occurred—most did not. This is a work of fiction. What is real and what is imagined is for you, dear reader, to determine through research, reflection and debate—an exercise not unlike our own journey through space and time. Enjoy.

"Anything short of God is not rational, anything more than God is not possible" – William James

"What we see depends on what we look for." – Albert Einstein.

"In the firmament above, and in the deep, on all the seven planes, and farther on, and all that's hidden to our eyes, and in all we see." – Baba Meher

VOYAGERS
OF THE GRAY DAWN

<u>Prologue</u>

Two years before the Wright Brothers flew at Kitty Hawk, physicist Ernest Lord Rutherford, a New Zealander, proved that radioactivity is a manifestation of sub-atomic change. While in the age of horse-drawn carriages, and as the world's pedestrians were dodging horse manure in city streets, Rutherford dreamed of splitting the atom. He had moved to the U.K. and taught college at the University of Manchester. In 1908 Rutherford's doctoral student, Hans Geiger, invented a device for registering the decay of radioactive isotopes. The Geiger counter would remain the gold standard for six decades, and versions of it are still in use.

In 1911 Rutherford drew the first model of the Atom. Six years later he would achieve his long wished for dream by splitting nitrogen atoms into oxygen atoms. As World War I was raging, with the cavalry still on horseback, the atomic age was born.

The truly remarkable advances in science that seemed to spark suddenly into existence around 1900 were shaking up not only the world's great thinkers, but also anyone within range of a newspaper headline. The general public was beginning to catch on to that which before had been formerly reserved strictly for the academics. Also truly remarkable is that these exponential leaps in the understanding of our universe were happening during the tail end of the Victorian era—a time when electricity was still a novelty and reserved for only the wealthiest. It was a time when the sight of an automobile sputtering down a dirt road enticed large crowds to gather. In these first halcyon days of the early 20th century, men and women were contemplating ideas and proving theorems that would have had them burned at the stake just a few generations earlier.

The Industrial Revolution of the 1800s permanently altered the way in which a large contingent of mankind lived its life. Wars became mechanized, larger, longer, and more global in their reach. Most of the great thinkers of the day would have rather used their brainpower answering mankind's greatest questions, but were instead recruited into mankind's greatest folly—its own self-destruction.

*****

Germany, September 1941

Not all the German scientists drafted by Hitler into the Wehrmacht, the German Defense Force, went willingly. In fact, most did not. But some did, and did so enthusiastically, especially after the discovery of nuclear fission in 1939. The USSR and the United States were already mining fissile material and creating heavy water needed to control nuclear reactions. The German war machine, too, was making technological progress and, under Chancellor Hitler, had proven its utter disregard for humanity. Despite this progress some leaders in the Wehrmacht remained unimpressed, to the dismay of those loyal scientists on the cutting edge of discovery who were glimpsing the atom's darkest, deadliest, and most extraordinary secrets.

Chapter 1

Stuttgart, Germany
6 p.m. September 15, 1941

"Nein, nein, NEIN! We must continue Uranprojekt," pleaded German scientist Hans Weissenberg. "We are close to the result der Führer is after. This will win the war and end all future wars."

Weissenberg, balding and rail thin, looked especially frail that afternoon. He hadn't seen the sunshine in weeks and had only eaten enough to keep from passing out.

"Don't you see? Don't you understand?" pleaded Weissenberg. "We must shift our focus from the laboratory to the industrial, and we need time!" The scientist flushed with anger. "We need resources! We need proper centrifuges, many of them!"

"I'm sorry," said Colonel Otto Ackermann, standing at the doorway of Weissenberg's laboratory and workshop. Ackermann's rotund frame blocked most of the late afternoon light coming through the door's window. Two guards stood behind him at attention. The Colonel unconvincingly feigned sympathy as he spoke slowly.

"We need to put our resources into other programs. Don't *you* understand?"

With deliberation and practiced ceremony, Ackermann paused to slip sausage-like fingers back into his favorite pair of leather gloves. He wore so much leather he squeaked when he moved.

"Do you not read the papers, Weissenberg?" asked the Officer, admiring his own hands, now sheathed in formfitting lambskin, "or listen to the wireless?

Germany is on the march. Most of Europe flies the Nazi flag. We do not need your wonder weapon." He nodded to the two guards to open and hold the door. He turned to walk out but stopped short, spinning on his booted heel.

"You are to report to Berlin in three days for reassignment. Oh, and by the way, there seems to be some pesky question regarding your... shall we say... heritage. Please bring your documentation. I apologize for the inconvenience, but all good citizens of the Vaterland must occasionally endure the injustice of a second background check. You understand."

This was not a question but rather an order from the Schutzstaffel, the SS, the most feared military division in the Third Reich. Ackermann and his escorts left the scientist with the bitter taste that came after every visit from the SS.

An hour later, at dusk, Weissenberg led two of his assistants in an action that would have had all three executed if caught. They gathered four large crates of material, two toolboxes, a generator, food, water, and a lead-lined container filled with a small quantity of enriched uranium-235, which, at the time, was the largest stockpile in the world. They loaded it all into a camouflaged Mercedes truck, and disappeared into the German countryside.

Four hours later, they arrived at Festung Schloss, a crumbling, overgrown stone structure that had been a nobleman's castle three centuries earlier. An ancient beech forest in a virtually uninhabited region of Central Germany surrounded the ruins, near Rhön; it was a place known to Weissenberg from his youth.

"When I was a boy my parents would bring me here, camping," he said, somewhat wistfully as the driver slowed and parked near a gaping entrance in what was left of the structure. "No one will bother us."

With the truck unloaded, just before midnight, the three men began to assemble a device without even the benefit of it having a name. After laying blankets and sleeping bags on the cold castle floor and hanging kerosene lanterns for illumination, the men continued in their mission to build the first nuclear device ever intended for warfare. They would work non-stop for 24-hours before resting briefly, away from the intrusions of disbelieving, meddling, so-called 'military advisors.'

"We have three days to prove that fat bastard wrong," said Weissenberg to his dutiful assistants, who were just as excited about nuclear fission as their boss.

On the morning of the third day at Festung Schloss, the gray skies overhead threatened rain, but Weissenberg was undaunted. This would be the day. The device was four feet long, three feet wide and three feet tall. A 1,100-lb. mass of metal and wire, it was not pretty, but what lay concealed inside was uglier still; a small, deadly, uranium core.

Too heavy and too dangerous to move, they left the device where it was, bolted to a reinforced table on the ground floor of the castle. A rudimentary wind-up clock timer, when activated, would give the men approximately 15 minutes to drive to the top of a nearby ridge to film and witness what they hoped would be the world's first uncontrolled nuclear chain reaction.

"If it works I'll be a national hero," said Weissenberg, with no particular concern to share any of the coming glory, "then there will be little bother regarding my heritage."

The three men, Weissenberg, the driver, and the other loading a 16mm film camera, raced as fast as the large vehicle would take them.

Less than two minutes into their trip and only about a kilometer away from Festung Schloss, the unthinkable happened.

"What's wrong?" asked Weissenberg, sensing a change in their speed. No one answered. The truck labored another 20 meters up the hill when it spit and lurched for a second time.

"What's wrong with this damned truck?" he screamed again, as the vehicle sputtered, slowed, and regained its speed momentarily only to falter once more.

"I don't know, sir," answered the driver. "It was fine earlier." Only then did he look at the fuel gage, firmly on the German equivalent of "E." His face went ashen.

"I think we're out of petrol," he said, as the truck's engine finally ceased and the vehicle slowed to a stop. He applied the brake to keep from rolling backward, downhill.

"Get out, now!" yelled Weissenberg, who had no need to convince his assistants of what they had irreversibly set into motion. "There's no time to stop this. Run! Run to the top!"

Still much too close to the castle below, the three men sensed they were in real danger and placed their only hope for survival in making it up and over the ridge before the device detonated. They scrambled straight for the top of the ridge, through the thick woods, camera in tow, with the castle and its ticking device less than two kilometers away below them. Stopping for breath, they turned to look at Festung Schloss and could still see the truck parked where it had quit, on the road 200 feet down the hill.

The forest smelled of rich earth and wet leaves. Weissenberg was momentarily lost in memories of boyhood explorations of these same hills until he remembered why they were there.

"Higher!" yelled Weissenberg, glancing at his watch. "We need to make the ridge!"

Eight minutes had ticked by since they'd activated the timer on the device. Even in the midst of their predicament, the scientist constantly recalculated formulas in his head. Would the implosion work? Would the lenses focus the energy as precisely as required?

Weissenberg's moment of scientific triumph, known just to himself and his two assistants, would come only from the benefit of dozens of scientists before him. He'd concluded, correctly he hoped, that bombarding a large radioactive isotope with a smaller one would result in a splitting of the larger, in a process called "fission." This had already been proven, theoretically. At the end of this process, in a sub-atomic miracle, the weight, or mass, of these particles would

3

be slightly less than before the fission. This so-called "mass defect," a term in use since the 1920s, had its consequences.

Weissenberg had simplified it and explained it to Ackermann weeks earlier in hopes to buy more time and to get his point across.

"As matter cannot simply disappear," he said, "it must go somewhere, or be converted into something else; in the case of fission, it's converted into energy, a lot of energy." Ackermann was unimpressed and dubious, but let the scientist continue his work, until their last meeting where he pulled the plug, suspecting Weissenberg had committed the mortal sin of being a closeted Jew.

Unknown to the scientist, and in an environment of paranoia and distrust, Colonel Ackermann had covert agents meticulously copying his notes, diaries, and drawings late at night after he closed up the laboratory, except, ironically, on the night he and has assistants escaped into the German countryside. Bugs were planted and conversations transcribed in an attempt to gain more information for a secret file code named: "Narrentraum," or 'Fool's Dream.'"

After weeks of effort, Weissenberg's team scraped together enough of the needed isotopes in rudimentary centrifuges to conduct the most important experiment of his lifetime, a culmination of four years' work. The device would use conventional explosives focused inward, concentrating the energy, compacting the core of uranium. This nuclear reaction, Weissenberg theorized, would result in critical mass, and an explosive force equal to the amount of radioactive material available and its mass defect. The sphere of uranium, though smaller than a baseball, weighed almost 100 lbs. Though untested, Weissenberg estimated that each gram of uranium would equal the force of 20,000 tons of TNT.

Eleven minutes and seven seconds after arming the device and starting the timer, it happened.

In a blinding flash of light 10,000 times hotter than the Sun, as fission occurred, the gray clouds parted momentarily to reveal blue sky. Any witnesses would have seen the color of the surrounding hills and the sky turn from a blinding white to purple, and green. As atoms changed their structure, on a sub-atomic level, splitting, creating a mass defect, a nuclear fireball and explosion vaporized the castle in a nanosecond. The blast was not much smaller than the U.S Trinity Test held at the White Sands Proving Ground, in southern New Mexico, years later, in 1945.

The explosion, though small in relative A-bomb terms, was still large enough to level two square kilometers of the Earth's surface in all directions. With it came a 10,000 degree firestorm extending outward to destroy some 3,200 forested acres. The castle, truck, Weissenberg, and his assistants, were instantly superheated to ash, and blown to the four corners of the earth by the shockwave, felt 100 kilometers away. The three men were eyewitnesses to their creation, if only for a split second.

Though the device went off three minutes and fifty-three seconds early, the men were doomed regardless. The extra time would not have been enough to escape Hell's fury, even in a properly fueled vehicle. Weissenberg for all his brilliance had underestimated the blast radius. He and his assistants didn't live long enough to see the goblet-shaped fireball, and the mushroom cloud overhead. When witnesses in the nearest town, some forty kilometers to the west, first saw the sky light up and minutes later heard the boom, a few farmers got in their trucks and drove in the direction of the column of smoke. A curious plume rose forty-thousand feet, some seven miles, into the air.

When the farmers arrived two hours later, they discovered the devastation and a smoldering, shallow crater where the ruins of Festung Schloss had previously sat undisturbed for centuries. The sandy soil in the blast zone turned to a greenish glass in the intense heat. Those closest to the site attributed the explosion to an abandoned sulfur mine. Beyond a little curiosity at the time, the story faded. No one was reported killed or injured. The truth of the detonation was known only to three Germans reported missing from a government lab three days earlier.

Colonel Ackermann suspected the truth upon hearing rumors of the explosion and of the disappearance of Weissenberg and his assistants. When an Allied air raid ended Ackermann's life two days after Weissenberg's disappearance, any investigations were stopped short. Only the secret Narrentraum file gave any hint to what may have happened.

Little hard evidence of the detonation ever turned up; no nearby eyewitnesses came forward with anything useful or credible. Geiger counters, had they been employed, would have detected residual radiation in patterns extending hundreds of miles in the direction of the region's winds. The site was mostly forgotten and naturally reforested itself.

Decades later cancer deaths spiked moderately in the wake of the fallout, leading some conspiracy theorists to suggest this first, formidable nuclear test took place in the forested lands of Central Germany, not the dessert in New Mexico.

No glory would come for Weissenberg. No headlines published by the Third Reich's propaganda machine would include his name. Details of his successes with the centrifuge, and in the laboratory had been smuggled out in whispers and rumors long before his disappearance, along with a top secret project file.

Locked in Ackermann's office, the Narrentraum file didn't see the light of day until it was rediscovered in 1942 by a group of industrious, desperate Nazi scientists, all members of the Uranverein, the Uranium Club.

Chapter 2

Princeton, New Jersey
7:25 a.m. September 5, 1943

The man puzzled over his predicament. He scratched his head and cocked it to one side like a dog trying to grasp the incomprehensible. He dismounted his recently disabled bicycle, which looked to be in about the same shape as the man himself. Like his bike, he was beyond middle-aged but not ancient, dented here and there, in disrepair, but still usually quite functional. The bike's chain had simply jumped its worn front sprocket. It took him several moments to comprehend what had happened, and set a course of action. Before initiating a repair, one any 10-year-old boy would have managed in seconds, he looked around for help. Seeing none, he rubbed his hands together and with some difficulty, eased himself to the ground. At 64, he moved carefully, slowly.

The early morning sun was warming the air in Princeton, New Jersey. The drowsy, small college town was waking with students, teachers, and business people all starting their daily routines, though in the late summer of 1943, not much was routine. The world had been at war for six years, with the Japanese terrorizing China and the Pacific since 1937, and the German's invasion of Poland in 1939. By late summer 1943 the U.S. was fully involved around the globe, and though Hitler was stunned by his defeat in Stalingrad, on the Russian front, he was far from surrender.

"Klar ich Grubeln diese (Clearly I am over thinking this)," said the man to himself in his native German, not the broken English he used in public. "Wenn nur," he said. (If only)

"Wenn nur…vas?" asked a young man, who happened upon the distressed cyclist. He repeated the German phrase he'd just overheard and added, "Was ist los?" (What's the matter?)

6

"Ahh, sprechen sie Deutch?" asked the man hopefully, standing, and smiling slightly.

"Nur ein wenig (Only a little)," he said.

"Vell, zhen let's not travel down zhat difficult road," said the older man, nervously twisting his bushy, gray and black mustache. "Tell me, vhat do you know about bicycles?"

"Well," began the neatly dressed young man, removing a tweed jacket. He dismounted his own bicycle, and laid it on the grass. "My father taught me how to repair my own bikes. I ride one every day and have ridden all my life, so—"

"So, zhen vhat have I done here?"

"Nothing too serious, Dr. Einstein. The chain has just popped off."

"Ah, ze chain has pooped off. Ok." He paused, eying the helpful young man. "So you have ze privilege of knowing how to fix bicycles, und of knowing who I am, yet I do not know you."

"I am Dr. Rollins, Henry Rollins," said the young man, extending his hand. Dr. Albert Einstein accepted the invitation, with an appreciative smile for the services rendered.

"Dr. Rollins?" asked Einstein, looking closely at the man who looked to be around the age of most of his students at the Institute, and who was wiping his grease-stained fingers on a handkerchief. He had short, dark brown hair, and wore it neatly parted on the left, in the style of the day; a sharp contrast to the free-for-all mass that sat upon Einstein's head. "You are a student? No," he corrected himself. "You must be a kollege at the Institute?"

"Well, no, actually yes," said Rollins, blushing. "I wouldn't say "colleague" exactly, though I am at the Institute, but only just recently, and we've not had the pleasure of speaking—until today. I've been hired as teaching assistant in the Math and Physics Departments. In fact I've covered your classes on a few occasions and have been meaning to speak with you."

"Yes, okay," said Einstein quickly, eager to get moving again. "Und now ve are speaking und meeting today, und now you will poop ze chain back on for me and ve may both finish our ride together."

Rollins, just 22, was the youngest post-doctoral faculty member the Institute had ever hired. He'd graduated from Princeton University at 20 and was gaining a reputation as a brilliant mathematician, theoretical physicist, and educator, though not even Rollins really knew exactly how to explain theoretical physics to the uninitiated. When asked, he told people that he simply "sensed that there was more to the world than the eyes could see, and more to the universe than a brain could imagine."

Rollins and his young wife, Margaret, experienced, first-hand, the mysteries of Euclidean Space—three dimensions of height, width and breadth, along with the fourth dimension of time. Together these dimensions create four-dimensional spacetime, and with it come all manner of possibilities.

An incident they rarely spoke of from ten months earlier traumatized them both. Margaret vanished and reappeared two weeks later, shaken, disoriented and convinced she'd gone insane. Henry Rollins, not so willing to dismiss her event as insanity, had other ideas and was eager to share his thoughts with the one man who could shed light on the mysteries of spacetime, the man who created the concept and might be willing to discuss multi-dimensional travel.

Dr. Einstein knew more about the mechanics of spacetime than anyone living, past or present. Rollins, like Einstein, was obsessed with quantum mechanics, and wormholes, in particular. He was convinced that math, science, and physics were the keys to unlocking the secrets of nearly everything, and that the mathematicians, physicists, and theologians were all on the same sacred path.

Though Einstein occasionally taught mathematics at the Institute, he'd been missing classes lately. He was preoccupied with the War, and the growing threat of something horrible on the horizon—something born of uranium and plutonium. It was all too frightening to speak aloud, but worrying enough to speak about in whispers, letters, and top-secret, closely guarded communiqués.

As the sun rose in the sky, the campus gradually came to life. Like salmon swimming upstream, students and faculty converged at the Institute's main door, as a growing din of cars and conversation began to fill the formerly quiet streets around Princeton.

In less than a minute Rollins had Dr. Einstein's bike back in working order and the two men resumed their commute to work, both lost in thought. Einstein was mentally preparing for a meeting with Robert Oppenheimer. The two men had begun a correspondence, friendship and working relationship that had involved the President of the United States, Theodore Roosevelt. Einstein's 1939 letter to Roosevelt had warned of the coming nuclear threat. In his letter he wrote:

> *"Sir, in the last four months it has been made probable—through the work of Joliot in France as well as Fermi and Szilard in America—that it may become possible to set up a nuclear chain reaction in a large mass of uranium, by which vast amounts of power would be generated. Now it appears almost certain that this could be achieved in the immediate future.*
>
> *This new phenomenon would also lead to the construction of bombs, extremely powerful bombs of a new type. A single bomb of this type, carried by boat and exploded in a port, might very well destroy the whole port together with some of the surrounding territory."*

Though a pacifist, Einstein's letter went on to recommend that the U.S. enhance its own enrichment programs and to locate uranium ore wherever it might be found. He suggested the government fund efforts to match the progress and knowledge already possessed by the Germans, who led the world in the nuclear race.

"I understand that Germany has actually stopped the sale of uranium from the Czechoslovakian mines, which she has taken over…"

His letter continued, and he closed,

"Yours very truly, Albert Einstein."

President Roosevelt responded, and with growing evidence to support Einstein and others, he approved the formation of the $26-billion Manhattan Project, a project in which Einstein was forbidden to collaborate. The top secret experimentation and testing that led first to the Trinity Test in 1945, and the first official detonation of a nuclear device, employed fission caused by a plutonium implosion, delivering a 20 kiloton yield, equivalent to 40 million pounds of TNT.

But that morning, still two years before Trinity, the sun was shining, and the Indian summer would not be denied its restorative power.

Rollins, bright-eyed, youthful and energetic, slowed his riding pace to be polite, and Einstein nodded in appreciation. The elder of the two peddled slowly, steadily. He looked ahead at the young man and envied his ignorance. Though the general public was war-weary, very few of them understood a nuclear threat. In 1943 the world lived blissfully in an age before Hiroshima and Nagasaki, and decades before the cold war and terrorism would dominate the media and the minds of nearly everyone old enough to read or listen to a news report. On that September day only a handful of men and women on the entire face of the planet understood the devastating potential of splitting the atom, and it weighed upon Einstein mightily.

*****

At the Institute, the two men, some 45 years apart in age, parked their bikes and parted company, each walking to a different office, on opposite sides of the large building. Einstein's first floor office had a view overlooking the park-like campus where the sugar maples were already threatening an explosion of vivid fall color. By contrast, Rollins' office was a windowless cell with a desk and file cabinet, and he couldn't have been happier.

An hour later, at a large table in Einstein's office, Robert Oppenheimer, who would later be known as "the father of the atomic bomb," sat, pencil in hand, pouring over notes and stacks of paper. Oppenheimer, like Einstein, was Jewish, and of German descent, though he'd been born in New York City, and was 20 years Einstein's junior. Taller than most men, thin and angular, Julius Robert Oppenheimer was a chain smoking overachiever, receiving his doctorate at 23. His brilliant mind for the burgeoning field of quantum mechanics, and theoretical astronomy was tempered only by his religious studies. He had taught himself the ancient written language of Sanskrit so that he could read the Bhagavad Gita, a 700 verse Hindu scripture, in its original form. Years later, when asked about his creation and the bombing of Hiroshima and Nagasaki, he would quote the Hindu god Vishnu by saying "Now I am become death, the destroyer of worlds."

Oppenheimer used personal finances to aid in the departure of German physicists fleeing Nazi Germany in the mid-1930s. Though a likely communist, if not an unapologetic sympathizer, Oppenheimer hated the Nazis and joined the Manhattan Project in 1942.

Two F.B.I. Special Agents assigned to surveillance of the scientist, sat in their car and watched the tall, thin man enter the Institute. In Einstein's office Oppenheimer lit another cigarette while one was still burning in the ashtray.

"Don't you see?" he said. "Albert, we can do this. It will work, and it will rid the world of its emperors and tyrants."

"Rid za world of its tyrants? Surely you're joking?" Einstein gazed out the window, and looked well beyond the acreage of the campus quad. "Zis vill create a new breed of tyrant vorse zan za last."

The phone rang loudly and intrusively. Einstein waited for the second ring, and then flipped a switch mounted to his desk. He had invented, designed, built, and installed the switch to cut the signal to the ringer. As an added bonus, whoever may have been calling whenever he engaged the 'Schalldampfer' (Silencer), as he liked to call it, first heard a loud painful buzz in his ear before the line went dead. Einstein's friends knew to call, let it ring once, then hang up and call again, letting Einstein know the call was friendly and from a pre-approved caller. He often said it was his greatest invention, and he usually took great pleasure in its use, but not on this day.

Oppenheimer knew of Einstein's aversion to the creation of the bomb, and understood the duality of his position; his conflicted sentiments. But allowing Hitler to be first out of the gate with an A-bomb was not an option. Of that they all could agree. Still, the creation of the bomb, by anyone, was only slightly less frightening. Oppenheimer, and to some degree Einstein, understood that being first with a viable nuclear weapon, one that the world could see, was the obvious, short term answer, though one with long term implications.

"It's coming one way or another, Albert," said Oppenheimer. "It will be better if it comes from us first."

"You're not even supposed to be in my office, Robert, let alone discussing zis wis me," said Einstein.

Sensing his colleague's lack of enthusiasm, Oppenheimer sighed, stacking his papers, putting them back into his briefcase, before leaning back and closing his eyes. He was to fly to Los Alamos, Nevada, the next day, having survived another round of questioning by the U.S. government who deemed him too important to the "project" to be removed because of his leftist leanings, but too dangerous not to be under constant surveillance.

Oppenheimer sat forward and looked at his troubled friend, who was still gazing out of the window.

"Albert, dear Albert," he said, taking a long drag on his cigarette. "It may be madness, but the one who draws first, and has the biggest gun, wins."

"Like za vild Vest?" Einstein asked, managing a slight grin.

Oppenheimer smiled back, crushed out his half-finished cigarette, stood and walked to the door. "I'll see you again, my friend."

Einstein listened to the man's footsteps echo down the hallway, while he sat, numb. Military plans and the folly of men saddened and angered him. Only math was pure. Only physics was infallible. Only light and gravity were chaste, uncorrupt, and innocent.

At the age of 15, while still living in Europe, Einstein wrote a paper entitled: "On the Investigations of the State of Ether in a Magnetic Field." By 17 he'd graduated from multiple universities throughout Europe, eventually renouncing his German citizenship, to avoid military service. In 1933 he immigrated to America with his second wife, who was also his first cousin, Elsa Lowenthal.

Early in his life, Einstein's reputation as a radical thinker and a man with an extraordinary mind was well known throughout academia and the scientific community. In 1911, using only his equations and mathematics, he predicted that light from any distant star could be bent by the sun's gravity. During a solar eclipse, eight years later, British astronomer and scientist Sir Arthur Stanley Eddington proved him right. Suddenly Newton was out and Einstein was in. But that was years earlier and a world away.

Einstein locked his door and returned to his desk. He sat, swiveled in his seat, and pulled open a wooden file drawer, producing a manila envelope with the initials "C.H." written across the top.

While the Manhattan Project was given to Oppenheimer, the U.S. government recognized Einstein as quite possibly the smartest man living, or whoever lived. If he had an idea for a military project that wasn't related to atom bombs, they were listening. His current experiment, one on which he focused all his time and energy, was one much closer to home—one pitting electromagnetism vs. gravity and light. These were the elements and properties of Einstein's oldest and fondest dreams.

He opened the file and spread it across his desk.

"Mein Gott," he said quietly. "Two days? Ver hast za time gone? Zey vant me to try in two days?"

He double-checked the U.S. Navy top-secret communiqué against a calendar on the wall, and rocked back in his chair. He put his fingers through a mass of unkempt hair that was in layered shades of black, gray, and white. He twisted his mustache. These habits helped him think.

"I need some muscle. Somevone smart, somevone young, somevone I can trust," he thought.

As if on cue, a light tap came at the door. Einstein shuffled his papers into one stack, and flipped them over, face down.

"Ya. Who's zhere?"

"Sorry, Dr. Einstein. I don't mean to bother you. It's Henry Rollins." He yelled through the closed door. "I wondered if you were going to class this morning or if you'd like me to cover for you. The Dean keeps calling me; says your phone is out of order."

Einstein guessed the call he'd ignored came from the Dean, whose right ear was probably still zinging from the Schalldampfer. He smiled broadly at the thought.

"He says he can't reach you and he needs an answer!"

"Rollins?" Einstein thought. He searched his mind for a face with which to put a name. "Rollins?" he asked aloud, this time yelling from across his office and through the closed door.

"Yes, it's Dr. Rollins! I helped you with your bike earlier...?"

"Ja, ja, Rollins! Of course. Just a moment."

Einstein unlocked the door and let Rollins in, closing and locking it behind him. Rollins looked warily at the Doctor, not accustomed to being locked in places, but said nothing.

"Sit down," said Einstein, leading him to the chair occupied by Oppenheimer less than 30 minutes earlier.

"So," said Einstein. "First things first. About class today? No, I von't be going."

"Okay. That's fine Dr. Einstein," said Rollins. "I'll be happy to cover for you. I think today's syllabus schedule has a lecture and study of Unified Field Theory. I'm sure the class will be disappointed to hear me babble on, rather than to hear it explained by the creator himself." Rollins smiled, expecting the doctor to smile back at the flattery. He did not.

"Tell me, Rollins. Vhat ist za Unified Field Zeory?"

Rollins hadn't expected to be quizzed so early and directly by the very man who'd spent his life in pursuit of the theory's completion. He wasn't sure if he should be offended or privileged to take a shot at it. He cleared his throat.

"Well, today's class is supposed to be an *introduction* to the theory, so to boil it down, I guess I'd say...the Unified Field Theory is a melding of the general theory of relativity as it relates to electromagnetism. That is, the theory of gravitation as a geometric entity and property of space and time, its curvature and how magnetic radiation might effect it. In its purist form it's the theory that ties all other theories together."

Rollins walked to a chalkboard and found a spot not already filled with equations.

"May I?" Rollins asked, picking up a piece of chalk, holding it in the air.

"Oh, zis should be gut. Be my guest," said Einstein, still not smiling. While Rollins wrote on the chalkboard Einstein reached into a paper sack, producing an apple. He took a bite, a bit of juice running down his fingers, which he wiped on his wrinkled, gray sweater.

Rollins wrote out the equation of Relativity in a series of letters, numbers, several equals' signs, and a pi figure, drawing on both Simple Relativity and General Relativity. He drew a line under it and wrote out the equation for Electromagnetism. The equation was not complete, as the Unified Field Theory had never been proven out, but in its simplicity, Rollins' diagram spelled out a basic level of understanding, one of which Einstein, its creator, approved.

Albert Einstein finally broke a smile. Then he chuckled, which led to an uncontrolled belly laugh and a slew of German words Rollins couldn't make out.

"Close enough, Rollins!" said Einstein, still laughing. "Zeher gut! You're hired."

Rollins also smiled, thrilled with the apparent sanction from his hero. He headed toward the office door, eager to get to class.

"Ver are you going?" said Einstein, "Sit down."

"So… you want me to cover your class today?" he asked.

"No, my boy, no class today. Ve'll cancel. I call za Dean."

No longer in a hurry to make class, Rollins stepped toward Einstein's desk, clearly with something on his mind. "Dr. Einstein, if you had just a moment, I wanted to ask you about the—"

"Nein! No time, go home, pack your bags. Ve're going to Philadelphia in za morning. By za way, how do you feel about boats?"

Rollins stood, confused. "I don't really like them," he faltered, as Einstein pushed him through the door into the hallway.

"Ve vill fix zhat in za morning! You vill love zis boat, I promise!"

Chapter 3

In Henry Rollins' small apartment, which sat not far from the northern edge of Princeton University's sprawling campus, a pretty, young woman fussed over the stove. The apartment smelled salty and rich from the meal being prepared. The woman had dark hair, short, and set with a permanent wave. She wore a form-fitting dress, and her porcelain complexion was set off by dark red lipstick. She looked as much like a fashion model as a recent college graduate and wife of a newly-hired college teaching assistant, one who had just been unexpectedly told he'd be leaving town the next morning.

"I don't know, Margaret," said Rollins to his wife. "Dr. Einstein just said 'You're hired,' and he'd tell me more in the morning, and did I like boats?"

"You hate boats, Henry," said Margaret, flipping two pork chops in a cast iron skillet. "You don't like the water and you don't swim well."

"I'm just as confused as you are, sweetheart, but I'm not turning down Dr. Albert Einstein. This is the opportunity I've waited for ever since you…well, you know."

"Not tonight, Henry," said Margaret. "I don't want to talk about it, I don't want to even think about it."

"Well, tomorrow I'll be in a car with *the* Dr. Einstein for three hours, and I'm not passing up the opportunity to discuss…*the incident*."

She didn't acknowledge his comment, still unwilling to talk about her disappearance from just over 10 months earlier and her husband's theories.

"And about the job, regardless of whatever it is he wants me to do, how could I say 'no?' If he said 'Rollins, my boy, you're flying to za Moon,' I'd say 'Let's go!'"

"Flying to the moon?" laughed Margaret. "Now that I could almost believe."

She turned the gas burner to low, and looked at her husband and smiled, though he didn't see it.

Meeting as freshmen in college, they'd fallen quickly, madly and deeply in love. They'd married at 18. Perfectly matched in temperament and intellect, they were best friends, lovers, and were both fascinated by science, though the mere mention of *the incident* still sent waves of nausea coursing through Margaret's body.

Decades later they'd call it P.T.S.D, *Post-Traumatic Stress Disorder*. In 1943 there was no such terminology. After combat, psychological stress was simply known as 'battle fatigue.' The best diagnoses the doctors could come up with for Margaret was a very generic 'nervous disorder,' for which they were too eager to prescribe seriously strong drugs or worse. One doctor had suggested Electroconvulsive Therapy, something the couple soundly rejected. Another doctor hinted at a lobotomy if her condition worsened, and another prescribed an insulin-induced coma.

In the end, she rejected all that modern medicine might offer. She suffered in silence on bad days, and felt she was returning to 'normal' on the good days. Mostly she let time and a loving husband help her into recovery. The occasional glass or two of wine or a stiff whiskey helped her to relax, but she was too smart to let the drinking get out of hand.

Margaret Rollins taught English part time at the local high school. As was becoming a trend among women of her generation, she moved easily between the roles of new wife and homemaker, and her career. Moving to stand behind her husband, who was pulling silverware from a drawer, she put her arms around his neck and whispered in his ear.

"How long will you be gone, my sweet, smart, handsome scientist?"

"The Great One didn't say. I hope only a few days."

"I'll miss you." She nibbled on his neck and he reached around to stroke her arm.

"I will count the seconds, my dear, and won't be gone any longer than I have to be. I do know we're going to the Philadelphia Navy Yard. I'll be working directly for the U.S. Navy. Beyond that—"

"Bring me back a sailor," she teased.

"Oh, you'd like that," he said, sitting, pulling her into his lap. "You've always had this thing for sailors." He kissed her and hugged her tightly.

"Dr. Rollins," she protested. "I'm a married woman, and there's food still cooking."

"Damn the pork chops. I want to taste the sweet fruit of your love."

"After dinner, my sweet. After dinner."

Princeton, New Jersey
9:40 a.m. September 6, 1943

The next morning two black cars, one following the other more closely than necessary, rolled to a stop in front of the Rollins' apartment. Two Navy MPs got out of their cars and walked toward the front door.

"You're so good to me, Henry," teased Margaret, peeking through the curtains in the living room. "Here's your ride."

Ignoring her sarcasm, Henry stumbled down the stairs, a small suitcase in hand, just as the doorbell rang. Three loud knocks made them both jump.

"I'm sweating like a pig," said Henry, beads of perspiration covering his face.

"Poor baby," said Margaret reaching for a cloth handkerchief from her handbag, patting dry his forehead, and cheeks. She looked him over and had to put her hand to her mouth to stifle a giggle.

"What?" asked Henry, sensing her amusement.

"It's nothing," she said, suppressing laughter. He glared at her and she gave in. "Oh, your argyle socks are mismatched, that's all."

A second loud knock spoke to the urgency and impatience of the men at the door.

"Coming! Be right there!" Henry looked at his feet and saw a bright blue sock on his left foot, and a red one on the other. He let out a moan as the men at the door knocked again.

"Don't worry about it, Henry," said Margaret. "Go. No one will notice. You'll be great. Just be careful."

"I will call you as soon as we get settled," he said.

"Okay," she smiled back. "Bring me back a present. At least get Dr. Einstein's autograph for me. Don't forget to call...I mean it!" They kissed quickly, and he turned and left the apartment, walking toward the street, leaving her to watch him awkwardly navigate in unfamiliar, military territory.

Rollins was escorted to one of two unmarked Navy vehicles, and was ushered into the back seat next to Dr. Einstein, who glanced out the window and smiled at Margaret still peeking through the curtains. A humorless naval officer sat in the front passenger seat along with a driver. Rollins didn't know the officer or the driver, adding to the mystery of the day ahead. They were in the lead car and made haste down the street as Margaret watched them turn the corner, and out of sight.

As she watched the two cars leave their Princeton neighborhood, she fought back pangs of anxiety. She'd learned to mask her distress when Henry was around. When he wasn't it was harder to fight off. The anxiety would take hold, like a school bully who could no longer be avoided. Sometimes the disquiet and fear blossomed into something much more crippling. She clutched the handkerchief like a prayer cloth, still moist from her husband's nervousness, inhaled his scent, and replaced it in her small handbag.

Separations were difficult for the couple, ever since *the incident*. Eleven months earlier Margaret went missing from the couple's country home in Maryland, one left to them by Margaret's family. Her disappearance, reappearance, and the tale she had to tell of a dreamlike world where things were similar, but not the same, resulted in this lingering emotional trauma that still haunted them both. While she was beginning to dismiss the event as pure hallucination, Henry was starting to believe her wild descriptions of this other world, and it became his obsession.

Nearly 11 months later she was better, and they were returning to some sort of normalcy, which led to confidence that she'd be okay during a brief separation. With the Navy vehicles no longer in sight, she closed the curtain, just as the phone rang, saving her from an all-out cry.

She picked up the receiver. "Hello."

"Mrs. Rollins?"

"Yes, this is Margaret Rollins."

"This is Principal Skinner from Sugarland, Maryland."

"Yes," she said searching her mind for a connection.

"You applied for a teaching position via mail a few weeks back? We've got an opening for you starting immediately, if you're still interested."

Margaret was silent for a moment, shocked by the call and the offer. Two months earlier she'd mailed out 30 resumes and had not received a single response.

"Yes," she said. "Yes! Yes! Thank you! I'm very interested! I have to talk it over with my husband, of course, and he's away on…on business. But if you can wait a few days, I'm sure the answer will be yes. So, yes! Thank you!"

They finished their short conversation, wherein the Principal had promised her the few days she'd requested, but no more. Then they talked about Sugarland, her childhood home, the job, and the salary. It was all she'd dreamed a first fulltime teaching job might be, in a place she loved more than anywhere in the world. The good news chased away most of her separation anxiety and she sat on the couch, pleased with herself, wishing Henry was there with her to celebrate. But he was not. Henry Rollins was caught up in his own euphoria at being with his idol, arguably the most famous theoretical physicist to have ever walked the Earth.

*****

"Guten morgen, Henry," said Dr. Einstein, more chipper than Rollins might have expected.

17

"Guten morgen, Dr. Einstein," answered Rollins, an ear-to-ear smile forming on his boyish face. "This is some mysterious adventure I've agreed to. When do you tell me what we're doing and where we're going?"

"A fair question," said Einstein. He seemed to be waiting for permission, which came in the form of a nod from the officer in the front seat.

"Ahh…he likes you," said Einstein. The uniformed officer ignored him. "Zis ist all very hush, hush, you understand?"

"Top Secret," corrected the officer, finally speaking. "Good morning Dr. Rollins."

"My apologies," said Einstein. "Henry, zhis ist Commander Koenig. He ist my keeper, my handler, und now he ist your handler, too."

"Good morning, Commander," said Rollins. Koenig nodded, and Einstein continued.

"Zis damned vore ist good for one zhing, Henry. Za government ist willing to pay for all manner of crazy schemes. Zis one ve're calling 'Canned Heat.' Zey vanted to call it 'Za Rainbow Project,' if you can believe zhat, but I talked zem out of it. If all goes according to plan, tomorrow around noon ve will bend light after turning za USS Eldridge into za vorld's largest electromagnet. Our hope ist to create a cloaking device, to render za ship invisible."

Rollins looked at Einstein, to see if he showed any signs that he might be joking. He did not.

"Ve're doing another simultaneous study in Norfolk, Virginia. We are trying to create an invisible port, if you can believe zhat!" Einstein chuckled as he said it aloud. "Ten, high-voltage, magnetic buoys are in place, und are tuned to match the electrical output of…vell I'm getting ahead of myself. It's all quite marvelous; und za U.S. government has spared no expense. I love zis country!" Einstein chuckled again, and twirled his mustache.

Rollins sat stunned, his mind racing. *Is what Einstein suggesting even theoretically possible?* Still unsure that he had heard Einstein correctly, he spoke.

"Invisible?"

"Ja, zhat's correct," said Einstein. "It's only an experiment, you understand. Ve needed somezing massive, made of metal, und za Navy needs to hide its warships. Ve are verking together on zis vun."

"What type of ship is the Eldridge?" asked Rollins.

Koenig spoke up. "She's a Cannon-class destroyer escort," he said. "We're trusting Dr. Einstein not to sink her quite yet. This will be her pre sea trial, no crew to speak of. He tells me we're only going 300 yards out into the river."

"How am I to help, Dr. Einstein?" asked Rollins.

"I'm not sure, yet, but you verked vonders vis a bicycle chain. I'd like to see what you can do vis two kilometers of copper vire und 100,000 volts of electricity."

They drove on in silence for a few minutes, while Rollins thought of the assignment. Then his mind drifted to a place from which he was never too far removed. He had spent the better part of a year grooming himself for a chance to have this kind of one-on-one time with Dr. Einstein, and now he was tongue-tied. He finally mustered his courage and spoke.

"Dr. Einstein," he began slowly, "I'm very curious about the Einstein-Rosen Bridge."

"You are? Gut for you. Me too," said Einstein. "My friend Nathan Rosen und I dreamed up zis one in 19…"

"In 1935," answered Rollins, assisting the Doctor's memory, eager for him to get to the point.

"Ja, it vas. Zehr gut, Henry. In 1935 ve published. It makes for wunderbar scary stories, no? The idea of tunnels through spacetime connecting parallel universes, it's too much fun. Und za math verks out pretty okay."

Rollins thought carefully about revealing too much, too soon.

"What are your thoughts on matter traveling through these...wormholes, un-accosted?"

"Un-accosted? Hmm. Matter? Vy not?" said Einstein. "Za math allows for it. Why do you want to know? Are you planning a trip?"

Rollins didn't laugh at Einstein's innocent remark.

"Actually, I believe my wife has already been. There and back again, so to speak." Rollins would leave it at that with the Commander and driver still in the car.

Einstein looked at his new assistant and determined he wasn't joking. "Ja, now zis I vant to hear more about."

"Perhaps we'll have an opportunity later?"

"Ja, ja. Sure ve vill, my boy. For now, we drive to Philadelphia, und I nap."

Chapter 4

Philadelphia, Pennsylvania
1:15 p.m. September 6, 1943

At the Philadelphia Naval Shipyard, a sprawling complex founded in 1776, two unmarked Navy vehicles were waived through a series of security gates. After weaving through a tangle of roads and checkpoints, they stopped at the waterfront at the confluence of the Delaware and Schuylkill Rivers. There, toward a remote section of the docks, the 300-ft, 17-ton USS Eldridge awaited her first active mission; one with which her commander was not particularly pleased.

"I won't let you do this," said the Eldridge Captain, Marcus Hammond. He spoke to Koenig through the car window before the vehicle had even rolled to a stop. "She hasn't even had her sea trials yet!"

Commander Koenig, Einstein and Rollins got out of the car, and stood awkwardly next to the angry ship's Captain.

"This is my tin can, and I have some say in what harebrained things are done to her," he continued.

"Are you quite finished?" asked Koenig. Hammond thought about continuing his tirade, but breathed instead, thinking it wise to listen to his superior. "Your tin can? I believe this ship is the property of the good tax-paying people of the United States of America, who paid for her, and who pay your salary." Hammond still was furious, but knew he'd protested as much as he dared.

A large crane moved into position, with a wooden crate, an eight-foot cube, attached by thick chains. The heavy smell of diesel fuel and river water filled the air. The unusual and pungent combination of odors made Rollins queasy.

"You don't look so vell, my boy," said Einstein. "Are you all right?"

"Yes, Sir. Just getting my bearings."

"Vell, get your bearings *und* your sea legs. Ve're going aboard."

An Officer's Assistant hurried to the men, giving each credentials to wear around their necks, and I.D. cards for their wallets.

"Follow me, Sirs," said the assistant, as the group followed him toward the gangplank.

The shipyard employed some 40,000 civilian and military personnel—this was wartime. Though a mass exodus was underway, the docks still buzzed with energy, supplies arriving by the minute. Activity aboard the Eldridge was high as the crew, preparing for a recently cancelled sea trial, was now pouring off the ship, full of delight and anticipation of unexpected shore leave. Onboard, Einstein and Rollins were escorted to special quarters, and each given a small, windowless birth, smelling strongly of fresh oil paint.

The Eldridge shuddered slightly when the first three-ton diesel generator was lowered to the deck with a resounding thud, just above their quarters. Einstein knocked on Rollins' door.

"We need to go up, Henry."

"Be right there," said Rollins, still not feeling quite himself.

On deck, 60-feet back from the bow, Einstein inspected the generator, now uncrated and gleaming, factory-new.

"See vhat your tax dollars can buy?" said Einstein. "Zis one machine could generate enough electricity to run a small town. Ve vill have five of zem vired in series."

A whistle blew as the crane began to swing a second generator into place. Within 20 minutes three more were loaded across the 40-ft beam of the ship, weight dispersed as evenly as possible.

Rollins, who finally got his work order, was charged with harnessing the power of the five generators together. He would prepare two points at which the nearly 1.5 miles of insulated copper wire would be attached. From the ship's bridge, Captain Hammond looked down upon the work, wondering what might become of his ship on this first, inconceivable, and infuriating mission.

Einstein, back on the dock, readied another crew who were moving eight spools of cable by forklifts, toward the ship. He noticed a quietness around the shipyard, not present just an hour earlier. Not a soul could be seen except for the crane operators and three or four men assisting them on the dock. Even the ship had become quieter now, reduced to a skeleton crew of less than 10 men. Rollins, too, observed a dramatic change in the level of activity.

"Where is everybody?' he asked of one of the engineers, sweaty and covered in grease from the installation. The crewman's face registered pure disgust.

"On leave," he said. "The whole damn ship was given leave except for me and a few other unlucky bastards. They've even cleared out half the shipyard. We're about it. Notice no one's around except us?"

"Yes, I do see that," said Rollins. "I'm not exactly here by choice either, if that makes you feel any better."

"It doesn't, but thanks for trying," answered the mechanic, dropping a giant wrench on the deck, and wiping his brow with a rag. "What are you guys up to, anyway?"

Rollins had been debriefed during the car ride from Princeton. Koenig had told him 'Tell no one of your mission. No one. Not your wife, your co-workers, your children ten years from now or your grand-children 30 years from now. Until this is declassified, if that ever happens, you are not to speak of this to anyone without clearance. This mission is top secret on orders directly from naval headquarters. The code name, that only those with the correct level of clearance will know, is 'Canned Heat.' Do you understand?' Rollins had understood. It was wartime and spies were most definitely on the prowl. 'If you are caught sharing information,' Koenig continued, 'no matter how innocently, you will be arrested, and if I have my way, executed for treason. What's our favorite motto?'

They all spoke in unison, as if in a grade school recital. "Loose lips sink ships." Rollins preferred the British version of the wartime phrase: 'Be like Dad, keep Mum.'

He looked at the hardworking engineer, but recalling the admonition, and in no mood for his own execution, lied to him.

"Damned if I know. They don't tell me anything."

*****

Later that evening Einstein, Rollins and the Eldridge's captain shared a meal in the Officers' Mess. The three struggled to make small talk.

"I apologize for the food," said Captain Hammond. "The galley is empty, except for one poor cook, and this was the best he could muster."

"I've had verse," smiled Einstein, as he swirled his fork around the reconstituted chipped beef, flour gravy and two pieces of toast. There was palpable tension at the table, and the bad food didn't help.

"Und I apologize for what you must perceive as a great indignity aboard your fine ship, Captain." Hammond did not respond.

"You really needn't vurry," continued Einstein. "Ve're simply proposing to pass electrical current around und through za ship's exterior. In fact, you could likely be aboard za ship vile ve conduct za experiment. As long as you're not grounded, it would cause you no bodily harm at all."

"I do not plan to be aboard while you turn my ship into a giant electromagnet," scolded the Captain, wiping gravy from the corner of his mouth.

"Nor do I," said Einstein, "but again, you needn't vurry. Und what if ve're successful? Do you know what it might mean? It could render your ship invisible to za human eye, radar, und any way of detection, aside from a strange trough, und a ripple in za water."

"Invisible? Really?" scoffed Hammond.

"Ja, invisible, really."

"How so?"

"Zhat vould take weeks for me to teach you za theories, und months or years for you to fully comprehend, but suffice it to say it comes from za basic understanding of zis question: 'Vhat ist visibility?' You look at your plate full of…vhat do they call zis? 'Scheisse und a shingle?'"

Rollins sputtered, blowing a poorly timed sip of water through his nose. The otherwise straight-faced captain couldn't hide mild amusement at Einstein's delivery and naming of the much-maligned military staple.

"Close enough. Go on," managed Hammond.

Einstein pointed to a single 60-watt bulb in a ceiling fixture.

"Light energy from zis small incandescent bulb, flies through za air in the form of vaves, bounces from za plate full of 'scheisse' und its 'shingles,' its image goes through your eyes' corneas upside down, to za retinas, to your brain, which processes za information, again, all using electricity. Anyway, large masses, with enough electricity, can bend zese light waves. If enough light is bent far enough around an object, in theory, you might render it invisible. Zhat's vhat ve're attempting. Ven your ship ist fully charged, to za observer standing 100 feet away, in any direction, ve hope it will simply appear not to be zhere."

Hammond, well aware of Einstein's reputation and resume, considered the military advantage of what he was suggesting.

"That would be something," he conceded. He paused to take a long, thoughtful sip of coffee. "Do you honestly think it will work?"

Einstein smiled and shrugged his shoulders. "Vhy not?"

Chapter 5

Rollins, hoping to engage Dr. Einstein in more wormhole theory discussion, sensed that his timing wasn't good. After dinner he made an excuse to separate himself and Einstein from the ship's captain.

"Dr. Einstein, would you join me on the deck for a moment? I have a few questions."

"Ja, sure Henry. Ve vill stretch our legs."

Einstein turned to Hammond.

"So, okay, ve begin again in za morning, say, around eight?" Hammond nodded.

"Shall we go up, Dr. Einstein?" asked Rollins.

"Please, call me Albert."

Rollins laughed. "No, I don't think I could bring myself to, but thank you. You've been my hero for too many years to be reduced to an "Albert."

"Breakfast here in the Officer's mess at 0700 hours," said Hammond.

"Oh gut Gott, vhat in ze hell is 0700 hours meaning?" asked Einstein. Hammond smiled at the world-renowned mathematician who didn't understand military time.

"7 a.m., Albert," said Hammond.

"Zhat's *Doctor* Einstein, if you please," he said with a twinkle in his eye. "I didn't spend 30 years in Genius School to be called "Albert" by every Tom, Dick, und Larry!"

The three men shared a laugh. Einstein was particularly pleased with his joke and chuckled all the way down the narrow gangway and up the flight of stairs.

On deck Rollins and Einstein walked to the still, silent machines just installed, and both men thought about the sheer power they represented. Rollins looked around the ship. It was big, and made entirely of metal. He recalled a popular child's science experiment where a wire-wrapped nail, attached to the opposite sides of a battery, turned magically into a rather strong electromagnet.

'Canned Heat' may have been the experiment of the day, but it was another theory of Einstein's that was never too far from Rollins' mind, and it showed on his troubled face.

"I sense somezing's on your mind," started Einstein.

Rollins nodded. "Yes, my wife's remarkable travels."

Einstein recalled Rollins' remarks in the car, just before his nap. "I must admit you're za first person to suggest they know of someone traveling in zis manner."

"Yes, no doubt it sounds quite implausible, Dr. Einstein," he said. "As I started to tell you earlier, I believe my wife Margaret has traveled through a wormhole, and I believe she's probably not the first or last to do so."

"Go on," said Einstein, intrigued, but skeptical. He'd heard from so many well-meaning but entirely misguided individuals over the years, he'd developed a natural armor against outlandish tales. But there was something about Henry he trusted.

"We own a house in the country, in Sugarland, Maryland, not too far from Washington D.C." Henry paused to take a deep breath. "Margaret vanished for two weeks a little less than a year ago. I was certain she'd been abducted, and I was insane with worry, frustration, even grief. I thought she was gone forever."

"I can't imagine," said Einstein.

"The police suspected me with involvement in her disappearance, but my alibis were truthful, and easily verifiable. Anyway, two weeks later she reappeared as suddenly as she had disappeared. We think…we think we've found…I don't know what words to use to describe it…a portal? She has no intention of ever using it again, but to the best of her recollection, she first disappeared in the den of our home in Maryland, and reappeared there as well. I know this all sounds crazy."

"Ja, ja, it does. But crazy ist right vhere all za best science lives. Continue, my boy."

"So, after the shock of her disappearance and reappearance settled, and we began to discuss it, it seems she had gone to a world like ours, but not ours."

"You're not suggesting…za Multiverse?"

"Possibly. I don't know. But I have to know. It's driving me…it's driving us crazy."

Einstein sat on a deck rail, and loaded a pipe with his favorite House of Windsor tobacco He struck a match and created aromatic clouds of smoke, which drifted around his head.

"Ze idea of za Multiverse has been around since, vell, a long time," said Einstein. "Zhere's Schrodinger's Cat paradox, za Many Vorlds interpretations, und others. Who are ve to say vis any absolute authority zhat your Margaret has not visited zis other place?"

"And not just Margaret," added Rollins, excited to be finally having the conversation with the one man who might not laugh at him. "Random disappearances, unexplained vanishings, even some forms of insanity…could this be why?"

"Sure, vhy not, Henry? But does za math prove it? Zhat's za key. Zhat's vhere your answer lay."

Einstein placed a fatherly hand on the young doctor's shoulder.

"You're togezzer now, you und Margaret, zhat's most important," he said, "und ve have a lot of werk to do tomorrow, so I'm turning in. Goodnight Henry."

"Thank you. Goodnight Doctor."

Rollins watched Einstein walk toward the hatch to the stairs and their quarters below deck. He contemplated what combination of factors might have made him the genius he certainly was. Einstein was a simple man, a man you'd not turn to look at twice on the street, except for his choice in hairstyles. He was simple, ordinary in many ways, yet he was a man with the greatest scientific mind the world might ever know.

Rollins turned his gaze to look at the generators strewn out on the deck of the Eldridge. Not wanting to disappoint his new boss, he focused and turned his thoughts away from wormholes, to Canned Heat.

"Mein Gott," he joked to himself, mimicking Einstein's accent. In the absolute quiet and stillness of the abandoned shipyard he was able to mentally calculate the amount of magnetic power to be generated, against Einstein's own equation of bending light. "Mein Gott," he said again. "It could verk. Vy not?"

He turned to head down to his quarters, and considered the Doctor's comments about the Multiverse and his proposition that possibly Margaret had indeed been one of its recent visitors.

"Margaret!" he said, stopping just short of the hatch and stairwell. "I'm in trouble."

At the far end of the Shipyard Rollins noticed two guards and a checkpoint blocking the only way in or out. He glanced at his watch. *9 p.m. I've got to find a phone.* A collection of buildings across the expanse of the abandoned dock, seemed as promising a spot as any for a payphone.

The dark and empty docks were eerily quiet; only the whistle of a distant locomotive made noise of any significance. Rollins wondered what kind of authority it took to shut down a shipyard of this size, in the middle of a war with shipbuilding at full steam. He wasn't the only one whose curiosity had been piqued.

Chapter 6

Within a workforce approaching 50,000 men and women it would be difficult to spot a single bad apple, but Heinrich Mueller, a.k.a. 'Henry Miller,' a recently hired civilian typist, was one of the worst, rotten to the core. When Mueller was first notified of the temporary closing of the shipyard, he took note. Something important was underway, and it was time for him to exercise a very specific set of skills. Not only could he type 70 words per-minute in flawless English, he knew the name, stats and position of every player on the 1943 squad of the New York Yankees. Perhaps more importantly, he could send newly developed German code, via a new form of longwave radio, as easily as picking up a phone.

Less than one year earlier, just four days after the Japanese bombed Pearl Harbor, Adolf Hitler declared war on America. German saboteurs had already been training for months to pass as U.S. citizens, at a camp near Brandenburg, Germany. The German Military Intelligence Corps would train and send these men and women to the U.S. in submarines, where they successfully came ashore at night. Aboard German U-boats these spies and saboteurs would make two known successful invasions of the U.S.—one along the south shore of Long Island, New York, in the town of Amagansett—the other would land near Mooreville, Florida, at Ponte Verde Beach. Both teams of spies self-destructed; their missions were foiled by capture, then claims of innocence, and unconvincing arguments that they never harbored any ill will toward the U.S. Six German men were executed after a secret military tribunal found them guilty. Two more were jailed.

Unknown to J. Edgar Hoover, then director of the F.B.I., a third team had made it across the Atlantic, to the East Coast of the U.S., landing near the summer resort town of Myrtle Beach, South Carolina. The team consisted of four men and one woman. One of the four men was 31-year-old Heinrich Mueller, and he was as loyal a Nazi as Hitler himself. Solid, with a prominent Germanic brow and cheekbones, but of average height, Mueller now found himself witness to a top secret mission, one in which the Wehrmacht would certainly be interested.

While watching the Eldridge, Mueller noted a lone figure headed his way. His three-story office building had a canteen on the ground floor, with a phone booth outside against the wall.

When Rollins eventually spotted and reached the phone, he made a collect call. In Princeton, New Jersey, at 9:08 p.m. the Rollins' home phone rang. Margaret picked it up before the first ring finished.

"Hello?" she asked. The operator sounded bored and spoke in a monotone.

"Collect call from Henry Rollins, will you accept the charges?"

"Yes, yes," she answered quickly. "Henry, are you there?"

"Yes Margaret, I'm here," he said, yelling into the phone, as if the distance between Philadelphia and Princeton required him to speak louder.

"Miss me?

"Yes, and I don't know why," she answered. "It's after nine, Henry, you were going to call when you got there."

"I'm sorry honey. We got very busy, and you know the military types. They don't give you much leeway."

"Henry, guess what? I got a job."

"What? A job?"

"Well, a job offer. Remember our last visit to the house in Sugarland this summer? And we both commented on how beautiful the countryside was?"

"Yes, I do."

"I sent the local high school a resume, about two months ago, when I sent all those others out. Well guess what? The Principal called, and offered me a job teaching high school English and History."

Henry Rollins was silent.

"Did you hear me, Hank? They offered me a job! $3,500 per year to start!"

"That's great, Honey," he said, trying to sound enthusiastic, which he was not. He'd just been hired on at the Institute in Princeton, and Sugarland was in Maryland, 200 miles away.

"You don't sound too happy for me, Henry."

"No, no, my sweet. I am, I really am, and I'm so proud of you. You'll be a fantastic teacher. But Sugarland…let's talk about this when I get home. There's just so much happening here, I can't think straight."

Margaret had been trying to avoid the elephant in the room. She didn't really expect Henry to quit his new job in Princeton. She knew it was unfair to even consider relocating, she had just been caught up in the moment. Sugarland had additional problems beyond its distance from Princeton. She fought to block out thoughts of her own unpleasant experience in the den of their Sugarland home, a place she loved but one that still made her uneasy.

"Well, so are you on a boat?" she asked, changing the subject.

Rollins thought about the stern warning regarding secrecy, and though he was dying to tell her every detail, he thought better of it.

"No, not at the moment," he said, not actually lying to her. She could see through his lies faster than anyone he'd ever known.

"Well, I figured that much, Hank. What are you there for? What's going on?"

Rollins sighed. "I can't tell you." There was silence on the other end of the phone. They always shared everything with each other, especially since *the incident*, no matter how mundane, or seemingly unimportant.

"I see," she said coldly, obviously hurt.

"Margaret, I want to, trust me, but they threatened me with execution if I breathed a word, and I just think it's better that we not discuss it, especially over the phone." She sighed, understanding the wartime need for secrecy. "It's just a silly Einstein experiment in Philadelphia," he said, "it's nothing to worry about."

"Oh, all right then," said Margaret. "I guess I understand. I just want you to be safe and come back in one piece from this…this Philadelphia Experiment of yours."

"With any luck I'll be home tomorrow evening." He thought twice about sharing details of his brief conversation with Einstein as it related to *the incident*, still so painful to them both, and decided it could wait.

"I'll call you if anything changes," he said. "I am so very proud of you. We'll find a way to make it work. I love you."

"I love you too, Henry. Call me tomorrow, the minute you can. Goodbye, my sweet."

"Goodbye, darling."

Margaret was disappointed that her husband hadn't been initially more excited for her, and that he couldn't explain what was going on. She hated not knowing, and wished he'd told her something more. She wasn't the only one who was hoping for loose lips from the young Doctor. Heinrich Mueller, a master at wiretaps, had heard the entire conversation, but was no better informed than he had been a day earlier when he'd received strange orders to type the '2 p.m. Evacuation' notice for the Shipyard.

Mueller had one small new piece of information, thanks to Rollins. He'd learned that Dr. Albert Einstein was at the center of whatever was going on. *The Dr. Albert Einstein,* he thought, *worthless Jew, traitor to the homeland.* With not quite enough information to send a new coded communiqué to Berlin, Mueller powered down the radio transmitter, and opened the cot he'd been sleeping on for five weeks, since first arriving in Philadelphia from South Carolina.

*****

USS Eldridge
5:55 a.m. September 7, 1943

Though Rollins had hoped to sleep until 6:45 a.m., just in time to make it to breakfast, the noise of trucks and cranes awakened him early. The clatter was beyond anyone's ability to ignore. Still groggy, he wandered into the narrow passage in front of their quarters, wearing boxer shorts and a tee shirt. He nearly bumped into Einstein, doing the same, also not dressed.

"Damnedest racket," said Einstein, looking somewhat jaundiced. His chronic health issues were never too far removed from daily life.

"Yes, sir. I couldn't agree more."

"Vell," Einstein yawned. "Let's get dressed und go see vhat kind of a mess zay are making up top." For Einstein 'getting dressed' meant throwing on ill-fitting, oversized, sometimes-filthy pants held up by a length of rope—not a belt—along with an undershirt, and sandals.

Topside, the morning light was shining brightly enough for Einstein, Rollins and Hammond to see that a 50-foot swing arm crane with a pulley had been attached to the center of the Eldridge, and that another crane was moving into place on the dock, just to the rear of the ship. According to plan, a team of five men led by an engineer was to begin tightly wrapping loop upon loop of copper wire from one end of the ship to the other, like an enormous, oblong ball of twine. The Navy reconnoitered the wire from the local utility company on authority of the U.S. government, with a promise to pay for it at the War's conclusion.

Six large spools, some three tons of high voltage copper transmission line, sat at the ready.

"Pardon me for saying so, Dr. Einstein," began Hammond. "But even if this works, these ships aren't designed to function with 15 tons of generators on the top deck, and another three tons of copper wire wrapped around her flanks. One medium sized wave would have us sunk with all this extra weight; look how low she sits in the water, and we're too top heavy."

"Ja, ja, good points Herr Hammond," said Einstein, "but remember, zis is just phase one. If it verks, ve'll fine tune za power und za vire to make za ships more acceptable to those who must sail them. Today ve do it zis vay. Ve go out into za river, away from za dock, und ve fire it up, und your ship appears to vanish. Poof! Or...maybe nussing but a loud buzz. Ve vill see."

30

Hammond, more distressed than ever, said nothing and watched as the crane began its first turn of wire wrapping lengthwise around his brand new ship-turned guinea pig.

Some 50 yards from the dock, on the top floor of a quiet building, looking through an unremarkable small window, the German spy, Mueller, took great interest in the activities outside.

Though he'd been ordered out of the shipyard with nearly everyone else, Heinrich Mueller stayed hidden in his office. The night before, he'd listened in to Rollins' phone conversation and now watched with binoculars the bizarre activity surrounding the ship. He turned on the shortwave and tested his codetone generator, a prototype even more advanced than the Enigma Machine. The codetone machine was a telegraph-styled instrument that sent sound waves, like musical notes, notes of various pitches and lengths. A machine on the other end deciphered the tones, which formed letters and words, and printed them on a page in the form of a message.

Flipping a switch on what looked like his desk typewriter, Mueller sent a test signal, typing the German word "sende" (transmitting). He waited a moment, then heard back through the radio a series of pitches, high and low, short and long. Mueller's ordinary appearing typewriter whirred to life, and printed a single word in German: "Bereit" (ready).

Since the code was indecipherable, even if the transmission was intercepted, he and his counterpart were confident enough in their security to begin each message with the time, date, and location.

"September 7 1943, 6:50 a.m., Eastern Standard Time,
Philadelphia Naval Shipyard. U.S. Navy conducting
experiment designed by Albert Einstein of unknown purpose
on Destroyer Escort, USS Eldridge. Stop."

Thirty seconds later Mueller's machine played its odd, mechanical song and his device began to spell out the once electronically coded but now decoded return message.

"Understood. Discover purpose of experiment. Stop."

Mueller frowned at the radio. "Easy for you to say," he said aloud. "Don't you think I'm working on that?" He sent a coded message back.

"Working on it. Will try to find a way onboard the ship. Out."

Still virtually abandoned, the Shipyard showed a little more activity than the afternoon and evening of the prior day. There were some 15 to 20 men, all with security clearance, operating the cranes and taking care of the vital systems

31

on board the Eldridge. It was as a common, low ranking sailor that Mueller thought he had the best chance of getting closer.

In the back of his office closet, Mueller pulled a false panel forward, revealing several sets of clothing he'd managed to steal over the previous five weeks. He decided on the uniform of a U.S. Navy Apprentice Seaman named David Sharp. Mueller had lifted the uniform from a laundry truck, after sizing up Seaman Sharp one afternoon and determining they were about the same size. He slipped into the uniform, hid his civilian clothing behind the false panel, and converted his coding typewriter back to something quite ordinary looking. Then he made his move.

With an efficient rhythm and procedure in place, the cranes were working smoothly, and the wire wrapping was well underway. Rollins, Einstein and the Captain managed to eat a quick breakfast in the Officers' Mess, and reconvened on the upper deck. Einstein and Rollins discussed the generators and how they would attach the copper cables. Sometime later Einstein sat and breathed hard, feeling every bit of his age.

"It's 9:15," said Einstein, looking at his watch. "I believe ve may be ready by 12 noon? Ja?"

"Yes, that seems about right," said Rollins, beginning to feel the excitement of seeing this odd experiment commence.

"Za Captain und a skeleton crew will maneuver za ship out into za middle of za channel und anchor her zhere," said Einstein. "Ve vill fire up za generators und set ze timer und interrupter."

"Once again, explain those devices, please?" asked Rollins.

"Ja, vell za first is a timer zhat vill give you fünfzehn minuten, sorry, 15 minutes, to set und leave za ship via za dingy. Once 15 minutes has passed, za generators will send current through za cables, und Canned Heat vill be set in motion. Captain Hammond says it vill take less than five minutes to get safely from za vaiting dingy und sail her back to za dock. Ten minutes or so later, und ve vill see, hopefully, nichts! Nussing! Ve hope to see right through her as light bends around za fully charged ship."

"Then what?" asked Rollins.

"Zen, some 10 minutes later, za interrupter, a circuit breaker, vill stop za current, shut za generators down, und allow you und za Captain und small crew to safely re-board za ship, und sail her back to her current position. Ja? Simple? Gut?"

"Yeah, sure, very good," said Rollins, not certain at all about anything. This was all happening quickly.

Though excited, Rollins was nervous. The September morning was cool, but he found he was sweating as he thought about what he was being asked to do. He could handle being on a boat moored to a dock, but one floating, or underway on the water, made him very worried, and he began to turn pale.

"Are you all right, Henry?" asked Einstein.

"Yes. It's just that… just…"

"Vhat?"

"I…"

"Spit it out, boy!"

"I can't swim, and I don't like boats very much."

"Ist ZHAT vhat's bozzering you?" laughed Einstein. "My boy, you needn't vorry. First, za Eldridge is a ship, a very sturdy und very large ship, not a boat, und ve'll get you a life vest zhat vill keep you afloat for days if need be. Oh my, but you are a funny boy, Henry. You make me laugh."

"Margaret tells me the same thing," said Rollins.

"You're lucky to have each other,' said Einstein, his smile diminishing slightly, as a memory took form. His thoughts drifted to his first cousin, who also happened to be his second wife, Elsa. His beloved died just a few years after the couple moved to Princeton. Lovers since 1912, married in 1919, Einstein and Elsa raised Elsa's two daughters from her previous marriage. She died at their home on Mercer St., in Princeton, and Einstein mourned her loss, never remarrying.

"So," said Einstein, snapping himself from the sadness that sometimes overtook him, "Ve should be close to ready, ja?"

Chapter 7

Philadelphia Naval Yard
United States of America
Morning, September 7, 1943

Though the football field-sized riverside quay was empty, compared to its usual hustle of men, Heinrich Mueller wasn't too worried; he knew his spy craft. *Walk with purpose, like you belong there, and everyone will believe you do.*

Mueller, at 36, looked a little older than the average Seaman Apprentice, but the stolen uniform fit well. He waited for an opportunity to leave a building the Americans thought had been empty. Cracking the door, he could see a bit of activity around the crane, now pulling back from the side of the ship. Each sailor in the small crew left to tend the ship was working double time, trying to accomplish the work of three. Even with all the distractions when Mueller walked quickly from the building straight toward the Eldridge, it didn't take long for him to be spotted.

"You, there!" yelled Captain Hammond from near the gangplank. Mueller froze in his tracks. "Seaman! You! We need you aboard, now!"

Mueller hoped he could fake it long enough to find out what was going on, make his escape, and make his report. For the moment he knew he had to play dumb, and play along. He ran to and up the gangplank, saluting Hammond upon his arrival on deck. It was the first time he'd ever been aboard an American vessel—an anti-U-boat subchaser, no less.

"Sharp," said Hammond, reading the nametag on Mueller's stolen uniform. "Get aft and help the Ensign ready the ship for maneuvers. He's short-handed. This whole damn ship is short about 200 men. They expect sea trials with eight of us. Damn the bureaucrats. Go!" Hammond was so busy he never thought to ask for credentials.

Mueller's English was exceptional. He knew "aft" meant the "rear," so he made his move away from the Captain, making mental notes along the way. He recognized the five large machines as diesel-powered electric generators, but he had no idea why the ship was wrapped in copper cable or where the crew was.

As he reached the back of the ship, he saw three men working on the ropes mooring the boat to the dock. The low rumble of the ship's engines indicated that it was running and preparing for something. But what?

Two large men in plainclothes, civilian contractors cleared for the mission, each brought a suitcase-sized device up the gangplank. Mueller watched as best he could from a semi-hidden vantage point, still confused.

"Gut," said Einstein, who, along with Rollins, was overseeing the installation of the timer and the circuit breaker they were calling the "interrupter." Both devices had been designed and built by Einstein himself. They were screwed into place on the deck and would run in the middle of the circuit in between the still unattached cable ends that were lying dormant, awaiting a tie-in to the series of generators.

With some difficulty Rollins, and an extra able-bodied Seaman, hoisted the heavy cables and made the final connections. With the last bolt tightened, project Canned Heat was ready for the critical phase of its test.

"I think that's it Dr. Einstein," said Rollins.

"Ja, seems to be. So, you sail out zhere to za middle of za river," he said, pointing, "you drop anchor, start za generators, enable za timer, und you all skedaddle back to za dock. Understood?"

"Yes, understood."

"You'll have plenty of time, so be methodical, careful, und you'll be fine."

Captain Hammond spoke from the bridge through the ship's P.A.

"All unauthorized personnel, please exit down the gangplank. The Eldridge is ready for maneuvers. Casting off in three minutes."

The Eldridge's powerful engines, smooth and certain, began an acceleration setting the whole ship humming. Einstein and a few other nonessential men left the boat, leaving aboard Captain Hammond, Rollins, six crewmen, and a German stowaway.

When the ship's whistle blew at the three-minute mark, Rollins jumped a foot into the air, as did Mueller, though no one saw him do so. Mueller hid amidships, just inside a hatch with a good vantage point. With the mooring lines retrieved, and the gangplank stowed, the Eldridge made her slow move away from the dock. After gaining his composure, Rollins donned the life jacket he'd been given and tied it snugly into place. He nonchalantly walked to the side of the boat, certain he was about to vomit.

With something not even large enough to call a skeleton crew, Hammond eased the ship toward the center of the channel. The port was empty, deserted; all shipping had been stopped for the day, with the port scheduled for reopening a day later. This was not Hammond's first command. He'd captained other Cannon Class destroyer escorts, and knew how to maneuver the ship, doing so with ease, confidence, and efficiency. The extra weight, however, was proving to be a new twist, though the relatively still waters of the river were forgiving toward a ship designed to sail the high seas.

On deck, Rollins depressed a green, electric start button on the first generator and it roared to life, humming with 25,000 volts produced by its 1.5 tons of spinning electromagnets. He repeated the process four additional times until all five generators were running, coughing diesel fumes into the air. He hadn't thought about noise protection until it was too late. With one generator running the racket was tolerable; with all five running it was deafening. He checked the gauges to confirm that all were producing between 23,000 and 26,000 volts. *Check.*

In a matter of minutes the ship was in position and ready to drop anchor, some 300 yards from the dock. A film crew stationed near all the watchful eyes on the quay set up cameras on a platform and signaled their readiness with a green flag. Rollins picked up the handset of a walkie-talkie provided just before departure. It was attached by wire to a 35-lb backpack transmitter. He dragged the entire apparatus along the deck, around a corner, so he could speak and hear over the roar of the generators. The two-way FM radio device had a range of some 10 to 20 miles and had just been introduced to the military by Motorola. On the dock a twin device signaled an incoming call.

Navy Commander Koenig, along with 10 other officials as eyewitnesses, sat on a small grandstand near the prototype communication device. He saw a red light flash, and looking pleased, picked up the handset and flipped a switch.

"Koenig, here." He looked to see that the other Navy brass were duly impressed by the new technology that he'd arranged to showcase.

"Yes, this is Henry Rollins!" he said, shouting to be heard.

"Yes," said Koenig.

"I work with Dr. Einstein and I'm..."

"I know who you are Rollins, for Chrissake. I can see you standing on the deck. What's your status?"

"Oh, yes, sorry Sir! All generators are running optimally! As soon as the anchors are set and the lifeboat is at launch-ready, I'll maximize their output and set the timer and the interrupter."

"Right. Well, get to it." Koenig put the handset on its clip and turned to Dr. Einstein. "So far, so good, says your boy, Rollins."

"He ist a gut boy und a smart man," said Einstein. "Brave, too. You know he can't svim?"

On board it was difficult to tell that the Eldridge's own engines had been reduced to an idle. The five generators running at close to full capacity dominated the sounds for a full square mile. They might turn the ship invisible, but unless the enemy were also deaf, it wouldn't do them much good. The Captain lowered two mighty anchors, one forward, the other aft, stopping the ship from drifting in the river's currents.

As the Captain left the bridge to meet Rollins on the main deck, he pointed aft toward a small manually operated winch that had already positioned a lifeboat ready to be lowered into the river. Once inside the lifeboat, the hand-cranked winch would lower them into the water, taking about three minutes. This would leave them at least ten minutes to make it to the dock in plenty of time to be out of danger, should something go awry.

The German spy and saboteur, Heinrich Mueller, was nervous, suddenly not so sure he'd made the smartest move by boarding the ship. It seemed to him, beyond all logic, that the Navy was planning to scuttle the Eldridge in the middle of the river, perhaps even dramatically by blowing it up. He pulled a small binocular from his pocket and noted the film crew and group of officers back on the dock. When he saw the lifeboat at the ready he rightly assumed the crew would abandon ship, and that he needed to be with them.

Just 40 feet away, Rollins made his final preparations under the watchful eyes of both the U.S. Navy and an uninvited representative of the Third Reich.

"I guess this is it," said Rollins to himself, setting the timer. "In 15 minutes we will witness a miracle or a mistake, one or the other." He gave his life vest straps one more tightening tug.

Chapter 8

"Let's go," Hammond said, arriving on deck from the bridge. He and Rollins ran to the lifeboat, with the remaining six seaman already aboard.

As one of the crewmen began to lower the boat, inch by inch, Mueller appeared and jumped in.

"Sharp! Goddammit!" said Lt. Hammond "Where the hell were you? We nearly left your sorry ass on board!"

"Sorry, Sir," said Mueller, with a more than passable American accent. The three crewmen looked at one another, and then at Seaman Apprentice David Sharp, not recognizing him, suspecting he was not who he claimed to be. Last in, Mueller was at the back of the lifeboat, avoiding anyone's gaze. One of the crew leaned into Captain Hammond's ear and whispered.

"Sir, we've never seen that man. In fact, we know Sharp, and that ain't Sharp. His uniforms were stolen three weeks ago."

Hammond played it cool, though all eyes were on the strange man sitting at the back of the lifeboat. Mueller couldn't help but notice he had become the center of attention.

The Captain watched Mueller while the lifeboat made its slow descent toward the water. He moved casually toward the imposter, ready to make a tackle. Too quick for the Captain, Mueller stepped back, and in one move steadied himself with the hanging ropes and pulled a German Luger handgun from inside his jacket. His eyes moved wildly, adrenaline pumping through his veins.

"Halt!" yelled Mueller, "Hands up!" His American accent was replaced by one that sent shivers up and down the spines of each of the other men on board. The sailor hoisting the winch stopped, as ordered, and the lifeboat hung some 15 feet above the water and 10 below the deck rail.

"Listen, it's over," said Hammond. "There're eight of us. You take a shot at one of us, the others rush you and you're down, and worse, you're down having shot one of us; it won't look good."

"You'll kill me either way!" cried Mueller, knowing what happened to German spies caught on American soil.

"Surrender now and it will go better for you," said Hammond trying to reason with the panicked German.

"What's the use…?"

Mueller held his breath and stared coldly at the Captain, aiming the Luger for a kill shot. This time Hammond was too quick and made a jump for him. Mueller fired, but missed and fired again, striking a crewman in the shoulder. In the scuffle Rollins reached for a rope to get out of the way of the sailors who seemed to be making progress subduing the German. The rope Rollins clung to with all of his weight and strength was the lifeboat's Emergency Bow Release Cable. When the front of the large craft suddenly tipped forward, Captain Hammond and the six crewmen tumbled out and hit the water, leaving Rollins and Mueller hanging on.

Mueller, needing both hands to keep from falling to the river below, dropped his gun. It hit the water, splashed, and sank irretrievably. With Rollins and the German swinging just a few feet from one another, the fight had changed from eight against one, to one-on-one in a split second. Rollins tried to figure a way out, wondering if he had gotten himself into something way above his pay grade. In the blink of an eye he'd gone from civilian teaching assistant to a combatant, fighting for his life with an apparent German spy.

"Rollins! Jump!" yelled Hammond. "He's unarmed! Swim for shore!" That was the wrong thing to say to a man who can't swim, even one wearing a life jacket. Panic took over and Rollins closed his eyes. He tried to muster the courage to do something, but jumping into the river was not at the top of his list. Unreasonably petrified of the water below, and with heavy ropes still attached to the stern of the lifeboat, Rollins climbed upward. Hand over hand he pulled himself back to the deck of the Eldridge. He'd have plenty of time to disable the timer, shut down the generators, abort the experiment, and regroup.

With his hands finally on the gunwales of the Eldridge, he looked down and saw the German scrambling up behind him, reaching for him. Rollins kicked at the spy, catching him with a lucky blow to the face. Rollins' upper body was now folded over the side of the ship, and with one final push he was up and over, but Mueller was not far behind.

Reaching for support, the German inadvertently grabbed the Stern Emergency Release Cable, sending the 16-foot boat crashing into the river, narrowly missing Hammond and the crewmen who were treading water. The captain and his crew climbed aboard the lifeboat, scrambled for its oars, and began rowing away from the ship, toward shore. Unarmed, Captain Hammond ordered their retreat for his crew's protection. He was worried about the crazed German, but even more afraid of what the Eldridge would become in the wake of Einstein's experiment, which now, according to his watch, was just five minutes from commencing.

Mueller, still clinging to ropes attached to the boom, pulled himself up and over the Eldridge's gunwales, unknown to Rollins.

From the water Hammond could see the German running to catch the lone scientist.

"Rollins! He's behind you!"

Rollins never heard the Captain's warning cries as the generators had fully warmed up and were running at top speed. The noise on the deck was deafening, Only 20 feet from the generators and the timer, Rollins felt a blow to the back of his head, which knocked him to the ground, nearly unconscious. The German kicked him in the side.

"For der Fürher, we will all blow up together, American pig!" Mueller was yelling to be heard over the generators' painfully loud churning.

"What are you talking about?" managed Rollins, still prone on the deck, dazed from the blows.

"Since I'm already a dead man!" yelled Mueller, "why not join me?"

"This ship isn't going to blow up!" said Rollins. "You don't have to die, neither do I. Jump in the river for all I care, make your escape. Let me shut this down!"

Mueller considered the offer but thought better of it. "No! It's a lie!" he yelled.

Rollins moved to a sitting position and glanced at his watch. *I still have four minutes to stop this.* When he stood he saw a PT boat with armed sailors racing toward the Eldridge.

"Look they're coming for you! Jump while you have the chance!"

Mueller turned to see the boat full of armed men, headed his way. He hesitated, considered his choices, and decided martyrdom was his only option. But before he could act, Fate played its hand.

Without warning, exactly three minutes and fifty-three seconds early, Einstein's timer opened its circuit, sending 135,000 volts coursing through 1.5 miles of copper cable. The load suddenly placed on the generators nearly shut them down, and they groaned under the stress of what was being asked of them. The efficient Fairbanks-Morse diesel engines, refusing to quit, came back up to speed, and the ship began acting as no ship before or since.

"What the...?" said Rollins, looking at the metal structure, which was beginning to hum, changing hue. Mueller, also stunned, tried to make sense of what he was seeing. As it got louder, the frequency and the volume of the humming caused Rollins and the Nazi spy considerable pain. They both tried in vain to lessen its impact by covering their ears.

The officials dockside, including Einstein, looked on in horror. They'd seen the entire incident, including the lifeboat crashing into the river. Through their binoculars they could see Rollins and what looked to be a U.S. sailor standing near the generators. They could hear the Eldridge screaming with unearthly wails, a quarter of a mile out into the wide river.

"Mein Gott!" yelled Einstein. "Za Unterbrecher! The interrupter!" He yelled in vain. "Come on Henry. Shut it down…"

"The interrupter…" said Rollins to himself, barely able to walk as the magnetic forces growing in the ship were playing havoc with his own physiology. He felt as if his internal organs were individually being shaken. He stumbled forward toward Einstein's device. He could feel his heart beating at twice its normal rate. Still many feet away from the only way to shut the experiment down, the ship shivered, then vibrated, creating ultrasonic vapor from the river water. The vapor rose into the still air, shrouding the 300-foot ship in fog. The Eldridge rattled and moaned with the sounds of tearing metal, as it began ejecting pieces of itself, and rearranging itself as if by unseen hands. As the physics of electromagnetism demanded, weaker metallic structures broke loose, reattaching themselves to stronger, denser steel elements of the ship.

A .50 caliber machine gun broke loose from its gunner's nest and flew across the deck as positive and negative charges moved it like an invisible puppet on a string. The gun had been preloaded for gunner's practice at the sea trial, and began spontaneously firing bullets, riddling the ship with holes, nearly killing Rollins and the German in the process. The men in the PT boat, recognizing the sound of machine gun fire, slowed just before reaching the now entirely shrouded ship. Unseen through the vapor, they feared crashing into the ship's side.

From the shore, now briefed by Captain Hammond on what had taken place, Einstein, Koenig, three Admirals and a film crew stared on in horrified disbelief.

"Henry. Oh, dear junge, my dear boy…" said Einstein quietly. "Vhat have I done?" The film crew kept its cameras rolling, shocked and thrilled at the images they were capturing.

"How long before the interrupter breaks the circuit," asked Koenig, emotionless.

"I don't really know. Four minutes or so," said Einstein looking at his watch, "but za timer circuit opened early, so…I don't know. I don't understand."

Within the shroud of vapor the ship rose out of the water, ripping the anchors from the riverbed. It lurched up and down, tilting left and right, once even bucking like a great steel stallion while the generators pumped on, doing exactly what had been asked of them. Structural steel threatened to buckle as the ship was thrown about, its outer hull superheated by the electricity, contorted in ways it was never meant to. The fluorescent blue-green glow, now an aura surrounding the ship, lit up the vapor cloud, and though it was midday it became bright enough to cast oddly-colored reflections on the buildings' walls behind the men on the wharf 300 yards away.

Just a few feet from the interrupter, Rollins pulled his hands away from his ears and noticed blood on his palms. He looked at his hands in shock, and then saw blood dripping on the deck. He wiped his face, realizing his nose was bleeding, too. The iron in his blood was reacting to the ship's intense magnetism. He wouldn't survive much longer. Behind him Mueller lay on the deck, unmoving. Rollins mustered every last bit of strength reaching for the emergency cut-off when his world went dark.

*****

At the Philadelphia Naval Shipyard the noise created by the generators aboard the Eldridge, along with the ship's own haunting vocalizations, stunned all who witnessed the ghostly specter. The metallic screaming caused by the tremendous electromagnetic properties generated, and its associated stresses, came to a sudden stop. The Eldridge's final groans echoed through the shipyard and faded quickly, leaving silence in their wake. All that could be heard was the gentle lapping of the water against the dock.

A light sea breeze blew in from the east, dispersing the water vapor cloud, revealing nothing. As if a magician had made a white dove disappear from plain sight in an instantaneous, flash-powder-filled misdirection, the Eldridge was gone. Canned Heat had been a success. The ship had vanished.

For a moment no one spoke. Then Koenig cleared his throat. "Congratulations Dr. Einstein," he said. "You've done it."

Three hundred yards out, where the Eldridge was supposedly still anchored and hidden by light waves bent by gravity, the PT boat moved slowly, as if looking for something that should be there. When the small craft made its way straight across the river, passing through what should have been the cloaked ship, Einstein breathed in sharply.

"Nein, Commander Koenig," he said. "I have not done it. Zis ist no mere trick of bending light. Zis is somezing…somezing else. I fear za Eldridge ist not invisible…it's gone."

Chapter 9

On the evening of her husband's second night away, Margaret Rollins was equal parts worried and angry. Certain Henry had just forgotten to call her, she fumed, turning on the radio so hard she almost ripped the power switch off the floor model Zenith. If she hadn't found Bud Abbot and Lou Costello so hysterically funny, she'd have sat and stewed. Instead she listened to her favorite comedy pair, and dreamt of their little country house in Maryland, where she hoped one day, sooner rather than later, she and Henry might be living permanently. She dozed in the large chair as the duo prattled on, hawking Camel cigarettes between each bit.

Two hundred miles away in a Philadelphia Naval Shipyard, no one dozed. An extensive search for the Eldridge, and for Rollins and the German, had been called off at 8 p.m., seven and a half hours after the ship's dramatic, unexplainable disappearance. Koenig, along with a few of his superiors and Captain Hammond sat at a table inside an office, with five guards at the door.

"Where's Einstein?" asked Koenig.

"Here I am gentlemen," said Einstein arriving late. "I vas told ve might be here for a vhile, so I had some laundry to send home."

Koenig and the others looked at the disheveled genius, and then around the room at each other. They were all thinking about how odd, in the middle of a crisis, that Einstein would engage his laundry service. He was never known for being overly concerned about his appearance. The far more pressing matters at hand kept them from focusing on his odd quirks, of which there were many.

"I realize you don't know for certain what happened, Dr. Einstein," said Koenig, his patience worn thin, "but please just give us your best guess."

"'Vhat happened,' you ask? Something miraculous und amazing," said Einstein, sitting, and loading his pipe, "but tragic. I fear for Dr. Rollins. It's my

43

fault he vas on board. He should have never been out zhere. He's not a soldier, or a sailor. He can't even svim. How vill I tell his vife?"

The officers at the table sympathized with Rollins' plight, but they were accustomed to losing good men in war. At that moment the officers in the room blamed Einstein for the loss of their ship and its unintended civilian passenger. Though they wouldn't say as much to his face, their displeasure with the world's most famous genius was mounting.

"You will not tell his wife," said Commander Koenig, waving away a cloud of sweet-smelling tobacco smoke. "May we remind you, Doctor, that this is still a top secret classified mission, not some Princeton University field trip gone bad. You've misplaced my $7 million boat. You will find the Eldridge and come up with a plausible explanation for what has happened. Those should be your only two concerns. Do you understand?"

"Ja, ja, I understand," he said, thinking only of Henry and Margaret, and of his own beloved Elsa.

*****

As if waking from a nightmare aboard a Coney Island thrill ride, young Dr. Henry Rollins inhaled sharply. He became fully conscious as his body violently reacted to the sudden cessation of a freefall. After a loud splash came a wall of water shooting 40 feet into the air on either side of the ship. Then came a calm and a gentle rocking. After the impact, he felt only the vibrations of the Eldridge's engines humming softly three decks below him. He tried to get his bearings but his head throbbed so badly he didn't want to open his eyes. After lying still for some five minutes or twenty minutes, Rollins didn't know, he rolled onto his back and stared skyward into the vast, inky blackness.

Heinrich Mueller, not much better off than Rollins, woke first, and rose from the darkened ship's deck. Trying to gain some composure after a traumatic and violent confrontation with the U.S. Navy, he decided not to immediately engage this odd American dressed in civilian clothing, who appeared dead, save for shallow breathing. Mueller disappeared in silence stumbling around a gun turret near the forebridge. Before Henry Rollins could even remember his own name, let alone what had just transpired, the German was gone.

Rollins sat up. *What the hell just happened?*

In a series of random flashbacks his memory began to return. *The Eldridge, the experiment.* The generators had stopped running, and all was relatively quiet, except for the fact that this ship was definitely under steam and moving slowly. *But where? How?*

Eventually he stood. He tasted iron from dried blood around his mouth, sharp and tangy. He reached to feel the smooth sides of the nearby generators

44

and found them cool to the touch. He assumed they'd been quiet and not running for some time. He looked at his watch, but only 10 minutes had passed since he last remembered checking the time just before all hell broke loose. *That's not possible.* He checked the generator's interrupter. *Well, you got that part right, Einstein.* The circuit breaker had flipped as planned, stopping the flow of electricity and the generators themselves. He looked at his watch again. It read 12:37. But the star field above him, and shimmering points of distant light in otherwise complete blackness, said nighttime, not lunchtime.

Looking around the ship, fore and aft, more bits and pieces of the previous hours began to coalesce as the fog around his memory lifted. *The noise was unbearable, the ship was howling, falling apart. Before that we were on a lifeboat. It fell into the river...the German.*

His heart raced as thoughts of the man who tried to kill him came rushing back to him. He looked left and right, just to be certain the German, dressed as a Navy seaman, wasn't standing beside him. With some stealth he traversed the length of the 300-foot ship, though none of the exterior lighting had been engaged. In nearly complete darkness, save the light from a few scattered small light bulbs marking hatchways and emergency gear, he saw no one at all. It was a big ship, but in 10 minutes time he'd covered a good deal of the upper deck, stern to bow. He began to think that he might be alone.

When he reached the pilothouse on the bridge, an ambient glow from radar screens and various pieces of navigational equipment helped him see a bit better. When he saw a panel with a clearly marked switch for the ship's floodlights, he flipped it, and the ship lit up like a small city. With a better vantage point, he focused his eyes through the porthole windows and thought he was seeing a lighthouse and the shoreline, still some few miles away, but everything was hazy. A semi-opaque film of ultrasonic fog, created during the teleportation, clung to the bridge's windows, making his view blurry. Through the window's haze he could just make out a dim, yellowish grouping of lights behind him in the distance. *Philadelphia? It must be.*

Without any technical training, Rollins was smart enough to attempt to use the ship's radio. *Nothing but static.* He flipped switches randomly trying several channels, still with no luck. He could read the gyroscopic compass and determine that the ship was pointed due east, but the distant lights on the horizon were due west. The captain-less ship was somehow moving. Even though it had been idling and anchored in the river, the Eldridge was now unmistakably underway but in the wrong direction. *I've got to get closer to shore, but I can't pilot this boat...can I? My Dear Dr. Einstein, what have you gotten me in to?*

He dared put his hands on what was obviously the ship's wheel—a flat brass disc the diameter of a car tire. He spun the wheel a quarter revolution. As it engaged electronically assisted hydraulic pumps, the rudders 200 feet behind him, just below the waterline, responded, though the ship showed almost no signs of turning. *I can drive a car, how hard could this be?* He figured he'd be able to steer, but he had no clue how the ship was moving without a crew. *Am I alone?*

"The German?" he asked himself.

Looking around the pilothouse he saw the ship's telegraph, a round, vertically positioned dial with brass handles, sitting atop a chest-high pedestal. The dial read "Stop," where the handles and an arrow were currently centered. *We're definitely not stopped.* He looked closer and read aloud "Full," "Half," and "Slow," which were clearly marked on both sides of "Ahead" or "Astern." *Ok...how about Ahead Slow? That sounds right.*

Rollins moved the telegraph's brass handles to "Ahead Slow," hearing the clicking and ringing like that of a bicycle bell. He waited for a moment but detected no change in the ship's speed. His knowledge of the required mechanics to pilot a 300-foot warship was near zero. As brilliant as he was, he didn't understand that an engine room crew was needed to receive commands from the bridge via the telegraph. This ship had no crew. The few sailors and engineers that were aboard had fallen into the river during the scuffle with the German.

During the first few minutes of the experiment, as the ship was lifted out of the Delaware River, and was being stressed, bent, and otherwise very badly treated, both drive shafts that employ the twin screws engaged without assistance. The 100,000 volts that precipitated the dramatic teleportation had managed to activate the ship's drive without help from a crew. As the ship splashed down a moment later, the screws remained engaged, moving it forward at about 10 knots. On calm seas, and a windless night, the ship glided through the water with ease.

"I'm still headed farther out to sea," thought Rollins. He spun the large wheel hard right expecting the ship to turn sharply and immediately, finding it did not. Rollins couldn't have known that even with the ship's rudder fully turned, a 17-ton vessel takes a moment to respond.

Further complicating any hopes of smooth sailing were the two fully deployed ship's anchors, dragging through the water underneath the Eldridge like some errant fishing lines attached to giant, bait-less hooks. The stern anchor hung 40 feet straight down, the bow anchor 20-feet. Because the anchors had been deployed in Philadelphia, they remained so in the ship's new location. Out in deep water the anchors hung well off the floor of the seabed. Despite their drag on the ship, she began to swing wide, slowly at first, then more noticeably.

"Ha ha!" Momentarily pleased with himself at piloting a Cannon Class Destroyer Escort with enough firepower to level a small city in 20 minutes time, he yelled out loud, just before his mind wandered toward what might come next. *First things first.* He made sure the wheel and the rudder were at maximum position, hard to starboard. Now, with his turn toward shore underway, his only concern was getting to dry ground. He tightened his life vest. *I hate boats.*

Chapter 10

Norfolk, Virginia
Gosport Navy Yard
Confederate States of America
11:16 p.m. August 13, 1864

At the Confederate States of America Navy Department Command Center in Norfolk Virginia, panic set in. Six minutes earlier a 300-foot sailing vessel of unknown class and origin appeared out of thin air and landed with a splash near the mouth of the James River in the Chesapeake Bay. Caught by surprise, it took the CSN Security forces 15 minutes to initiate a response. Several eyewitnesses watched, disbelieving, as a massive ship of metal seemed to appear out of nowhere, and land with a mighty splash. The over wash from the waves generated swept some unwary seamen off the nearby wooden docks.

Although it was night, the Naval officers looking through binoculars could see large cannons on the strangely well-lit ship. In an era before electricity, seeing the brightly illuminated ship out on the horizon, just past the channel, was a new and frightening sight. They recognized multiple gun turrets, and cannons as weapons of great power, though they also noted they were curiously not under fire, at least not yet. If this was an act of war from the United States of America, they'd blown their chance to wreak havoc.

"What's the status of the Virginia?" asked CSN Commander John Powell.

"She's at the ready, Sir," answered one of the half-dozen Confederate Naval officers poring over charts. The command center office smelled of kerosene and hickory firewood. It was warm enough that evening so that no fire in the iron woodstove was burning. The room was lit by several portable lanterns and permanent gaslights hung on four walls and from a hanging centerpiece fixture.

Powell looked at the charts, but his mind was on the CSS Virginia. Her storied career was already naval legend, having beaten back and prevented new Union blockades of the Port. After sinking the Union ironclad, the USS Monitor, at the Battle of Hampton Roads in 1862, every port, and every southern coastal city wanted the CSS Virginia at the ready. Gosport was fortunate enough to have the warship call her port home.

The 275-foot long ship was not much smaller than the USS Eldridge, but most of her 4,000 tons of displacement sat below the water. All that showed above the waterline was her ironclad angled casemate shell, the stack, her nine cannons, and a 1,500-pound iron ram at her bow.

The Virginia had been converted from a recovered Union ship, named the Merrimack. When the State of Virginia seceded from the Union in 1861 the U.S. Navy attempted to scuttle the Merrimac in order to keep it from falling into Rebel hands as they abandoned the base. The U.S. forces were unsuccessful. The Rebels captured the base and salvaged the Merrimac. Engineers retooled and rebuilt the wood-hulled, ironclad ship, putting her back into service for the Confederate Navy. They'd suffered one Union blockade; they weren't about to let it happen again.

"How about her Captain? Brown, isn't it?" asked Powell.

"Yes, Sir. Captain Brown. As far as I know, he's on base, probably sleeping."

"Wake him immediately and ready the crew. I want shore batteries and artillery crews at high alert tracking that thing out there, whatever it is. I want this entire base at full alert, now!"

"Yes, Sir!" said the officer, who nodded at three junior officers. They were quick to move out of the Command Center, stationed on the top floor of the tallest four-story building at the base.

"We also have the David, Sir," said the officer. "She was brought in by train from Charleston and arrived yesterday with her captain and crew. In fact they just finished loading her into the water."

"The David?" asked Powell, intrigued.

"Yes, Sir," said the officer. "Shall we prepare to launch?"

"By all means."

As the tide of the U.S. Civil War had turned in the favor of the Confederate States of America, the once scrapped submersible program had been re-launched by order of CSN Navy Secretary, Stephen Mallory. The David's predecessor, the H.L. Hunley, was the first submarine to ever seek out and destroy an enemy ship. She was lost in 1864 in the Charleston Harbor after sinking the USS Housatanic, a Federal blockade ship.

Unlike the Hunley, which was operated by seven crewmen hand-cranking a propeller, the David had a small boiler, which burned smokeless anthracite coal. At 50-feet in length and with a 6-foot beam, the David's crew of four could deliver a payload of 60 kilos of gunpowder from the end of a spar, a long, tapered spear.

Ever since the massive detonation at Gettysburg in July 1864, word spread about a new, deadly cocktail of chemicals created by a C.S.A. Artillery officer. The ordnance expert, a young, brilliant chemist from Charleston South Carolina, managed to invent and create an explosive mix of chemicals so deadly that it was considered immoral by many the world over. As word spread about the extreme lethal force, which decimated much of the U.S. Army of the Potomac at Gettysburg, the C.S.A. began to employ its use everywhere it could.

Aboard the David, the 134 lbs. of gunpowder, mixed with this new formula containing nitroglycerin and dynamite could sink anything afloat. The David's single-use weapon, and one spare charge packed aboard, could destroy almost anything of any era, ancient to modern.

*****

Rollins didn't see the launching of the CSS Virginia, or of the CSS David, after he appointed himself captain of the Eldridge. His focus was steering a 300-foot Naval Destroyer closer to the lights in the distance. He desperately wanted his feet on solid ground and to get back to Margaret. *You must be worried sick, my love. I'm so sorry.*

As the Eldridge finished its 180-degree turn it overcorrected by nearly another full 180 degrees, requiring Rollins to spin the wheel again in the opposite direction. Making slow progress, the ship loomed ever closer to what was indeed Norfolk, Virginia, though Rollins was certain it was Philadelphia. He worried about his steering, though he was getting the hang of it, with fewer overcorrections on each try. More worrisome was his inability to change the speed of the ship, of which he was now the reluctant Captain.

Watching every awkward and puzzling move of the strange ship, some three miles out to sea, the Confederate Navy Commanders considered the gray behemoth, and worried, anxious for the two brave crews just launched against it.

The Virginia and the David, even at top speed, around six knots, moved slowly and awkwardly through the water; they were not designed for the open sea, but the dead calm of the channel worked in their favor. Though speed was not a part of their chief design, their four-inch-thick iron hulls made them impenetrable to most shells of their day. They were formidable warships in their defensive positions but could pack a brutal offensive punch as well.

The Virginia's armaments were considerable: six cannons with bores between six and nine inches, along with two 12-pounder howitzer cannons. She was the finest warship in any Navy, on any coastline, anywhere in the world. While the Virginia could be seen easily, steaming along, low in the water, the David in the dark of night was all but invisible. Only the slim conning tower and boiler stack would give her away. Not a true submersible, it might as well have been, as 95-percent of her was well hidden beneath the sea's surface.

In the Eldridge's radio room Heinrich Mueller tried desperately to raise a U-boat, any U-boat, via shortwave. He knew they were always prowling the Eastern coast of the U.S., and if he could only reach one. Nearly suicidal after his cover had been blown, he was frantic to earn a place on der Führer's short list of war heroes before his likely death, but the radio would be of no help in getting him there. He heard nothing but static, not even the American swing music he'd grown fond of. He pounded his fist on the table and pushed his chair back away from the bank of receivers and transmission equipment.

"Let's see what that dummkopf American is up to," he said as he worked his way back to the main deck. On his way he searched for a handgun, ransacking the quarters of every officer; until he located an American Colt .45 in a bedside table drawer. The seven-round clip was full. Once on deck Mueller saw that the Eldridge's exterior lights were lit, but the stark lighting didn't stop him from seeing beyond their glare. *We're headed for shore.* Through his binoculars he could also see that at least one ship was steaming in their direction.

The curious vessel, not among those he was trained to identify, was metal of some sort and sat very low in the water. It flew an odd flag at its stern, one he'd only seen a few times before. He searched his mind and could see the beloved, illustrated, historical naval books he'd devoured as a child. He had to look twice to be sure. *The Confederate States of America? A Navy Jack?* He dismissed his memory, certain the flag was more American insanity.

In the pilothouse, Rollins, frustrated with the poor view through the hazy porthole windows, took his binoculars and flew up a set of stairs taking a ladder to the top of the crow's nest, the highest point on the ship. Once he'd steadied himself, he trained his focus toward the lights. He, too, spotted the Virginia nearly two miles out, but had no idea what he was really seeing. He was certain the ship, no matter how odd, was coming to greet them, and was almost giddy at the prospect of a rescue.

Like a schoolboy, from the nest at the highest point on the ship he slid down the rails of the ladder, skipping the steps altogether. Back on the bridge he pulled the telegraph levers back and forth in an attempt to stop or slow his forward movement, but just as before, the ship did not respond. He took the opportunity to straighten out his course, but his biggest concern was how to actually stop the ship. At some point, sooner or later, the ship would have to come to a stop, one way or another.

"Where are the damned keys?" he said. "A parking brake, maybe? There must be a way…"

Mueller, seeing Rollins, hid from his view. He looked through his binoculars again, certain the mysterious ship had to be the American Navy coming in to render assistance to the Eldridge. Capture was something he would avoid at all cost.

A gunner, before being reassigned to agent, Mueller knew the basic operation of nearly every weapon known to man from the latest high-tech armaments back to ancient Anglo-Saxon javelins. He was especially knowledgeable of German, French, Japanese, Soviet, and American weapons. He was adept at the blindfolded disassembly and reassembly of some 50 models of handguns, the loading and firing of 20 models of machine guns, and basic operating principles of virtually all large shell cannons, including the cannon gun he was hiding behind on the Eldridge. With a trained crew, the large gun could accurately hit a target six miles away—Mueller could handle the job by himself.

Watching for Rollins, the German snuck into the nest of the forward-mounted cannon. Mueller could have fired upon the Navy Yard if he'd chosen to, but he wanted to save his shots, and with the element of surprise sink the boat coming to greet them. He'd have fired upon Rollins and the bridge of the Eldridge if the guns hadn't purposefully been designed with stops to keep them from shooting at its own superstructure.

Two steel bunkers held a supply of 100 shells, each weighing 13 pounds, and Mueller knew just what to do with them. A chill ran down the German's spine as he spotted the battery of Hedgehog anti-submarine projectiles. *Wasserbombs...* This was the weapon of British design that German U-boat captains feared more than any. Stacked in such a way that the battery resembled the spiny back of a hedgehog, each of the semi-aerodynamic depth charges could be launched from the ship thousands of feet. They were deadly to U-boats. He tingled at the prospect of being able to fire the Hedgehogs at the American's own ships. *Alles zu zeiner Zeit. All in good time.*

To load and fire the onboard cannons according to regulations was normally a six-man operation. Mueller was by himself, and though he could load and fire a shell, he lacked significant training in sighting but he'd do his best. When the German fired his first shot in the direction of the CSS Virginia the sky lit up with a bright muzzle flash. The noise was deafening not only to Mueller, but also to Rollins, who suddenly realized he was not alone on board the ship. He had an idea who might be with him.

The first shot fired marked the beginning of a sea battle unlike any before. Nineteenth century warships with well trained, battled-hardened crews, vs. twentieth century innovation and a lone gunman—in other words, an even fight.

51

Chapter 11

The shell fired by Heinrich Mueller flew through the air at 2,700 feet per second. The Confederate Artillery Corp on the ground, and the officers within the observation deck, saw the flash before they heard the report that followed. The shell's trajectory, at a 35-degree elevation, missed the CSS Virginia by 1000 vertical feet, but had in its sights an accidental target much further west along the coastline, just short of three miles away. When the 13-inch shell landed almost six seconds after being fired, it detonated, missing the Confederate Navy onshore artillery batteries by 400 yards. The strike was not close enough to do much more than psychological damage, but it got everyone's attention.

Still the Virginia and the Eldridge headed straight for one another, neither varying their speed or course, in an apparent game of 'Chicken.'

When Rollins peered out of a window on the bridge, he looked to the big guns below him, and could see Mueller in the turret of the largest, his suspicions confirmed—*The German is on board. Not good.*

Spotters on the CSS Virginia hadn't missed noticing the shot over their heads, and thought it might have been a warning. Undaunted and with no plans for surrender, the Virginia's forward gun, already trained on the well-lit Eldridge, fired from two miles away. This was no warning shot; this was engagement. Mueller and Rollins both saw the incoming shell from the 12-pound howitzer. It flew in a straight path, but was a near miss, just splashing into the water 200 yards short of their bow. While Rollins could understand why the stowaway German might be firing at a Navy ship, he couldn't quite understand why the U.S. Navy, or so he assumed they were, would fire back. *Maybe the near miss was a warning?*

Mueller, with the aid of his binoculars, saw the explosion he'd created on shore and adjusted his sights, lowering the elevation. All he could easily see of the Virginia was a vague outline and her stack spewing a thin stream of smoke and steam—this was all that separated her from the expansive, dark water of the Bay.

On board the Virginia, Captain Josiah Brown, with a scope in hand, finally got a good look at the Eldridge. Though in his 50s, he appeared to be much older. He was of average height for men of his era, around 5-foot 6-inches, and stocky. A snow-white beard was cropped close to his round face, now pale with shock. He was speechless as the Eldridge came into close-up focus.

"My Lord in heaven," he said quietly.

"Pardon, Sir," said one the officers, unable to hear over the din of the engines and yelling from the crew.

"I don't know what I'm seeing out there," said Brown. "This is…I don't know what. You look."

He handed the scope to the Lieutenant, who had the same stunned reaction. In 1864, nothing as extraordinary as a WWII Destroyer Escort could even be imagined. Face to face with a monster ship he'd never seen the likes of, the otherwise stalwart ship's captain showed fear.

"It's as if Satan himself has created a great metal beast in the depths of Hell," said Captain Brown, "and he's unleashing its fury upon our small Navy."

Mueller reloaded and fired again. The next shell was off before Rollins could think of what he might do. This one landed in three seconds, much closer to the Virginia, and detonated just under the surface of the water. The concussion rattled the ironclad as 20,000 gallons of seawater was displaced, seconds later raining down upon her deck. The detonation did nothing to disable the Virginia or dissuade the Captain from the battle at hand.

Unseen to all but the spotters on shore, the semi-submersible CSS David was only 300 meters behind the Virginia. The David's captain watched carefully for an intercept point. It would be difficult to attach a barbed spar to the metal monster's hull. Most of the surface ships in both Navies, even the ironclads, were wooden below the waterline. The David's spar torpedoes required ramming the iron spear-like spar into the side of a ship below the waterline, then backing away and igniting the fuse from a safe distance, via rope. If the Eldridge didn't stop or slow its movement, it would be improbable that the David could land a deadly blow. *Improbable, but not impossible*, thought the David's captain, Alexander Robertson. A quick thinker, and able to improvise, Robertson considered how he might take out the gray beast, and decided to flank her.

"We're changing course," said Robertson, a 42-year-old U.S. Naval Commander-turned Confederate when his native Alabama seceded from the Union. "Five degrees port. Prepare to release the spar!"

He stepped down and turned from the small tower that allowed him to see outside his experimental stealth craft.

"I need a volunteer to go out the hatch, and deploy two life vests underneath the charge to float it."

"We're going to release the spar and charge?" asked the second in command. "We're nowhere near the ship."

"I'm well aware of that. She's moving too fast. It seems that this great beast may be all metal, and we'd not be able to lodge the spar into her side. But we can lay it in the water and await her arrival. She seems to be headed straight into Port, and we can't let that happen. It's a long shot, but it's all we've got."

"Aye, aye, Sir."

The commander looked over his frightened, but well-disciplined crew. A sturdy 17-year-old plantation owner's son from Georgetown, South Carolina, stepped forward and volunteered for the mission.

"All stop!" yelled the Captain. Steam and pressure hissed out of the boiler valve, causing the engine, drive shaft, and propeller to cease turning. The David came to a slow idle and floated quietly and unseen in the water.

*****

Aboard the CSS Virginia Captain Brown ordered a new course. When facing the enemy bow first, the ship became a much smaller target, and so, was the preferred, safest defensive attitude in the water. But with only one forward-mounted gun, the position was wide of the mark for offensive maneuvers. Each side of the Virginia had four mounted guns, offering four times the firepower of a head-on offensive, but in trade becoming a much larger target.

"We're the ship of the line right now," said Captain Brown, making reference to the term denoting the forward-most ship in a flotilla. "We're going to turn broadside, wait for range, and fire everything we've got."

The Eldridge and the Virginia were now less than two miles apart and slowly closing the gap. As the German was readying himself for another shot, loading the third shell into his gun, he saw Rollins about to exit the bridge. Mueller raised his Colt .45 and fired two rounds at the American, one bullet grazing Rollins' left leg, surprising him. Rollins yelled out in pain, retreated and watched helplessly as the German loaded another large shell into the long gun.

As the Virginia was now fully perpendicular to the Eldridge, in a David and Goliath blockade of sorts, Mueller saw his opportunity. He dialed in the elevation the best he could and was ready to fire but hesitated when the Eldridge changed course, suddenly turning to the left. It wasn't a fast turn, but it was enough to force Mueller to abort the shot and re-aim. This wouldn't do at all. *The damned American is turning this ship.* He pulled his pistol out, prepared to stop Rollins permanently. Mueller jumped from the gun turret and snuck along the forebridge. He climbed the stairs quietly and had just about reached the hatch door when the sky lit up, followed a second later by the unmistakable sound of multiple cannon's firing.

Three seconds earlier Captain Brown had yelled "Fire!" and all four of the Virginia's portside guns let loose a volley with a singular target in their sights.

Mueller instinctively ducked when the first shell flew over the deck, just missing the bridge. A direct hit would have killed him and probably destroyed, and maybe even sunk, the Eldridge. He'd be okay with the sinking, but he wasn't quite ready to die. A millisecond later a second shell struck the Eldridge clipping the rear stack, and detonating, but not knocking out any of the ships' vital systems. The third in the volley missed the ship altogether, but the fourth was a direct hit.

The Virginia landed a 12-pound Howitzer cannon shell, from the distance of one and a half miles, taking out one of the Eldridge's big guns. Miraculously, the shell did not detonate the remaining 97 unused shells in the nearby reinforced armament bunker, whose hatch had been left wide open. Still, the shot from the ironclad warship, using 80-year-old technology, packed a serious and unexpected punch. The ship rocked with the explosion, knocking Rollins to the floor of the bridge, and throwing Mueller from the stairwell.

Only shaken, Mueller was undaunted and uninjured. There were plenty of additional guns on the Eldridge, and he knew how to fire them all.

*****

The young volunteer aboard the CSS David stripped to the waist and dove into the relatively warm August water. He was holding on to the boat's hull, waiting to be handed the life jackets and rope. When the Virginia fired upon the Eldridge, the sight of the volleys flying through the air, detonating and leaving the monster burning and smoldering brought a cheer from the young sailor, who relayed the news to those on board. The officers watching from the Naval Base on shore also cheered, breathing new hope into the very real possibility of defeating the beast. Though the Virginia had landed an important, and direct hit, the fight was far from over.

The David's spar and explosive ordnance sat three feet below the waterline. The sailor tied the two life jackets in place underneath the 145-lb explosive. The crew released the spar and it floated to the surface, just as intended. Once back on board, the teenaged sailor dried himself near the boilers, which were rekindled and running at full steam.

"Well done, Sailor," said the Captain. "Now we wait to see where this monster is headed and we'll drag the charge across her bow, like a mine. We have to be a good 200 feet from her when we detonate, but we can do this. We *will* do this, that is, unless the Virginia sinks her first!"

Enthusiastic agreement came from the men aboard the David who wanted nothing more than to see the Virginia do the job. They knew all too well the fate of the eight Confederate sailors lost on the H.L. Hunley, which sank for unknown reasons after detonating her explosive charge. It had long been suspected that a hull breech from being too near to her target sealed her Fate.

Much had been learned since the Hunley's loss, but these were new tactics with new technologies, and none of the crew wanted to sink in the process of trying, though try they most certainly would.

Mueller, bound and determined to sink a U.S. Navy ship before he himself was killed, ran to the .40 mm twin-mounted, air-cooled machine gun turret. Primarily an anti-aircraft weapon, the machine guns were useful for blasting at just about anything. Though they were accurate, it was their unrelenting firepower at 120 rounds per-minute that was their real threat. Mueller loaded a long chain of rounds into the weapon and spun the turret in the direction of the Virginia.

"She's still coming at us!" yelled the ironclad's helmsman.

"Fire!" ordered the Captain, watching through a protective observation port. He and the helmsman alone shared the conical pilothouse.

When the next volley of shells came at them from the Virginia, Rollins and Mueller both feared certain destruction. If the Eldridge's rear anchor hadn't hit an underground reef stopping their forward movement suddenly, they'd have been hit. For the first time since Rollins had regained consciousness 20 minutes earlier, the ship had come to a full stop, though the screws were still turning. Within a few seconds the Eldridge broke free of its hold and was moving again.

Each of the Virginia's four rounds fell just short of the Eldridge—the unexpected sudden stop was to blame. The nearest shell detonated upon striking the water peppering the Eldridge with shrapnel. A two-inch piece of red-hot iron spun and buzzed like a hornet flying across the deck, striking Mueller in the forehead. The blow knocked him to the ground and, while not life threatening, the injury filled his eyes with blood. He struggled to his feet and wiped his face, turning his stolen uniform sleeve from dirty white, to blood red.

With a penknife Mueller cut a ring of material from the bottom of his tee shirt, turning the cloth into a bandage for his still bleeding forehead. Once he could see again, and timing in his favor, he took advantage of the Virginia's misses and began firing the .40 cal machine guns. The shells, with a maximum range of 12,000 feet, easily reached the ironclad, strafing the water and finally hitting the Virginia with such force and clamor that the Confederate Captain ordered his ship to turn bow-first, losing her firing advantage, but making her less vulnerable.

Now less than one mile away, each round from the Eldridge that hit the Virginia echoed across the water. Sounding like a tin duck firing range at the county fair, most of the bullets ricocheted off the iron hull, but occasionally one would sneak through the cannon ports. Three crewmen were killed and the boiler pierced in the first 90-second barrage before the Virginia could turn.

Scalding steam created mayhem on board the ironclad, even as more seemingly relentless rounds from the gray monster continued. Engineers managed to patch the boilers with steel bands, like giant hose clamps, and helped her regain steam and maneuvering power.

"I don't know how much more we can take of this, Captain Brown!" yelled the Virginia's Second in Command.

"Ready the forward pivot gun!" yelled Brown. "We won't go down without a fight!"

"The gunner's been wounded, we're replacing him!"

"Make haste!"

When a shell, lobbed from an on-shore cannon, flew over the Eldridge, just missing the radar and antennae arrays, Mueller turned his guns toward the coast. Now that the Eldridge, still steaming straight for the Port, was much closer to shore, Mueller could better see his targets. The flash from another cannon in the battery helped him narrow his aim in the crosshairs. From positions on the shore the machine gun fire was nearly inaudible, but as the shells landed and hit their targets those in the artillery batteries had to take cover. Sand and dirt flew from the earthen fortifications protecting the cannons and crews as each whizzing bullet came ashore. Mueller kept up his fire for 45 seconds, killing four out of the crew of sixteen, wounding five more, and disabling three out of eight cannons.

Helplessly watching from the bridge, Rollins knew the German was attacking U.S. soil, and he felt utterly helpless. For the first time he could also clearly see the ship nearest to them, and it looked remarkably like a Civil War-era ironclad. He struck the notion from his head, knowing it couldn't be. When he focused his binoculars on the odd ship he saw a Confederate Navy Jack flying from the stern, though at first he didn't recognize it as such. Confusion further clouded his thinking as both the ship and the partially destroyed batteries on shore were clearly trying to sink the USS Eldridge. *If only I could stop the German, and stop this damn ship from moving, maybe they'd stop firing at us.*

Rollins made his move from the bridge while Mueller was engaged firing the machine guns like a man obsessed. He wasn't sure what he could do unarmed but he was brave enough, and desperate enough to try something, anything.

Chapter 12

"Time," Albert Einstein would say, "is relative." The passage of time for one person may be different for another, relative to the speed of light. "The past, present, and future, are all an illusion," he also once said. To Einstein, and a host of other physicists, including Henry Rollins, reality was not necessarily a single, unfolding history, leading to a momentary present, and eventual future. There may be many realities unfolding simultaneously. The Multiverse, a possible product of quantum decoherence, allows for de-phasing and entanglements that are incomprehensible, except to the genius minds. To those of average intellect, the Multiverse and its intricate, sometimes mischievous complexities are wondrous, even miraculous, but rarely expected to be understood.

The fact that Rollins, Mueller and a 1,300-ton warship traveled from 1943 to 1864 was remarkable, to be certain, and represented a previously unknown form of inter-dimensional time travel—great minds had been suggesting that possibility for centuries. The fact that their travel was also extra-dimensional, that is, traveling out of one universe into another parallel universe, part of the Multiverse, made it even more remarkable.

To an outside observer, standing back, looking at two neighboring universes in the Multiverse, September 7, 1943 and August 13, 1864 might be occurring simultaneously. A Child named Adam may be playing in the forest in August of 1864, and that same Adam, in another part of the Multiverse, to the distant observer is a 79-year-old man playing with his great-grandchildren. Further, a trillion billion Adams might each be doing something altogether different.

While time may be relative, and the Multiverse may contain an incalculable number of similar versions of itself, they rarely interact with one another in the ways created by the stumbling experiments of the U.S. Navy Department and Albert Einstein in the late summer of 1943.

World War II had been going badly for the Nazis. In their desperation they became more inhumane with every passing day. The 'Jewish Question' became the 'Jewish Problem,' which led to the 'Final Solution,' and mass genocide on a scale the likes of which the modern world had never before seen. As his inevitable defeat became more obvious, Hitler would not surrender, and instead stepped up his efforts to exterminate the Jews, and other groups he deemed unfit to inhabit the Earth.

Even though the reign of U-boat terror had already peaked and was waning, the Battle of the Atlantic still raged on. The Allies were finding new ways to thwart the efforts of U-boats, even as the Kriegsmarine was deploying newer, faster, and quieter boats built in the shipyards of occupied France.

As people across Great Britain and Europe were literally starving, America, chiefly, regularly sent convoys of troops and tons of food on slow-moving freighters, which were too often sitting ducks for the Luftwaffe and the unterseeboots, known forever to the world as 'U-boats.' Despite the German's devastating successes, serving aboard a U-boat carried a 75-percent likelihood of combat death. By 1943 some 400 U-boats had already been sunk. Just in 1943 alone, through September, some 190 U-boats had been sent to their watery grave, and dozens more crippled and captured. The duty was getting more hazardous with each passing day.

The U.S. Navy's Destroyer Escorts were designed to escort and protect slow-moving convoys made up of Liberty Ships, merchant marines, and troop carriers. They had become faster, more maneuverable, more technologically advanced with better radar, sonar, weapons, and highly developed techniques to detect and destroy U-boats. These Allied advances had taken a terrible toll on the once seemingly unstoppable U-boat fleets, who had relied on secret messages passed from spies, air-born reconnaissance, and decoy ships, but the Allies had a secret.

Unknown to the Germans, their supposedly unbreakable Enigma Codes had been cracked by British cryptologists two years earlier. The Germans eventually got wise, and even the MI-6 British Secret Service, and the Bletchley Park cryptologists, were unaware of the Kriegsmarine's newest code machines, which made Enigma look like a Sunday crossword puzzle.

*****

September 8, 1943
Cape Fear, Frying Pan Shoals
North Carolina
1:15 a.m.

U-boat Commander Walther Zoeller lay on his bunk while his ship silently maneuvered off the coast of the Carolinas along the Eastern seaboard of the United States. Zoeller's 6-foot-3-inch frame was not well suited to the cramped quarters of a U-boat, nor a bunk 5 inches too short. Zoeller was solidly athletic, and wore a close-cropped blonde beard that matched his hair, rarely seen, hidden under his visor cap. His 225-foot U-boat, one of the newest in Hitler's fleet, carried 20 torpedoes and a 57-man crew. U-4713 represented the best German engineers could manage.

The 36-year-old Captain was quiet, though short-tempered. He could be simultaneously contemplative and deadly. Like most officers in the German Navy, he was of upper-middleclass origin and in the top two percent of his university class. Zoeller was an Olympic track star, and the physically fit picture of the supposed Aryan superiority Hitler so loved. Under his command, during three previous U-boat assignments, he'd sunk 14 ships with a loss of 390 souls. Included with the men and women who lost their lives, 49,000 tons of food and goods were sent to the floor of the North Atlantic, the Caribbean Sea, the Gulf of Mexico, and the Mediterranean Sea.

Zoeller was used to the smell on board U-4713, though he didn't like it. Two bathrooms for 50 men who wore the same uniforms for months at a time, and were not afforded fresh-water to bathe, created a stench that earned U-boats a particularly pungent reputation.

Having narrowly missed detection by bombers flying out of the Myrtle Beach Air Force Base in South Carolina, Zoeller was spooked, and extra cautious. He'd delivered two saboteurs to the Little River Inlet, and a nearby remote, sandy strip of coastline on the North Carolina – South Carolina border without incident. The mission was one of six he'd successfully accomplished over the previous 18 months. The two spies he'd delivered were in steady communications with a German infiltrator posing as a P.O.W. and operating, with near impunity, from a prison camp located on the coast of northern South Carolina in Myrtle Beach. The resort town swelled to overflowing in the summer, and shrank back to a handful of hardy locals in the off-season, who regularly co-mingled with the German prisoner trustees.

Zoeller's mission had been risky but well coordinated. He'd avoided detection from American subs, merchant marine ships, and air reconnaissance. When it looked clear, he surfaced to deploy an inflatable raft within 300 feet of the shoreline. A passing shrimp trawler narrowly missed entangling its nets in the conning tower as the U-boat submerged and made its escape. Zoeller was sure they'd been seen, and the radio chatter confirmed it. Bombers and fighters were scrambled, and ground forces investigated the region but turned up nothing. Just three hours later he was on a new mission, steaming to a rendezvous point 300 nautical miles west-northwest of Bermuda. The coded message ordered Zoeller to meet U-4710 for a transfer so classified neither U-boat Captain could identify the cargo. They steamed at full speed toward the coordinates, avoiding allied enemies even as a new enemy approached.

The weather in the region was deteriorating, which was rarely of great concern to submariners who were able to ride out the storms in the relative calm of the undersea world. Hurricanes, however, became more problematic. Even at depths of 300 – 400 feet, the rolling waves from the surface effected underwater currents and could turn an unlucky U-boat upside down. Surfacing during these storms was even more difficult, and Zoeller's mission would require plenty of periscope observations at the surface. This worried him.

A knock on the door roused the reclining Captain from his bunk.

"Yes?" he asked, standing.

"Oberfunkmeister Kempler, Kapitän."

The Captain had summoned the Senior Petty Officer radio operator just a few moments before he laid down to rest.

"The last transmission said '*U.S. Navy conducting experiment designed by Albert Einstein of unknown purpose on Destroyer Escort, USS Eldridge,*" said Kempler. He'd re-read Heinrich Mueller's entire coded transmission.

"High Command wants us to investigate, Sir."

"Ja, High Command..." said Zoeller, his contempt oozing for the leaders in Berlin, who had no idea what it was like patrolling the U.S. coastline. "Did you tell them we're meeting U-4710 for a classified transfer, first?"

"Yes, Sir."

"Are they aware that the weather is turning to scheisse? Have you told them that?"

"I did, Sir," said Kempler, "and they responded, 'continue as ordered.'"

"Very well," said Zoeller. "Dismissed."

*****

Norfolk, Virginia
Gosport Naval Base
Confederate States of America
August 13, 1864

With the gun barrels glowing red-hot, Mueller kept up the machine gun fire, alternating between the CSS Virginia, three quarters of a mile away, and the on shore artillery batteries less than two miles away. Both Rollins and Mueller wondered why air support was missing from all the fighting. Both men kept looking into the night sky, expecting to see fighter planes and bombers at any moment, but 25 minutes into the battle, no planes had yet been spotted.

As Rollins had successfully moved from the bridge, and had made it behind the machine gun turret, he looked for a weapon of any kind. The irony of being without a gun aboard a sophisticated warship, filled with enough munitions to destroy a city, wasn't lost on him. The best he could do was to detach a small fire extinguisher from the bulkhead and sneak up on the German. As more shells from the onshore batteries and from the Virginia were headed his way, Rollins concluded that taking out the German would be the only way to stop the shelling, and save himself. *Be brave, Henry.*

With the course of the Eldridge still headed more-or-less toward the channel leading to the Gosport Naval Base, Rollins stayed hidden and moved only when Mueller was actively firing the machine gun. The German was doing a good job at keeping the incoming shells to a minimum. Those that did fly their way lacked the accuracy of the earlier volleys. Rollins, just a few feet behind the unaware German, raised the blunt end of the steel fire extinguisher fully prepared to crush his skull, or at least knock him unconscious.

Before Rollins had a chance to finish the swing, the Eldridge lurched, one of its anchors again grabbing at the sea floor. The ship groaned with the sudden impediment, sending Rollins into the gunner's nest and on top of the German spy, who was still dressed as a U.S. Navy sailor. The ship screamed as the anchor chains stretched against the force of her mighty diesel engines, threatening to snap. The sudden halt left Rollins and Mueller locked in a wrestling embrace on the deck behind the turret's shields.

"Now! Fire!" Captain Brown shouted, taking advantage of the Eldridge's cessation in forward movement, and break from the onslaught of machine gun fire. The Virginia's forward pivot gun fired and at one mile away took only a second to reach the target. The shell hit the base of the 40-foot tall antennae array, snapping it in two, equivalent to shooting a toothpick off a floating sandwich with a pistol at 100 yards. If the Confederate shell had been just five feet lower, it would have taken out the bridge.

When the powerful screws pulled the anchor free, the Eldridge lurched again, sending Rollins backward into the bulkhead, knocking him nearly unconscious. Mueller, fearing new shelling from the ship and from on shore, left Rollins where he lay, and resumed the machine gun fire. Through luck and voluminous firepower, Mueller was once again the master of this battle. He'd already killed 12 artillerymen inside the Virginia by lucky shots through cannon ports. Even if 90 percent of the bullets were deflected from the Virginia's angled casemate iron shell, the 10 percent that made it inside were deadly. Even more serious was the damage caused from the constant barrage of armor-piercing bullets just below the waterline, into the Virginia's unprotected wooden hull.

"Sir!" shouted the Virginia's Engineer up to the pilothouse. "We're taking on water! We're keeping up for now, but I'm not sure for how long!"

"What about the boilers?" yelled the Captain. "When are you going to get me some more power?"

"We're working on that, too. I reckon 10 minutes. Maybe more."

"We don't have 10 minutes! We have 5 minutes, if we're lucky. That great, gray beast is still coming straight for us!"

From the Eldridge, Mueller was devastating the artillery batteries on shore. He'd blown up armament and powder stockpiles, killed or injured half of the cannon crew, and disabled more than three quarters of their weapons with an almost non-stop salvo of large caliber machine gun fire.

It seemed that the technology of 1864 was losing to that of 1943, but the battle of the Chesapeake was not over.

With the Virginia's engines out, the forward guns disabled, and with no one left to operate them, the great ship sat dying, but not yet dead in the water. It was time for the David to play her role. Meanwhile, the Eldridge, free of her snag, resumed her slow, methodical course toward the Gosport Navy Yard.

*****

Aboard the David, Captain Robertson put down his scope and turned to speak to his crew of four.

"Looks like it's up to us. The Virginia is down. We're going to need full steam to cross the bow of that thing out there, towing the spar and the ordnance behind us. With any luck she'll pull the rope under her bow, we'll detonate it and see if we can't send that monster to the seafloor. All hands ready?"

"Aye, aye, Captain," came the response in unison. With the ship's boiler at full steam, the David set herself on a near collision course with the most terrifying warship any of them had ever seen.

As Rollins came around he stood slowly, gaining his wits and his footing, though the many blows to the head he'd endured in the previous 45 minutes left him dizzy and with blurry vision. He took advantage of Mueller's preoccupation with the machine gun to slip away unseen. *I've got to stop this ship.* Knowing the bridge's telegraph had been unresponsive, Rollins worked his way below deck toward the engine room, hoping to figure out some way to stop the engines.

As the Eldridge loomed ever closer to the disabled CSS Virginia, Mueller was getting careless. When he stood above the turret's shield to reposition another belt of ammunition, the Captain of the Virginia saw him through his scope and took note.

"Sharps to the cannon ports!" ordered Captain Brown.

Five highly trained sharpshooters, with their muzzle-loaded, rifled Enfield muskets at the ready, took position aiming their barrels out of the ironclad's cannon ports. They took a bead on the well-lit gunner aboard the monster ship, now 700 yards away and closing. The distance for these sharpshooters was at the far extreme of their ability to accurately hit a target, but the Virginia had to try anything and everything. The Captain couldn't maneuver broadside without the engines and his forward gun was out. The sharps were his only hope.

63

"We're not going down without a fight," said Brown. "Ready! Aim! Fire!!!!"

The almost perfectly in unison percussion from five simultaneous shots rang out as one with a volley of lead Minie balls flying through the air toward their target at 1000 feet-per-second. The conical Minie ball would flatten slightly and provide a bone-crushing injury when it hit, if it hit. All of the five bullets from the sharpshooters hit the steel bulkhead in a tight pattern just over Mueller's head one second after having been fired. None were a direct hit, but a piece of ricocheted shrapnel caught Mueller in the ear, stinging like a thousand wasps as it took a small chunk of his earlobe.

"Ahh! Scheisse! Scheisse!" he yelled, holding his bleeding ear, wincing at the extreme pain.

The sharps had already reloaded and were at the ready, but not before Mueller wisely ducked out of sight. As the distance between the two ships lessened by the minute, avoiding more of the same accurate and deadly small arms fire would be his biggest challenge.

In the Engine Room, Rollins saw the massive diesel engines, and heard their purring, and they seemed perfectly content to run on until they ran out of fuel. While no obvious "off" button would make it easy for him, he was beginning to make sense of the electronics and straightforward engineering before him.

"If I can isolate the fuel supply and electrical components," he reasoned, working his way around the engine room, "that should stop the engines and propellers. Maybe it will buy me some time?"

The Engine Room was situated amidships, on the lowest deck. Beside each of the mighty diesels he found banks of valves, gauges, electric boxes, high voltage switches and warning placards. He closed what he thought had to be the fuel valve to the starboard engine. The diesel sputtered and stopped as hoped, even while the port engine and its screw spun on. With only one propeller driving the ship, the Eldridge began a slow right turn, slightly away from the Virginia but still headed more or less straight into the Confederate Naval Base, now less than a mile away.

On the open deck above, Mueller managed to reload his weapon and stay low, avoiding more musket fire. When he resumed his machine gun assault on the Virginia, a cannon shell from onshore arced its way to the ship, just missing her by a few feet. Mueller focused his fire back on shore and shut them down momentarily.

Riding low in the water, the unseen CSS David was in final position for its intercept.

Through the conning tower, Captain Robertson piloted the David at top speed, some eight knots, threading the needle between the still disabled Virginia and the slowly turning Eldridge.

"This will be close," said Robertson. "Can you get me any more speed?"

"I can try Captain," said the Engineer, "but we're at 97-percent now."

"Give me 115-percent or we're not going to make it across that monster's bow in time, and she'll crush us. It's too late to abort or turn. We have to beat her to the mark!"

"Aye, aye, Sir!" said the Engineer opening a steam valve, watching the gauges closely, while another crewman loaded more anthracite coal into the burner.

Aboard the Virginia the Captain smiled slightly as he watched the slow, but obvious new tack being made by the Eldridge.

"She's turning away from us," he said, sounding hopeful for the first time since the start of the battle. "Prepare the port broadside guns!" Without moving his ship, it seemed the Eldridge wouldn't ram her after all, and would even come along her side, offering a perfect close quarter opportunity to blow a few holes in her gunwales, maybe even below the waterline.

When a shell launched from the onshore battery found the Eldridge, hitting the forward most starboard anti-aircraft gun and its magazine, the explosion rocked the ship. Rollins, still weak and dizzy from too many concussive blows, fell to the Engine room floor unable to move.

The CSS David emptied her ballast tanks, riding higher in the water, gaining needed speed. The spar and deadly explosive charge dragged behind a fully extended 200-foot rope. The David's crew knew the rope-activated igniter wouldn't work in this configuration. Turning the spar charge into a floating contact mine, it was hoped that this new, experimental and highly volatile explosive mix, would impact with the enemy ship's hull and detonate.

Unknown to the two Captains aboard the CSS Virginia and CSS David, or to Rollins and the German, the Eldridge was returning to a particular coordinate, the mouth of an interdimensional portal, in which she'd entered these waters 40 minutes earlier. Rollins had taken the ship in a wide circle and had managed, quite accidentally, to return it to the exact place of its original, sudden admittance into 1864.

Quite by accident, or perhaps Fate, the Eldridge was aligning itself perfectly with a set of magnetic buoys placed in that same, exact location 79 years later; the fact that they did not yet exist wouldn't matter to the quantum physicist, who understands that "time is an illusion." This secondary part of the Einstein's and the U.S. Navy's Top Secret Canned Heat experiment, was yet another failed attempt at cloaking. This time it was hoped that the magnetic buoys would create an invisible port. It did not, but it did create a sympathetic location that acted as a terminus between points, in this case, Philadelphia and Norfolk.

As the Eldridge moved unwittingly forward, not unlike an aircraft approaching an unseen landing strip, the Captain and crew of the David held their breath. As they cleared her bow, missing a collision by seconds, Robertson turned to his crew.

"We're clear," he said with a relieved sigh, his men cheering. Now all they could do was hope to be far enough away from the Eldridge when the spar would hit, trigger the nitroglycerin, and detonate the 140-pound mix of explosive chemicals.

On board the Virginia, her broadside cannons were loaded, primed, and ready to unleash their considerable firepower against the hull of the Eldridge. In seconds the two ships would glide past one another, side-to-side, with less than 100 feet separating them.

Mueller rose to his feet and was shocked to see not one, but two ships at the bow, both low in the water. Now that he could see close-up, both curiously looked to him like replicas of Civil War Naval vessels. He tried to maneuver his anti-aircraft machine gun to target the Confederate ships, but couldn't reduce elevation enough to hit either of them. The ships were too low and too close. All he could do was watch in horror, and wait for their expected shelling. Then he remembered he had one more trick up his sleeve.

Der wasserbombs!

He abandoned the machine gun nest and ran to the Hedgehog Weapons Battery. Intended for use against his own Wehrmacht, if he could figure out the proper launching sequence in time, he'd use them against this American Navy instead. The spiny array of 24 mortar bombs was located dead center of the beam of the ship, just in front of the forebridge. They'd been designed by the British Royal Navy a year earlier and had been proven effective against U-boats, but they'd detonate with deadly power upon contact with anything they hit.

The Virginia, nearly in position to fire, would be far enough removed from the bow of the Eldridge to avoid damage by the David's powerful ordnance. Once it smashed into the hull, it would hopefully blow a hole under the waterline. With the double-pronged attack imminent, both Confederate Captains dared consider victory against the curiously understaffed, but no less terrifying and fierce, intruder. Without warning or any comprehension of what they were seeing, their optimism was thwarted by the seemingly impossible.

"My God," said Captain Brown, as he and many of his crew watched the bow of the Eldridge disappear. This was no fog bank or trick of the light. The ship simply vanished, inch-by-inch, foot-by-foot, seemingly into thin air. Captain Brown could see the gray metal specter from amidships to stern, but with each passing second, more and more of what he eventually came to think of as an apparition, disappeared until all 300-feet of the Eldridge was simply gone.

The David's explosive package, still attached to its 200-feet of rope, floated untouched in the Eldridge's wake. The only trace of the spectral ship was a trail of glowing bioluminescent propeller wash on the surface of the dark sea.

Chapter 13

Chesapeake Bay
Confederate States of America
11:25 p.m. August 13, 1943

When Mueller launched the first round of Hedgehog mortars, they flew with a bright orange fiery tail, but short arc, toward the spot where he last saw the CSS David. He watched in disbelief as the mortars plunged harmlessly into the sea.

"Scheisse! Scheisse!"

Mueller ran to the side of the Eldridge, which was still moving toward the channel but also continuing its long, slow turn. Though its rudders were still straight ahead, only the port screw still spun, pushing the ship into an unintended wide circle. The German scoured the surface of the water looking for targets, anything, but found that both of the odd little American ships had disappeared.

"Wo sich die Fuchse gute Nacht sagen?" *The hare and the fox have said goodnight?*

A moment later when sirens blared and floodlights bathed the channel in bright light, Mueller suspected some new battle was imminent. He abandoned his guns for one more try on the radio. *If only I could reach U-4713.* Mueller knew U-boat Captain Zoeller, as it was his perfectly executed mission that landed him on U.S. soil one year earlier in South Carolina. He knew the U-boat was somewhere in the region, but exactly where and how to reach her were two vital pieces of information he lacked. The Radio Room, located just beneath the bridge, squawked with bits and pieces of random conversations, a vast improvement from the static heard in earlier attempts.

"Die Funkgerate arbeiten!" *The radios are working!*

The radios may have been working, but there was plenty on board the Eldridge that was not.

When Henry Rollins pulled himself together, he stood, head still pounding. He tried to shut the fuel valve off to the portside diesel engine but found it stuck solidly on, welded shut in the Canned Heat experiment. When he heard the sirens from outside he worked his way up two decks and cautiously opened the hatch door. *No sign of the German.* Up two more flights of stairs he was back in the pilothouse, and was shocked to look out the window.

"We're going to run aground."

*****

Norfolk, Virginia
Central Naval Command
Confederate States of America
11:30 p.m. August 13, 1943

"Get your crews mobilized, now!" shouted Vice Admiral Charles Campbell, who'd been awakened by phone, at home, with the startling news. As ordered, in less than five minutes crews of three quick response CSN gunboats were aboard their vessels rushing out of the Navy Yard to engage or attempt to capture, or at the very least, make contact with an invading naval force.

"She's making a slow turn back out to sea!" yelled an Ensign, binoculars glued to his eyes. He was stationed at the bow of the CSS Virginia, named for its predecessor, an ironclad first commissioned in 1864. This modern namesake was a 200-foot gunship, loaded with expert marksmen and a trigger-happy captain. They, along with two other ships of similar disposition, raced fearlessly toward the unknown intruder.

In the Radio Room, just one deck below and one wall away from Rollins, the battered and bruised German spy managed to lock on to a little used German-monitored station. He wasn't sure exactly what he'd say even if he was able to raise anyone; all sides monitored all channels. Frustrated he threw the handset down and wiped his brow with the bloody sleeve of his stolen American uniform. He slowly spun the dial through all the possible frequencies and stopped when an authoritative voice speaking English caught his attention.

"…you are intruding in the Confederate States of America's jurisdictional waters. Stop, drop anchor immediately, and prepare to be boarded or you will be fired upon. Attention, ship of unknown origin, you are intruding…" The voice, one with a distinct southern drawl, repeated the orders.

"Ship in the Bay, identify yourself. You are in C.S.A. waters. Stop, drop anchor, and prepare to be boarded or you will be fired upon."

Completely bewildered, Mueller tried to wrap his mind around what had happened, and what was still happening. Neither he nor Rollins even realized the ship's anchors were already making contact with the seabed. He dismissed as impossible the correct notion, that Einstein and a crew of Americans had developed a time travel or teleportation device.

Mueller ran the possibilities through his throbbing head. *Teleportieren? Nein. Zeitreisen?* (time travel) *? Nein! A wunderwaffe* (wonder weapon) *Nein! Nein!* Not a fan of science fiction, Mueller preferred cold hard facts away from the realm of supposition. But what he'd experienced flew in the face of everything he thought he understood. His head spun with these twisted realities combined with the pressures of battle, and the very real possibility he was facing his own mortality.

Through binoculars Rollins saw the oncoming gunboats, and focused his attention on the lights from shore. He opened the still hazy porthole windows to better see outside where he saw a lighthouse, operational, but damaged from some unknown battle. Then he trained his eyes to the right and saw the lights of the Navy Yard. *Where's the Philadelphia skyline?* He didn't know Philadelphia well, but he knew it well enough. *This is not Philadelphia.*

"What the…?" He never finished his sentence, catching sight of something quite unexpected.

Countless Confederate States of America battle flags and Navy Jacks could be seen on the buildings, flying from flagpoles, trees, or just about anything that didn't move. The iconic flag of the Southern rebellion and the nation's bunting was everywhere. The city appeared to be preparing for a celebration of some kind. Across the narrowing bay he could see the lights from Hampton, Virginia, with its buildings also bearing the C.S.A. flag and bunting. As he looked again, he saw the three ships, traveling at high speed, headed straight for the Eldridge.

Rollins hoped against hope. "Thank, God," he said. "Finally, my rescue."

*****

"We're trying to reach that…that whatever it is…by radio," said one of the CSN personnel working from a tower at the Naval Base. Six officers, two of whom were communications experts, along with an Admiral, were gathered in front of transmitters and receivers, and nautical charts. The room buzzed with anxious banter.

"Well, dammit," said Admiral Josiah Brown III. The station's commander was the great grandson of Captain Josiah Brown I, who had first commanded the ironclad CSS Virginia before retiring in 1870.

Like his great grandfather, he was a well-educated Scotsman. Like the rest of the men in the room, he couldn't imagine what this monstrous alien ship was, or from where it came, but the memory of some long forgotten legend called out to him. He tried to ignore the unsettling recollection but couldn't completely. Through binoculars he spotted a U.S. Naval Flag, one he knew had been retired 70 years earlier.

"It's her..." said the Admiral, finally admitting his suspicions. "The Gosport Ghost Ship."

Seventy-nine years earlier, to the day, some three hundred crewmen and forty from the artillery units all swore that they had battled a giant all-metal warship for 40 minutes, and that she had vanished as quickly as she'd appeared. The tale of the ghost ship spread over the next few years, but despite sworn affidavits, the Confederate States military elite, who'd not been there in person, eventually had the Battle of the Gosport Ghost Ship stricken from the record. They claimed 'mass hysteria induced by excessive intoxication' as the explanation for the event.

Anyone who didn't recant his claims of battle was stripped of his rank, lost his pension, and threatened with the sanatorium. Most recanted officially, including the Admiral's great-grandfather, who'd been supposedly directly engaged in the battle, as the acting captain of the ironclad. But after retirement, Josiah Brown entertained his grandchildren and great-grandchildren with tales of the battle. The legend of the battle and of the Gosport Ghost Ship eventually fell into family lore and tall tale status as the last few resolute eyewitnesses died off.

"I never really believed him..." said Brown to himself, suddenly convinced he was looking at the same ship his great-grandfather once engaged.

Even if it wasn't the spectral ship of legend, it hoisted colors not seen for nearly 70 years. When the northern aggressors, the United States of America, conceded defeat in the War Between the States, their leaders rewrote their constitution. What remained of the Union became the Federated States of America, and the new country, wholly separate from the Southern states of the Confederacy, adopted a new flag, and this ship was not flying anything resembling it.

"I'll be damned," said the admiral, still lost in thought.

"What's that, Sir?" asked an officer.

"Nothing, nothing...just thinking about my great-grandfather," he cleared his throat, and turned to look at the lieutenant. "How close are our gunboats?" he asked.

"Closing fast, Sir," said the officer. "Less than a minute until rendezvous."

"How about our destroyers?"

The three remaining officers in the room looked anxiously at one another, no one wanting to incur the Admiral's wrath.

"Well?" he demanded.

"Sir," said the lieutenant, speaking for the rest. "All the ships, all 11 of them, are without a full complement and are at least an hour from being ready to deploy. Most of the crews are on shore leave on account of the holiday."

"Do you mean to tell me they've caught us with our knickers at our ankles and we've got no real firepower besides the three gunboats out there?"

"Yes, I'm sorry to say so," answered the officer.

"Call the crews back from shore leave. I don't care if it is Armistice Day, or if it's Christmas! Call them all! Every sailor, every officer, every powder monkey! I want everyone back on board their ships yesterday! We've had National Prohibition for 60 years. If any sailor is too drunk to man his station, I want him thrown in the brig and court-martialed! Any man who doesn't make it back to his ship in one hour is to be considered a deserter."

"Do I make myself clear?"

"Yes, Sir!"

"Sound General Quarters." The Admiral looked back out to sea, studying the massive, brightly lit monster. "We are sitting ducks if that abomination decides it's coming back around, or God forbid, comes into port and turns its guns on us."

"Aye, aye, Sir," said two of the junior officers in unison, scurrying out the door with the message and the admiral's orders.

The Admiral leaned down to get the radio operator's undivided attention. He spoke softly, with a calm chill. "Tell our gunboats to fire one warning shot, demand surrender, and then…God help them, try to sink her."

In the dark of night three ships raced toward an uncertain encounter. Aboard the CSS South Carolina, now the lead gunboat, the captain ordered the ships in the formation to slow to 10 knots. Their radar indicated that they were less than a mile from the intruder. The Captain had been given an order to fire a warning shot toward the Eldridge and to continue trying to raise her by radio. Before firing at the behemoth in their harbor, which all on the bridge could clearly see easily outgunned them, he placed his hand on the radio operator's shoulder.

"Try again," said the Captain. "One last time."

"To the ship in the channel. This is the CSS South Carolina. Identify yourself. You are in C.S.A. waters. Stop your engines, drop anchor, and prepare to be boarded or you will be fired upon."

They waited for a response. Hearing none, the Captain ordered the shot across the bow.

When Rollins heard the cannon and saw the trail from the shell fly overhead, he knew the battle was back on. Mueller, too, heard and felt the cannon's report. He ran from the Radio Room, to the nearest .50 cal machine gun, one of six on board.

Rollins, still on the bridge in the pilothouse, thought he could make the small flotilla of gunboats aware that he was friend, not foe.

He ran to the deck, toward the bow of the ship. A collapsible emergency water bucket made of white canvas sat clipped on to the bulkhead near the ordnance locker. He ripped it from its hooks to crudely attach it to the end of an eight-foot-long boat hook. *I'll surrender. They'll have to see this.* All the captains, all the players in this most unusual unfolding drama were all close enough to clearly see one another. Rollins furiously waved the white flag from the bow of the ship, which caught the CSS South Carolina Captain's attention, as well as the German spy's.

Mueller used the American's own preoccupation against him, easily sneaking up from behind. He checked his Colt .45, with five shots left in the clip, still tucked into the waist of his pants. He thought about simply shooting the odd little American troublemaker in the back to be finally done with him, but he wanted him to suffer a little first and maybe get a few answers. With a chop to the back of his neck from the butt of his revolver, Rollins was down but not out. Struggling to stand, he turned to see the Nazi with a gun pointed at his chest.

"Just who the hell are you, and where the hell did you come from?" asked Rollins, wincing in pain.

"I did not come from Hell. My name is Heinrich Mueller, and I come from the most glorious place on Earth, Austria. I am the future of the Fatherland and a loyal officer in the Third Reich, und your end is at hand."

Rollins dropped his gaze, looking down at the deck, waiting for the inevitable. No shot came.

"And who are you and what has that traitor Albert Einstein created with all this, this mess of cables and generators."

"I'm afraid I don't know what you're talking about," said Rollins, who sensed his death was inevitable, with little now to stop it. He wouldn't give the German the satisfaction of an answer. *I'm sorry Margaret.*

"Don't feel like talking?" asked Mueller, raising his arm and pistol taking a bead on Rollins' head. Before he could squeeze off the round the Eldridge shuddered and lurched to a stop. Now in much shallower water, the ship's bow anchor again snagged a rock. The momentary catch and release caused just enough of a jolt to once again send the men into an unintended embrace. When Mueller's gun flew from his hand, Rollins threw a punch and missed. Each of the men, already exhausted and bruised, fought with all they had. Mueller, a bit larger than Rollins, had combat training. Rollins, 13 years younger, had youth and a fierce will to live on his side. With the ship still underway, both men, with locked arms, were caught in an even match that had them leaning over the forward-most gunwale at the starboard side of the bow.

Strong vibrations rattled the ship just before the stern anchor grabbed the rocky seafloor firmly, and this time permanently, on an unmovable shoal. Both men went over the gunwale, one hanging on, the other never having a grip.

Rollins fell through the air, and hit the water hard. Mueller hung onto the rail with one hand as the ship pivoted on the snagged anchor. Moving slowly but steadily, the ship swung in a sharp turn, leaning hard with its one remaining operational screw now churning and chopping the water at the surface. The ship, smoldering from two direct hits, groaned at yet even more indignities she was being asked to endure.

Rollins had the wind knocked out of him but was still in his life jacket. He coughed out seawater as he struggled to catch his breath and make sense of what he was hearing. Even before he could see it coming, a horrible, loud, chopping noise, like a dozen giant butchers madly slicing at the water, filled his ears, and then his vision.

"My God," he said when he saw from just where the noise was coming. Like a school of ravenous steel piranhas, the ship's screw, half in and half out of the water, churned and chopped, ready to turn him to shark chum. He tried to swim, but the ship was coming at him too fast. There seemed to be no escape.

Mueller managed to pull himself back on board but had to hang on to keep from falling off the severely listing ship. He saw his revolver on the deck, and managed to retrieve it as he secured his position. The Ship screamed as it pivoted and pulled against the two-ton anchor snagged on the seafloor.

Rollins flailed desperately, trying everything he could to get out of the way of the ship. Forty feet and closing fast, he watched in horror, finally giving in to the inescapable, certainty of death. He closed his eyes tightly but he couldn't block out the ever louder, ghastly, rhythmic slapping of the nine-foot diameter propeller slashing its way toward him.

Then all went quiet. The sea's surface no longer churned as it became as smooth glass. All was still. Just that quickly the Eldridge was gone, leaving Rollins safe from the German and the wrath of the ship's screw, but bewildered and disoriented. When he allowed himself to once again breathe, and after thanking God for sparing him from the propeller, he realized he was in the last place he really wanted to be—floating in a sea of uncertainty.

A moment later Rollins heard voices. The crew of the CSS South Carolina called to him, and readied a lifeline.

Chapter 14

Philadelphia Navy Yard
1:30 a.m. September 9, 1943

As Dr. Albert Einstein and five U.S. Navy officers exited the dockside administrative building, having agreed to reconvene at daybreak, they stopped suddenly, unable to speak or move. What they were eyewitness to next, would, like the rest of the Philadelphia Experiment, forever remain classified. The USS Eldridge, like the phantom Flying Dutchman she surely was, returned through an unseen hole in the sky with engines running, one propeller chopping the air, and two anchors swinging from massive metal chains.

The ship splashed down hard into the river. There'd been no fog, no blue-green fluorescence, just the ship gliding through the sky and splashing down. At first there'd been little noise, but when the forward anchor grabbed the riverbed, the ship let out a wild lament. When the still spinning screw wrapped itself in the stern anchor chain, an unearthly metallic screech reverberated through the quiet shipyard and half of Philadelphia.

"Mein Gott," said Einstein, pointing. "She's back!"

The men, along with a handful of Navy personnel, ran to the edge of the dock having witnessed a second miracle: the return of a 17-ton ship out of the night sky. If they hadn't seen it with their own eyes, it would never have been believed.

In the shallow waters of the Delaware River, the one free anchor found purchase of the riverbed, and even though the ship was at "Slow Ahead," she held fast. Smoke billowed from the rear of the ship as the still operating diesel engine finally seized. Koenig immediately ordered Captain Hammond, a fire team, and an armed crew into a nearby PT boat to secure the Eldridge, suppress any fire, and search her for two missing men.

74

In moments the crew of 12, some more reluctant than others to climb aboard, had erected emergency boarding ladders and made it onto the deck. Captain Hammond and three men ran to the bridge. There he tripped the emergency fire suppression system and six armed guards began to sweep the ship looking for anything.

Mueller, who'd managed to hang on through the ship's violent reentry, saw the men coming. He couldn't take the time to be awed at the miracle of teleportation, something of which he'd twice been a participatory eyewitness. Armed guards were there to arrest him. Within the nest of a twisted .40-calliber machine gun, Mueller hid. When a guard rounded the corner, the German rose from his hiding place and fired his handgun. The guard dropped to the deck, having been hit in the right leg. The shooting, heard by the other guards, prompted a short firefight, before Mueller's Colt ran dry, but he had other weapons at his disposal.

Though the machine gun was designed so it couldn't accidentally strafe the ship, there was no reason it couldn't fire across the river.

"Hit the deck!" ordered Commander Koenig from on shore, pulling Einstein and himself prone to the dock. A strafing round of .40-cal bullets chewed up 20-feet of the concrete dock, just missing the men. Mueller fired at anything and everything, even taking out the window in his own office three floors up in the same building where Koenig, his staff, and Einstein had been meeting. From around the Eldridge's bulkhead, one of the guards snuck up on the German from behind, and pointed a revolver at his head.

"It's over, Kraut! Hands up!" yelled the Navy guard. Mueller stopped firing and spun slowly, raising his hands. His compliance was short lived.

"Alles hat eine ende (everything has an end)."
In a lightning-quick maneuver Mueller swung at the guard, but not before the crewman got off one well-placed shot. After the smoke cleared, two American Navy Seaman, and the Nazi spy and saboteur, Heinrich Mueller, lay dead. The German took with him secrets and information those waiting on shore and in Norfolk, Virginia desperately wanted, but would never get.

*****

When Henry Rollins still hadn't checked in with Margaret by the next morning, her anger diminished and was replaced by her worry, which had grown in magnitude. This was not like Henry. He knew how much communication meant to her, still tender from their separation during the incident. At 9 a.m. she called the Institute to try to reach Albert Einstein. He'd been the last man with her husband, and the only one she knew by name.

"I'm sorry Mrs. Rollins," said the operator. "Dr Einstein's direct line here hasn't been working for weeks. Try his secretary, Helen Dukas. I can connect you from here."

When Helen Dukas answered the phone and Margaret Rollins told her of her concerns, she was silent for a moment. "I'm sorry Mrs. Rollins. Dr. Einstein is…still not back from his trip."

Margaret sensed the woman was lying, or hiding something.

"It's been two days and I've heard nothing," said Margaret, on the edge of tears. "Don't you know anything? Please help me." Her suspicions were confirmed by a longer than normal hesitation from the secretary.

"Can you meet me at the corner of Witherspoon and Wiggins Street in 30 minutes?" asked Dukas.

"I can be there in 10."

"Okay, 10 minutes. See you there. Goodbye, Mrs. Rollins."

The F.B.I. may not have known everything, but they did know about the Philadelphia Experiment, as they'd nicknamed it, and nearly all who were involved. As soon as Henry Rollins had been given clearance by the Navy brass, the F.B.I. had a file on him. They knew his wife, Margaret Rollins, the couple's address in Princeton, bank account numbers, and checkbook balances. Hearing Dukas' and Rollins' conversation, two mid-level agents, who had long been engaged in the warrant-less wiretapping of Einstein's phone, mobilized in an unmarked car. From their small office on the outskirts of Princeton, the two women they surveilled would beat them to the rendezvous point but not by much.

Margaret Rollins and Helen Dukas, who'd never met, easily found one another at the entrance to the Princeton Cemetery at the corner Dukas had suggested. After cursory, awkward introductions they walked through the gates of the century old burial grounds.

"I'm sorry for the cloak and dagger," said Helen Dukas, a sweet, quiet, 60-year-old woman who had worked for Einstein for nearly 15 years. "We know our phones are tapped, and what I'm about to tell you is probably classified and could get us all in a lot of trouble." She spoke with a German accent, but unlike her boss, was better at hiding it.

She motioned for the two of them to sit on a bench. Before speaking again, she looked left and right nervously. "Dr. Einstein has a messenger he uses to get me information he wants only me to know about. The man comes and goes in a dry cleaning truck. He picks up and delivers clothes, along with notes, and the F.B.I. is none the wiser." She looked more worried than before. "I'm sure I'm not supposed to be telling you this."

Listening to Dukas struggle to get the words out only multiplied the fear and anxiety on Margaret's face. Dukas sensed it and took Margaret's hand in her own.

"Apparently there's been an accident in Philadelphia. It appears that the Project Rainbow—no, that's not it—the *Canned Heat* project didn't go well," started Dukas. Margaret sat numb, speechless. "Dr. Einstein's brief note arrived yesterday." Dukas opened her purse and produced a small slip of folded paper and handed it to Margaret. It had been written in German, but Dukas had translated it to English.

'Ich werde noch ein Tag sein. Nicht gut gelaufen, Henry Rollins ist verschwunden – A.E.'

Margaret stared at the note, and finally read the translation aloud. *"I'll be another day. Didn't go well. Henry Rollins is missing.- A.E.'"*

She burst into tears at the news she feared more than any. "No, no, no..." she sobbed while the secretary did her best to comfort her.

"Albert is good man," said Dukas. "He'll find your Henry. Try not to worry."

The words meant to comfort her, did not.

"How can I not worry? Why don't you ask me not to breathe?"

"I know, dear," she sighed. Margaret cried for a few moments while Helen Dukas rubbed her back. "How can I help?"

Sitting straight up, Margaret tried her best to regain her composure. "You can't, but thank you. Do you know anything else? Anything at all?" she pleaded.

Dukas shook her head, no.

Margaret, still shaken, stood to leave. "Thank you Mrs. Dukas." She pulled a pencil and a slip of paper from her purse, writing quickly. "Here's my number. Please keep me updated."

The women parted company leaving the F.B.I team certain that Dukas had told Margaret Rollins of the Philadelphia Navy Yard fiasco. The young scientist's wife's tears proved that now she likely knew the worst of it.

"Dja see that?" said one of the F.B.I. Special Agents to his partner. The two agents watched through binoculars from across the street. "They're trading notes. I'll betcha a bottle of Tennessee hooch the German dame told the Rollins woman about the Eldridge and the missing Doc. But how? Einstein is still in Philly, and we haven't missed any calls?"

"I dunno," said the other agent, not nearly as engaged as his partner. "I am beat. My kid was up all night. You hungry?"

******

A major inspection and overhaul was underway as soon as the Eldridge was towed to the dock. Divers with underwater lights inspected her hull from the bow to stern, and found no serious damage, except to the portside propeller. The steel was riddled with pockmarks from cannon shells, musket ball fire and all the signs of battle. Though she was beaten up pretty badly, it seemed to the engineers that she'd made it through the teleportation and whatever mysterious enemy had engaged her.

By their careful records, the Navy said the Eldridge had been missing for 13 hours and 17 minutes. The clocks aboard the Eldridge, however, all agreed that only 2 hours and 12 minutes had elapsed. This was just one of the many mysteries they wish they could explain. Einstein, though sick over the disappearance of his young friend, Henry Rollins, was thrilled by the time discrepancies. The anomaly represented faster than light travel, or something even grander.

The repairs had been ordered and begun with as little explanation to the work crews as possible. The rumors were vague, only that she'd been part of a top-secret mission, and obviously in a battle, but how – there'd been no crew – and with whom? The evidence was hard to ignore. Thousands of rounds of spent 40 mm machine gun ammo casings littered the deck, six shell casings from the 50 mm cannon were found, and one round of 24 Hedgehog mortars had been fired.

Behind closed doors Captain Hammond, his junior officers, and his superiors debated just what might have taken place but could come to no consensus. There'd been no report of any hostilities along the East Coast, and without confirmation from one or both of the last two men they knew were aboard the ship, they remained clueless.

After the copper cables had been removed from the Eldridge, the scorched and mangled weapons were removed, awaiting replacement. One of the repair crew found something not seen aboard a U.S. warship in some 80 years.

"Would you look at this," said the sailor to another on the repair team. "That don't look too familiar."

"No it don't," said his coworker, "and we better not touch it. Could be live."

It took a team of four Navy specialists to defuse what was eventually identified as a Confederate Artillery canister shell, circa 1864. It was likely fired from a rifled 12 pounder Napoleon, and had it detonated it would have sprayed dozens of iron balls in a devastating shotgun effect.

Additional repairs included the replacement of one diesel engine ripped apart internally when the anchor chain seized the drive shaft. After replacing three big guns and the antennae array, along with a few cosmetic fixes, she was certified as ready to go. The Shipyard reopened under heightened security. There was a war going on and the Department of the Navy didn't have the luxury of waiting any longer.

The office once inhabited by German spy, Mueller, along with his shortwave transmitting radio, were discovered, but not the code machine. Unlike the Enigma Machines, which were big and obviously nefarious, by design this new model code device looked and operated like a standard Smith & Corona typewriter, and so went unnoticed. The Navy made repairs to the office, replaced the windows, fixed the holes in the walls and had a new typist in place in less than 24-hours. The woman from the Navy typing pool complained of the typewriter's abnormal weight, but was soon typing memos, unaware of the technology cleverly hidden within.

On the ground floor of the same building in which Mueller's office had been, Commander Koenig and his staff met again attempting to sort out what details they could of the disastrous project code named '*Canned Heat*.' The experiment left a brand new, very expensive Destroyer Escort needing a million-dollar repair, 12 Navy Yard windows shattered from machine gun rounds, and a good chunk of the dock riddled with bullet holes. Worse, the project left two crewmen dead, two more injured, and a valuable German spy as a corpse. And there was the troubling matter of a missing civilian mathematician, whose wife had probably already begun to ask questions no one could answer.

"Go back to Princeton, Dr. Einstein," said Koenig. "Tell no one of this. It's still top secret and highly classified. We will contact you if anything develops here."

Koenig rose and opened the door where a waiting driver stood by. "Be thankful we don't send you a bill," he added.

Einstein was quiet, depressed, and feeling guilty. But somewhere deep inside his brain, a new synapse had formed and was growing, calculating, and opening up new lines of thought.

He turned to the disheartened and angry group of officials, and spoke. "I vill go back to Princeton, Commander. I vill go home und sink about zis. In za meantime, I suggest you keep your eyes und ears open. Check around Norfolk Virginia. I'm not sure, but za magnetic buoys in place zhere just may have had something to do vis vhat has transpired here. It vas no accident zhat zhey generated und shared ze exact same voltage und output as did za five generators on board za Eldridge."

"Funny you would say that, Dr. Einstein," said Koenig. "We just received word from Norfolk. Those electrified buoys you mentioned apparently sizzled and created quite a spectacle at the same moment the Eldridge went hot."

Einstein walked out the door, his great intellect working at full capacity. He motioned to the driver, who opened the car door for him.

"Of course I don't know…," started Einstein, fluffing his hair and twisting his mustache. "…no, probably not, but I can almost see young Dr. Rollins in my mind, und sense zhat he may be zhere, or near zhere. Vishful thinking, perhaps? But one can hope."

*****

Norfolk, Virginia
Confederate States of America

11:58 p.m. August 19, 1943

At the mouth of the Chesapeake Bay, the Cape Henry Lighthouse shone as the brightest light in the night sky. The CSS Virginia idled down as it approached the floating scientist. Henry Rollins' mind was lost in thought chasing down a thousand rabbit trails as he tried to make sense of the upside-down place in which he had been thrown. He floated, kicked lazily and wondered why he wasn't freezing. He expected the September water temperature to be much colder. *Maybe this is Florida?* What he didn't know is that it was not September. The last date he remembered in Philadelphia was September 7. But here, somehow, in the middle of an especially warm summer the ocean water was a very comfortable 78 degrees. He tried to take stock of his health. *Am I bleeding? Am I even still alive?* Save a few goose egg bumps on the back of his head, Rollins was otherwise okay.

Most of the crew aboard the 50-foot CSS Virginia gunship, had seen the Eldridge vanish, and Rollins flung into the water. With 12 rifles aimed at him, they came to within 30 feet and threw a floatation ring attached to a lifeline.

"You, there in the water!" yelled a voice from a bullhorn. "Hands in the air!"

Rollins chuckled at his predicament. Here he was thrown a lifeline, and then ordered not to touch it. He bent his arms at the elbow, and showed that he was unarmed.

"Keep your hands visible, and grab the life ring!"

He did as instructed and was pulled toward the gunship. When the sky above him flashed from black as night, to gray, back to black, he blinked rapidly, his eyes involuntarily trying to adjust. A bright flash from a suddenly visible noonday sun caused him to shield his eyes with his hands, and let go of the ring. With some momentum still carrying him toward the ship, the sky turned again to the black of night. When he removed his hands from his eyes and refocused, the ship was gone, the lifeline was gone, and he was alone treading water in the Chesapeake Bay.

Rollins scanned the surface of the water, and looked toward shore. There were no ships nearby, save a few towers visible from vessels moored well inside of the port. Still clueless as to where he was, he knew one thing for certain. *I've got to get out of the water.*

Floating on his back, Rollins did his best to paddle toward shore, three-quarters of a mile away. Occasionally he would stop to rest, looking to make sure he was still on course. Closer to shore, Rollins could make out individual streetlights, and saw the occasional car's headlights pass by. The glow of a town hovered just behind the lighthouse, and gave him hope that civilization, though perhaps one hostile to his nationality, was almost at hand. Just where he was, he couldn't say, but he was glad to be headed toward solid ground. *I've got to get to a phone, call Margaret, call Einstein. They're not going to believe this. I don't believe this.*

After an additional 30 minutes of backstroking, kicking, resting, repeating, Rollins was close enough to hear small waves crashing on the shoreline. The steady outward gaze of the lighthouse was somehow reassuring, and he nearly cried when he passed through the last of the breakers and was finally able to stand in chest-deep water and walk with aching legs up to the beach.

Tearing off his life jacket, he collapsed, and lay in the warm sand, but only for a moment. *Margaret.* As he struggled off the beach toward a road, he saw military vehicles in the distance. He took his shoes off, and walked barefoot. The wet leather of the shoes rubbed his feet raw. He stopped to rest at a park where he saw a plaque commemorating the Battle of Hampton Roads, a Civil War era fight between the two steam-powered ironclads, the USS Monitor and CSS Virginia. The Confederate imagery he had first seen from the bridge of the Eldridge was plainly visible, though the bunting and celebratory excess wasn't quite as he remembered.

"Maybe Philadelphia is hosting a Civil War reenactment?" he mumbled to himself.

When he looked again around the park he saw, for the first time, hard evidence that maybe he wasn't in Philly. *Norfolk. How in the hell...Norfolk? Dr. Einstein, what have you done?*

An odd looking Jeep-styled vehicle passed him, driven by military personnel he couldn't see too well. Instinctively he moved behind a hedgerow to watch another small convoy of trucks roll past, all with the same Confederate Southern Cross emblem. As he looked closer he could see a round Navy Department seal that read "Confederate States of America Navy Department." It contained the image of a three-masted sailing ship in its center. Blood rushed from his face, and his breathing became rapid.

"This can't be," he whispered. "What has happened?"

He found that by walking through the Stephen Mallory Memorial Gardens, named for a Confederate Secretary of the Department of the Navy, he could get closer to a heavily guarded gate. Some 20 yards in the distance he saw a large sign, lit up by floodlights: "Norfolk Naval Station, C.S.A."

"What the hell?" he again whispered to the air, desperate to make any sense of what he was seeing. He searched his line of sight for any signs of normality, any U.S. flag, anything, but saw nothing that gave him any hope that he'd be able to understand anything, anytime soon.

Chapter 15

Princeton, New Jersey
8:27 a.m. September 9, 1943

On the morning of the fourth day after the disaster, Dr. Einstein was delivered by Navy personnel to his residence in Princeton. His home office, one he far preferred to the one at the Institute, was there waiting, as was the ever-dutiful Helen Dukas.

"Guten morgen, Herr Doctor," said Dukas helping him with a small bag. Einstein managed a smile, and flopped down in his favorite chair in the living room.

She played dumb for the unseen ears that were certainly listening in. "You're trip was uneventful?" she asked, knowing that it had been anything but.

"Ja, ja, uneventful," said Einstein. "Perhaps you could help me pick some flowers from za garden. Za place needs a little cheering up." The garden was the closest, safest place they could speak without fear of being overheard.

"Certainly, Herr Doctor," she said, as the two went through the back of the kitchen and out the back door.

With a pair of pruning shears in her hand, she bent by a rose bush filled with bright yellow blooms. She snipped a few and looked up at her boss and spoke quietly.

"These may be the last of the season, Albert." He didn't look at her or the roses in her hand. "Margaret Rollins has been to see me," she continued. "She tracked me down through the Institute." Still he remained silent. "Albert, she's beside herself with worry and knows that you must know something about Dr. Rollins'…absence."

"I vish I did," said Einstein quietly. "It vas all very messy, Helen. I don't know vaht I'd tell her if ve met. I don't know how za Navy is going to handle zis, either."

Helen Dukas snipped a few more stems, enough to fill her favorite vase, one that had been shipped from Austria. Einstein packed his pipe, struck a match, and blew lazy smoke rings in the morning sun.

*****

A knock at the front door of her Princeton apartment startled Margaret Rollins, who ran to answer. When she saw two Navy officers, her heart sank. She invited them in, but they stood just inside the doorway.

"Mrs. Rollins," said one of the officers. "The Secretary of the Navy regrets to inform you of your husband's Missing in Action status."

Margaret stumbled backward, clutching at the back of a chair. Though she already knew her husband was missing, to have the Navy admit to it couldn't be a good sign. The officer helped her to take a seat.

"What do you mean "missing in action," asked Margaret, weakly. "To what "action" are you referring? He was in Philadelphia."

The officer cleared his throat while pulling a telegram from a folder. He read it aloud.

"Dear Mrs. Rollins, we share in your frustration and sorrow regarding the disappearance of your husband, Dr. Henry Rollins. Credible evidence exists to support his likely death. While Dr. Rollins was not employed directly by the U.S. Navy, he was under our care at the time of his disappearance, and we regret this loss deeply. Signed Commander William P. Koenig, Commander, U.S. Navy"

Vacillating between angry and sad, Margaret's blood boiled.

"You tell me what the hell happened, and where he is…right now!" She screamed at the officers, and raised her fists, as if to beat them. One officer gently grabbed her wrists, and led her back to the couch. The other officer followed them just inside.

"We understand you're upset, Mrs. Rollins, but we weren't there. We don't know exactly what happened."

"Then you tell me who does!"

"We don't know that either. We are very sorry. Do you have anyone here? Or anyone you could stay with?"

"Go!" she said, doing her best to control her urges to scream again. The men moved toward the door. "Get out!" she yelled, pushing them through the door with all her might. They replaced their hats and walked down the steps.

She yelled at the men retreating to their car. "I know damn well someone who does know! Tell the Navy I'll be happy to do their jobs for them! I will find my husband!" As the car drove off, she cried out. The scream was something instinctive, primal, her voice echoed throughout her Princeton neighborhood, reverberations of which could be felt a universe away.

"Einstein!"

*****

"Einstein..." laughed Henry Rollins, "you crazy old bugger. Just exactly where have you sent me?"

Henry Rollins was as missing as anyone on the planet had ever been before or since, and no one knew of his whereabouts. Even he himself couldn't make heads or tails of his location. Finding a quiet, dark corner of the Mallory Gardens, he stretched out on the grass near a park bench, removing his wet outer clothing in an attempt to dry it out. The warm night was comforting, even if the mosquitoes threatened to feast on his exposed flesh. Not intending to, he fell fast and hard asleep. When he awoke the sun was bright in his eyes, and he turned to look at his watch. It read 4:17, which clearly it was not. This was a morning sun and he guessed it might be 6 or 7 a.m. When he felt a kick to his side, he sat upright with a bolt.

"What do you think you're doing here?" asked the voice coming from above, face obscured, backlit by the bright morning sky.

He reached for his shirt, which was mostly dried, though stiff with salt residue. He managed to stand up, wearing only his boxer shorts. The two policemen waited for an explanation.

"I fell into the ocean?" asked Rollins, hoping it might be a suitable lie.

"Go on," said the cop, humoring him.

"I got lost, was wet, and slept here until my clothes dried?" Even as he made the statement, he turned it into a question.

"You mean you slept one off here," corrected the cop. "Well this ain't the Salvation Army soup kitchen, Pal. Get your damn clothes on and get the hell out of here."

Rollins was relieved he wasn't going to be arrested, but had so many questions that part of him wished they would take him away. As he pulled on his pants, also still slightly damp, he thought *maybe crazy will work*.

"Where am I, Officers?" he yelled in the direction of the policeman, who had started to move on, before turning to look at him.

"Huh?" asked one cop in disbelief, looking at his partner.

"Yes," answered Rollins matter-of-factly, "I'm asking. Just exactly where am I? I'd really like to know."

"Are you messing with us, boy?" one of them asked.

"No, Sir, I just get confused sometimes, and forget." It sounded polite and quite reasonable for someone delusional.

"You're in Norfolk, Virginia, in the Mallory Park. Where are you headed, anyway?" asked the lead officer, as they walked back to where Rollins was still dressing.

Rollins, starting to wish he'd left well enough alone, finally answered with honesty thinking, why not? "Philadelphia, Pennsylvania, and then Princeton, New Jersey. Or maybe the other way around."

The cops laughed. "Oh you are, huh? You a Fed Stat spy?"
Rollins didn't understand, so he didn't answer.

The other cop tried. "So what about it? You a misplaced Yankee? You kinda sound like one."

Rollins, still unsure what they were asking, thought he'd better play along.

"No, no," he laughed. "I just have family up there. Distant family. Some Yankee cousins I'd like to see."

The cop laughed out loud. "Good luck crossing the border. And Pennsylvania is a long walk from here." He spun his Billy club and it snapped into his palm, pointing toward the Park's entrance. "You'd best get going."

Rollins slipped on a red sock and looked for the other, a mismatched blue argyle. He remembered laughing with Margaret about it, but couldn't find it. Not to be found, and with the cops waiting, he slipped on his shoes, smiled, and nodded, walking toward the gate and into the unknown.

*****

Hell hath no fury, thought Margaret Rollins as she raced across town in her car. She would camp on Albert Einstein's front doorstep if she had to. The address of Einstein's house was well known, as paparazzi, fans and autograph seekers, and even the F.B.I. often camped out by his front gate for a glimpse of the world's most famous genius.

When she arrived, she was alone. No throngs were there at the moment. She marched through the gate and before she could knock on the door or ring the bell, Helen Dukas opened the front door.

"Come in Margaret," she said, looking up and down the street. She held the door, and let her inside.

Margaret, loaded for bear, softened some at the surprisingly warm welcome, but her improvement in mood lasted only a few seconds.

"Where is he, Mrs. Dukas? Where is Dr. Einstein? He's going to tell me right now about this…this Philadelphia experiment, and just where Henry is."

"I am right here, Mrs. Rollins," said Einstein, appearing from around the corner. "Let's get some fresh air? No?" He led her through the house to the back door, out into the garden. The abundance of late summer blooms from dozens of rose bushes, though fading, still perfumed the garden.

"I've just arrived back from the Shipyard in Philadelphia," he said. "I don't know vaht to say. I feel awful. I'm so sorry…"

"For what, Dr. Einstein? Sorry for what? What has happened to my husband?" Even outside, the volume of her voice was too loud for Einstein's comfort. He pointed toward the house, and then put his fingers across his lips.

"The truth is, Mrs. Rollins, I don't know." He almost whispered it to her. "I vill tell you zhat I am responsible. He vas verking for me vhen he…vhen he disappeared."

The very word 'disappear' was a trigger sending chills throughout Margaret's body. Einstein saw the discomfort on her face, and motioned for her to follow him deeper into the garden. They sat on an old iron bench near a birdbath that was getting a workout from two chipper sparrows.

"Ve vere conducting an experiment," he continued, "und Henry vasn't supposed to be anywhere near za ship. He vas supposed to have gotten off vis za crew and been beside me on za dock, safe und sound."

"What ship?" asked Margaret, still frustrated.

"The USS Eldridge, a Navy ship, like a smaller version of a battleship. A bad situation erupted caused by an…shall we say "enemy of the State," und the spy und Henry vere on board vhen za test began."

"The spy? The test?" she asked.

Einstein sighed, knowing full well the U.S. Department of the Navy was probably already correctly guessing at what was transpiring in his back yard. Giving in, he told her everything he knew. He felt he owed the couple that much. He told her about Henry, the German, and the ship, which vanished in an electromagnetic fog, reappeared 13 hours later, and that the German, now dead, was on board, but Henry was not. Margaret listened in stunned silence. She and Einstein sat for a moment, neither talking.

"Don't ask me vhy," said Einstein, looking up at his traumatized guest. "But I don't sink your Henry ist dead, und I sink you might know vhy, from your own experiences, even."

While sitting in Dr. Albert Einstein's flower garden Margaret Rollins was forced to face head on the reality of her own two-week disappearance and how it had shaken the foundation of everything she and Henry and the world believed.

"If you can, Mrs. Rollins," said Einstein. "Please tell me vaht you faced zoes many months ago. Henry has told me some of zis already, and of his theories on the Multiverse."

"Please, call me Margaret," she said, before closing her eyes, taking a deep breath, preparing to say aloud that which she had repressed for so long.

*****

The morning was already hot and humid, and as Henry Rollins walked through town, he limped from the pain caused by still damp shoes and tender feet. He fought through the pain from muscles and bruised bone that had not recovered from man-to-man combat aboard the Eldridge. Two blocks down the street, he had to take off his shoes and one sock. His feet needed air.

No one paid him much attention, as he looked every bit like a young, drunken, homeless man. They didn't notice his clothing was odd, not quite a style anyone had before seen. Passersby might have guessed he was European, but no one really looked too hard, or made eye contact with him. He was just another obviously unstable, barefoot man walking aimlessly down the sidewalk.

He stopped in front of a drugstore, and wiggled out a newspaper from a tied bundle that had just been thrown on the sidewalk.

August 20, 1943. He breathed in sharply, knowing it was not August, but September. Then he read the name of the paper; *Norfolk News.* Though incredible to comprehend, the fact that he was in Norfolk made at least some sense. He dared put words in his mind that might explain what had happened. *Einstein's experiment has teleported me, the Eldridge and the German, 250 miles to Norfolk, Virginia.* Though all of this was confusing and fantastic to comprehend, it paled in comparison to the headline. *Fed - Stat and C.S.A. come to Agreement on Funding Border Fence.*

The annual Armistice Day celebration had been a week earlier on August 13, and had been in honor of the surrender and ceasefire in 1866 of the United States of America, in effect, granting victory to the Confederate States of America.

When the Confederate gunship and the lifeline thrown to Rollins in the water all disappeared, and the sky flashed around him he'd traveled again and, though he didn't know it, found himself seven days later already a fugitive in a foreign land. The C.S.A. was still searching for the mysterious sailor and enemy combatant who'd vanished before their eyes.

The sound of cloth gently flapping in the warm summer breezes caught his ear. When he looked up he noticed more Confederate flags, with the same basic design as the Civil War-era Southern Cross flags known to every history student and child of the South. But, they were everywhere. Waving from tops of streetlights, in front of the bank, the post office, and on the license plates of passing cars. All the vehicles seemed to be the same make and model, one he'd never seen before.

"It must be a dream," he said, the reality intoxicating, manifesting itself as vertigo. He looked for a friendly face, but none of the busy commuters on the sidewalk seemed willing.

*****

Helen Dukas arrived in the garden with a tray stand, a pot of coffee, two cups, and some fruit. She placed the tray near Einstein and Margaret Rollins, and then excused herself back inside.

"Dr. Einstein, it was the single most horrible experience of my life. I was certain I had gone mad. I'm still not completely sure I haven't."

"Ja, ja, I can't even imagine," said Einstein. "Vehn did you first realize somesing vas...off.?"

"I was standing near the den in our home in Sugarland, Maryland," she continued, "and then it was as if I was in someone else's home. Oh it was the very same house, and looked very similar, but I got the strangest feeling right away that it was different, that something wasn't right. When I walked into the hallway it all really fell apart. I saw photographs of Henry and me hanging on the wall that I'd never seen before. Pictures of us in places we'd never been. Terrified and shaking I called out to Henry, but he wasn't home. I was in the house by myself."

She paused, trying to catch her breath. Einstein patted her forearm.

"My heart is beating out of my chest just from retelling this story."

"Go slow, my dear. Have some coffee," said Einstein, pouring cups for them both. "Henry told me much of zis. He has a zeory, well actually I have the zeory, und he's verking on proving it. He vanted to see if your experience matched a very unusual mathematical postulation."

"What, Dr. Einstein?" she asked, looking for any scrap of good news on which to hang her last vestiges of hope.

"Za Multiverse. Parallel universes. Vermhole travel. It seems my relativity equation from 30 years ago has stirred za pot."

Some of the terms were not entirely new to her. Henry had been obsessed with relativity long before *the incident*, and afterward he had tried to tell his wife about the other theories, possibly explaining what had happened to her, though she hadn't been ready to listen. They were not the kinds of things taught anywhere, or ever even discussed, and she pleaded with him not to bring up the subject. Now she wished she'd listened more and stayed open to what he was asking her to consider.

"Today is a new day, Doctor," she added rationally, while smoothing the front of her dress. "Today I'm ready to hear, and try to understand. It's all I have."

Einstein paused and sipped his coffee. The sparrows, still fussing with one another and splashing, created a momentary distraction, bringing smiles to both of them. Then they flew off leaving Margaret to wait for some sort of explanation from the only man, other than her husband, who might be able to help her make sense of any of this.

"Very few people understand za zeoretical possibilities," said Einstein. "I am one of zem. I sink your Henry ist another."

"So you're talking about some sort of, what? A parallel existence?" she asked.

"Ja, somesing like zhat. Zese ideas date back as far as recorded history. Za Greeks, Taoists, Hopi Indians, even Jesus himself talks about heaven und earth. Zese are all places vhere ve might exist, different than our own. Some sink ve might be able to travel back und forth. Not in some craft, but by simply aligning ourselves with za portals, za vermholes that allow for it."

"Wormholes?"

Einstein smiled, with difficulty over emphasizing the 'W'. "Ja, WORMholes."

He picked up an apple off the tray, and held it in the air.

"A verm crawling along za outside of this apple wants to get from here to there," he said, pointing from the stem at the top, to the bottom. "He could crawl along za outside, und it might take him, say, 20 minutes. But zhen it dawns on him he could eat his way straight through, cutting travel time, und have a full belly. When he's done, you still have ze apple, but you also have a tunnel, connecting two points in space. Zis ist de wurmloch…pardon me, za vermhole."

He took a bite from the apple, and looked up at Margaret.

"I believe the Eldridge traveled through time und space. Ve know Henry vas on board—ve saw him clearly. I know it's unfazamable, zis possibility, but I believe."

"Henry definitely believes," said Margaret, her thoughts never too far from her missing husband. "I wonder if he's safe? I wonder if he's…where I was? Oh, my Henry…"

Chapter 16

Norfolk, Virginia
Confederate States of America
10:37 a.m. August 20, 1943

"I just don't believe what I'm seeing," muttered Henry Rollins as he walked through downtown Norfolk, Virginia, a city he'd visited before, but that now looked very different. Though he had a hunch it would be futile, he tried to find a phone. After a few more minutes of walking, he did locate a phone booth with 'C.S.A.' stamped into its metal exterior. It was nearly identical to the red telephone boxes of England, something he'd never seen in person, but still recognized. It was much too near the police station for his comfort, but he entered the closet-sized phone booth and took a deep breath.

Remarkably, he still had change in his pocket, but it slipped through the coin mechanism, rejected. It seemed U.S. coinage had no place in a Confederate payphone. He pressed "O" and waited. When an operator picked up, so did his spirits.

"Operator. May I help you?" asked a sweet voice, dripping with Southern charm.

"Princeton, New Jersey. Collect call to—"

"My, aren't you the funny one?" she laughed, interrupting him. "I don't have time to play, Sugar. How can I help you?"

"I...I'm not playing. I'm trying to reach Princeton, New Jersey."

After a loud click the line went dead, followed by a dial tone. The operator was gone. Rollins assumed that long distance calls might not be in the cards. Frustrated he slammed the phone receiver into its cradle, and the plastic earpiece broke into shards. From the front window of the local police substation, an officer saw what had transpired and quickly ran down the five steps to the sidewalk.

"You! What are you doing?" asked the cop, arriving, opening the phone booth door to see Rollins with the broken phone still in his hand.

"I didn't mean to," Rollins started. "It just broke."

"It just broke because you just broke it." The cop looked at him, and in another stroke of bad luck recognized him. "You're the half-naked drunk from Mallory Park this morning," he said. "Let me see your hands. Now!"

Rollins dropped the shattered phone, raised his hands only to be spun backward by the wrists and promptly handcuffed. Moments later he was marched a few feet down the sidewalk, up a short flight of stairs, and forcefully introduced to the Norfolk City Police Department. It was the first time he'd ever been arrested. The charge was 'Destruction of State Property' and he was booked at 11:07 a.m. and thrown in a holding cell.

"Your I.D. says you're Doctor Henry Rollins, and that you live in Princeton, New Jersey?" asked the arresting officer through the bars, not quite believing it. He was holding Rollins' wallet and a clipboard.

He examined the I.D. and lanyard that had been around Rollins neck, which surprisingly stayed put through his antics on and off the Eldridge. It had been held in place by his life jacket. "This one says you're working for the United States Navy, United States of America?"

"That's right," said Rollins. Lying at this point wouldn't help. *Maybe there's an Embassy?*

"Is this a joke? If you're a doctor, I'm the Queen of Canada. The United States of America? Really?" The cop sneered, assuming the I.D.s were fake and the property of a mad man.

"I am. A PhD. I'm a Doctor of Applied Science. I teach at Princeton University and the Institute."

"You're a damn Yankee liar is what you really are. Or just plain crazy." He ran another possibility through his head, but dismissed it. "You're too stupid to be a spy."

"I assure you, Sir, I am none of those things. I am not a liar, I'm not crazy, stupid, or a spy. I will admit to being a little confused and frustrated. I seem to have…blacked out."

"Uh huh," said the disbelieving cop, scribbling notes on forms attached to his clipboard.

The small police station was getting busier, and two officers brought a handcuffed man through the front door. Henry guessed he might have been 50 or so, and observing his countenance, along with the unmistakable odor of liquor, he guessed very intoxicated.

"Your wallet is empty, except for $22 in play money," said the cop nearest to Rollins. "I'm guessing you won't be able to make bail, pay a fine or restitution to the State Telecommunication Authority?"

Rollins sighed. "No, I guess not, but maybe—."

"Maybe won't cut it. Welcome to the Norfolk Correctional System. You'll be our guest for…mmm…my guess, maybe 60 days, if the Judge is in a good mood."

"Sixty days!" screamed Rollins, standing and pushing against the bars of the jail cell. "No! My wife. My job. This can't be happening."

"Oh, trust me," said the cop. "It is."

A jailer led the newly arrived, drunken prisoner toward the cell, and told Henry to step back. The cell door was unlocked, and the drunk unceremoniously pushed in before it slammed shut behind him. Rollins spotted a small platform, large enough for one man to sit, and he did so, head in his hands. The drunk looked around, looked at Henry briefly, mumbled something, and sat hard in the nearest corner, snoring almost the second his backside hit the filthy floor.

"My God," said Henry softly. "My Margaret."

*****

"Henry."

Margaret Rollins kept repeating his name, even while Einstein was talking to her. It didn't matter whether she was alone or not. His name kept forming on her lips, even without her realizing it. She'd never experienced anything as heartrending as this separation, not even the difficulties from her own disappearance almost one year earlier. Her worst nightmare was repeating itself.

Not a woman to be denied much of anything, Margaret coaxed out every last bit of information Albert Einstein had to offer. Reluctantly, Einstein found himself repeating details of highly classified meetings regarding the nature of the experiment, of the Eldridge's disappearance, its reappearance, of the German spy; he felt he owed her that much. The two talked for an hour before she was finally satisfied that she had wrung every detail from the man she had last seen with her husband.

"Thank you, Doctor" she said, sincerely, though she had to fake a smile. She was trying her best not to blame him, though Einstein was already blaming himself. She found his own distress over her husband's disappearance to be in earnest, but she couldn't disagree with him. Albert Einstein was complicit in the mess that she was about to take into her own hands.

Back home in her Princeton apartment, she didn't pack a bag. She gathered up $200 saved in a canvas bag stuffed in the back of their closet, grabbed the car keys, and left Princeton at noon, for Philadelphia, and, she hoped, some answers.

On the drive she ran Einstein's comments through her head. Over and over she replayed his telling of the Eldridge story, Henry's heroics, the vanishing, and the reappearing. It made no sense, but then neither had her own disappearance and reappearance. What she'd do upon arrival at the Philadelphia Naval Yard, she hadn't a clue, but she hoped and prayed that's where some answers might be found.

Margaret Rollins was not the only one headed from Princeton to Philadelphia. Two F.B.I. agents assigned to Einstein and any other local persons of interest had added another to their ever-growing list. Especially after long visits to Einstein's home, and secret meetings in the cemetery with his secretary, they were taking a keen interest in a young woman named Margaret Rollins, deciding to tail her.

The specific details and news of the Eldridge and the ship's magic act had managed to stay out of the chatter within the intelligence community. Aside from the handful of officers present, and highly vetted security guards, for the moment, no outside law enforcement agency, including the F.B.I., knew of the experiment or its dramatic unfolding.

The agents followed her on the 90-minute drive to Philadelphia without much difficulty and watched her pull as close as she dared to the first security gate at the shipyard. She knew she'd not be able to drive right in and start demanding answers. Though the heavily guarded gate would be impossible for a civilian to breech, she knew from Einstein's spilling of secrets, that the USS Eldridge was birthed on the river, on the Shipyard's southwest side.

Sitting in her car, she thought about with whom she might hope to speak, and what she might ask. This focus, this obsession with finding answers was the only thing that kept her from breaking down and sobbing. Her husband had been missing for three days, and even the Navy said they didn't know where he was. *How far could he have gone?*

"What am I doing here?" she asked herself. A single tear ran down her cheek. When an hour dragged on, she felt heavy with sleep. A hotel near the shipyard promised some rest, and she drove from her secluded spot near the gate to check in.

The Hotel Franklin, named for Philly's favorite son, Benjamin Franklin, was moderately priced at $14 per night. In a big city hotel it was unusual, but not unheard of, for a young woman to check in alone. The clerk was polite, and told her he had only one room available, and it was on the top floor of the seven-story hotel.

"Room 703. You'll have a nice view of the river," said the clerk. "And you can see some of the shipyard activity, too."

She wasn't sure why, but that information resonated with her. She said she had no bags and would like to buy a few basic toiletries. The clerk raised his eyebrow, and pointed with a suspicious sneer. At the Hotel's concierge shop she found what she needed for an overnight, and something else— the Hotel's lost and found. A pair of cheap binoculars, probably used for a show at the nearby opera house, sat dusty and ignored in a box with an assortment of odd gloves, and even a women's single, red high heel shoe.

When the store clerk wasn't paying attention, Margaret slipped the binoculars into her purse. After paying for a toothbrush and a hairbrush, she left the ground floor taking the elevator to the seventh.

She found her way to room 703 and entered with a sense of unease and hopelessness that would not go away. Under different circumstances she would have enjoyed a hotel stay in the city. She and Henry would visit Baltimore, or New York once every couple of months and find the most expensive restaurant in town. Then they would order the cheapest items on the menu and laugh at the dirty looks the snobby wait staff would give them. They'd go to the local movie house and argue about which feature to see. She'd lean toward a drama or a love story. Sometimes she suggested war flicks like "This is the Army" with Ronald Reagan, or "Sahara" starring Humphrey Bogart. Henry, on the other hand, was all about horror. "I Walked with a Zombie," and "Frankenstein Meets the Wolfman," were his favorites from earlier that very summer. She smiled at the memory of him trying to convince her that it was a love story and that both Frankenstein's monster and the Wolfman's motives were driven by love.

"Yeah, pure Shakespeare," she said, teasing him to the point that he got mad. They spent the rest of the night making up, and making love.

Henry

A glow came from across the darkened hotel room from a slight part in the window curtains. Margaret walked over to see the view, and when she opened the curtains further she was surprised to have such a clear view of the Naval Shipyard. *Good thing I'm not a sniper.* She almost gasped when she saw what looked like a small battleship, which was indeed a Destroyer Escort, the very same ship upon which Henry Rollins was last seen.

She reached for her purse and the binoculars, hands trembling as she cleaned the lenses with her shirtsleeve, and put the cold metal to her eyes. She fumbled with the focus ring. Then it was there, as clear as if it were 10 yards away.

"USS Eldridge," she said aloud. "Henry's boat."

*****

Henry Rollins wasn't sure how long he'd slept. Five minutes or five hours, he couldn't tell. The police substation was quieter now than it had been, he noticed, though it was still light outside. Through the cell bars he could see a clock on the wall. It read 4:22. He looked at his wrist instinctively, and then remembered the jailer had taken his watch along with his wallet, and I.D.s, and gold wedding band. The uninterested officer placed everything in an envelope with Rollins' name on it, stuffing it into a file drawer.

"4:22," he said quietly to himself and the mostly empty jail cell. "I guess I slept for a few hours."

"You did," said a man from the shadows. "I know, because I listened to you snore for three hours and…" He strained to see the wall clock outside the cell. "…forty-five minutes."

"Sorry about that," said Rollins. "You snore, too, by the way." That ended the conversation for a few minutes, before Henry spoke again.

"It's been a long couple of days."

"Tell me about it," said the stranger. He sat in a darkened corner and Henry could not make out his features.

"Name's Hickok, as in Wild Bill," said the man. "People call me Hitch."

"Okay, Hitch," said Henry, actually glad to be finally talking with someone who didn't want to kill him, arrest him, or use him as a guinea pig for radical, electromagnetic experimentation.

They sat in silence for a few moments, each considering their own situation. When Hitch became tired of running the endless loop of problems through his head, he spoke.

"Who's Margaret, by the way?"

Henry figured he must have been talking in his sleep. "My wife," he answered with a sigh.

"Hmm. You said her name more than a few times."

"Yeah, I'm kind of missing from home. I know she's really worried and I can't reach her."

"Sorry to hear. Where's home?"

"Princeton, New Jersey."

Hitch was quiet for a moment. "You're a Yank?"

"Why do people keep asking me that?" said Rollins.

"Well, because you're in the Confederate States of America, and Yankees, generally speaking, are somewhat rare down here."

At this bizarre revelation and reminder of the flags he'd seen earlier, his pulse quickened and stress hormones once again coursed through his veins. *How could this be?*

"Are you speaking metaphorically or literally?" Rollins asked of the man in the corner.

"You are one unusual Yank…I guess I didn't get your name."

"Henry Rollins," he answered, still shaken. "This is Norfolk, Virginia, right?"

"Yep," said the voice, still covered by shadow. "Lived here all my life."

"And you're saying that Virginia is in the…" he had a hard time bringing himself to say the words, "the Confederate States of America?"

Hitch paused, sizing up his cellmate. "You sound kind of educated, Henry," he said. "Are you not feeling well? I mean, how could you not know that? The C.S.A. capitol is just up the road in Richmond. You probably came through Richmond to get here."

Henry chuckled slightly. "That's not exactly the route I seem to have taken. By the way, where's the U.S. capital?"

Hitch wondered if the man he was speaking with wasn't really a European spy, perhaps even German. Three weeks earlier the C.S.A. had unceremoniously hung three alleged spies from Austria without so much as a hearing. But Hickok prided himself on being a good judge of character, and Rollins seemed innocent enough, if not perhaps mad.

"The U.S. capitol?" asked Hitch, puzzled. "There's no such thing as the 'United States,' at least not since 1866. If you mean 'Where's the *Federated States* capitol?'—it's in D.C. But you knew that, right, Henry? Washington, D.C.? You've heard of it?"

"Of course, yes," said Rollins, having barely comprehended what the man was saying. "I, ahh…look, Hitch…I've had a blow to the head." Rollins turned to show him, parting his hair to reveal two scabbed-over goose eggs. "I'm still a bit confused, but I'm coming around."

"That must have been a mighty good blow? Sure you're not recuperating from an Armistice Day hangover? But I shouldn't laugh. I'm just a lousy, hopeless souse who's been on a three-week bender. It finally caught up with me."

They could hear some activity picking up around the building, inside and out, but the two men were still very much alone.

"So what are you in for?" Rollins had always wanted to ask the question; the question all the tough guys from the movies asked. Though still shaken from Hitch's statement about this upside down geopolitical reality in which he'd landed, he took some small piece of macho pride in the asking.

"Drunk and disorderly. How about you?"

He almost wished he could say 'murder' or 'racketeering,' or something truly gangster-worthy, but the truth came out instead.

"I guess I destroyed the payphone out front. I was trying to call Princeton and the operator gave me a hard time. I got upset and accidentally smashed the phone up pretty well. A cop happened to see me do it, and didn't like my explanation."

The conversation stopped again, the two men taking a moment to soak in and process all the information each had offered. Hitch, finally, was first to speak.

"What do you do?" he asked "Are you employed?"
"I am, or I was…," said Rollins. "I'm a teacher. Mathematics, physics. I'm on a…break"

"You don't say," said Hitch. "So am I. A teacher, that is. High school history for the Ol' Dominion, the great State of Virginia. I too am on a break, a permanent break, you might say."

Rollins thought about Hitch's background, and as a trained historian, he would likely be loaded with useful information. He, stood, stretched, and walked across the cell to finally see the man, still hidden in the shadows. He extended his hand into the darkness. Hitch returned the gesture.

"Nice to meet you, Hitch," said Rollins.

"Likewise."

Rollins sat on the floor, and the two got a good look at one another. Hitch was tall, thin, and hadn't shaved in weeks. His dark hair was speckled with gray and the bags under his eyes could have been from age or hard living. Henry leaned in and lowered his voice.

"Umm...do you mind if I ask you some, what I'm sure will sound like strange questions about the C.S.A. and North American history?" asked Rollins.

"Sure, what the hell. I've got nothing better to do."

*****

With the binoculars gripped tightly in her hands, Margaret Rollins peered through the window from the top floor of the Hotel Franklin. Not missing an inch of the 300-foot Eldridge, she looked from stern to bow, hoping beyond reason, she'd see Henry, or at least some sign of him.

While she came up empty, she did notice plenty of activity. It looked to her like mostly maintenance crews. Welding torches and their showers of brightly glowing molten steel lit up the deck of the boat. Her eye caught one man, in particular, who seemed to be in charge. She couldn't exactly make out officer's insignias on his uniform, but the man pointed and other men obeyed. *Maybe he's Einstein's Captain Hammond?*

She watched him closely. *If I can't get to the ship's captain, maybe he can come to me?* She watched the man for an hour, and at 8 p.m. when he walked down the gangplank, and toward the guard shack, Margaret mobilized.

Running as fast as she could out of the room, down the hall, to a miraculously waiting elevator, she made it to the Hotel's lobby in a matter of 90 seconds. Flying out the front door, which was just around the corner from the shipyard, she looked anxiously for the officer. With a stroke of luck she just saw the tall captain disappear into a shady looking rathskeller around the corner from the hotel.

Unashamed about traveling and checking into a hotel alone, and now bar hopping, she mustered additional courage and walked in the front door of the Ship-n-Shore Lounge. She was no more than two minutes behind a man she hoped might bring her one step closer to her missing husband.

The bar had some 20 or so sailors, of all makes and models: baby-faced boys, older sea-worthy veterans, and at the bar by himself sat Captain Hammond, as identified by a nametag. She'd made an educated guess, and had gotten it right. After a quick glance around she suddenly felt self-conscious, noticing she was the only woman in the place, and she wasn't the only one making the observation.

"I'll have an Old Fashioned," she asked the bartender, who had already pegged her as a prostitute, though she was missing the low-cut advertising garments most of the working girls wore. When the bartender looked dubious about ever receiving payment from her, Margaret reached into her purse and produced a one-dollar bill, more than enough for the 35-cent cocktail.

"Keep it," she said, to the bartender, who looked only slightly less judgmental.

She sat two seats to the left of Hammond, who saw her from the corner of his eye, but made no acknowledgement. He drank a beer, lost in his own thoughts.

Two young sailors from across the dimly lit bar took note of the only woman in the place and approached, placing themselves on either side of her. They were young, Margaret thought, very young, maybe even teenagers. The Navy regularly recruited 17-year-olds during the war; some even younger than that managed to sneak in. For most it was their first time away from home. With a few bucks in their pockets, smart looking uniforms, and fresh haircuts, these kids were known for their bravery in combat, bravado on the streets, impulsivity, and raging hormones.

"Hello sweetheart," said the one to her left, placing his arm around Margaret's shoulder and getting close enough that she could smell the alcohol oozing from his pores.

"Not interested," she said, smiling, quickly removing the young man's arm. His friend laughed heartily at the rejection.

"Maybe I'm more your type?" asked the other sailor, swooping in from the other side.

"No, I'm sorry, you're not," she said. "Please, boys, I'm not in the mood. No offense."

"Not in the mood?" asked the first sailor, incensed. "Since when is a whore not in the mood? My money ain't good enough for you?" he was getting louder and angrier. The drunken sailors' antics caught the attention of Captain Hammond.

"Leave the lady alone," he said, standing, "or I'll knock your teeth out, then have you court-martialed. Understand?"

The sailor was just sober enough to get it. "Sorry. Sir," he said looking at the Captain, just noticing his rank. "And sorry, Miss. We meant no harm."

"That's okay fellas," said Margaret, trying to defuse the tension. "Just please remember that every woman traveling alone isn't necessarily working or looking for a date."

Both young sailors tipped their hats, and backed away. Hammond sat back down and smiled at Margaret, who smiled back. A minute went by as she decided best how to approach him.

"Excuse me," she said, turning slightly in his direction. Hammond turned to look at her. He noticed how pretty she was, and how troubled. It was the bittersweet combination of emotions upon her attractive face that had him so enchanted.

"Yes?" asked the Captain, politely.

"First of all, thank you," she said, with a quick nod toward the sailors in the corner.

Hammond smiled and nodded back.

"I'm not sure this is the best place to talk," she continued, "...but. I'm Margaret Rollins. Dr. Henry Rollins' wife."

The Captain's face went pale. The very thing he'd been trying to erase from his memory came rushing back. He knew better than to say a word to her, and knew exactly why she was there.

"I'm sorry Ma'am. I don't know a...Dr. Rollins." Margaret confirmed his identity by double-checking his nametag—Captain Hammond—and she was sure he was lying.

"I understand your hesitance to talk with me, Captain Hammond. But I saw you on the Eldridge, and already know about the ship's disappearance, the German spy, the electromagnetic experiment, and I know of the various gunfights on board, and of the ship's return to port a couple of nights ago, so you needn't worry about spilling Navy secrets. I already know most of them."

He was stunned by her brazenness and impressed with her level of knowledge. Though he was unable to discern how she could have known, he accepted the fact that she might possibly know more about *Canned Heat* than did he.

"Where is my husband?" she asked plainly.

He sighed, and looked straight into her sad eyes, genuinely sympathizing. "I wish I knew, Mrs. Rollins. I really do wish I knew."

She took a sip from her drink, and wiped the corners of her mouth with a cocktail napkin.

"Nobody seems to know," she said. They sat in silence for a moment, both lost in thought, before she turned to him.

"He had a small suitcase with him," she said. "The Navy came to see me two days ago, but failed to return my husband's belongings."

"It might still be on board, in the guest quarters," Hammond offered. "We're...umm... retooling the ship after the..." He didn't know what to call the events of the past two days.

"*The incident*?" said Margaret. It's the phrase she and Henry had settled on after her own terrifying disappearance less than one year earlier. The Captain nodded. It was as good a word as any for something as bizarre, and difficult to explain, as teleportation, if that was even what it was.

"I'd like to get it back," she said, "the suitcase and whatever clothing might be with it." Her voice trembled, while her eyes glistened and threatened tears.

"I understand," said the Captain. "I'll see to it personally."

"When?" she asked again, not letting him off the hook so easily. It almost sounded rude, but given the circumstances he excused the directness.

"Well, I'm not staying on board," he said, "too much noise. I'm at the Hotel Franklin. I will check to see if Dr Rollins' bag and personal effects are indeed on the ship, and meet you in the Hotel lobby in say…20 minutes?"

"Yes," answered Margaret. "I'm staying at the Franklin as well." She sniffled, holding back her emotion. She finished her drink in one quick gulp, and stood.

"Thank you Captain. I'll be waiting in the lobby and will see you in a few minutes."

As she left the bar, two F.B.I. special agents watched from the shadows across the street. When Captain Hammond left a moment later, one of them scribbled a note in a black notebook. *Hammond met with Rollins woman, 7:45 p.m. at the Ship-n-Shore, Philly.* The agents quietly discussed what they'd seen.

"First Einstein, now the good Captain," said one agent to the other. "This Rollins dame is getting around. Wonder what she knows?"

"A hell of a lot more than we do, I guarantee it," said the other agent, stepping backward out of the streetlight and into the shadows.

Back on board the Eldridge, Hammond did find Dr. Rollins' clothes and a small suitcase. He was glad to be able to offer at least this much, and to see, once again, the prettiest young woman he'd met in a long while.

*****

A depressed and bewildered Henry Rollins was sitting in a jail cell, one from which Margaret and the entire U.S. military would be unable to rescue him. For now he would have to attempt to assemble the puzzle that was his current predicament, one oddly shaped piece at a time.

"So you were saying we're in the Confederate States of America, as in U.S. Civil War Confederate?"

"Yeah," answered Hitch, with a tone in his voice that said without saying 'why wouldn't you know something everyone with a third grade education would know?'

"Humor me, Hitch. How long has this been the C.S.A.?"

"Since Independence Day, August 13, 1866. Are you from Europe or something?"

"You wouldn't believe me if I told you," said Rollins.

"Word to the wise," said Hitch. "Curb your crazy talk around the police and the military. They've been known to hang anyone they suspect of being a Fed-Stat or foreign spy. No trial, no nothing, just a quick and straightforward hanging. Then your body goes in an unmarked grave. Got it?"

This sent a chill through Rollins. "Thanks. I will." He looked around and saw they were still very alone in the darkened corner of the police station. "Since it's just the two of us, a couple more questions?"

"Sure, fire away," said Hitch, beginning to get bored with the history lesson.

"Where do all the Yankees live, if there's no United States of America?"

"In Fed-Stat."

"Fed-stat?"

"Yes, the Federated States of America," whispered Hitch, uncomfortable with this particular line of questions. "It's what they replaced the United States of America with at the end of the Civil War, after they impeached Lincoln."

"Oh my," said Rollins. How could he tell his cellmate that Lincoln had not been impeached, but rather assassinated? He chose not to mention it and stopped quizzing his new and only friend in the world, but now Hitch was curious.

"So where are you from, again?" he asked.

"I live in Princeton, New Jersey," said Rollins. "But I suspect it's not the same town I once knew."

"Oh? How long have you been gone?"

"About 14 hours, the best I can guess, but I know I left in September."

"Oookaaay," said Hitch, with some condescension. "You do know it's August?" Henry didn't answer him. Hitch took a deep breath. "Listen…my head hurts. Let's take a break on all this."

Henry nodded, ready for a rest as well.

"I'll sure be glad to get the hell out of here and back to my apartment," said Hitch.

"When will that happen?"

"Tomorrow morning, I hope. They always just let me go out the front door after I've slept it off. Have they told you anything about your release?"

"Not much," answered Rollins. "One cop mentioned 60 days, but I think he was trying to make a point. At least I hope so."

"Maybe not," said Hitch. "They can be sons of bitches when they want to be."

"I'm a little worried. They have my wallet, which has some…what may look to them like strange I.D. cards. They know I'm from New Jersey, for starters. I guess that won't help."

"No it won't."

The men sat in silence for a moment, and though his head was pounding Hitch couldn't help himself, his curiosity fully piqued.

"Why the hell are you in Virginia, anyway?"

"I don't really know," answered Rollins honestly enough. "I have a suspicion, but it's too wild to even contemplate, let alone try to explain. Let's just say I'm involved in the war effort."

"The war? You mean in Europe?"

"Yes."

"I thought Fed-Stat was staying out of it, staying clear of ol' Adolf?"

Rollins puzzled at this. He knew the Allies were fully involved in the War, both in Europe and against Japan. Hitch, who seemed well educated and who claimed to be a high school teacher, would have known this. His mind spun, trying again to reconcile this twisted retelling of current events.

"Ahh, yeah...ol' Adolf," said Rollins, trying not to stir any more doubt in the mind of his new friend. Everything Hitch was saying had a ring of familiarity, which he could not quite place. He'd heard details from Hitch that somehow he knew, but didn't know how he knew.

His thoughts turned away from the greater issues of a world turned upside down, and toward his immediate problem; getting out of jail without proper I.D., any money, or a credible story. He dared not let himself think about his greatest challenge—getting home to Margaret.

"You've been in before, Hitch?" asked Rollins.

"Afraid so. I don't always know when to stop with the sauce, and my big mouth gets me in trouble. So, yeah, I'm what you'd call a 'regular.'"

"Your arrests don't interfere with your teaching job?"

"The hell they don't. I was fired a year ago. Been doing odd jobs ever since."

"Sorry to hear that."

"Well, shit, I guess I got what I deserved. I'd have fired me, too."

"I hate to bring you into my world of crazy problems," said Rollins, "but if you were me, knowing what you know about how they run things here, and you wanted to, let's say..." he lowered his voice to a whisper, "...escape, how would you do it?"

"I wouldn't," said Hitch, also whispering. "Not worth it. You're looking at 60 days now? Add in an escape attempt and you'll be doing hard labor in the North Carolina gold mines for 10 years, in shackles no less, if they don't decide just to hang you."

Rollins didn't like the prospect, but he continued his line of inquiry.

"Humor me, just for kicks. How would you do it?"

Hitch sighed. "Well, I'd be the model prisoner for starters. Lots of 'Yessirs' and 'Nosirs' and make them comfortable with you. It wouldn't hurt if you sounded less...Yankee. Can you put some twang in your talk?"

Henry Rollins, born in Rhode Island, knew he couldn't fake a southern accent if his life depended on it, which it probably did.

"The best time might actually be tomorrow morning," continued Hitch, "when they come to transport you out of here. They'll strip you down, put the stripes on you—that's your prison uniform—handcuff you inside the cell, and then lead you down the hall to see the judge. After the arraignment, you'll be transported to the county detention center. If you're lucky, and it's just you, they'll only have two guards leading you into the van. If there's a big group of prisoners, that means more guards, and more chances to get shot.

"Okay," said Rollins, "so let's say I'm handcuffed, walking freely to the truck. I can't just make a break for it, can I?"

"That's what I'd do," said Hitch. "I'd look for my opportunity and run like hell. There's a spot where they park the trucks to pick up prisoners. Lots of twisty, turning, back alleys, places to get lost. But they'll be after you fast and you'll be handcuffed. They'll come hard, guns blazing. They won't give a good God damn who they run over to find you, and they will kill you."

Rollins sighed. "That's the best you've got?"

"'fraid so, sorry."

After a dinner of chicken and rice, and a little more small talk, both men nodded off to an uneasy sleep; Rollins' fitful and Hitch's interrupted by a stage five hangover.

Chapter 17

Norfolk, Virginia
Confederate States of America
Norfolk Police Substation 1
7:12 a.m. August 21, 1943

The next morning, just as Hitch had predicted, prison stripes were thrown to Henry with an order to strip and put them on. Hearing the guards, Hitch rolled over, surprised to see a second set of stripes thrown in his corner, with the same order. The guards disappeared.

"What the hell..." said Hitch, looking at the prison garb he'd never before been asked to wear. "Guard!"

"What do you want, Hickok?" asked the unseen guard from down the hallway.

"Umm...is this a mistake?" he asked pointing to the black and white striped prison uniform. "Isn't it time for me to get out of here?"

"No mistake. Judge wants to see you this time. Said he's tired of you wasting the taxpayer's money, and our time and space, and eating our food without so much as a kiss on the lips. He says since you seem to like it here so much he wants to formally extend your stay."

"No, no, no!" Hitch protested. "I've got to get out of here."

"Too bad," said the guard. "Shouldn't have gotten your filthy ass thrown in here to begin with."

Hitch sat back, staring at the uniform in disbelief. Rollins was silent; there was nothing for him to say about his cellmate's miscalculation of his good standing and status, let alone his personal hygiene. Rollins reluctantly stripped to his underwear, folded his street clothes into a neat pile, and donned the prison uniform.

"If she could see me now..." he grumbled, thinking that Margaret would have to smile slightly at the wardrobe. She loved to laugh, especially at his expense, but did so out of endearment and love, the way a little girl adored and laughed at a new puppy.

"This is bullshit," said Hitch, putting on the stripes. "They've never held me or sent me to County before."

An hour later a guard slid two pie tins of gruel through the food slot, and handed each of the men a glass of water through the bars. Six long hours later, in the middle of the afternoon, the guard reappeared. Both men were asked to put their hands through a slot in the cell where they were unceremoniously handcuffed. When the cell door was opened, a single guard led the two men down the hall.

"The Judge is at County this afternoon," explained the guard as they walked past the courtroom. "We're headed straight there. He'll want to see you tomorrow morning. I don't want any trouble from you guys."

"Yes, Sir," answered Rollins. Then added "No trouble," with a poor attempt at sounding less 'Yankee.'

"How 'bout you Wild Bill?" asked the guard.

"Yeah."

When they stepped outside, both men tried their best to shield their eyes from the bright late afternoon sun. They came upon an armed guard and an idling prisoner transport truck. The driver walked toward the truck's front door while the prison guard opened the back.

"Get in," said the guard.

Rollins climbed up and sat on a bench. Before Hitch got in behind him, he stopped and looked down toward the tightly packed gravel road. "Guess you're not planning on making it to County?" he asked.

The guard looked at him cautiously. "Why do you say that?"

"Tire's flat, or just about."

The guard looked under the truck.

"Which one?"

"Driver's rear."

"Don't look flat to me," said the guard. "Maybe a little soft. I don't know. Richie, come out here and look at this tire."

The driver got out of the truck and walked to the back.

"Get on in Hickok," said the guard, gesturing toward the open hatch. Hitch sat on the back gate of the truck, as if to help himself in, unable to use his shackled hands. When the two guards had their heads and necks strained to look at the back tire Hitch jumped. With a perfectly placed kick he caught the driver in the jaw, sending him dazed into the prison guard, both hitting the ground. When the guard tried to stand, Hitch kicked him again.

"Hold on, Henry!" yelled Hitch as he jumped from the back of the truck, and made a beeline for the open driver's door. When he put the truck in first gear, and popped the clutch hitting the gas hard, Rollins almost flew out the open back.

The truck screamed down the alley, as the less injured guard stood, retrieved his sidearm from his holster, and began firing.

The bullets, four or five in rapid succession, whizzed into the vehicle and through the steel, narrowly missing both men. As Hitch wheeled the prison van as best as his manacled hands would let him, Rollins was thrown hard to the left and right, like a rag doll in a washing machine. Once they rounded the first corner, the gunshots stopped, but that was only a small victory. Soon the entire Norfolk Police force would be after them, and if they managed to elude capture from the police, then the C.S.A.'s federal forces would join in. Escaped prisoners were simply not tolerated, no matter how minor their original offenses. Death or capture of any escaped prisoner was of the highest priority. The two guards allowing the escape faced dereliction of duty charges, and were in danger of imprisonment themselves.

Even in the midst of the chaos, Henry's thoughts were never too far from the, kind, strong face of his wife. Hanging on the best he could, he thought of her, replaying snippets of conversations, laughs, even her tears after returning from who knew where. She had sounded like a woman possessed, when she told him of the strange places and world events of her temporary dislocation. He'd tried to pay attention, but she was confused and rambling. After she calmed down, she'd just refused to talk about it at all. But here in the middle of a prison break, some of the things that Margaret had said were clicking inside Henry Rollins' brain.

"I'll be damned…that's it!" he shouted a little too loudly. "My God, I think I'm there. This is Maggie's other world! It has to be!"

"What?" shouted Hitch from the driver's seat. As he piloted the van and raced through alleys, around sharp corners, Henry was hardly aware of their peril. He felt that for the first time, he really knew for certain where Margaret had gone: The C.S.A., Fed-Stat, Hitler's Europe. In the swirling dust behind the speeding van, he thought he saw her image, and then heard her voice, as if she were about to climb in the back of the van with them. *Henry, you sweet fool, hang on and come home!*

*****

In the lobby of the Hotel Franklin, Margaret Rollins sat, gazing down at the floor. Her eyes were open but she did not see anything. As if in a trance, her slow breathing and lack of awareness were two indicators of shock. Her beloved was gone, and it seemed no one could help her, not even the handsome Captain Hammond who had just arrived.

She heard his voice as if he were speaking through a bale of cotton.

"Mrs. Rollins. Mrs. Rollins? Are you okay?"

"Hmm? What? Oh yes," she said, finally coming around to find Hammond standing before her. She saw a small suitcase sitting on the lobby's marble floor and she recognized it as Henry's.

"This is it," she said. She clutched the small overnight bag as if it were Henry himself.

"I wish there were more I could do," said Hammond. "Please don't hesitate to call, though I'm hard to reach. We're headed out in 24 hours, trying to beat some bad weather. They tell me my ship is, well, ship shape. But I don't believe them. If you'd seen the mess…"

Margaret looked away, imagining Henry in the midst of some horrible experiment. Hammond immediately wished he could take back his words.

"Sorry…," he said. "Anyway, we're headed out to sea, but I will find a way to get word to you if I hear anything, anything at all."

"Thank you Captain," she said. "You're being very kind. Maybe I'll just stay at the hotel for a few days, see if he…see if anything changes."

"You could do that," said Hammond, who struggled to find the better side of his nature, denying his growing infatuation with the vulnerable young woman, "but why not just go home. You'll be more comfortable there, and we can certainly reach you easily enough."

"Maybe you're right."

Margaret took the Captain's advice and checked out, though she didn't go back to Princeton.

*****

As U-boat Captain Zoeller and crew steamed toward coordinates halfway between the Carolina coast and Bermuda, the skies around them were gray and humid. A strong wave of tropical moisture stirred the pot of September weather in the Atlantic, shooting warm, moist air up the Gulf Stream.

Zoeller's U-boat, like all the others of the 1940s, was not a true submarine. It ran on the surface, primarily, to take in fresh air, and run its diesel engines, which recharged a series of batteries. The batteries were used to power the vessel when submerged to avoid enemy fire, detection, or occasionally, the weather. But with no oxygen scrubbers, or a way to recharge the batteries once under water, a U-boat could only stay submerged for 16 to 24 hours, unlike modern submarines that can manage to stay under for months at a time.

The dawn was breaking, and Zoeller, up top in the open air, saw the gray skies beginning to show just how massive the storm to his south and east might become. The water was already choppy and the swells had started to grow, although the strong winds and rain had not yet arrived.

"What's the latest weather report look like?" he asked his First Officer.

"Last we received, about 15 minutes ago, it seems the storm is headed north-northeast at 18 knots."

"Isn't that just wunderbar?" asked Zoeller, not expecting a response. He turned to Oberleutnant Fritz Dengler, his First Watch Officer, and asked him to make sure the ship and crew were ready for the transfer in two hours' time.

"What is it we're transferring, Sir?" asked Dengler, annoying the Captain, who was not privy to the information himself.

"You'll know when I know, Dengler. You have your orders."

"Yes, Sir!" said Dengler, who at 33 years old was just a few years younger than the Captain. His position as First Watch Officer was the equivalent to that of an Executive Officer, the second in command, in the American Navy. Being treated like an errand boy, instead of a confidant and an officer worthy of the Captain's respect, was beginning to take its toll.

In the radio room a teleprinter whirred to life and chattered like a thousand birds pecking at a pie tin as it printed from a roll of paper. It read:

"For Kapitän Zoeller's Eyes Only. Signal when ready."

A red light flashed awaiting the sign indicating Zoeller would be the lone observer of the incoming message.

Zoeller followed the officer into the radio room and knew the protocol—wait until he was alone, and then depress the flashing "Erhalten" receive button and await transmission. The machine rattled back to life and Zoeller, alone in the small room, read the top secret communiqué as it rolled off the teleprinter.

"To Kapitän Zoeller. For your eyes only: You will be transferring radioactive cargo from U-4710 at the previously agreed upon coordinates. Trade with U-4710 to make room for the G7e-UP1, a nuclear-tipped torpedo. It will match the specifications of your current arsenal of G7e torpedoes, except for its hidden uranium warhead. Your gunners will not be able to discern its difference. It is untested, and dangerous, with the potential explosive power of 15 kilotons, some 30 million pounds of TNT."

"15 kilotons..." said Zoeller in disbelief. G7e torpedoes were standard aboard mid-WWII U-boats, but the 'UP1," which stood for 'Uranium Projekt #1' classified it as the only nuclear torpedo in the German Arsenal. It was the only one of its kind. Its designers and engineers promised catastrophic destruction. Still years before the Trinity Test and the Japanese bombings, no weapon had been dreamed of or seen by any living human boasting that magnitude of destructive power. Zoeller continued reading the communiqué.

"You are to maintain firing readiness of this weapon. A target, yet undetermined, will be given to you in a timely manner. When you fire from your aft torpedo tube, you must be a minimum of two kilometers away, stay submerged, and maintain a maximum speed away from the blast zone. The warhead is set to detonate 20 minutes from deployment. It will not detonate upon impact, nor use a magnetic trigger. This is a timed trigger detonation system engaged automatically at the time of launch. Repeat: It is essential that you be a minimum of two kilometers away before firing, and be underway in the opposite direction, which should put you four to five kilometers away from the blast zone.

Captain Adler of U-4710 does not know the torpedo is nuclear. You, the G7e-UP1, and an operative, who will be made known to you at a later time, must maintain absolute secrecy. END."

It seemed after all that Weisenberg's work had made sense to someone in the Wehrmacht, and that the Narrentraum file had been put to use. Zoeller sat stunned for a moment and considered the implications. It was an honor to be chosen for this mission, though he was beginning to suspect it sounded like suicide. *A nuclear torpedo? I'll be damned.* There'd been plenty of talk, rumors and whispers of the nuclear program, Uranprojekt, but this was the first confirmation he had that a weapon was ready for testing. Weapons grade uranium and plutonium were so rare and hard to come by that those in charge of the clandestine program decided an American target made the most sense. With the War going badly, the consensus was: why not test the device where it might do the most damage, in hopes of it actually working? London was chosen first, but it seemed the Americans were the bigger threat, so U-4713 and its spotless record and ruthless Kapitän were chosen.

Zoeller rose from the chair, and opened the hatch door where the radio operator stood guard. He folded the message and placed it inside an interior breast pocket and said nothing, and revealed no emotion, leaving the curious officers very dissatisfied.

An hour later the radio operator indicated they'd made contact with U-4710 and would be at the meeting coordinates in 15 minutes. The deteriorating weather had kept air patrols grounded, making their surface rendezvous less dangerous. With both U-boat Captains on their respective decks, standing in the observation towers, they spotted one another and ordered preparations for rafting and the transfer.

The two gunmetal gray warships, far from home, and far from any air cover or help of the Luftwaffe, slowed while the two Captains greeted each other with a wave.

The swells were manageable, but the conditions were far from ideal, making the simultaneous transfer difficult. When the G7e-UP1, hoisted by winch, banged against the side of Zoeller's U-boat, he was certain the end was near, and cursed the winch operators.

"Verdammte idioten! Dumkopfs!"

After no immediate, or even delayed, 15-kiloton detonation occurred he breathed again. The two captains conferred from their outdoor conning towers, yelling the 20 feet between them.

"Seems like once again we are to do the bidding of high command without much to go on," said Captain Adler.

"Ja, Captain. It seems so," answered Zoeller. "I know very little about this torpedo," he lied. "Do you know anything?"

"Nein. Nothing," answered Adler, "only that I'm glad to be rid of it. We sail for Gibraltar as soon as the transfer is complete. I hope to avoid the worst of this weather."

"I'm afraid we'll be in the thick of it," said Zoeller. With the small talk of weather behind them, neither Captain had much else to say, except for some news from home. Zoeller enjoyed hearing salacious rumors about Germany's favorite starlets and about Adler's bit role in a Joseph Goebbels full-length propaganda film entitled "Titanic," a movie that suggested inferior shipbuilding from the Irish.

In 30 minutes the crews managed to swap torpedoes without detonating either one or losing them to the bottom of the sea. The ships de-rafted, and each went on their way, U-4710 east, toward Europe, and Captain Zoeller's U-4713, west toward the mid-Atlantic coast of the United States, with Phil-adelphia its next destination.

Seven hours into their voyage west, the helmsman reported in. "We're 59 kilometers due east of Kitty Hawk," he said.

"Kitty Hawk?" asked Zoeller. "These Americans und their ridiculous names. Where do they come up with such a name?"

"I don't know, Sir."

Still traveling on the surface, where they could maintain maximum speed, the swells had grown more pronounced and the wind had picked up, making the ride bumpy and miserable.

"With any luck we'll stay west of the worst part of this scheisse," said Zoeller.

"Yes, Sir," said the helmsman who was conferring with the radar and sonar operator. "Und it seems shipping traffic has slowed to a stop. As far as I can tell, we're alone."

"Lucky for them they'll live to see another day," said the Captain, who rarely missed an opportunity to puff his chest and exercise his bravado.

"Air traffic is null, too, Commander. All weather-related, I'm sure."

"So it's just us fools out here?"

"Seems so," answered the helmsman.

"Okay then, we'll continue on to the City of Brotherly Love and find out what the genius Jews are up to—Einstein and Oppenheimer, both. They make me sick. I can't stand the thought of them."

"Yes, Sir."

*****

Philadelphia, Pennsylvania
1:22 a.m. September 9, 1943

Margaret Rollins consulted a road atlas, and piloted her small car south and west to her favorite place, one of comfort, and one also of great mystery and trauma—the ancestral home of her parents and her grandparents in Sugarland, Maryland.

Three hours later Margaret pulled into the long driveway of the modest, but well-kept country home. After opening a few windows, she felt the cooling, restorative breezes and freshness of the country air doing her some good, and found herself with a new, clear-headed resolve to find Henry. She repeated her new mantra: *Until there's a body, he's alive and trying to get back to me. I know he is.*

Inside the two-story, three-bedroom home, mustiness from being unoccupied required a quick but thorough cleanse. Though she was tired, she knew she wouldn't be able to sleep. She opened every window she could reach and dusted the entire two floors. Every room, with one exception, the den, got a good cleaning. Finally exhausted, she flopped down on the sofa in the living room. She found a pencil and pad, and began to scribble absentmindedly.

"Let's take stock," she said aloud, folding her hands in her lap. In her mind she played out scenarios. *He wouldn't have voluntarily jumped off the boat, that's for certain. And he'd be wearing a life jacket, as scared as he is of the water. Since I know he's not on the Eldridge, maybe he did make it into the water. But then what? Did he somehow manage to scramble ashore? God, I pray so...but where? Where did that damned boat go?* Her brain, sorting through any little detail from what she'd learned from Dr. Einstein and Captain Hammond, suddenly focused on a place. She sat bolt upright.

"Norfolk, Virginia!"

It would require some real detective work, but Margaret Rollins was smart and energized. The desk in the den was set up with a phone, and a comfortable chair, the perfect place from which to work. From her spot on the couch she looked into the den, and her stomach tightened. It was the very place she'd experienced her own disappearing act, one that convinced her she was mad, an incident from which she was still very much in recovery.

111

"No, no," she said, squeezing her eyes tightly, trying to will the memories out of her brain, though they kept screaming back to her consciousness. Despite her best efforts she was the narrator of a movie she couldn't stop playing in her head. She relived, in chronological order, the traumatic events of her incident, most of which she'd just shared with Albert Einstein.

One ordinary day some 10 months earlier, while Henry was in Princeton, she simply walked into the den and felt an odd sensation. She wrote it off as a fleeting bit of indigestion. She dropped a stack of mail on the desk, turned to leave and walked back out. The dis-ease she felt stayed with her when she walked back into the den, curious about a letter, she discovered that the mail she'd put on the desk seconds earlier was gone, and that items on the desk were rearranged. *That was my first clue that I was losing my mind, or that something even more extraordinary was happening.* The simple stack of missing mail began a trip into madness that still haunted her nearly a year later, but the missing mail had been just the beginning.

She considered that perhaps she'd been daydreaming and put the stack of mail elsewhere. She checked the house, wandering, as if in a dream. Things were out of place. Items she didn't recognize populated each room. When she walked back into the den the missing mail rematerialized on the desk before her eyes, as if from some magician's trick or Hollywood special effect. She gasped at the unsettling sight, and grabbed hold of the chair to steady herself, worried her heart would beat out of her chest. Panicked, she pushed the desk chair aside, and left the room to catch her breath.

She walked to the middle of the living room and glanced up at the mantle over the fireplace. Photographs of her and Henry standing with people she didn't know stared back at her. *My hands trembled and I felt faint. I thought I was dying.* As her eyes darted from one end of the house to another she knew something was very wrong. This began a two-week trip into someplace she couldn't understand, where, in the midst of her seemingly growing insanity, people, places, familiar objects, even world history, especially world history, were all skewed, twisted into a torturous, teasing version of reality. It was a place where she felt alone, even though she lived with a man who looked like her husband, but who may as well have been a complete stranger.

Just as quickly as her ordeal began, it ended, though she didn't know how or why.

Nearly 11 months passed, and her life returned to something resembling normal. In fact, she and Henry were the happiest they'd ever been. She'd been offered a dream job in a town she loved. The version of Henry that seemed so different had been replaced with the one she knew. He confirmed her absence, and they made up a story for friends, family, even the police, about her needing to get away to clear her head.

While she'd been missing, Henry was the number one suspect in her disappearance, which was as hard on him as it was on her. In her sleep she'd mumble things about the Confederate States of America, and a border between the North and South of what was once the United States. Henry dismissed the ramblings as bad dreams, and she refused to speak of it when awake and coherent.

After a week of bed rest, and with Henry's corroboration and full support she began to accept that maybe she wasn't crazy. The massive geopolitical upheaval of wherever she'd been, had returned to what she'd known to be true her entire life. She felt the only way to get better was to deny it ever happened, but that proved to be impossible. She dealt with it by refusing to talk about it. Henry, however, couldn't leave it alone.

Obsessed with new theories of spacetime and something he was calling the 'Multiverse,' he thought he was helping her by describing, in scientific terms, what she'd been through. Though the incident was something she tried her best to forget, Henry wouldn't let her. Finally, when it seemed the worst of the trauma was behind her, Henry himself vanished. Once again, in an instant, her life full of love, joy, and anticipation for the future had crumbled. But this time she was stronger.

Sitting in her living room, staring at the desk in the den—the place she was sure was the vortex of her worst nightmares—Margaret faced her fears.

"Could he be...no," she asked and answered herself, dismissing the notion, even though something was telling her to continue. She stood and walked toward the arched entryway into the den, stopping just short of crossing the threshold between the rooms. She spoke in a clear, loud voice.

"Henry, listen to me. Hang on."

Chapter 18

Norfolk, Virginia
Confederate States of America
Morning, August 21, 1943

Fugitive Henry Rollins, once again in a fight for his life, heard the sweet clear voice of his dear Margaret.

"I am hanging on the best I can, Margaret," he said aloud.

He and Wild Bill "Hitch" Hickok were officially on the lam. Racing through town, jumping curbs, breaking every traffic law they could, a low profile was hard to maintain. Rollins had been able to secure the doors and make it toward the front of the van's holding area. Through a small window and a locked door he could see and talk to Hitch, who hadn't yet slowed down.

"Hitch!" yelled Rollins over the sound of the racing engine and considerable rattling and road noise. "Don't you think you're going a little fast?"

"How do you like that?" he yelled back. "I give you the jailbreak you requested and you criticize my driving?"

"I just don't want to be mangled in the process, and, by the way, thanks. I have to admit I didn't see that coming."

"Neither did the guards, that's why I moved when I had the chance."

Hitch steered with his knees and managed to twist his body enough to open the door, which could only be unlocked from his side of the cab. Rollins scrambled into the front passenger seat.

"What's our next move?" asked Rollins.

"See if you can find a key to get us out of these cuffs."

Rollins looked around the cab of the van, checked the glove box, over the visors and saw no keys. When they hit a pothole the van bounced so hard the ignition keys clattered against the steering column.

"How about on the key ring?" asked Rollins. "Looks like maybe?"

Hitch smiled. "I knew I was glad I brought you. We'll have to stop to get to them."

"We need to stop anyway," said Rollins. "We've got to ditch this van and find something a little less obvious."

Hitch didn't have to agree; it was understood. It had been clear to them both that they stood out against all the other traffic in Norfolk, but where to hide the van and how to get a replacement vehicle was the most urgent new challenge.

Looking in the side mirrors Hitch could see that, so far, no one was on their tail, but that wouldn't last long. Soon every cop in the area would be hunting them. Five minutes into their escape they were almost on the edge of town.

At first Rollins couldn't be too concerned with the overall oddity of the place. The maniac at the wheel and the certainty of hanging or a firing squad awaiting him were his chief worries. He began to survey his surroundings, eyeing good hiding places and looking for a vehicle to steal. That's when he again took stock of his environs, noting that things were not as expected. What should have been a bustling city was not. It looked more like a turn of the century rural village that stretched on further than most small villages would. The Southern Cross Confederate flag of the C.S.A. was still popping up on street signs and in front of retail establishments, but not in the same frequency as in the city center.

A few minutes further down the road wooden shacks lined the streets, fewer cars could be seen, and when they were, they all looked nearly identical to one another. They had big, rounded fenders, and were many feet longer than the cars Rollins was used to seeing. He noticed they all carried the same emblem, a large "M" at the center of an ornate logo.

A hundred yards ahead, down a long gravel driveway, a small house and a large barn, in disrepair, caught his eye.

"There!" he pointed with both hands, still cuffed together.

Without even seeing what Rollins was pointing at, Hitch slowed the vehicle for the first time since the jailbreak.

"What? Where?" he yelled.

"Over there, turn right!"

Hitch slammed on the brakes, nearly sending Rollins through the windshield, while making the turn. They drove past a small house, which may have been abandoned, it was hard to know, and straight into a large barn. Its pale-red, aged wood gave it away as something quite old.

When the van came to a lurching stop, both men took a deep breath. They were well inside and hidden from view. It was dark inside the van and so Hitch found the interior light and switched it on. Reaching for the keys he found the one for the handcuffs easily. It was not the first time he'd seen the specialized key. He un-cuffed Rollins first, and gave him the key for the reciprocal favor. They each rubbed at their sore wrists and were grateful for a moment that felt like a step in the right direction.

"Okay," said Rollins. "What now?"

"Clothes and a car," said Hitch. "That won't be easy, but it's our only move."

When they exited the van the smell was almost overwhelming. Smoldering brake dust mixed with the scent of an engine on the verge of overheating, were accented by whiffs of old horse manure, and filled the air inside the barn.

"Guess the tire was in better shape than I thought it was," said Hitch, pleased with himself and his clever ploy. Rollins tried to smile, but couldn't.

"What about that house?" asked Rollins, as the men made their way to the edge of the wide open barn door, staying as hidden as possible.

"Maybe," said Hitch. "Seems like if anyone had been home, they'd have come out to see what the hell just flew into their barn."

The old structure was a pale gray, two-story antebellum farmhouse. Though not in as bad a shape as the barn, it wasn't cared for, either. Weeds grew tall around its corners, and the yard was mostly dirt with a few ragged bushes.

"Let's check it out," said Hitch, clearly the more impulsive of the pair. As they crept out of the barn, three police cars raced by. Bubble-gum red lights mounted on the roof were flashing, but with no siren. Both men dropped to the ground.

"Shit, that was close," said Hitch. "This is one of the main roads out of town, and it'l only get busier."

Unseen, the men hunched low and made their way to the back door of the house, hidden from the road. The outer screen door opened, but the back door was locked. Hitch looked inside and saw a small entryway leading to a large kitchen. It looked lived in. Without consulting his partner, Hitch knocked loudly and Rollins jumped.

"Crap, Hitch!" he yelled, trying not to be too loud. "What if someone *is* home? We aren't exactly dressed like Fuller Brush salesmen."

"I guess we'll find out." He knocked again, and after a moment's silence he looked at Rollins and smiled mischievously at the real discomfort he was about to cause him. He reared back and with a large booted foot, the same one that had taken out the guards ten minutes earlier, kicked open the door. The deadbolt smashed through the doorframe and the door swung open with a violent shudder. Both men went inside.

The darkened kitchen was tidy, clean, and looked like someone had been there recently. Neatly stacked dishes sat next to the sink, and the percolator coffee pot was still warm to the touch.

"I think we're in luck," said Hitch. "Find the bedrooms, and we might find some street clothes."

They ran through the bottom floor of the house and realized the bedrooms were all upstairs. At the top of the stairs the first room to the right seemed to be for storage. It was full of boxes, and had nothing of immediate value, except for a window that afforded a long view toward the city center. Rollins could see the Chesapeake Bay in the distance and thought for a moment about the strange twist of events that had led him to this place.

"Here!" yelled Hitch. "I found a closet loaded with men's clothes." Rollins ran toward the sound of his voice and into a bedroom sitting at the front of the house, facing the road. Hitch had already found a shirt and pants that were surprisingly almost too big for his 6-foot 3-inch frame.

"This guy must be a giant," he said. "I'm swimming in these."

Rollins shuffled through the closet and found all the clothing to be big enough to fit three of him.

He held up a pair of pants that were a foot too wide and two feet too long. "Crap," he said. "This won't work."

He ran to another bedroom and found a closet filled with a young boy's clothing, which was much too small. Hitch could hear Rollins cursing from the other room. "Crap!"

"There's one more option," said Hitch. "Get in here, Henry."

Rollins returned to the room where Hitch had finished dressing. He looked much more passable out of his prison stripes. He was holding up a women's dress still on a hanger.

"No," said Rollins. "Absolutely not."

"Look, it makes sense," said Hitch. "It will probably fit you for starters, and no one is looking for a man and a woman, they're looking for two men. You're clean-shaven, you have an almost feminine, baby face, and you're on the scrawny side. And here's a pretty pink scarf for your head."

Rollins looked at him, horrified and insulted. "Ahh, thanks for all that."

Hitch tried to reason with his reluctant partner. "And you'd look even more ridiculous in these giant men's clothes than in this lovely floral print."

"No. Hell no, no way, no how."

"Henry, we're out of time and out of options."

Disgusted that this was his only option, he finally gave in.

"Okay, okay," said Rollins with a sigh. "I'll try it on, but if you laugh, I'll spend my dying days, which will probably be today, cursing you and hunting you down. I'll call the cops myself." He grabbed the garment from Hitch and walked toward the other bedroom to change. "And this is only temporary," he yelled down the hall toward Hitch who was grooming himself in a mirror, "until I can find something that fits me."

*****

At the Norfolk City Police Department, an emergency meeting was underway. Police Chief Martin Jensen led the task force, which included the officers already on the hunt, and the 20 or so sitting before him. Within minutes of the escape every available unit was put on alert. With no two-way radios in any of the police cars, the telephone was law enforcement's best weapon.

Roadblocks had been set up, police substations for 40 miles surrounding Norfolk were on high alert, and photos of the criminals were being printed to distribute by hand as far out into the state of Virginia as necessary until the fugitives were apprehended.

Jensen held up a large, somewhat distorted black & white photograph. "Okay, here's what we got. Bill Hickok, a.k.a. "Wild Bill" and more often "Hitch." He is the goon who stole the prisoner transfer van and single-handedly took out these two morons, while he was handcuffed, I might add."

Chief Jensen pointed at the guards with swollen faces and black eyes standing at the back of the meeting room.

"He's 53-years-old, has no known family, a bit of a drifter, and was fired from Norfolk City School system six months ago. He's been on a bender ever since, and we've had him in for Drunk & Disorderly five times in five months."

Jensen looked down at the bulletin he was holding.

"We don't have a picture of this 22-year-old Henry Rollins, the other escapee, but we do have the I.D.s he came in with. He's the one that worries us the most. I'll let Agent Serio tell you about him."

Serio, a Special agent with the C.B.I., the Confederate Bureau of Investigation, was a tall, brooding, dark haired, and dark skinned Italian; a first generation immigrant who spoke with a pronounced Sicilian accent. He served in Mussolini's Secret Service before deciding he didn't like the direction in which a Europe, ruled by Adolf Hitler and the Nazi Party, was headed.

He took a few steps forward, looked through a stack of papers in his hand, and spoke.

"Firstly, the reason we don't have a photo of Rollins to distribute is because you guys didn't bother to photograph him or book him properly, so nice going there."

The City cops and State Troopers in attendance bristled at the admonition from this C.S.A. Federal agent. They didn't like big government telling them how to handle their affairs. There'd even been talk from among some right-leaning politicians to push the State of Virginia to secede from the C.S.A. because of that very kind of intrusion. The movement hadn't made too much headway, the irony all but lost some 75-years removed from the state's last successful secession attempt.

"If we believe the information we have is accurate," he continued, "this Henry Rollins lives in Princeton, New Jersey, and is, or was, working for…and this makes no sense to us, the United States of America." A rumble went through the group, with a few laughs.

"Settle down," said Serio. "He had a civilian driver's license, which said 'Dr. Henry Rollins,' and it had his Princeton address. He also had this I.D. for the Philadelphia Naval Shipyard and something called the U.S. Navy."

Loud conversations erupted among the men in the room and threatened to stall the meeting. Everyone was coming to the same conclusion.

"Alright, quiet!" yelled Serio. "I know you all heard about the large ship near the port ten days ago."

"I saw it with my own eyes!" yelled the cop who's beat took him through Mallory Park and the waterfront. Several of the men laughed at him.

"And you watched the big bad ship disappear, right?" said a disbeliever from the back of the room. He was one of many.

"Yes, I damned well did," said the cop. "Me and 200 other guys."

Before a fight broke out and the yelling got out of control, Serio resumed command.

"Shut up and listen. As of this second, Rollins and Hickok are the C.S.A.'s most wanted. This guy thinks he's from the United States of America, and that's got to mean trouble. Big trouble."

The grumbling, laughter and conversation grew even more pronounced. Everyone in the room knew the United States of America had been dissolved at the end of the U.S. Civil War, some 75-years earlier. What was left of the Northern states was renamed the Federated States of America. The 13 Southern states, plus a few more, became the Confederate States of America. This was taught in every school, on both sides of the border. Only those in a terrorist or reunification group would call themselves U.S. citizens.

Serio turned his attention to the cop who'd busted Rollins. "So, you picked him up yesterday after he smashed a payphone?"

"Yes, Sir, that's right."

"Chief Jensen tells me you'd questioned him the night before. He was sleeping near his wet clothing, in Mallory Gardens Park, like he'd just swam in out of the ocean?"

"Yes, Sir."

"You didn't think his I.D. was a bit strange?"

The cop didn't answer.

"Well?"

"We didn't I.D. him. He looked like a bum sleeping one off."

"I.D. everybody, every time!" yelled Jensen. "Why do I have to keep telling you guys this?"

Serio interrupted the rant. "What's done is done. We're moving forward. So, one working theory is that this so called 'U.S. Navy' is an underground reunification group. There's more and more activity on both sides for reunification. We're not here to discuss politics, so regardless of how you feel about the prospect, we're considering Rollins to be a spy and throwing every asset we have into his capture. We don't need to tell you how important this is."

Serio looked at his watch. "As of 26 minutes ago Dr. Henry Rollins, and his accomplice, which we believe is one of convenience, have escaped your custody. They are wanted alive, preferably, but dead if necessary. Move out!"

Chapter 19

Sugarland, Maryland
United States of America
8:21 a.m. September 9, 1943

It had been ten months and two weeks to the day since Margaret or Henry Rollins had entered the den in their home in Maryland—Margaret had forbidden it for either of them. She'd even talked of bulldozing the house, and selling the land. But now, four full days after the disappearance of her husband, she stood at the small room's entryway, mustering courage, determined to break her own rule. She didn't know how or why, but something within the room had taken her to a place, real or imagined, where the impossible became possible. *Maybe, just maybe...*

Part of Margaret's speedy recovery from the trauma of her two-week disappearance came from the unexpected and complete belief of her fantastic story by her husband. Henry Rollins was absolutely convinced that Margaret had traveled through a vortex of some sort, into a realm, a place not quite like our own, but very similar. Not only did he believe her, he set to work proving the theoretical, and finding the mathematical and tangible evidence of the Multiverse's existence. She once told him "Having your partner in life fully believe in the craziest things you've ever dreamt of, or spoken aloud, or whispered in your sleep, may be unsettling, but it made all the difference. Thank you for proving to me that I'm not insane."

Margaret Rollins was far from insane. But now she was alone, though determined. *I'm not crazy.* She looked out the window at the purple-blue sky as the sun was about to rise; and then she focused her attention straight ahead into the room where all the real insanity seemed to be centered.

"For Henry," she said, smoothing the front of her favorite dress, and taking three steps forward.

The cloudless dawn was replaced in an instant with a crash of lightening, blackened skies, and torrential rain. Terrified, Margaret stood absolutely still, and felt like she was in one of Henry's favorite horror films. The wind whipped the trees in the yard, and rain pelted the window so hard she thought it might break. Nearly immobile from fear, she took two deep breaths and made a logical choice, reversing the three steps she'd just taken. Just as suddenly as the storm appeared, it disappeared.

Back in the living room where she started, she stood just a foot from the arch of the den's entryway. In a feat of courage and desperation, she repeated the process, with the same results. After repeating the action five times, fear slowly gave way to revelation. Now that she apparently had some control over her fate, moving between worlds at will gave her the head-to-toe energy of one who was experiencing, first hand, something that could only be called 'miraculous.' *By God, Henry. You were right...*

She tried the experiment a few more times and found that it didn't always work. Through trial and error she discovered that she had to be facing in a fairly exact direction to implement the travel. She moved the desk chair once and momentarily got stuck in the rainy, stormy version of the cosmos. Though panicked, she figured out what was wrong, and moved the desk chair back into place, its feet having made convenient, and life-saving, divots in the carpeting.

On what may have been her tenth visit to the strange world in less than 20 minutes, just as she crossed over she heard a knock on the door, startling her. Instinctively she went to the hallway and placed her hand on the dead bolt, not knowing who might be on the other side.

"Good afternoon, Ma'am," yelled a Maryland State Trooper, looking through a small window at the frightened woman. "May we come in?"

Speechless, Margaret opened the door and stood back as the officers, dripping with rain, stepped into the entryway.

"You're Margaret Rollins?"

"Umm...Yes, I am?"

"We're a little surprised to see you," said the Trooper. "You've been reported as a missing person for the better part of year? And now your husband, Henry Rollins, hasn't been seen in several days." Margaret stood, jaw agape, struggling for words that wouldn't come.

"After your disappearance your husband moved into town, but we check on this house periodically, and this morning we saw movement through the window. Can you explain any of this?"

The cross-dressing Dr. Henry Rollins and Wild Bill "Hitch" Hickok had suitable disguises but no easy way to get out of town. Fearing that the occupants of the house might return at any minute, the men were anxious and ready to move.

"Before we worry too much about moving, we need to know where we're going," said Hitch. "How 'bout it Doc?" he asked, using a new nickname given Rollins upon learning more about his degree.

"I guess north toward the border into…what's it called…? Fed Stat? I need to get to New Jersey."

"You're on your own going there, Doc. They routinely arrest and sometimes shoot people trying to cross the border without papers."

Rollins tried to wrap his head around a border crossing apparently bisecting the U.S. and the North from the South. "Well how about you, Hitch? Where do you want to go?"

"I'm thinking about heading south for the winter. Maybe Florida, or South Carolina. I'll get a new identity and start over somewhere else. Nothing to tie me to Virginia, that's for certain."

"So is this where we part company?" asked Rollins. "You get me all dolled up and dump me? I go north, you go south?"

"No, not yet. I think we need to stick together a little longer, until we're well west of Norfolk. We'll be less suspicious as a…don't hate me, a couple."

"How do you propose we do that?" asked Rollins. "We can't exactly just walk down the road?"

"We can't?" asked Hitch. "People do it all the time. Not everybody can afford a car, like you Yankees," he teased. "We might even find a horse to…borrow."

"A horse? You've got to be kidding me."

Hitch looked at Rollins as strangely as Rollins had been looking at him.

"Yes, a horse. Four legs, broad back, eats hay, poops a lot. A horse. We're in farm country. Please tell me you know what a horse is?"

"Yes, of course I know what a horse is."

Hitch looked at Rollins, and would have laughed at him in his dress, but thought better of it. "It shouldn't be too hard to find one."

Rollins shook his head in disbelief. Horses hadn't been used for transportation in 50 years. Dressed like a woman and likely to become a horse thief, his optimism had all but disappeared.

"If I'm not mistaken," continued Hitch, "about a mile or so north of here, through these fields, behind the barn, another road runs parallel. It's a lot less busy and there are more farms. We've got to get out of here, and unless you can think of anything better, I think the time to go is now."

Rollins nodded. Although eager to leave the house, he was not at all happy with his wardrobe, or the underdeveloped plan on which they were embarking.

"Let's go then," he agreed.

The two men filled their bellies with drinking water from the tap, and each took an apple and two slices of bread from a tin breadbox on the counter. They left the farmhouse and headed toward the barn. The afternoon sun was still strong, but it would be dark in a couple of hours.

Through fields and gullies, across ditches, over barbed wire and through brambles, they hugged the tree line and managed to stay hidden. They heard sirens in the distance, and were pretty certain the manhunt was in full swing. Rollins' stolen dress was full length and mostly covered his shoes, which were again soaked, causing him great discomfort.

"Hold up, Hitch," he said. "I gotta take these off." He grimaced from the pain and pointed to his damp shoes.

"Bad idea. You cut your feet, you're done, we're both done."

"I can't walk any more. I'm getting blisters on my blisters."

"Suit yourself, but I ain't carrying you."

Another 45-minutes heading approximately due north, using the setting sun on their left as a reference, the men began to see and hear farming activity. At the crest of a cultivated hill, they watched a farmer shoo the last of his cows into a large barn. Unlike the one where they'd stashed the prison van, this barn was five times the size, modern and active. They ducked low to avoid being spotted. They'd be hard pressed to explain the tall man and the not so comely woman by his side in the middle of a plowed field.

"Stop!" said Hitch with an urgency Rollins hadn't before seen.

"What?"

"Susshh!" he yelled though a husky whisper. "Do you hear that?"

"Hear what?"

Just then the unmistakable baying from a dozen hounds rolled over the fields coming from the direction of the just-stashed prison van.

"Dogs!" yelled Hitch. "Move it!"

The men ran, Henry barefooted, as fast as they could toward the barn in the distance. There was no sign of the lone farmer, though the twilight and setting sun made seeing details difficult. Once Hitch dared to look behind him and saw the light from swinging lanterns a mile or so behind them.

"Stay low, Doc!" said the six-foot-plus man doing his best not to make a convenient silhouette for whoever might be chasing them. When they made it to the barn and stopped long enough to regroup, the baying hounds could still be heard, though in their haste they'd managed to put a little more distance between them.

"Do you think they saw us?" asked Rollins.

"God, I hope not," said Hitch. "But they sure as hell smell us. They must have found the van and our prison stripes. Damn! We should have stashed them. If they found the van, which seems probable, and they saw two figures running, we're in big trouble. Let's hope they only picked up our scent and are just following the trail. This doesn't look good, Doc. They'll be on us in a few minutes. Find us a vehicle or a horse; either will do, or they're going to start throwing lead."

"I've never…I've never ridden a horse," declared Rollins with more than a little worry in his voice. "Margaret's tried since we first started dating to get me on one, but I never would. I don't know how to ride."

"Do you know how to hang on?" Hitch managed to laugh. "Proper riding techniques should be the least of your worries, Doc!"

*****

Sugarland, Maryland
Federated States of America
9:40 p.m. August 21, 1943

The Maryland State Troopers questioned Margaret, who had officially been a Missing Person for almost 11 months.

"I needed some time away," she said, turning on a lamp by the door. "I've been visiting my aunt in Ohio." The officers took notes and looked at her with mounting suspicion. She had no aunt in Ohio, and no siblings, though the police wouldn't know this.

"Uh huh," said one of the Troopers. "And how about Henry Rollins, your husband? He was reported missing from work four days ago. Any idea where he is?"

"I'm sorry," she answered, confused. "You know about my husband's disappearance?"

The two troopers looked at one another, and then back at Margaret.

"Yes. The Post Office called after the third day of him not showing for work. We came to your house, and found no sign of him, or you, until this morning. Your parents are quite worried, as well."

"My parents? The Post Office?" said Margaret, her head swimming.

"You'd better come with us Mrs. Rollins," said one of the Troopers. "We have some more questions for you and the detective will want to see you."

"Wait. What's today?" she asked, looking faint.

The officers helped her to the couch. "It's August 21."

"August twenty first?" she asked, knowing it had just been September ninth less than 10 minutes earlier.

"What year?"

"Ma'am, are you okay?"

"What year," she demanded.

"1943."

Gaining some composure, Margaret stood. "Yes, officers, I'm okay. I'll come with you. Let me grab my purse."

She walked toward the den, took three steps in through the archway and disappeared before the eyes of the two seasoned Maryland State Troopers.

"Whoa! Did you see that?" shouted one trooper, his hand instinctively moving to the handle of his sidearm.

"I...I...think I did," answered his partner. The two men scanned the den for exits, and saw none but a closed window. They searched their minds for some explanation of what they had just seen, and found none. They searched the house, including the basement where they hoped to find a trap door, anything to explain the vanishing, but they found nothing.

An hour later, sitting in their patrol car, one officer broke the silence.

"I don't know how we're even going to report this."

"We're not," said the other.

"We're not what?"

"We are not reporting that we watched a woman vanish into thin air. No one would believe us, and it wouldn't do any good anyway. I'm not even sure we saw her at all."

"So you're going to pretend this didn't happen?"

"What? Something happened?"

The other trooper was not happy about his partner's decision to ignore what they had both clearly witnessed, but a part of him understood the logic of staying silent.

"If it will make you feel any better, we'll continue to keep an eye on the house, but this is NOT going in any report, and neither of us will say a word to anyone. Agreed?"

"Agreed."

With the understanding of secrecy settled between them, they sat for a moment, still in shock and disbelief. Thinking that Margaret Rollins had somehow magically vacated the home, they finally drove off, but they were wrong.

Through a small opening in between two curtains in the den, Margaret, having returned, spied on the two officers. She'd watched them sitting in their idling patrol car for 10 minutes, before finally driving off. She knew they were trying to make sense of what they'd just seen, while she did the very same. She tried to comprehend what it meant that the Henry she'd lived with for two weeks a year earlier went missing from his job at the Post Office, and the talk of her parents. There was enough maddening confusion to set her on edge.

"How many Henrys are there in the universe?" she asked herself. "I can only miss one at a time."

*****

With twilight just about over, and nighttime racing in, Henry and Hitch snuck up to the edge of the farmyard. Having just come down off of a rise in the field, the baying of the hounds could no longer be heard, but they knew the dogs were behind them and headed in their direction. Hitch lifted the latch on a large wooden swing gate, and they crept cautiously toward the barn. A few small utility lights spread just enough dim, yellow light inside that the men could see. The cows noticed their presence and mooed with a restlessness they were afraid might alert the farmer they'd seen earlier.

"Shhhh baby cows," said Hitch, doing his best to calm them. "It's just Uncle Hitch and Aunt Henrietta."

Rollins ignored the humor, too frightened to make or appreciate jokes. At the far end of the large barn they saw the horse stalls.

"There, Doc," said Hitch pointing. "There're our rides. You're going to mount up, right? I know I am."

"I'll figure it out," said Henry, who had never before ridden a horse, or even been inside a barn. "How hard can it be?"

"That's the spirit," said Hitch as the two quickly made their way toward the horse stalls.

From through the far gate they saw the red lights of a police car zip past the farm. Another police car, also with red lights flashing, slowed and turned into the driveway.

"Crap," said Hitch, pulling Henry out of view, hugging the interior wall next to the horses.

Just 50 feet away, a Virginia State Police car, emblazoned with "Old Dominion" and the C.S.A Southern Cross, stopped near the side door to the farmhouse. Hitch and Doc Rollins watched two large troopers exit the vehicle and walk to the door. They knocked, and while waiting for someone to answer, one of the troopers shone his flashlight into the barn. The beam just missed revealing the fugitives.

"What are we supposed to do now?" whispered Rollins.

"Same as before," said Hitch, more confident than he had a right to be. "We're leaving by horse. There's a half-a-million acres of wilderness out there, with just a few roads and a railroad track. It's our only hope at this point."

The farmer opened his door and engaged the officers in conversation, most of which was inaudible to the men in the barn. Hitch slowly and silently opened a stall door holding two fine-looking Arabian stallions. The agitated horses snorted and shook their heads with disapproval as he approached.

"Hello fellas," said Hitch, stroking the horse's flanks. "Try this." He reached into his pocket and produced a lint-covered apple. Using his teeth, he split it into two pieces, feeding one to each horse. They nickered appreciatively.

"That was handy," said Rollins.

"That was dinner," said Hitch. "Put to good use, though. We'll save your apple and the bread for later. Never know who else we'll need to bribe."

Outside, the troopers and the farmer talked a minute more, when all three looked toward the barn. The farmer pointed just before the flashlight beam again came sweeping through the open barn door.

"Hurry, Hitch," said Rollins while his partner grabbed the tack hanging from the wall and placed a bridle over each of the horses' noses. Outside the farmer and the trooper stopped to look out over the property, before continuing toward the barn. Hitch retrieved saddle blankets, saddles, and had the horses ready to go in 45-seconds.

"How do you know what you're doing?" asked Rollins, wishing he weren't in this predicament but grateful for someone as resourceful as Hitch to have as an outlaw partner.

"We had horses growing up," whispered Hitch. No sooner had he finished speaking when both men saw the farmer and the troopers just a few yards away from the barn door.

"Crap," said Hitch, buckling the last saddle in place, securing the straps beneath the horses' large bellies. "It's now or never."

Hitch backed the two horses out of the stall, and he and Henry walked them through the shadows as quickly and quietly as they could away from the troopers and the farmer, toward the opposite end of the barn. As they passed by an interior holding pen with 50 head of cattle, Hitch unlatched the gate, though the cattle didn't move.

"Crap," he said.

As the troopers and the farmer approached the other end of the long, wide barn, the trooper with the flashlight began sweeping the beam around the barn's interior. Before Henry and Hitch could mount their steeds, the blood-curdling, unmistakable baying of the hounds echoed through the barn as 10 officers and 20 dogs crested the hill just outside.

With the Trooper on one end and the dogs on the other, Hitch yelled. "Now, Doc!"

The two men jumped up on their horses, Hitch making it look easy, Henry struggling, stuffing the long dress between his legs the best he could. He slipped off the stirrup, kicking his horse in the leg before just managing to pull himself up. His horse let out a long, loud high-pitched whinny, and then reared, Lone Ranger-style while he hung on to the saddle horn with one hand.

The troopers and the farmer, hearing the horse, ran toward the sound. The flashlight beam shone on Henry and Hitch, while the dogs howled in delight from the other end of the barn. Trapped between the hounds and their fully armed handlers at west entrance, and the troopers and their shotguns on the east entrance, the fugitive outlaws on horseback had to make a decision.

"Follow me!" yelled Hitch, kicking his horse to a run, leading him parallel to the cattle corral.

He yelled at the cattle like a crazed cowboy, reaching down to slap one on the rump as hard as he could, spooking them into a stampede out of the coral. Hitch, Henry and 50 head of cattle all moved toward the barn door. Fortunately for Henry, not at all a horseman, his horse followed the other, and, like Butch and Sundance, they were off. Gunshots came from the officers with the dogs, while the troopers inside the barn were caught in the dust kicked up by the spooked cattle.

Hitch and Henry raced around the side of the barn at a full gallop, while the men on foot shot at them, missing, but running to try to catch up. They let the dogs free, who gave a gleeful, ferocious chase. The horsemen passed the parked Trooper's car as they sped down the driveway toward the road. With Hitch in the lead, they slowed momentarily while considering their next move.

"Which way?" yelled Rollins, looking left and right at the dark road in front of the farmhouse.

"Neither!" yelled Hitch. "Follow me!"

Hitch urged his horse to jumping speed, and led him straight across the two-lane road, over a four-foot wide ditch, a three-foot high fence, and out into an open field illuminated only by the fading twilight and a rising moon. Henry, and his dutiful horse, just a few feet behind the leader, followed in his first ever steeplechase escape attempt.

After blindly riding for an hour as fast as they dared in the dark, through creeks, into meadows and forests, and in what they hoped was generally away from civilization, the baying of bloodhounds on their trail faded.

"I think they're giving up," said Henry. Every muscle in his body silently screamed for him to give up as well.

"Keep moving. You don't know these people, Doc," said Hitch. "They'll never give up."

Chapter 20

Atlantic Ocean
Coastal Waters off the United States of America
11 a.m. September 9, 1943

Outside in the elements, at the top of U-4713's conning tower, Capitan Zoeller and two officers watched the sea, which had grown in magnitude. With waves topping 12 feet, and some higher that crashed over the top of them, Zoeller and his officers were forced down below, sealing the hatch behind them.

"We can stay surfaced for a bit longer," said Zoeller to his Chief Engineer. "But if we get bounced around much more, we'll have to dive."

He turned to the navigator and helmsman. "If this storm comes up the coast we'll have to stay submerged and try to ride it out. I'll check KURT in a moment."

On a mission three months earlier, an unmanned German land weather station, a Wetter-Funkgerat codenamed "KURT" for the scientist that developed it, was deployed on a barrier island near the Frying Pan Shoals off North Carolina's Cape Fear. From a 30-foot antenna, the equipment, powered by nickel-cadmium batteries, used telemetry to transmit barometric pressure, wind speed and direction, once every three hours. The Germans who installed the array scattered spent packs of Lucky Strike cigarettes and LOOK Magazines around the station's base, to make it appear as if it were an American installation, should anyone happen upon it.

The top-secret weather station automatically switched frequencies, and its broadcasts were of such a short duration, that radio triangulation was nearly impossible. A new report was due in, and Zoeller wanted to be there to hear the latest readings for himself.

"Set a new course, west-northwest."

"Ja whol, Captain," said the Navigator. Using the onboard compass and exact chart positions, the Navigator turned the U-boat toward the west, headed closer to the mid-Atlantic region of the U.S. coastline, on a slightly different course than the one that would have taken them to Philadelphia.

"I'm headed to the radio room," said Captain Zoeller, but before he left, he pulled Oberleutnant Dengler just out of earshot from the helmsman. "By the way," he said to the officer, "what do you know about the new man. The transfer happened so quickly I didn't get a chance to study his file."

They were both watching 29-year-old Junior Lieutenant Luca Adams, who was assisting the Navigator with charts.

"That's Adams, Sir. As you know we picked him up near Myrtle Beach. He'd been posing as a P.O.W. for three months, gathered some useful intel. I didn't know him well but his references are without blemish. He seems to be up to the task. He served as Navigator on U-4701 before they changed his assignment. His English is spot on so the Kriegsmarine turned him into an intelligence operative. He's due for leave after this mission is over, when we sail back to France next week."

Zoeller looked annoyed. "I determine whether he's due for leave or not, Oberleutnant. He's had a three-month vacation basking in the sunshine at Camp Myrtle all summer. The mutterficker has a gottferdam suntan. Welcome him aboard for me, would you?"

"Of course."

By 1943 some 170,000 German P.O.W.s were interred at 750 camps across the U.S., including some 20 camps in South Carolina alone. The P.O.W.s, by most standards, were treated well, fed well, and became agricultural and infrastructure laborers for communities that were not always too welcoming. They ate as well or better than the average American citizen. They had canteen privileges where they could buy and consume beer. They enjoyed recreational activities, concerts, and were "coddled" according to many. It was hoped, and to some degree proven, that word of a relaxing Myrtle Beach vacation awaiting German P.O.W.s encouraged many battlefield surrenders.

With their freedoms came access to local radio and newspapers, and overhearing American guards' wartime banter. This afforded certain well-trained spies lots of opportunity for observation and reporting, under the very noses of their captors.

A carefully documented list of Adams' fellow prisoners, who dared to declare themselves "anti-Nazi," and who were segregated into less ideological barracks, was the most valuable piece of information Lieutenant Adams was charged with obtaining. The "traitor's" names and hometowns were to be turned over to the Gestapo for special retribution—namely the harassment, or worse, of their families.

Captain Zoeller was eager to retrieve the list from Adams, and relay the names himself, but it would have to wait. When a rogue 20-foot wave broadsided the U-boat, it almost capsized. Cups and plates flew out of the galley, crashing around the interior of the ship, while alarms sounded, and the crew struggled to stay upright. They survived the hit without any serious damage, but frayed nerves led to worry about what the next wave might bring. Zoeller worried most about his precious uranium cargo.

*****

"We lost them, Sir," said a red-faced Trooper, back at the Norfolk P.D. command center. Some 15 agents filed back into the room and took seats, while the two Troopers who'd been with the farmer, told agents Serio and Jensen, what had transpired.

"How?" said Serio, shaking his head in disbelief. "By your own reports, they're unarmed, and so never fired a shot. You had guns. You had them cornered…inside a barn. How?"

"These guys are good," said the Trooper. "Real pros. They spooked the cattle and blocked us in on one side, and they escaped from the other end of the barn on horseback. The dogs finally gave up. After about three hours, they wandered back."

Serio sighed, his head in his hands, as a new face of authority entered the room, this one wearing a Confederate Navy uniform.

"What's this about a woman?" asked Jensen.

The Trooper cleared his throat. "We think one of them is dressed as a woman."

"The smaller one, probably," said the other Trooper. "The Yank named Rollins. The couple from the first farmhouse where we found the P.T.V said that—"

"The what?" asked CSN Navy Admiral Josiah Brown, interrupting. What in the hell is a "P.T.V.?"

"The P.T.V.? That's our Prisoner Transfer Van," answered the Trooper.

"Gentlemen, this is Admiral Brown," said Jensen, introducing the newcomer. "He is one of our permanent neighbors from the naval base here in the great City of Norfolk. Seems he now has operational jurisdiction surpassing that of even the esteemed C.B.I.'s Agent Serio, here."

Jensen nodded toward the expressionless Serio, whose command authority had been usurped by order of the C.S.A. and the third highest-ranking official in national governance—the Attorney General.

"Continue, Trooper," said the Admiral, who had taken a keen interest in the case six hours earlier upon hearing, through the rumor mill, about an alleged escaped Yankee spy who showed up wet and salty in Mallory Park, and who was now on the run.

"Yes, Sir," said the trooper. "The couple at the farm house reported missing a men's shirt and pants, and a floor-length, floral print dress."

"A floor-length, floral print dress?" repeated Jensen, acting impressed by the detailed description. "Do we know what color the lovely flowers are?"

The room erupted in laughter.

"You fat heads think this is funny?" yelled Serio, fuming. "Have you been drinking rot gut?" He turned to look at agent Jensen. "You don't think this is funny, do you Special Agent Jensen?"

"I certainly do not," said Jensen, straight-faced. The room quieted.

"You know…we all have bosses," said Serio, feigning serenity. "You have to answer to yours, Agent Jensen has to answer to his, and I have to answer to mine, the Confederate States of America. My boss is the head of the C.B.I., the goddamned Confederate Bureau of Investigation, and his boss is the Attorney General, who is fourth in line to the Presidency. Now Admiral Brown is the boss. Tonight I have to write a report that tells how you idiots first lost two unarmed prisoners and a P.V.T. Then you lost them again, on horseback, while one of them is in a dress—a floor length floral print dress, as was so skillfully ascertained." He looked at the men's faces, daring one of them to smile.

"Do you know how that makes me feel?"

No one answered.

"Mad as hell!" screamed Serio. "No one goes home! No one sleeps, no one pisses, or takes a crap, or calls their wives, or does anything until we find these bastards. You are the laughingstock of the entire C.S.A. As word spreads about this, and I'm going to make sure the world knows, you'll be lucky to have jobs in the morning. Your only task and your only hope of redemption is in finding them!"

******

"The horses are tired," said Hitch. The clear night sky, a bright moon, and hard ground had mercifully helped them in their escape. The horses moved at intervals between a cantor and full gallop for three hours across mostly wilderness land and a few dusty farm roads. "We'd better stop."

"Amen to that," said Rollins. "I haven't heard the dogs for a couple of hours."

"That's a good thing, but it doesn't mean they're not still looking for us. They're probably quite upset with our little stunt."

The two men dismounted near a small stream where they, along with the horses, all took their fill of water.

"Where are we?" asked Rollins.

"Not sure, but my best guess is we've gone 40, maybe 50 miles west of Norfolk, so that puts us somewhere near…between Franklin and Emporia. You're still a long way from New Jersey, Doc."

Henry wiped his mouth with the sleeve of his dress after another long drink. "And you're no closer to Florida." Hitch's horse let out a sneezing snort.

"What's their next move, the cops?" asked Rollins, assuming Hitch would know, because he seemed to know almost everything about everything.

"They've got the telephone circuits jammed up good, I'll bet. The good news is they didn't see us turn west. When we crossed the road we were heading north, and they know you're a Yank, so they might not expect us to be where we are. I made a mental note of where west was, and I think I have a pretty good sense of direction. So, considering we're traveling by horse, we may have bought us a little time. But not much."

"Hitch, you're kind of a natural at this," mused Rollins. "Are you sure you're a school teacher and not an outlaw, like Jesse James?"

"Jesse who?"

"Never mind," said Rollins. "I'm just very impressed with your gangster-like abilities."

"What the hell is a gangster?"

Henry didn't answer. He watched the horses grazing and drinking. They seemed no worse for the wear after a long hard ride at night. He, however, was in great pain. Muscles that hadn't ever been used ached, and he didn't even want to think about the serious chafing and blisters that had formed in places he'd never seen before. He was exhausted, sore, raw, and suffering the indignity of wearing a floor-length, floral print dress.

"If we survive this, I'm going to kill you," said Henry to his only friend in the world. They both allowed themselves a long, hard, laugh.

"It's getting cold, Hitch. Do we dare a fire?"

"Sure, I think a small fire would be okay. But are you going to start one for us?"

"Good point."

Hitch walked over to his horse, and rummaged through the pockets on the saddle, coming up with a skein of twine and nothing else. "Try yours." Henry did the same, and managed to hide a smirk before producing a single box of wooden matches.

"I'll be," said Hitch. "Good job Henrietta. But let's not bed down here. Another hour or two west, and I'll feel a lot better."

"I prefer 'Henry,' thank you. Or, 'Doctor Rollins' is also appropriate. I didn't manage to graduate four years early with a PhD to be called 'Henrietta,' I don't mind telling you."

Hitch smiled as he bent down toward a pool of water at the stream's edge. "I could use a Highball, I don't mind telling *you*."

"A Highball?"

"I realize you're a little wet behind the ears, and that I've got few years on you, but you've never had a Highball?"

"Nope."

"It's bourbon and a splash of ginger beer, and it's delicious." He leaned in for one last drink from the stream. "I guess this will have to do."

After another long drink, the men mounted their horses, Rollins groaning when he hit the saddle. They followed the stream, keeping their ears and eyes open.

"There's Polaris, Doc. The North Star," said Hitch, pointing up into the night sky at the constellation Ursa Minor. "Follow it straight to Fed-Stat if you want. Bet that makes you a little wistful for home."

"You have no idea."

Chapter 21

Sugarland, Maryland
United States of America
8:15 a.m. September 9, 1943

Margaret Rollins was beginning to wrap her head around the fact that she was traveling, at will, between two universes, that also jumped in time. In the few discussions she'd allowed, Henry spoke of the 'Multiverse.' Margaret had been completely unwilling to consider any of it, but now she was knee-deep in it, facing her demons. It was exciting, frightening, and confusing, but it also gave her hope that maybe Henry had traveled as well. She tried to establish in her head the two similar but distinct places, and to make sure she never confused them.

"Okay, there's this place," she said aloud, sitting in her living room. "My home world."

She knew for sure she was "home" by checking the photos over the fireplace mantle. There were pictures of her and Henry at Coney Island, and on their wedding day at a church not far from where she sat, and their honeymoon at Niagara Falls. These were events in places she categorically knew, and could recall countless details; these were her life's stories.

"Then there's the other place, my second home world," she said. In this 'other place' the photos on the mantle were slightly off. Oddly, though they were photos of her and Henry, they'd been taken in places she knew they'd never visited: St. Louis, the top of the Chrysler Building in New York City, standing at the base of the Washington Monument. These were the memories of some other couple, for which she felt no immediate kinship, even though the haunting faces called out to her across unknown dimensions of space and time; a place almost without comprehension.

There were plenty of additional confusing, and even disturbing, additions or omissions to this 'other' home. There were photos of her and Henry with people she'd never met before, all laughing and hugging like they were best friends. There was an urn filled with ashes on a table near the fireplace. She dared not think of whose cremains they might be. She decided Henry might be in that 'other' place, her 'second home world.' *Maybe I can look for him there? But how?* The Maryland State Troopers were sure to be watching for her and ready to arrest her. Until she was sure the police weren't sitting, waiting out front, she'd travel at night. She hoped that in the early hours of morning she'd have the best chances of traveling unnoticed. There were no guarantees, but it was the start of a plan.

She walked upstairs, very alone, very tired, and very afraid.

*****

The next morning, the sixth day since the accident on the Eldridge, Margaret Rollins woke up screaming. When she sat up and opened her eyes, whatever terror she'd been living in her subconscious disappeared. All that was left was a feeling of isolation, and of being alone. There was no one to talk to, no one to help her figure out what, if anything, she could do with this new parlor trick she'd learned. Her next move would come after getting up, washing, and changing while listening to the radio.

"My Fellow Americans," began President Franklin Roosevelt, "if we lose this war, it will be generations, or even centuries before our conception of democracy can live again. Never before have we had so little time, to do so much." Margaret pondered the words of the President, who for years had engaged in periodic 'fireside chats' over the radio, and Margaret, like most of America, listened intently.

*So little time...*she thought. *But what is time? Who knows?* She buttoned her blouse and looked into the mirror as the answer came.

"Einstein!"

"Dr. Einstein," she said his name again and packed her car for a trip back to the one man, besides her husband, who might have a clue what to do. "Back to Princeton," she found she was talking to herself more and more. "At least someone's listening," she said, before getting into her car to leave Maryland for the drive back to New Jersey.

*****

Since neither man had a watch, it was difficult for the two fugitives to know just what time it was. "My best guess," said Hitch, "is that it's around midnight. I guess we should stop."

"I could eat a horse," said Henry, who immediately regretted his words and felt obligated to scratch his horse behind the ears. "Sorry boy."

Among a long and growing list of skills, it seemed Hitch could navigate, more or less, by using the little dipper, and its most prominent star in the handle, Polaris. The stream they'd been following had a westward branch that they followed and soon found its source, where it had forked from a larger river. They dismounted and liked their chances to stay hidden in a ravine along a shale bed, surrounded by hills on either side. The location would help hide any light from a campfire, which they both agreed was needed.

After tying the horses up along the bank where they could graze and get at least some sustenance, they spent 30 minutes gathering firewood, which, fortunately, was abundant. Hitch tried to think along what river they might be camping. He claimed to know Virginia like the back of his hand.

"I think this is the Meherin," he said.

"The what?"

"The Meherin River. It runs from way up past Emporia all the way down to the Chowhan in North Carolina, then to the Outer Banks. Gotta be the Meherin."

"Okay, if you say so."

"And I know there's fish in here."

"Don't mention food, please."

"Fish would taste good," teased Hitch, just as hungry as his partner.

"Yeah? How do you propose we get the fish out of the river and into our bellies?" asked Rollins.

"Fire first, fishing second," said Hitch.

The men gathered tinder, and the driest wood they could find, putting it into a pile where the shale formation met the riverbank.

"Matches?" asked Hitch. Henry produced the box and handed it without hesitation to the best Boy Scout he'd ever met. Within a few minutes a small, efficient, nearly smokeless fire warmed the campsite. They had placed the fire pit near a spot not far from an outcropping of earth. The reflected heat from the fire and coals should keep them warm through the night, which was turning cool. The mound of shale, made up of tons of small, flat, gray rock, was surprisingly soft and forgiving, and nearly as comfortable as any bed.

They sat without talking, mesmerized by the flames. Finally Rollins broke the silence.

"What was that you were saying about fish?"

"I knew that was coming," said Hitch, who had been sharpening a piece of shale into a workable knife. He went to his horse and retrieved the large skein of twine. On his way back to the campsite he sawed off a piece of buckthorn branch and returned to his spot near the fire. Rollins watched him fashion six fishhooks using thorns from the bush. He stripped a foot-long piece of the twine into dozens of individual threads, winding the base of the hooks into a secure, sharp, check mark shaped piece of homemade fishing gear. Then he braided a 10-foot section of twine into something 10 times the strength it had been, and attached the homemade fishhooks at two-foot intervals, using knots worthy of a first-class midshipman. This took about 20 minutes.

"Worms," he said. "You're on worm detail, Dr. Henrietta. Check the loose soil in that riverbank. Grubs will do if you can't find any worms. Dig through the dirt, in and under rotten logs, just get me six good ones."

"Don't call me Henrietta," said Rollins, who got up to do his part.

"Okay, sweetheart, sorry."

Henry had pretty good luck in the bright moonlight finding three worms and three fat grubs in just a few minutes time. Soon the trotline was complete. Hitch scouted the river for an eddy, a slow-moving swirl of water near a bend, or some flat, still water under a large tree branch. He found the perfect combination of both. He weighted one end of the trotline with a large chunk of shale, and secured the other end to a nearby willow tree trunk, lowering the business parts in the middle gently into the water. The grubs and worms wriggled, suspended 10-inches below the surface, glistening in the moonlight, daring the fish not to bite.

"Now what?" asked Henry, salivating.

"Now, we wait."

Hitch was not nearly as skeptical as the city boy he'd been paired up with. He'd been doing this, or some manner of this kind of fishing, since he was nine years old, but it was often hit or miss. Rollins stayed on fish watch, while Hitch prepared a bed of coals, and fashioned two long, sturdy green cooking sticks from the nearby willow.

After 15 minutes with no signs of activity Rollins was certain the fishing expedition was a bust and had mentally prepared himself to try to sleep through the hunger pangs.

"Hey, Super Scout. Nothing is happening," he complained.

"Patience, young lady," said Hitch, his outward confidence never waning.

"I'm starving. I had an apple and a slice of bread 12 hours ago – that's it!" said Rollins.

"First of all, that's more than I had, and I'm twice your size, and yelling at me is probably not a great idea, even if you are starving."

Looking at Hitch, instead of the water, Henry missed seeing the first telltale ripple. Then he missed seeing the first splash around the trotline, but he heard it.

"What was that?" he asked.

"What was what, Apricot?" said Hitch, still working on the cooking utensils.

"I heard a splash."

"Oooh, that's a good sign," said Hitch, walking to the water's edge. "Let's see what we caught."

Hitch pulled in the trotline and found a broken hook and a missing grub.

"No!" Henry said, louder than he should have.

"It's okay," Hitch said. "We know they like the grubs, and that they're hungry tonight. That's good." He threw the remaining five baited hooks back into the river, and they watched in amazement as three large trout flipped out of the water, ravenous for fat beetle larvae. One small trout took a grub and escaped, but the two largest were hooked. The fishing line, fashioned from twine and skill, was stretched to its limits but Hitch deftly retrieved it along with two 15-inch rainbow trout attached at the mouth by a buckthorn hook.

Henry Rollins would never be as impressed by anyone or anything for the rest of his life, as he was that very moment. Hitch and his impromptu fishing expedition led to the finest dinner he thought he'd ever eaten. Hitch even managed to char several small hickory sticks, finely grating them over the fish adding a salty, smoky spice to its tender, juicy perfectly cooked flesh. He threw the remaining two baits back in the water for a chance at a second helping, but the fish had been spooked, and wouldn't bite again.

"Where'd you ever learn this stuff, Hitch?" asked Rollins, mouth full of tasty, steaming hot trout.

"I dunno. Just comes natural to boys growing up in the country. Every one of my friends could have done the same."

"They're really remarkable, your skills."

Hitch laughed. "I picked up a few thing along the way, I guess. My stint in the Navy taught me the most."

"You're a Navy man?" asked Rollins.

"I was a Navy man, until they told me my services were no longer required after one particular shore leave in 1939, in Charleston, South Carolina. I don't remember much, but what I do...let's leave it at 'we had a little fun', and I took the rap for the whole gang. I really loved the Navy, and working on the water. Really I don't care if it's a river, a lake or the wide, blue ocean, I just love the water. I'm really going to love Florida."

Henry couldn't help but to recall the quite unbelievable Naval battles he'd just made it through. He wanted so badly to tell Hitch, to tell anyone, but it was all too bizarre and incomprehensible to put into words.

"I feel badly about the horses," said Rollins. "They've got to be hungry."

"Their alright," said Hitch. "Plenty of grass to graze on and good water. They could live out their lives without another single bucket of feed. Don't you worry about them. They're amazing survivors. Just like we are, alright Doc?"

"Yes," he answered, "and thank you."

The men finished their meal, mostly in silence, sucking every last piece of flesh from every last fish bone. They slept warm, somewhat satiated, and for the moment content, although a new set of challenges would greet them with the sunrise.

Chapter 22

In Princeton, New Jersey, two F.B.I agents became tired of waiting for Margaret Rollins. They'd missed her driving off to Sugarland, Maryland, two days earlier, assuming when she left the Hotel she was headed for Princeton. They confused her car with a neighbor's, so they expected her to be home. With no activity after 36-hours of surveillance, it was time to move on. They left their vantage point near the Rollins' apartment, just as Margaret rolled around the corner unseen. She stopped long enough to eat. It was 10 a.m. the morning of the sixth day after the Eldridge disaster.

The Federal agents instead staked out Albert Einstein's home on Mercer Street. They were both caught off guard when Margaret Rollins pulled up in front and parked.

"Well, lookie what we got here," said the taller agent.

"It's the Rollins woman," said the other, powdered donut residue still on his chin.

Margaret, greeted by Helen Dukas at the front door, was ushered in.

"Good morning Dr. Einstein," said Margaret. "I'm sorry to come unannounced."

Einstein smiled warmly at Margaret, grabbed his sweater, and led the way to the back yard garden. They sat on either end of Einstein's favorite garden bench.

"Any word, Dr. Einstein?" she asked, noticing that he looked older, even though she'd seen him just a few days earlier. He looked to the ground, still feeling guilty about ripping apart this young couple's life. He looked sad when he finally looked up and into her eyes, shaking his head, 'no.'

Margaret put her small, youthful, perfectly alabaster hand upon his, which showed its age, spotted and with signs of arthritis.

"Me neither," she said, "and…I don't even quite know how to tell you this. But I have an idea. It's crazy, for sure, but…something's happened." Margaret told the great Dr. Einstein about "the incident." It had not been easy to tell the story, but she had to tell someone, and Einstein was a good listener, and the perfect choice. Besides Henry, he was the only choice.

"Vhat could you possibly be smiling about?" asked Einstein, himself smiling.

Margaret took a deep breath. "I have hope, and I have a gut feeling about Henry. As I've told you, about a year ago I…disappeared from my family home in Maryland. I was gone for two weeks."

Einstein nodded. "Yes, both you und Henry have told me of your frightening experience."

"I vowed to wipe it from my memory, because it was so terrifying and so disorienting. I thought I'd gone mad."

"Learn from yesterday, live for today, und hope for tomorrow, my dear."

"I'm working on it, Doctor. Anyway, yesterday I went back to the place of my disappearance, and reappearance, the den of our home in Maryland…and…" She couldn't quite say the words, trying but unable to form them on her tongue.

"Und vhat?

"And I've been able to recreate the…the traveling. That's what I've been calling it. I can travel back and forth, at will, without any ill-effects, that I know of."

"Remarkable," said Einstein believing every word he was hearing. "Perhaps zhere ist a rip in spacetime, or a vermhole?"

"You mentioned those before," said Margaret, "and that's your department, Doctor Einstein, but what I'm wondering, what I'm praying is true, is—"

"Ist our dear Henry in zis other place? Zis other universe? A good assumption, my dear."

Einstein reached for a nearby pad and pencil, and scribbled an equation. He showed it to her. To her untrained eyes it was as mysterious as Mandarin Chinese. A series of mathematical, algebraic and geometric formulas made perfect sense to the genius who'd helped create the theory. Working from the theories of dozens of physicists before him, collaborations with colleagues at The Institute, and his own amazing intellect, he'd developed the Einstein-Rosen Bridge wormhole theory; a rip in spacetime allowing for interdimen-sional and time travel.

"Zis is vhat it might look like, stripped down to…how do American's say it…'za nuts und bolts."

She smiled, tears forming in her eyes. "So it is possible?"

Einstein laughed. "Possible? You tell me. You're za traveler among us." They both felt lighter and Einstein smiled again. For the first time in days he felt some hope for his young friends. He leaned in toward Margaret, taking both her hands in his. "Yes, my dear. Anything ist possible. If you say you can travel back und forth unmolested, zhen maybe you should go zhere, und focus all your attention on—"

"On what?" she interrupted.

"Finding Henry."

*****

Rural Virginia
Confederate States of America
6: 12 a.m. August 22, 1943

While somewhere west of Norfolk, Virginia, the morning broke without incident, no hounds, no posse, just a warming, orange sun, rippling water and smoldering coals from the night's fire. Sometime overnight a large, lazy catfish attached itself to a hook on the trotline, and hadn't bothered to get himself free, offering himself up as another meal for Henry and Hitch. Not nearly as tasty as the gourmet, hickory-seasoned trout, the catfish was still good, and had large hunks of protein-rich flesh and fat in the skin, providing another badly needed boost of calories and energy.

"Coffee?" asked Henry, rubbing his arms, realizing he was still wearing a dress.

"I may be good, but I'm not that good," answered Hitch.

"We've got to be somewhat near a town, somewhere, don't we?" asked Rollins.

"Why, you want to check into a hotel and order room service?"

"Yes. I want a shower, and bacon and eggs, a telephone, and a change of clothes, so yes, a hotel would be nice."

"Probably Emporia is not too far," said Hitch, "but it's likely to be crawling with cops. They've seen us, and they know that you're in a floor length floral print dress."

"Thanks again for that. This is beginning to really bother me."

Hitch smiled. "At the time it made sense. Still might come in handy, but you look more like a whore that's been dragged through the mud, as opposed to the proper young lady you started out."

"You've taken me across farmland, through cow manure, on horseback, down dusty roads, and camping on rocks – what do you expect? It's not easy for a lady to stay nice looking under those circumstances."

"That's the spirit," said Hitch. "Embrace your femininity."

"Oh, how I'd like to punch you right in the mouth."

"After all I've done…"

142

The men and horses all had long drinks from a nearby smaller, clear-running tributary stream. After they remounted, they moved slowly at first giving the horses time to graze in fresh greenery along their direction of travel. The early morning sun showed them where east was, so they knew how to head west, and kept moving opposite the rising sun.

"Hitch, this is 1943, correct?"

"Here we go again. Yes, 1943."

"So aren't we involved in World War II with the Germans and the Japanese?"

"Ahh…no. Hell no. That's Europe's problem. And the Japs? The Japs are all but gone, and the Chinese are next. The few million Japs that survived the second holocaust are refugees, spread all over the word. Yep, Hitler flattened Japan with the bomb."

"The 'second holocaust?' The bomb? What do you mean?"

"First he hit the Jews, Doc. They're all gone—at least in Europe—some think there may be ten to twenty thousand in hiding, maybe more. And the bomb, the Atomic Bomb? Hitler flattened Japan with five of them. Killed 50 million. He threatened to use it on Fed-Stat and the C.S.A. if we involved ourselves with Europe. So we didn't. After China, Russia's probably next to get nuked. They have a peace treaty, but I hear it's not holding. Hitler wants their oil and other natural resources."

"My God," said Rollins, stunned at the revelation of the wholesale destruction and loss of humanity, and that a nuclear-fueled 'Atomic Bomb' had been created. There'd been talk for years, and he studied radioactivity and knew of the potential energy from fission's 'Mass Defect' but still, no one had a bomb. In less than 30-seconds Hitch had informed him that in this backwards universe, in many ways suffering from arrested development, the Nuclear Age was upon them.

"How about Albert Einstein? Ever heard of him?"

"Sure, smart physics guy, executed in Austria 10 years ago."

The color drained from Rollins' face. "What for?" he dared to ask. "Whaddayathink? For being a Jew and for speaking out against Hitler. Many think it's because he wouldn't play along with Hitler's other scientists and help develop weapons."

Hitch could sense his companion's awe and his uneasy digestion of the facts. "I swear, for an educated man, you are the most uninformed person I've ever met. I had you as a spy early on, but you're definitely not the spy type." Hitch twisted and tried to stretch the knots from his body while they rode on lazily. "What's going on with you? Don't ask me to believe that little goose egg on your head knocked all the sense out of you."

Henry sighed. "Hitch, I would tell you everything about the last six days I possibly could, but if you have a hard time believing me now, you'd really not believe me five minutes from now."

"Try me," said Hitch. "What have you got to lose? You owe me that much."

Henry started at the beginning with the basic historical facts of home, including the fact that the C.S.A. had been defeated in U.S. Civil War in1865, when General Lee finally surrendered to Grant at the Appomattox Courthouse. He told him that the United States still existed and had grown to some 48 states, and of his understanding of World War II and the U.S. involvement with the Allies. The Japanese bombing of Pearl Harbor in a protected territory in the Pacific Ocean called Hawaii. He was about to continue when Hitch interrupted.

"You do know that I'm a history teacher, or was, anyway?" asked Hitch.

"Yes," said Rollins, "and I told you this would sound crazy, but all of it is true, and you asked. I'm spilling my guts here, Hitch."

"Okay, keep going. I'm kind of enjoying it. But the big question is, what about you? How did you get here?"

"That is perhaps the biggest question of all, and the basis of my field of study, quantum physics—I dabble as a theoretical physicist—and I think I've been thrown headfirst into the Multiverse."

"The multi…what?"

"The Multiverse. It's an old concept. Goes back to 1895, when William James first used the phrase. It takes a leap of faith, but a lot of smart people, smarter than you or me, believe that we exist in one of many or possibly an infinite number of universes, all progressing in basically the same way, with changes appearing along the timeline, here and there. The hypothetical theories of parallel universes have been around for a long while, but traveling between them, that's completely new territory."

Hitch was silent, not buying a word of it.

"I know it sounds crazy, but you asked, and I'm answering. I believe my wife traveled to one of these universes about a year ago. In fact, I'm starting to think that she traveled to this one. I think that maybe that's my answer, too; that maybe this is the next closest universe to my home, and that I'm a…a traveler of sorts. I'm just not sure; but I do know one thing for certain, this place is not where I belong."

*****

Norfolk, Virginia
8:12 a.m.

"We've searched 300 acres and 50 miles from the farm all morning," said the Virginia State Trooper in charge of the K-9 unit. "The dogs seem to have lost any scent." He was speaking to Agent Serio of the C.B.I. "The horses were too fast."

144

The Command Center in Norfolk was buzzing with activity. Maps with concentric circles emanating from the farm where the fugitives were last seen, showed the slow progress the police were making in their systematic search.

Three officers; Admiral Brown, an Army General and a Colonel, dressed smartly in C.S.A. gray entered the room, commanding attention as they stood near the doorway.

"Good morning men. I'm General Hannaford. This is Colonel Johnson. You already know Admiral Brown. We're joining your party here and came down from Richmond to try to understand this major...well there's no way else to say it, this major fuck-up. This goat rodeo you call a manhunt is the most inept, fouled up thing I've ever heard of. The Admiral has kindly granted jurisdiction to the Army. This is a ground operation. You all will answer to me. Do I make myself clear?"

The cops who'd been literally beating the bushes for any signs of the fugitives, and who had worked the case from minute-one, rolled their eyes and were especially insulted, but no one argued. The men in the room looked to Serio and Jensen who made no counter-claims of jurisdiction. General Hannaford was most certainly now at the helm of this ship.

"Bring me up to speed," he said.

Serio led the officers to the large wall map of Virginia and portions of four adjacent states.

"We lost them on horseback here, last night, around 7 p.m.," said Serio, pointing to a black dot west of Norfolk. "We gave chase on foot, but the dogs lost the scent."

"On foot?" asked Hannaford.

"Yessir. They didn't take the roads. They went north through farmland, and basically wilderness. My men drove to the few intersecting roads they could find, but couldn't detect any sign of them, except for this headscarf." He held up a pink cotton scarf, covered with splashes of mud. "The woman from the farm identified it as hers."

"What else have you managed to do in the last...," he looked at his watch, "...thirteen hours?"

"We alerted every P.D. in the state, we've delivered photos of Wild Bill, and a description of Rollins, and made them both 'C.B.I. Most Wanted.'"

"Who the hell is Wild Bill?"

"William Hickok. He goes by 'Wild Bill,' or 'Hitch.' He's a nobody. A drunk who ignores prohibition, and happened to be sleeping one off in the same jail cell as Rollins."

"No photo of Rollins?"

"No sir. Norfolk P.D. didn't make one," he glared at Jensen. "We have his wallet and his I.D.s, but they make no sense. His driver's license says he lives in Princeton, New Jersey. The other I.D....well that's another story altogether."

"So he's another Yankee south of the border. Does that make him a spy? Is that really so odd?" asked the General.

145

"Not normally, but both of his I.D.s said the 'United States of America.'"

"Hmm, okay, so he's a radical, probably a reunificationist."

"He's more than that, General," chimed in Admiral Brown. "By now you've heard of the ship we encountered on Armistice Day?"

"Pretty wild tale," said Hannaford with a small grin. "They're having a good laugh up in Richmond, calling it the 'Return of the Gosport Ghost Ship.'"

"A wild tale maybe," said the Admiral, not seeing the amusement, "but it's a tale corroborated by 200 eyewitnesses, including me."

"Okay, go on, Admiral," said Hannaford, humoring him.

"The ship, a gray metal monster some 350-feet in length, five decks tall to the bridge, with 20 or more guns, appeared out of nowhere."

"What do you mean 'appeared out of nowhere?'"

"Just that," said the Admiral. "Clear skies, calm seas, one minute it wasn't there, and the next it was. It was lit up like a Christmas tree. Our spotters should have seen it from 10 miles out."

The Admiral looked past his Army counterpart, and out the window to somewhere far away.

"The ship, which I am telling you right now I saw through binoculars with my own eyes, perfectly matched the descriptions from my great-grandfather's diary accounts, to the letter. The crews of three gunboats saw it, and the Virginia fired a shot across the monster's bow. This is not speculation, this is not a rumor, these are the facts. What you want to call it is up to you, but I believe this was the Gosport Ghost Ship from 1864, whether that makes a lick of sense or not."

The room had gone silent, every man hanging on each word of the Admiral's account. Too many credible witnesses were making it harder, even for skeptics, to disbelieve.

"The Virginia's Captain and three officers say they clearly saw a man, in civilian clothes, surrender, waving a white flag. There was some kind of a scuffle with a sailor, and the civilian fell overboard. The ship had no other visible crew aboard. It was in severe distress, maybe hung up by an anchor, with her screws still spinning, one of them hanging out of the water as she listed 40-degrees. Anyway, that's when it happened."

"What?"

"The monster vanished just as quickly as it had appeared. That, too, I saw with my own eyes."

"Vanished? As in gone?" asked Hannaford.

"Gone without a trace."

"What about the man overboard?"

"My crews threw a lifeline into the water, and then they watched him vanish as well."

"Perhaps he drowned?" asked Hannaford, ignoring the greater part of the story involving a 350-foot metal monster that came and went before hundreds of witnesses.

"He was wearing a life vest," said Admiral Brown. "It's my belief that he did not drown, but rather, just like the ship, simply disappeared, until, I believe, he showed up here yesterday."

Hannaford hid any sign that he believed the tale as it was being told. He wouldn't allow himself to become one of the 'Ghost Ship crowd,' as the eyewitnesses were already being labeled.

"That's all well and good, Admiral," said Hannaford. "I'm sure something out there spooked your men, but weren't they really all in town, celebrating?"

"No!" shouted the Admiral, annoyed at the dismissal. "Not all. As I said 200 perfectly sober men, and a four-star Admiral, witnessed what I have just told you."

"Let's say for a moment it's all true," conceded Hannaford. "The Gosport Ghost Ship was back, and dropped off a passenger, who made it ashore. Fine. But what's done is done. The task at hand is finding him. Let's worry about how he got here and what he was doing, after we find him and interrogate him. Can we agree on that?"

"Yes," said the Admiral. "Agreed."

"Let's move on." Hannaford turned to the lead Virginia State Trooper. "What can you tell me about this piss-poor excuse for a manhunt?"

"We've got roadblocks up and checkpoints out to 100 miles," answered the trooper. "We're running radio bulletins across the state."

"Expand the checkpoints out to 200 miles," said Hannaford. "I'll supply any extra men you may be short. What else do you know?"

The Trooper didn't answer.

"Just great," said the General. "Let me see Rollins' I.D.s."

Serio snapped his fingers and an aid ran to a file cabinet retrieving a large envelope. Serio dumped its contents on a table. The General studied the driver's license, and emptied the rest of the wallet finding his Princeton University I.D. listing him as 'Doctor Henry Rollins, PhD.' He picked up a gold wedding band, looked at it carefully, and put it back on the table. He did the same with a wrist watch. When he found the Navy Yard I.D. and neck lanyard, he handed it to Admiral Brown.

"That's not good," said Brown. "I think the damn Yanks are up to something. I'm putting the Yard back on high alert."

"Up to what?" asked Hannaford.

"Not sure. My guess…preparation for war."

Hannaford dug a bit further into Rollins' wallet and pulled out a small photo featuring a pretty young woman standing in front of a small house in the countryside, rolling hills in the background. He flipped the picture over and read the inscription.

"Margaret, my love. Sugarland, Maryland, 1942."

"She looks young. Maybe his wife," said Hannaford.

He looked to Colonel Johnson. "I believe Rollins may be headed to Princeton, but he also might be going to this Sugarland, Maryland. I never heard of the town, but we know it's north of the border. You've got men up that way. Can we reach your operatives?"

"Yes, Sir," said Johnson. "They're at the Cottage."

The Cottage was a safe house for C.S.A. undercover operatives north of the international border, not far from the Federated States capitol, Washington, D.C.

"We have a new assignment for them," said Hannaford. "Find this woman." He handed the small photo to the agent. "Whoever she is, she's important to this Rollins, and at the moment is our only lead."

Chapter 23

Rural Virginia
Confederate States of America
10:40 a.m. August 22, 1943

When a train whistle blew from an unseen locomotive, Rollins and Hitch almost jumped off the backs of their horses. From the other side of a wooded ridge, the stack from a locomotive could be seen bellowing thick clouds of white steam mixed with tallow smoke. The men halted.

"I guess we're not in the wilderness any longer," said Rollins.

"No, and that whistle means there's a crossing nearby. We're getting close to a town."

They tied the horses off and climbed up the ridge, hoping for a better vantage point. They were no further than 50 yards from the train below them. As soon as the caboose passed by they watched heavy vehicle traffic a half-mile ahead start to move across the tracks.

"Well, Doc, we're here."

"Here?"

"Welcome to Emporia"

"So, now what?"

"Much as I hate to say it, we've got to get you out of that dress."

"Amen to that. But how?"

"Well unless you've got a purse full of cash, we'll have to borrow some clothes. Maybe we let the horses run free and go on foot."

"Won't two horses wandering around town give us away? Surely Norfolk has alerted police here to be on the watch."

"Hope not. We'll tie them loose, so when they get really hungry they'll pull free and head home."

The men tied the horses using their reins in a slipknot. The horses would think they were tied, but even a gentle tug would set them free. They stayed in the woods following the tracks toward town. A few ramshackle houses let them know they were getting close to a population. A neighborhood on the outskirts showed some promise. Some 50 or 60 identical, small, tidy homes, each with a small garden, surrounded a church in the neighborhood's center. When the church bell rang 10 times, they knew it was 10 a.m., and they watched a long stream of black men, women and children make their way through the church's small front door.

"Must be Sunday?" asked Rollins.

"Good guess," said Hitch. "That means all the coloreds are at church. Let's go."

The two men moved cautiously out of the woods, across the train tracks, and into the neighborhood. They couldn't be sure that every household was attending church, and there was a real risk of being seen. Like cat burglars who didn't know enough to work at night, the men snuck around the outskirts of the neighborhood looking for an optimal home to enter.

They tried two backdoors, finding them both locked, but they were able to help themselves to tomatoes and cucumbers from a flourishing vegetable garden.

"Third time's a charm," said Hitch, letting himself into the backdoor of the next house down the row. Rollins followed. They stood in a small kitchen and nearly passed out from the good smells of food on low simmer.

"Somebody's home," whispered Rollins.

"No, everybody leaves supper slow cooking for after church. Trust me. We're good."

They walked through the tiny kitchen, into a room that served as dining room and living room, and saw what they hoped were bedroom doors hiding closets full of clothing.

They stopped dead in their tracks when an elderly black man opened one of the closed doors, and walked into the large room, apparently not seeing the men who were less than five feet away. The man had a cane, and tapped the floor before settling into a large chair next to a radio. The dark-skinned black man, with white scraggly hair and beard to match, looked quite old and frail, and was obviously completely blind, and maybe deaf.

"He can't see us," whispered Henry.

"Who's there?" asked the old man, alarmed.

"No, but he can hear us, darling," whispered Hitch. "We mean you no harm, sir. Sorry to frighten you. We knocked, but you didn't answer."

"The hell you did," said the man, fear and anger growing on his craggy face.

"We just need a change of clothing," said Hitch, "a bite to eat, and we'll be on our way."

"Who are you?" asked the man.

"We're just two folk passing through," said Hitch.

"And you thought it'd be alright to pass through my house, and steal from my family?"

"No sir, it's not alright at all," said Henry, "but we've no choice. We have no money, and are trying to escape...some bad people who are after us."

"What bad people?"

"The C.S.A. and C.B.I for starters," said Hitch.

The old man relaxed a little. "Whadja do?" he asked. "Rob an old man?"

"No, sir," answered Henry. "My friend and I are both school teachers, and they didn't like what we were teaching, so they threw us in jail. We escaped yesterday, and are trying to make it out of the state."

"You say the C.B.I after you?"

"Yes," said Hitch.

"I got no use for the C.B.I., but still I don't like you just comin' in here like you done."

"We're very sorry," said Rollins, "but can you help us? Please."

The old man chuckled. "I wish I could. The clothes on my back, and one more set in the closet, is all I got, and you ain't gettin' 'em. I live with my daughter and two granddaughters, so you boys is outta luck, unless you want to wear dresses."

Hitch and Rollins shared a glance.

"I will tell you this," continued the old man. "Church gets out around 1:00, and the girls will be back to feed me. So stay for supper, I'll tell them what's going on, and then we'll get y'all to the church. They have clothes and food for the needy, and y'all seem pretty needy."

This was not what Hitch and Rollins had hoped for, but the plan had merit. A fresh set of clothes, a proper meal, and a sympathetic safe house, might just be workable.

"It beats sneaking around town," said Hitch. Rollins nodded.

"For now, go wash up. You both stink to high heaven and are ruining the smells coming from my kitchen. Go on now. The bathroom is right there."

Each taking their turn, Hitch and Henry stripped down and luxuriated in soap and hot water, wishing they didn't have to re-wear dirty clothing. Both took the time to wash their underwear in the hot soapy water, and wring them out to dry. Henry decided not to wear the dress, and stayed in his clean but damp boxers and undershirt. He'd had quite enough of Wild Bill's teasing, and their host would be none the wiser.

In the living room, they sat with the man listening to the radio, and telling his life's story. His name, they found out, was Cecil Washington, and he was 87 or 88, he didn't know for sure. The youngest of two sons of an escaped slave from Georgetown, South Carolina, he'd lived in the area most of his life.

"My pappy tried to get us north after the C.S.A. won in '66," said the old man, "but the borders were shut tight—couldn't even hardly sneak through the woods. There was a bounty out—$5 for every nigger, dead or alive. The south couldn't afford to lose us. The north didn't really want us either. We made it as far north as Emporia, and settled here."

"I told you we were in Emporia," said Hitch, proudly, looking directly at Henry. "You look different since your sponge bath, Henry. Have you done something with your hair?"

Rollins ignored him, but the old man's face showed he was having second thoughts about the two men in his living room.

"If you don't mind," asked Rollins, changing the subject, "how did—"

"How'd I lose my sight?"

"Well, I was going to ask about the tattoo on your wrist."

Cecil was silent, and stared in Rollins' direction, a quizzical look upon his face.

"He doesn't know about all that," said Hitch.

"Every Nigger got a number, boy," said Cecil. "You know that. I know mine by heart; 5-8-1-1-4-2-0-9."

Rollins couldn't believe what he was hearing. *Is it possible blacks are required to be...registered?* Rollins lied about not knowing.

"Well yes, of course. The numbers...how about your sight?"

"Courtesy of your friends at the C.B.I. It was around 1870 or '71, and I was still a boy, 14 or so. We was living as freedmen right here in Emporia. I was just old enough to start workin' for the railroad. Word got out to somebody somewhere that my pappy was escaped from South Carolina 10 years earlier. He died when I was a little fella, but they still didn't like our family too much. One day coming back from the rail yard they flashed their badges, stopped me and my older brother, checked our numbers, asked us who our pappy was. We told 'em, and then they beat us somethin' horrible. My brother died four days later. I went into the long sleep, and when I come to, five days later in the ward, I was blind. They'd crushed my skull in six places, tried to kill me, but I was a tough little bug. So as you see, I don't have no use for the C.B.I."

"That's awful, Cecil. We're sure sorry," said Rollins.

"Yeah, lots to be sorry about, young man, but that don't get you nowhere. It was a long time ago. Anyway, I made my peace with it. A pretty girl, my nurse, decided she liked me. A few years later, when I was 17, and she was 21, we married, had two daughters, one of them lives here, along with her two daughters, my granddaughters. Life's got a way sometimes of giving you little pieces of happiness here and there. My wife died 15 years ago, and I reckon I'll be joining her soon."

"Well, not too soon, I hope," said Rollins.

The men stopped talking when Cecil turned on a large floor model, wooden radio. He said he preferred the programs coming from New York better than the local Richmond shows. But he did have one favorite from Richmond that aired every Sunday at 12 noon, *The Old Time Gospel Hour* with Reverend Billy Hallelujah.

"Sure that boy can preach alright," said Cecil, "but you should hear him sing!"

The music swelled, and Cecil leaned back just as the announcer began to speak.

"This is Richmond's WWJD with the Ol' Time Gospel Hour featuring Reverend Billy Hallelujah, brought to you by Marathon Motor Works of Nashville, Tennessee. We will begin programming after this important message."

A detached monotone voice, with a distinct, strong southern drawl began reading a prepared statement:

> "Citizens of Virginia be on the lookout for two white men, one in his early 20s, the other in his 50s. They are escaped convicts and fugitives from the law. They are considered armed and dangerous and should be reported at once to local law enforcement. The younger is 5-foot 9-inches tall, the older 6-foot 4 inches. Both are of slender build. The smaller man may be wearing a full-length, floral print dress. Contact law enforcement if you've seen these men, or know of their whereabouts or activities. Thank you."

The announcer came back on the air. "Now back to regular programming with Reverend Billy Hallelujah and the Gospel Kings and Queens of Richmond!"

Cecil lowered the volume on the radio and was quiet for a moment. "So...y'all armed and dangerous?"

"As God is my witness, Cecil," said Rollins. "We are neither."

His highly attuned sense of observation led the man to believe that Rollins was the younger, smaller man, as described in the police bulletin. He turned his head toward Rollins as if he were looking at him.

"Young fella...are you still wearing a dress?"

"No, Sir. Not at the moment."

Cecil rubbed his whiskers and leaned back in his chair. "Hmm, that's not good. 'Not at the moment' you say?"

"No, Sir, not at the moment."

"Then...what *are* you wearing?"

Rollins sighed, embarrassed, and then in frustration heaved his story in one long sentence. "I'm in my underwear, Cecil. I know it sounds strange, but after the escape we had to get out of the prison stripes, we found a farmhouse, and the dress is all we could find that would fit me. Look, I'm trying to get home to my wife in New Jersey, and Hitch is trying to get south to Florida. We haven't hurt anyone, and wouldn't hurt anyone. They're mostly mad at us because we escaped their jail in Norfolk."

"Does your wife know you like to wear dresses?" asked Cecil, without a hint of a smile.

Hitch snorted and choked on his own laughter.

"No!" protested Rollins.

"No, she doesn't know you like to wear dresses?" asked Cecil, seeking clarity.

"Oh my God!" yelled Rollins, now laughing with the others. "Please can we talk about something else?"

"Let's talk about jail," said Cecil. "You had to do something to get put there in first place, didn't ya? I doubt that teachin' tale you told me is true."

"We are teachers, or rather were teachers," said Hitch, "My crime was that I had too much to drink and was pulled off the sidewalk for singing too loudly. I had become a regular, and they were going to throw the book at me, give me some serious jail time."

"And I broke the telephone receiver on a Norfolk City payphone," said Rollins. "But because I'm from New Jersey, with no papers allowing me across the border, they wanted to throw me in jail for 90 days. I guess they think I'm a security threat."

"Are ya?"

"No, Sir."

"Well in that case, let's listen to a little Gospel music and wait for Ophelia and the girls to get home and serve up supper. Afterward, we'll get you into the church and find some proper clothes for ya. Maybe we can get you a new dress?"

"Sir!" protested Rollins at the continued teasing.

"Be quiet, boy, the Rev is about to sing," said Cecil, leaning back in his favorite chair.

Chapter 24

Philadelphia, Pennsylvania
United States of America
12:01 a.m. September 10, 1943

At the Philadelphia Naval Yard, preparations were underway to re-launch the USS Eldridge. It was touted as the 'maiden voyage' but many knew that it wasn't. The rumors around the shipyard were that she was a part of some sea trial and shakedown experiment, and maybe had been in battle, but details were scarce. Only a handful of men and women, less than 20, knew of the Eldridge's spectacular trip to somewhere quite unknown.

Considered a failure by the naval brass, the Philadelphia Experiment was shelved, permanently classified and buried. Einstein, the pacifist, was unceremoniously sent home to Princeton. Because the Eldridge was desperately needed on the high seas to protect convoys of troop ships and merchant marine vessels from German U-boats, which were still a threat, the repairs had been hurried. The teams of engineers all signed off on the inspection, confident that the Eldridge was ship shape and ready to do her part. Captain Hammond wasn't so sure.

A small group of officers stood on the deck in the bright sunshine. Elsewhere on the ship, men readied themselves and the Eldridge for sea.

"I wouldn't have believed it if F.D.R. himself told me it was so," conceded Captain Hammond to the Chief Engineer, who'd been cleared for a full debriefing. Hammond looked around and lowered his voice. "The ship was hanging 50-feet out of the goddamn water, levitating and groaning like the metal was being ripped and bent. I can't believe there wasn't more damage. I can't believe she still floats."

"We've gone through her, bow to stern," said the engineer, "every deck, with a fine-tooth comb, and other than a few popped rivets, the busted antennae array, a twisted propeller shaft, and the guns we had to replace, she's lookin' pretty good."

"We set sail at 0630," said Hammond. "You're telling me she's good to go?"

"She's a fine ship, Sir. As far as I can tell, yes. Good to go."

Hammond made his way to the bridge, where he sat and reviewed his orders. He was to take the ship to Norfolk to do just what the Eldridge's class of ships was designed to do, escort convoys across the treacherous Atlantic Ocean.

The Eldridge's Executive Officer, 28-year-old Phillip Moore, a new man, came to the doorway of the bridge and stood at attention. He was blond-haired, square-jawed, fit, and looked like an Aryan poster child.

"You must be Moore," said Hammond, standing, and saluting. "At ease."

"Yes sir. Permission to enter the bridge."

"Of course. Glad to have you on board. We were getting worried about you."

"Sorry, Sir. Trains are running slow out of the Carolinas. Glad to be here. Looking forward to 0630."

"That makes one of us," said Hammond under his breath, but loud enough to be heard. It was an unusually candid remark, and not considered Naval etiquette or good form for an officer, especially the captain of a ship.

"Sir?" asked Moore, not sure he'd heard him clearly.

"Oh, nothing, Moore. Just mumbling to myself. Yes, 0630. We'll be headed south then a bit west to meet up with the Battleship Texas and a small supply convoy. We're headed to England."

"Right, Sir. Haven't been there before."

"Well, if the Krauts have their way you won't make it to see jolly old England; they'd like you to be fish food for the North Atlantic cod. The latest intelligence says the Atlantic is still crawling with the bastards. They sank the *Francis Marion*, a 20-ton cargo vessel, last night in the Celtic Sea, 225 nautical miles south of Ireland, smack dab in the middle of our route. And, there was a possible U-boat sighting last night off the South Carolina coast."

Moore was quiet, contemplative.

"This is your first shot at XO, isn't it Moore?" asked the captain using the 'XO' abbreviation for 'Executive Officer.' The XO was the second in command of a ship, and was supposed to be the captain's right hand man, confidant, and sounding board.

"Yes, Sir, but I've been sailing for eight years. I graduated at the top of…"

"Never mind the resume, I already know it. I like the fact that you're green in this position. That means some other captain didn't transfer you to me because you were screwing up his boat. We can do things my way, the right way. Agreed?"

"Absolutely, Sir."

Moore walked a few steps to the traditional seat of the Executive Officer, and sat.

"Permission to speak freely, Sir."

"Permission granted, and don't ever ask for permission again," said Hammond. "You are required to speak freely. It's your job to, and I expect nothing less. Never mince words with me. If something's on your mind, just say it. Life's too short, Mr. Moore."

Moore smiled. "Okay." He paused and smiled. "Will every answer to every question I ask come with its own tutorial and lecture, Sir?"

"Okay, that's a little *too* free, sailor," said Hammond finally cracking a smile. "And no, I'll try to do better on that front."

The two men were alone on the bridge, while crews below them scampered with duffels, and crates of supplies readying for departure. With the ice broken, Moore asked the captain a burning question, one that had been on his mind for three days, ever since receiving orders to transfer.

"Is it true?"

"Is what true?" answered Hammond, uneasy with what he knew was coming.

"Is it true what they're saying about the Eldridge? That she was Dr. Einstein's bathtub toy?"

Hammond looked straight ahead, and decided to answer honestly.

"More or less."

"What happened to her?"

"You're probably not cleared for this, but nobody, not even Einstein, can say for sure." Hammond swiveled in his chair and stared out at the empty sky. "She went somewhere, alright. We just don't have a clue where. The only two aboard her at the time are either dead or presumed dead. We're very short on answers."

"Besides the German, who else was on board?" asked Moore.

A chill ran through Hammond at the question. He'd never mentioned the German. That detail was at the top of a long list of particulars that were exceptionally sensitive. Only he, Dr. Einstein, an Admiral, and eight security officers knew about the German operative. Even with all the rumors floating around, the accepted story was that the Eldridge had been vacant of sailors, or anyone, during the experiment. He decided not to call out Moore on his knowledge of this detail, but his question made him uneasy.

"A civilian," answered Hammond, finally. "An engineer of sorts, a young scientist working with Einstein."

"No sign of him?"

"None."

"These are strange times in which we live, Captain," said Moore. "Strange indeed."

*****

"Verdammt diese wetter, und damn our luck!" yelled Nazi U-boat Captain Zoeller from the control room, as his ship struggled to stay on course. He'd just received more bad news while in the radio room. Transmissions from the nearby secret German weather station, combined with radio shipping chatter, all confirmed something he already sensed.

"The wind has shifted direction," he told the helmsman and the three officers who were holding on to anything solid. "It seems there's been a fairly pronounced turn to the west. In essence, we're near the northwest outer bands and the storm is following us. We can't out run it. It's too big and too fast. We can't go backward as we'd be running straight into the worst of it."

The Captain and his officers huddled around a chart of the East Coast of the U.S. Mid Atlantic. Everyone's best guess, assuming the storm followed its current path, had it making landfall in seven or eight hours somewhere between Norfolk, Virginia, and Cape May, New Jersey.

"We can dive and ride it out," said Zoeller, "but I don't like our position. We're too damned close to that Naval Base."

"At least the American's air-cover will be down," said a Jr. Officer. "There's no way they would risk flying in these winds."

"I hope you're right," said Zoeller. "How are the batteries?"

"Fully charged, Sir."

"And how long can we safely stay submerged?"

"At least 15 hours, perhaps a little longer—it depends."

Zoeller thought about the worst-case scenario, and spoke plainly and truthfully to his officers. "If this storm is as bad as we think it might be, we'll have to dive to at least 50 to 60 meters. I'm not too worried about that, but if we have to surface for any reason, and that storm has stalled, or hasn't passed us…I don't need to tell you how difficult that will be."

"Yes, Sir."

"Well then…Zoeller was interrupted when another giant wave crashed over the top of his 294-foot ship, and almost turned it on its side.

Zoeller struggled to his feet. "Enough of this! Alarm!" he yelled. "Dive! Dive!

******

Had Dr. Einstein's health been better, if he'd not felt so weak, he would have asked to visit Maryland and witness Margaret's new trick, and perhaps even try it himself. But after she drove off, he told Helen Dukas he was going to take a nap, which he did promptly.

Around four-and-half hours later Margaret Rollins pulled on to the country road, leading to the house in Maryland. She watched for police, and even unmarked cars. When the coast looked clear, she pulled into their driveway and parked in the barn in back, hiding the car under old horse blankets.

She put one of the blankets to her nose and inhaled deeply. The musty scent of horse and hay brought her back to her childhood. She'd loved horses, but Henry was scared to death of the big animals, refusing every time she'd suggested they go riding. She was so unlike him in so many ways. He'd lived a sheltered, conservative, strictly academic life, nose buried in books since he was three. She'd been an adventurous girl, breaking the rules and smashing stereotypes of what a proper young woman should or shouldn't be doing. Despite their differences, or perhaps because of their differences, they were drawn together as if from some mystical, magnetic force that insisted upon their union.

Her mind drifted to the versions of herself and Henry in the other place, the ones she'd seen in photographs. She wondered how their lives were the same or different, and how they'd found one another in that twisted translation of home. She never told Henry that she'd lived with some version of him for the two weeks she'd been missing. She hated keeping that part of the tale to herself, but it was more than she was ready to share. *All in good time.*

"Explain the love equation, Dr. Einstein," she said aloud, as if he was there. She'd grown fond of the eccentric genius, even if she still blamed him a little for Henry's disappearance. "Put 'love' into a mathematical formula, then I'll really be impressed."

When she reached the back door, she took her key to unlock it, and was alarmed when the door pushed open, unlatched. Her heart raced, and she backed away. When she could muster the courage she peeked through the kitchen window and saw no one. She did see an open box of cereal spread out on the kitchen floor. *Not the cops, I don't think. A thief?* She walked to the front of the house, looking in each window along the way, still seeing no one. After walking to the front of the house, she went up the porch steps, unlocked the door, stepping cautiously into the foyer.

"Hello?"

She heard scrambling and something that sounded like nails being dragged and tapped along the hardwood floor. When a skinny dog, tail between its legs, came from the living room, sleep still in his eyes, she breathed a sigh of relief, and smiled.

"Well, hello. Who are you?" The dog wagged the back half of his body, and lay on the floor, rolling on to his back. A Golden Retriever, not at all afraid of the human whose house he'd been borrowing, enjoyed the belly rub and a kindness that he might not have experienced for a while, or possibly ever.

She guessed she'd left the back door ajar, the door didn't always latch, and the dog found his way inside. Other than the cereal on the floor there seemed to be no damage.

"Well, how do you like that?" she said. The dog had no collar and so she wasn't sure where he belonged. His hair was matted and he was skinny, too skinny, to have been properly cared for.

She opened the back door, and the dog looked outside, and wagged his tail. He showed no desire to leave the house. Margaret found dry goods, powdered eggs and powdered milk, along with canned hash that she turned into a lunch for them both. She took the dog up the stairs to the second floor, into the bathroom.

"You need a name," she said while running a tub full of warm water. She found some mild soap and gave him the spa treatment he deserved and relished. She relished giving him the attention as it distracted her, even for a moment, from her sadness.

"It's not easy being a dog lost in the country," she said to him, her thoughts turning to Henry. She sat on the closed toilet lid, dried him, brushed his matted hair, and returned him to some level of dignity.

"I'm calling you 'Hank,'" she said, patting him on the head. He wagged his tail and seemed pleased enough. "I call Henry that sometimes." She got up and moved, staving off the tears, which seemed always ready to flow.

"Okay, downstairs, Hank. We've got to go find our Henry."

Chapter 25

Southwood, Virginia
Confederate States of America
2 p.m. August 22, 1943

When two loud chimes rang out from the Southwood African Methodist Episcopal church, just a few blocks away, the three men in the house knew the women would be returning soon. They all worried about the reception they might be given. Ophelia and her daughters were fiercely protective of Cecil, and wouldn't be happy to see two white men, one in his underwear, sprawled out in the living room. When they found out they were fugitives, all hell would break loose.

"They'll be here shortly," said Cecil. "You two wait in the bedroom. Close the door. I'm going to warm them up to the idea of y'all being here, and us maybe helping you."

That made sense to Hitch and Henry, who moved quickly, happy to get out of sight. Cecil grabbed his cane, and walked to the kitchen and waited near the back door. His acute hearing picked up the women's voices even before they came through the back yard, a short cut from the church. He made an unconscious mental note of whom he heard: Ophelia, his granddaughters Augusta and Clarissa, and another voice he hadn't expected. A moment later, they all arrived.

"Hello Daddy," said Ophelia walking through the door. "Church was splendid today. Did you stay out of my stew? How was Billy Hallelujah? I know you love to hear him sing."

Ophelia was a large woman, with a heart to match. Her pretty smile was partially hidden by a hat covered with white feathers over a royal blue, crushed velvet brim and crown.

161

"Hello Pappy," said the two girls in unison. They were both teenagers, Augusta 14 and Clarissa 17. They both made a beeline for the living room and changed the station, looking for music.

"Daddy, you remember Sheriff Brooks," said Ophelia. She led the Sheriff, who was last to enter the house, by his right elbow to her father, so that the two could shake hands.

"Sheriff Brooks?" asked Cecil, stunned, his face showing concern.

"Yes, Daddy. Smile a little, he won't bite you. I invited him over for supper."

"Hello Cecil," yelled Sheriff Brooks, overcompensating, thinking he needed to shout at the blind man.

"Hello Sheriff," answered Cecil, unsure how to proceed with this new challenge.

"Y'all go to the living room," said Ophelia, "make yourself at home while we get supper ready. Girls! Come help your momma."

The teens rolled their eyes and stood up, again speaking in unison; "Yes, momma."

The middle-aged Sheriff Brooks carried his potbelly proudly girdled by a uniform shirt at least one size too small, and tightly belted pants to match. He was a large black man, whose size and personality were matched only by his obvious affections toward Ophelia. Those tender feelings had grown, and gone unrequited for two years. He began trying to get close to Ophelia six weeks after her husband died, and it had put her off, but she was beginning to warm to him.

Brooks was not particularly well liked in the community, but he kept things on an even keel. He was sometimes criticized for bending over to the white authorities who ruled the town, literally from the other side of the tracks. Sheriff Brooks didn't suffer fools or criminals and, along with his two part-time deputies, could be tough as nails when the job called for it. They were the only law enforcement in Southwood, and their jurisdiction ended at the town's borders.

The small, overwhelmingly black community had a population of 375. It was made up of around 70 families who kept to themselves, only heading into downtown Emporia when they needed something not supplied by local merchants, which was rare. Since the end of slavery, just before the turn of the century, the plight of former black slaves improved only marginally. Under a strict and severe apartheid system, and with mandatory identification tattoos, the blacks were considered even less then second-class citizens, unable to vote, freely associate, or hold elective office, beyond the Sheriff, making Brooks the king of Southwood.

"So, Cecil," started Sheriff Brooks. "How you been?"

Cecil would have normally enjoyed small talk. Though not all that fond of Brooks, he loved visitors. But with Hitch and Rollins, less than five feet away, he was a wreck. He knew harboring fugitives was never a great idea, and them being white, made it potentially worse.

"I'm good, Sheriff. You?" said Cecil. He looked anything but 'good.'

"Fine, just fine." That was the end of the awkward conversation, which led to an uncomfortable silence.

In Cecil's bedroom Hitch and Rollins heard every word of the conversation. They could tell by Cecil's tone, that he was as surprised and horrified by the Sheriff's arrival as they were.

"That's not good," whispered Hitch.

"No kidding. What are we going to do?"

"There's the window?" said Hitch, pointing to a small four-paned window that might be big enough for Rollins to squeeze through, but not likely large enough to accommodate anyone Hitch-sized.

"I think we wait it out," said Rollins.

"For now, I guess."

"Supper!" shouted Ophelia. "Come on boys."

Cecil and the Sheriff stood, and made their way to the dining room.

"Daddy, you sit here next to me," said Ophelia, "and Sheriff Brooks, you sit on my other side."

"Please Ophelia, can't you call me Bobby?" said Sheriff Brooks.

"You're a man of the law, Sheriff," said Ophelia, blushing slightly, "and I like to address you with the title and recognition of the authority God has placed in your most capable hands."

They all sat, said a grace, and dug into chicken stew and sweet cornmeal spoon bread. The clinking of utensils, and the slurping of thick stew, along with the comments of how wonderful everything was, was tortuous to Rollins and Hitch. Smelling the food and listening to the mealtime activity from just on the other side of the bedroom door, sent them both into dog-like salivation that only got worse by the minute.

The dining room conversation lagged when a loud knock at the front door startled them all.

"My goodness," said Ophelia, pushing away from the table. "What in the world?"

She opened the door to see the round, ruddy face of Emporia's newest Sheriff, Randal Overstreet. His nearly 300-pound frame didn't appear as if it would fit through the door. Even with his crisp Emporia Sheriff's Department hat perched on top of his bald head, he stood no taller than Ophelia's 5-foot 6-inches, and they stood eye to eye.

"Good day, Ma'am," he said through a false smile, removing his hat. The young deputies didn't even try to hide their disgust with being in Southwood.

"So sorry to bother you. May we come in?"

Ophelia backed away from the door, just as Sheriff Brooks stood.

"Why, Sheriff Brooks," said Overstreet. "Sorry to interrupt your midday meal. We missed you at the Church and heard you might be dining here today."

"Sheriff," said Brooks, nodding. "What's this all about?"

"Oh, well, Sheriff Brooks, you see it seems that our good colleagues at the C.B.I. are after their most wanted #1 and #2 men, both on the loose for about two days."

"I heard the bulletin. Got the phone call last night," said Brooks.

"And wouldn't it be our luck, that two men fitting their description were seen in Southwood just this morning."

"Two white men in Southwood?" asked Sheriff Brooks, with a chuckle, disbelieving.

"Yes, I know it seems unlikely, Sheriff Brooks, but to further complicate things they were seen around the backyard of Miss Ophelia's house here."

The three women looked nervously at one another, and the girls held each other's hands under the table. Cecil remained quiet.

"We were gone to church all morning," said Ophelia. "Daddy's been home, but we haven't seen anyone."

"How about you sir? Mr.—"

"This is my daddy, Cecil Washington. He didn't see anything."

"That so?" Overstreet turned sideways, and pushed into the house further. His two deputies followed. He walked around the table to face Cecil, whose back had been to him, and saw his cane leaning against the chair and his sightless eyes.

"I guess you didn't see nothin', now did you?" he laughed, looking at his deputies, who remained stone-faced. No one else saw the humor in his cruel joke.

The Sheriff looked around the room and got a strange gleam in his eye. "You don't mind if we check y'alls numbers, do you?" asked Sheriff Overstreet. "Strictly routine, you understand?"

Mandated by law in 1901, every black baby was to receive a C.S.A.-registered I.D. tattoo at birth. Though the girls were too young to have ever suffered the indignity of a random, unwarranted check, Ophelia, her father, and even Sheriff Brooks had all been put through the humiliation before. They stared into space, and bared their upturned palms. The deputies wrote down the series of numbers in a notebook and checked them against a list of outstanding warrants.

"So what's wrong with them?" asked Overstreet, nodding toward the non-compliant girls, whose hands were still clasped tightly, as they stood against the wall. "They deaf? You got a blind one over here and two deaf ones over there?" Again he roared at his own joke, his face turning bright red. Even though it was the Lord's Day, Ophelia wished the man would die from a stroke. She imagined him gasping for air sprawled out, right then and there on their dining room table. Overstreet's round face turned so red from his choking and sickening laughter, she thought the Lord may grant her this wish.

"Girls, let the Sheriff see your numbers," said Ophelia. The teens unclasped their hands and raised them into the air, turning their palms upward, allowing the deputies to write down each set of I.D. numbers. They sat in silence while their numbers were checked against the list. The deputy nodded they were okay and Overstreet almost seemed disappointed.

"Guess y'all passed with flyin' coloreds! Did I say coloreds? Get it?" said Overstreet once again the only one in the room laughing. He was not particularly concerned, or to have taken note of the fact that no one else thought his jokes were funny. Even his own deputies tired of his offensiveness, but he didn't care.

"My God, woman, but that chicken stew sure smells delicious." He looked at his deputies. "Don't it smell good, boys?"

"Yes, Sheriff," said one of the deputies. "It does smell mighty good."

Ophelia nodded slightly in recognition of the remark. An awkward silence filled the room. *Surely he's not expecting us to ask him to stay?* She couldn't imagine that man at her table.

"It is delicious," said Brooks, breaking the silence scowling at the Sheriff. He threw his napkin on the table, no longer able to hide his anger. "We'd like to get back to our meal, if you don't mind."

"Well, thank you very kindly," said Overstreet, oozing sarcasm, "but we can't stay, though your hospitality is overwhelming. You'll let us know if those white boys show up on your doorstep, won't you?"

"You'll be the second to know," said Sheriff Brooks.

"I mean they could be hiding in some corner of this house, and y'all wouldn't even know it, so consumed by this fabulous meal, and all. My, but it does smell good."

"We ain't seen nobody!" yelled Cecil at the top of his voice, standing, his glass of ice tea crashing to the floor. "Nobody!"

"Now, now, Mr. Washington, no need to get upset. We're just doing our jobs," said Overstreet. "Ain't that right Sheriff Brooks? A lawman's gotta do what a lawman's gotta do."

Brooks didn't answer. Overstreet motioned to his deputies to leave the house, and he tipped his hat, and followed them to the front stoop.

"Stay safe, Washington family. You, too, Sheriff Brooks," he said before finally walking back to the patrol car.

As soon as Overstreet and his men had driven off, Sheriff Brooks hugged Ophelia, while the girls cried a little and cleaned up the broken glass and puddle of tea. It had been the first time the girls had ever been asked to show their I.D. numbers. As traumatic and humiliating as it was, if any of the family hadn't had 'nigger numbers' as some called them, they would have been immediately arrested. Under apartheid, it was the law of the land throughout the C.S.A.

"I'm so sorry Ophelia, Cecil, girls. Men like that have no right to wear a badge. They're the real criminals. Those white boys are probably lucky to have escaped. There's no justice here for any of us." They all sat back down, but no one felt like eating.

"I'm glad to hear you say that, Sheriff," said Cecil.

Peering out the front window, Margaret watched for any sign of surveillance.

"Have I gotten paranoid, or what?" she asked Hank, who never answered her questions, but wouldn't leave her side. She stood before the archway to the den, knowing she'd have to travel again to this other place, a place like her own comfortable world in so many ways, but one she thought may as well have been on another planet. *Maybe it is?*

She put a bowl of water on the front porch, and struggled to put Hank outside. "Maybe you better go home, Hank," she said. "I can't have a dog right now, and I don't know how long I'll be away." The dog looked at her, and seemed to understand they were about to separate. He whimpered softly as she closed the front door leaving him on the porch.

She pointed herself toward the desk in the den.

"Henry, here I come."

She walked three steps, and held on, knowing she would pass from one point in space and time to another, as easily as waving hello. Only this time she didn't travel. She knew right away it hadn't worked, because before there had always been some change, no matter how subtle, in the light and atmosphere, room temperature. She double-checked herself by looking backward at the fireplace mantle, which had all the right pictures, right where they belonged.

"Huh," she said aloud. "That's strange." She walked back out and tried again, still with no luck. She sat on the couch to think. She knew from previous experience that everything had to be just so. *I haven't touched anything in the den, so that's not it.* She folded her hands on her knees and looked at the slacks she was wearing. *My clothing?* She wondered if it could have something to do with the dress she'd been wearing. *No, how could it be?* She thought back. *I was wearing the same dress every other time I traveled. Maybe? But I changed clothes in Princeton, so it's not here.*

Disappointed she wouldn't be traveling that day, and certain after 10 additional tries that it was probably the dress, she had no choice. *Back to Princeton.* As she retrieved the car, and pulled down the driveway, Hank barked, and followed. She rolled down the window.

"Go home, Hank. I can't take care of you. Go on!" Both she and dog looked sad, but there was just too much going on in her life to deal with a big dog, regardless of how much she enjoyed his company. She pulled down the gravel driveway, Hank never more than five feet from the bumper. When she hit the paved two-lane road, she did her best to outrun the dog, who was bound and determined to keep up. He wasn't a particularly old dog, but was weak from malnourishment.

"I'm not going to look in the rearview mirror," she said, looking straight ahead down the road. "I can't have a dog to worry about. I just can't." Not able to help herself, she glanced in the mirror and saw Hank, too worn out to continue the chase, at the top of the hill.

"Dammit!" she yelled, pounding the steering wheel with her fist, slamming on the brakes. "I knew I shouldn't have looked." She spun the wheel of the car, and made a U-turn. Hank waited patiently in the middle of the road, and hopped in on the passenger side when the car door was opened for him. He licked her face, and sat upright looking out the window, like the co-pilot he knew he was meant to be. Margaret smiled at him and scratched his neck with one free hand.

"Ever been to New Jersey?" she asked him. Hank looked out the window, marveling at how fast they were moving.

Chapter 26

"Come on out boys," yelled Cecil toward the bedrooms. There was no movement, and the others looked at him like he'd lost his mind.

"Daddy," said Ophelia. "Are you alright?"

"Yes, yes, I'm fine. I just got a little surprise for you all."

When he called again, Henry and Hitch knew it was futile to stay hidden. They opened the door and walked through the living room to face a stunned audience.

"Oh my God," said Ophelia. "Daddy, what have you done?"

Sheriff Brooks, off duty and unarmed, stood, in shock, and looked at the strangers standing before him.

"Oh no, Mr. Washington," said the Sheriff, "what have you gotten this family mixed up in?"

"Everybody relax," said Cecil. "They came knockin' this afternoon, and it bein' the Lord's Day and all, I decided the Christian thing to do was offer some help."

"That man has no draws," said Ophelia. Henry was feeling underdressed in boxer shorts, a tank-top undershirt, and black shoes with no socks. The girls giggled.

"It's a long story," said Henry, taking a step closer to the table to introduce himself. Sheriff Brooks, in one quick move, tackled him to the ground, and twisted his arm behind his back. The women screamed and got up from the table, and ran to the far side of the dining room. Hitch stayed where he was, and put his arms out, gesturing calmness. Sheriff Brooks cursed himself for being unarmed, and not having handcuffs.

"Stop it, Sheriff," said Cecil, standing. "These boys are guests in my house. We've been together all morning, and I trust my gut on this one. They okay."

"Okay?" asked the Sheriff, still kneeling on Rollins' back and watching Hitch for any sudden moves. "How do you know they're okay? They're wanted by the C.B.I. and are armed and dangerous."

"No we're not!" yelled Rollins' his voice muffled, face pressed against the floor.

"You might have just landed me and your whole family in prison, Cecil," continued Brooks.

"How are *you* in trouble?" asked Cecil

"They won't believe I didn't know anything about this. My God, aiding and abetting fugitives. Cecil, you have no idea what this government can and will do to us. They are capable of destroying you, Ophelia, and the girls, in the worst ways."

"We have no intention of letting anything happen to anyone but us," said Hitch. "We're not armed, we're definitely not dangerous. Do we look dangerous?"

"Then why the statewide manhunt from the C.B.I?" asked the Sheriff.

"Because the man whose back you're kneeling on is from New Jersey," pleaded Hitch, "and he doesn't have a passport or papers. He doesn't even have an I.D. anymore. I don't have I.D. either."

"Why not?"

"Because we broke out of the Norfolk City jailhouse two days ago," said Hitch, "just before they were going to take us to State Prison, for no good reason. I was in the drunk tank one too many times, and with his Yankee I.D. and crazy talk, they probably think he's a spy, which, for the record, I'm not so sure he isn't. All he did was break a payphone, for God's sake. The C.S.A. is out of control."

Brooks eased up slightly.

"I will tell you this, Sheriff; neither of us have any respect for the C.S.A. or the C.B.I and the way they treat the coloreds. It's not right. The entire system is plain wrong, and I believe you feel the same way."

None of the Washington family, nor Sheriff Brooks had ever met any white men who spoke so boldly about the injustice suffered by blacks. Brooks was skeptical, but he let some pressure off Henry's back.

"Sound's nice and all, but those are just words," he said. "You are holding this family hostage just by being here."

"We are very, very sorry," said Hitch. "But we were desperate. If they catch us now, they'll torture us for information we don't have, and then hang us for escaping and making fools of them." He glanced at Henry. "Lord know what this one might say if he let loose."

Disgusted and angry, Sheriff Brooks released Henry, who sat up first to catch his breath, before standing, coughing, and then brushing himself off.

"Them boys need some clothing, some food in they bellies, and a ride out of town," said Cecil. "Hell, out of the State if possible. You know how I feel about the C.B.I. We gonna help 'em, an that's all there is to it."

Sheriff Brooks walked quickly around the house closing every curtain he possibly could. He then told Hitch and Henry to sit and wait in the living room, and to stay away from the windows.

"You've already been seen and reported in Southwood, on this street, and near enough to this house that that fat son-of-bitch came calling today. Sorry for my language Ophelia, sorry girls." He turned back to Hitch and Henry.

"From this point forward, if you get seen in this house, you've destroyed this family, and there won't be a damned thing I can do about it. Their safety is all that I care about. I don't give a good goddam, sorry again Ophelia, about how you think us poor colored folk are treated. You put us all in danger by coming here. I am not sympathetic to your situation, but getting you out of here and out of my town, quickly, and quietly seems to be in everyone's best interest."

*****

USS Eldridge
Philadelphia Navy Yard
5 a.m. Sept 10, 1943

A wind-up alarm clock sitting on the tiny table next to Captain Hammond's excuse for a bed rang out unmercifully at 5:00 a.m. He rubbed his eyes and was almost happy to get off of the uncomfortable single mattress hung from the ceiling on a wire rack. They called them "beds," though they were far from anything anyone would willingly choose to sleep on; and these were the officer's quarters. The rest of the crew slept on bunks stacked three high, 50 men per room. Even brand new modern ships were not built for comfort.

He turned on the light and stood, his mind engaging with the day ahead. This was the morning he had once hoped for, when he first got the assignment to command the Eldridge. While he and his crew were ready for the 'maiden voyage,' he couldn't shake the feeling that he was being asked to take command of a ship that was damaged goods, and maybe should have been scrapped. It was an awful feeling for a captain, who was supposed to love his ship, defend her and protect her. He tried to put the thoughts behind him while he washed, and got dressed for the launch.

At 0530 the sound of a shrill boatswain's whistle blasted through a few dozen P.A. speakers around the ship. The call let those men who were among the186-strong crew know it was time for muster. They had 30-minutes to use the bathroom, dress, eat some chow, and be at their posts for an 0630 departure.

Normally an event of this type came with a bit of fanfare, though the Eldridge's launch would not. One of the two Admirals who'd witnessed the calamitous operation "Canned Heat" first-hand, along with Commander Koenig and a few dignitaries, began arriving. They gathered near a small platform that had again been staged with a microphone and P.A. system, and room for a U.S. Navy film crew. The footage taken would be used for newsreels, and shown in movie theaters around the country, some continuously throughout the day.

The film crew was glad to be back shooting the Eldridge. The last time they'd seen her, their cameras captured her disappearance in a cloud of blue-white fog. The cameras weren't operating upon her dramatic reappearance hours later; the missed opportunity for obtaining the world's first photographic proof of cloaking, teleportation, or whatever it was, was deeply regretted. They quietly hoped things might go spectacularly wrong, and that their good luck and timing would capture it on film. They weren't eager to see anyone hurt, they were just hoping for some fireworks of the kind they'd witnessed a week earlier. It seemed the Eldridge, not even yet fully commissioned, was gaining a reputation, albeit one best fitting sci-fi pulp magazines.

Precisely at 0630, after a few remarks from Admiral Grant, with all hands on deck, the Eldridge shoved off from the docks. No Navy band played, or families waved their goodbyes. The Navy brass had scrapped all public spectacle, a little afraid of what might happen. They certainly didn't need 186 mothers and girlfriends watching their boys and men disappear in a cloud of blue-white fog.

Cruising at 12 knots it took the Eldridge 7 hours to make it down to the mouth of the Delaware River, with the Cape May Lighthouse to her starboard side. The windy day and the open water rocked the small ship. For the unaccustomed, it could be treacherous walking the deck or negotiating tight spaces above or below deck. Though Destroyer Escorts could sail in all weather, just about anywhere in the world, their relatively short length and narrow beam made them especially susceptible to rocking in strong seas. It was easy to spot Destroyer Escort crews on leave, as they were the most battered and bruised sailors to ever serve.

The Executive Officer Moore, nearly banged his head on the port bulkhead of the ship's bridge when a 15-foot swell sideswiped the ship and sent it listing 20-degrees.

"Easy there Moore," said Hammond, hiding a smile. He knew how to stay sure-footed on smaller ships.

"Yes, for sure, Chief. Choppy today," said Moore.

"This?" Hammond laughed out loud. "You ain't seen nothin' yet. Just remember, keep your stance wider than normal. But you served on the Alabama, right?"

"Yes, Sir. Much bigger ship."

"Well, size doesn't always matter," said the Captain. "We can sail circles around, and out- maneuver any battleship out there. That's our whole reason for being, Moore. We're the little guys protecting the big guys from those nasty little Kraut U-boats." He paused. "I'm doing it again, lecturing, right?"

"No, Sir, not at all." Moore smiled, looking on a clipboard at the assignment. He walked to the navigator's station, and looked over the man's shoulder at a panel full of electronics and a radar screen. Moore noted the navigator's name tag, "Lebowitz," and made a mental note. Next to his station sat a small table laden with charts.

"We make our rendezvous at 1730, or thereabouts?" asked Moore.

"Yep," said the Captain, that's what we figure, and from there out across the North Atlantic. Eight ships expected to be in the convoy: cargo, Marines, munitions, a battleship but we're the only DE around. Better get those sea legs working. You're going to need them. We're getting reports of potentially nasty weather out there well to our south, but we think we can outrun it."

Hammond walked to the hatch door and opened it. The rush, of salty mid-day air, away from the City's stagnant smells was refreshing. He was starting to like his ship and his assignment a little more with each passing hour.

"The Conn is yours, Mr. Moore," said Hammond, "I'll be in my quarters."

"Yes, Sir," said the XO, who would, for the first time in his career, be commanding in a Captain's absence.

"Oh, Mr. Moore," said Hammond. "I know we're still close to home, but keep your eyes peeled for anything unusual." Moore knew he meant 'watch out for German submarines.'

"Aye, aye, sir."

After the hatch door to the pilot house closed, and the Captain's footsteps echoed down the metal stairs, Moore pulled a navigational chart and looked to his left and right to make sure he wasn't watched too closely by the two other men on the bridge. He had to steady himself. Feeling faint, he closed his eyes, took a deep breath, and managed to subdue the mounting anxiety of what was ahead. He was well trained and had prepared for this, but still the stress was taking its toll.

"For Der Führer," he whispered.

*****

Sheriff Brooks hovered over Hitch and Rollins, hurrying them to finish their meals of Ophelia's chicken stew. The women needed to get measurements for clothes, but getting them to the Church was out of the question, and an unnecessary risk.

"We'll wait for dark," said Sheriff Brooks. "The girls can go for the clothes, but it ain't safe for you two to just wander around Southwood. You stick out like sore, white thumbs."

"Okay," said Hitch. "We'll wait until after dark, then what?"

"After dark you get the hell out of my town." The Sheriff wasn't softening much, and may have been getting more agitated as the afternoon wore on.

"Trust me Sheriff," added Rollins. "We don't want to be here anymore than you want to see us gone. Any ideas for...escape?" He hated using that word, but it seemed to be the only one that fit. 'Escaping' while in his own country, to another country, one that was also supposed to be his own, but wasn't, was complicated and something hard to grasp.

The more Henry Rollins thought about it, the more he considered the obvious likelihood, as bizarre as it was, that he was in the same realm in which Margaret had once been lost. With each story about a fractured Union, with each detail about a former United States, the plight of blacks, and additional fuzzy details that agreed with Margaret's descriptions, he was becoming certain of it.

"Where you headed, again?" asked the Sheriff?

"I want to go south," said Hitch. The Sheriff looked at him like he was crazy.

"Why anyone would want to do that is beyond me. Wachu wanna do that fer?"

"Florida, beaches, warm weather, good cigars, Latino women...need I go on?"

Sheriff Brooks cracked a slight smile, the first since he'd sat down for supper hours earlier. "And how 'bout you, Rollins?"

"I've been thinking about that," he answered. "I had it in my head to go to New Jersey, Princeton, but as I'm thinking about what's been going on—I think I want to go to Maryland, a little four corners hamlet just west of Washington, called Sugarland. I'm hoping to meet someone there."

"Okay, you're headed south, and you're headed north. As long as both of you are headed out of Southwood I don't care where you go. But you listen to me. If you get caught, and you probably will, if you mention Southwood, or me, or Cecil or Miss Ophelia, even if they don't torture you, and they probably will, I will kill you myself. You forget you ever saw this place. Understood?"

The men nodded in agreement.

"In trade for your promise to keep your mouths shut, I will help you leave. That's the deal."

"It's really more than we could have hoped for, Sheriff," said Hitch. "Thank you."

Ophelia had returned to the darkened living room, to retrieve the empty bowls and had heard what had been said. She looked at Sheriff Brooks, waiting for him to respond to the sincere thanks, which she could tell wasn't coming any time soon.

"You're welcome, Boys," said Ophelia, shooting a look at the Sheriff. "We may be the first Underground Railroad for white folk in the history of the South." She managed a chuckle, but the dread they all felt from the looming danger, wouldn't be quenched with a laugh.

"Speaking of railroads," said the Sheriff. "I've got an idea. The rail yard is here in Southwood, on the outskirts of town. Most of the folk that live here work there. The white bosses keep tabs on everyone, but I think I can get you two aboard the 10:05 in a freight car. It's a quick stop for the 10:05, so that means fewer people working and fewer eyes watching. You take it west to Lynchburg, hop off, and hop another train north for you," he said looking at Rollins, "and a straight shot south for you," he added with a nod toward Hitch.

"Lynchburg it is, then," said Rollins

"Lynchburg's a big city," continued the Sheriff, "with a huge rail yard, lots of trains going north and south. Hobos jump the trains all day and all night. Do what they do, and you should be able to manage. It will be easier for you to get to south," he said to Hitch, "but you, young man, you've got to get across the Fed-Stat border. That's going to be tricky—not impossible—but tricky."

Rollins and Hitch looked at one another, and shared a nod of agreement for the plan as laid out.

"Thanks, again," said Rollins. He'd been eying a small bookshelf in the Washington's modest home. One title particularly intrigued him. 'The Rise and Fall of the United States of America.' Ophelia was just around the corner, so Rollins asked if he might look at it.

"That ol' thing?" she asked. "It ain't been moved off that self in 15 years. You can have it."

"Thanks Miss Ophelia," said Rollins. "Again, your hospitality is overwhelming."

"Nonsense," she said, while Sheriff Brooks looked on, not able to hide his displeasure with all the niceties. "You take it, and you take this candle, too, to read by." She reached in a drawer and produced a single, decent sized candle, and a box of wooden matches.

She looked down at the book detailing the rise and fall of the United States of America. "That's a sad story, if you ask me," she continued. "I wish it all hadn't worked out like it did. The South never shoulda won that damned war."

Chapter 27

Margaret Rollins, knowing not what else to do, had decided a trip back to Princeton to retrieve the dress she'd worn before, might help her to travel to wherever it was she'd been before, and maybe find Henry. Back home she packed the dress, a floor-length, floral print, along with a few other items, She let Hank wander around the apartment, on an expedition of his own, which included a long drink from the toilet.

Princeton was bustling, but things had been quiet at the Einstein home, so the two F.B.I. agents in their large black sedan did a drive-by to see if their other mark had returned. Right away they noticed Margaret Rollins' car parked out front and circled the block for a better vantage point. When they saw her leave the apartment with a small suitcase, they knew they might be in for a long tail.

"Damn," said the taller of the two agents. "I guess we're in it for a while. She's got a suitcase."

"And a dog," said his partner. "When did they get a dog?"

"Beats me. You didn't have anywhere important to be, did you?"

"Nah, you know me. I got nothing going on. Let's go."

As Margaret pulled down the street, headed toward the road that would lead her back to Maryland, she happened to glance in the rearview mirror just as the Federal Agents pulled out. She didn't make them right away as a tail, but she'd seen the car in the neighborhood so many times before, she wondered about it. And with all the cloak and dagger when visiting Dr. Einstein, she'd been suspicious. She drove cautiously, but made five random turns, as a test, all of which the black sedan made too.

"Well," she said to Hank, who was again thrilled to be riding in a magic machine. "I think we've got company."

Bound and determined not to lead them to Sugarland, she thought of ways she might lose them, but it was a long trip, some three to four hours, and she could wait for the right moment.

As she drove through Trenton, New Jersey, and followed along the Delaware River, her thoughts turned to Henry. Soon she'd pass by the Philadelphia Navy Yard, and it would take all her strength not to crash the gates and drive to the dock where she'd seen the USS Eldridge. It was the last place anyone had seen Henry. She knew better than to try it, and that it would be a waste of time. Henry wasn't there. But where was he?

"Maybe you're through the looking glass, Henry?" she said aloud, referencing her favorite childhood storybook character, Alice. She understood all too well what it was like to leave one reality for another.

An hour later the traffic had really gotten heavy; Baltimore was up ahead. She looked in the mirror and saw the same black sedan, weaving around fast-moving cars and trucks, to stay near, but not too near. She made sure to keep her driving steady and natural, so as not to tip them off, but in this traffic she sensed opportunity.

"I think it's now or never, Hank. Hold on!"

She punched the gas and maneuvered like a stunt driver, crisscrossing the four-lane road, even driving on the shoulders. A cloud of dust from the dry, loose gravel on the shoulder slowed the traffic behind her, almost causing a pile-up. Before long she'd put an additional half-mile between her car and the black sedan, but every few moments she caught a glimpse of them in the mirror.

A quarter-mile ahead she saw an exit, with three possible turns at its end. If she could make this exit unseen, they'd never know where she went. It would be as if she simply vanished, something she'd been getting very good at.

"This is it, Hank," she said to the excited dog sitting beside her. "If I blow it, we're done for." When she got to the exit, driving much faster than she should, she checked one last time in her mirror.

"I don't see them. I'm going for it."

When she whipped the wheel hard to the right, the car skidded and threatened to roll, but she held on. She made the right hand turn, and then another hard right, back underneath the road she'd just left. When she was under the overpass, she slammed on her brakes, and pulled off the road, unseen by the traffic whizzing overhead. She had a clear view of the exit and the three options: straight ahead toward Baltimore, left toward Essex, or right toward Towson. If the agents had seen her get off the main road, and were really committed to following her, she'd see them get off the exit, before they saw her.

After three full minutes there was no sign of the sedan. *Maybe. God I hope so.* She'd try driving through Baltimore, instead of around it, and pick up the road to Sugarland on the southwest side of the city. She made a U-turn and followed the signs toward downtown Baltimore. She'd ask directions out of the city and to the west once she was sure she'd truly lost the tail.

"I think we did it, Hank!" she said rubbing the dog's head. "What do they want with me, anyway?" Hank twitched his eyebrows expressively and sneezed before lying back down on the seat.

"You're probably getting hungry and have to pee," she said, and he sat bolt upright, confirming her guess. She'd never known a dog to drink more water than this one she'd just adopted. Even though they were new to one another, an immediate bond had formed and both were equally in love.

"Fine, then. I'm hungry too."

It was late in the afternoon. The sun was falling low on the horizon, and it peeked through the buildings making up the cityscape. Baltimore was an old city, first settled in 1661 by the English. Nearly 300 years later the city had close to one-million inhabitants. Many were black, direct descendants of slaves. But thousands of immigrant German and Irish also populated the city. Margaret loved the excitement and energy of big cities, almost as much as she liked her quiet countryside.

As she drove deeper into the city, she saw children playing stickball in the streets, waiting to be called in for supper. They looked happy and carefree. She envied their simple joy in life, and longed for the end to the ache she'd felt every minute of every day since losing Henry.

*****

Southwood, Virginia
Confederate States of America
6:45 p.m. August 22, 1943

When Ophelia and her daughters returned with two carefully bagged outfits, and two pairs of shoes, all hidden, wrapped and tied in brown paper, Henry and Hitch knew their time to leave Southwood was at hand.

"I'll donate this dress, not that anyone would want it in the shape it's in," said Rollins to Ophelia.

She looked it over and smiled. "I'll patch up that hem and give it to the church. It's right pretty."

Rollins looked at her and spoke warmly. "Thanks for the food, the new set of clothes, and, well…for everything."

"You're welcome, child," said Ophelia. "Everyone needs a little help sometime. I'm glad we could help you boys."

"We're leaving here at 7:45," said Sheriff Brooks, "that's an hour from now. I'm going to take you in my patrol car, and drop you by the freight dock. I have a man there, named Curtis. He'll lead you to an empty freight car when the 8:05

arrives. You'll get in and find a spot to sit. It's not going to be a first-class ride, but it's just under two hours to Lynchburg, and you'll be off the streets."

"Can't thank you enough," said Hitch.

"Just remember our deal," said the Sheriff. "You don't know nothing."

"Nothing," said Hitch, his inner schoolteacher ignoring the Sheriff's double negative.

"I packed you some food, and each a Mason jar of tea," said Ophelia.

The men hadn't heard much from Cecil. They looked over to see him in his chair, sound asleep.

"Please tell Mr. Washington how grateful we are," said Hitch. "You all have taken a chance on us."

"Just repay the deed somewhere down the road when you have opportunity," said Ophelia. She wrapped her arm in the Sheriff's, which surprised not only them, but the Sheriff as well. It was the first sign of affection they'd seen her show the man who was obviously smitten with her. She smiled at him, pleased with the help he was offering these strangers. He smiled back.

"No ladies in your lives, boys?" said Ophelia.

"Mine left me long ago," said Hitch.

"I'm trying to reunite with my wife," said Rollins. He held out his left hand. "I lost my wedding ring, or rather it was taken from me. It's sitting in the Norfolk City Jail."

"You'll get another," said Ophelia, "It's just a ring. Make sure you find her."

"It's going to be tricky," said Rollins.

"Yes," said Ophelia, "but everything worth getting in life is tricky and sometimes hard. Where is she, anyway?"

"That's part of the problem," said Rollins. "I'm not sure. I have an idea, but it might be a place that's impossible to get to."

"Nothing's impossible, child."

They killed time chatting for another 20 minutes, until Sheriff Brooks looked at his watch, and then nodded at the men.

"Time to go. I'm going to get in my patrol car, circle the block. When I come back around, I'm going to flash the interior lights if it's clear. If there are people on the street, or any sign of that bastard Overstreet, or anyone else, I'll just keep going, and you'll have to wait it out. Understood?"

The men nodded, and Sheriff Brooks left the house, headed for his car parked on the street out front. He took off slowly and disappeared around the corner. They peered through the window, waiting for his return. When they saw his patrol car come around the corner from the opposite direction, they watched it slow. When they saw the interior lights, their bellies did a flip-flop. Hitch and Rollins knew what was at stake for all of them.

"Okay, here we go," said Hitch. "Quick and straight to the backseat. I'll go first and slide all the way over. You come right behind me, get in and shut the door quickly. Agreed?"

Rollins nodded.

"You ready?" said Hitch.

"Ready," said Rollins who turned to look at Ophelia and the girls who were standing by her side. "Thanks again."

"Good luck boys," she said, and they were out the door.

*****

Even after the once nearly indestructible U-boat Wolf Packs had become less of a threat to the Allies by late 1943, the Germans remained relentless in their attempts to stop supplies from reaching England. New classes of German submarines, better equipped and more technologically advanced, were starting to enter the North Atlantic, giving new worry to Naval commanders.

The small convoy of ships awaiting the arrival of the USS Eldridge, left the Norfolk Naval Base for a rendezvous point some 60 miles out to sea. While still close to shore, the officers aboard a Liberty Ship, the *USS Teddy Roosevelt*, watched a flotilla of engineers and barges working on an odd buoy configuration.

The rows of buoys and lights, a part of *Operation Canned Heat*, looked as much like an airport landing strip as anything else. Each buoy jutted 20 feet out of the water, and each had sizzled and fried out in a spectacular display of fireworks at the same time the Eldridge first vanished. The array and its mission were so classified that none of the officers had a clue what they were, what had happened, and why they were being repaired. While sailing out to sea the curiosity surrounding the buoys seemed less important than the mission at hand, a mission that had an added twist.

A tropical depression, on the edge of hurricane status, had first formed 150 miles off the coast of Florida, near Jacksonville. The storm moved slowly up the Eastern seaboard, but was forecast not to reach Virginia until well after the Eldridge and the ships she was to escort had left for England. They hoped to miss the outer bands of the storm and the largest ocean swells by 15 hours. Under different circumstances the mission would have been postponed, however the goods and personnel aboard the ships needing escort, were so badly overdue and critical for the war effort, losing a day was not an option.

Executive Officer Moore, still on the bridge, continued to study the charts, and did so with such intensity, that the helmsman noticed his obsessive interest, and commented.

"Anything I can do to help?" asked the Helmsman, who was a 32-year-old veteran of countless actions at sea, and an experienced navigator who'd already served 12 years in the Navy.

"If I need your help I'll ask," said the XO, not quite snapping, but obvious he didn't care for the question or the implication.

179

The helmsman didn't comment, but took an even keener interest in what might have had the XO wound so tightly. He glanced over his shoulder, and noticed Moore was using a pencil and plotter referencing a point two days out, a point halfway across the North Atlantic.

A call came in to the loudspeaker on the bridge from the radio room two decks below.

"Radio room to bridge," cracked a young man's voice, one that sounded like it came from an adolescent in the throes of puberty.

"Bridge here," said Moore, through a handset. "New weather advisory, Sir. The tropical storm has strengthened and picked up speed. It is expected to affect our rendezvous area at 1130 hours."

"1130?' said Moore, surprised. "That's 10 hours sooner than the last report."

Though radar and hurricane hunter storm forecasting was in its infancy, the forecasts were getting better, and were earning some degree of trust. Still storms had minds of their own thwarting even the best meteorologists' efforts.

"Yes, Sir. New information just in," said the operator. "We should clear it okay if the convoy is ready to move out when we arrive. The first real swells will just be rolling in."

"Great," said Moore sarcastically. "Understood, out." He clicked off the microphone, and reached for a handkerchief, which he used to wipe sweat from his brow. The helmsman, an Ensign, noted this as well, and wondered if the new XO was up to the job of second in command. He'd heard the updated weather report, and was waiting for Moore to phone the Captain, which he didn't.

"Shall I communicate this to Captain Hammond, Sir?" asked the Helmsman.

"Ensign you are to navigate, and only navigate," yelled Moore. "I will call the Captain if and when I think he needs to be notified. Increase speed to full ahead. Do we have a problem here?"

"No, Sir," answered the Helmsman who rang the command for speed via the ship's telegraph to Full Ahead. He'd been berated two times in the past 10 minutes, and was feeling a little picked on. "Just trying to help, Sir."

"Help yourself, and help me, by shutting up," said Moore. The Helmsman didn't respond.

The XO went back to his charts, and scribbled notes on a piece of paper. "You have the bridge, Helmsman," he said just before scrambling down the stairs.

In his officer's quarters below deck, Moore closed and locked the door. He reached into his locker and retrieved a shoebox-sized device along with a collapsible radio antenna and a small hand-cranked generator and battery, enough to fire up and operate a short-wave radio free from the ship's electricity and internal systems. He double checked the already locked door, and turned on big band music programming from a small radio on a shelf.

In less than five minutes he had an operational radio, capable of transmitting and receiving. He cranked the small generator using 40 fast turns, and it came to life. A red power indicator glowed softly, and he dialed through 20 locations until he reached the frequency he was after. The specialized radio included all the standard, monitored shortwave bands, as well as newly discovered longwave bands, allowing freer communication.

Speaking in German, Moore began transmitting to the Kriegsmarine, the German Navy.

"Hello, hello, crossroads west. Crossroads west, come in. Come in." He dared turn the volume up slightly, but still heard only hissing static. He tried again, with the same result. He moved the antenna around the room, trying the call several times, until a faint voice responded.

"Crossroads west here."

The voice spoke in German, and sounded a million miles away. In fact it was coming from an Unterseeboot, a German submarine, some 1,200 nautical miles north and west of the Eldridge. A U-boat patrolling the waters of the North Atlantic was one of several dozen between Europe and the east coast of the U.S. It dragged an antenna buoy, and stayed in longwave radio communication with two saboteurs operating in North America. One of the operatives, Heinrich Mueller, had ceased transmitting abruptly a week earlier for reasons unknown. His mission had been classified as 'compromised' and his whereabouts were 'unknown.' The other, an American born Nazi sympathizer named Phillip Moore, had infiltrated nearly to the heart of the U.S. Navy Atlantic Fleet.

Over the course of 10 years, Moore had first managed to obtain an appointment to the United States Naval Academy where he graduated in the top two-percent of his class. He began his Naval career at 22, and worked his way up through the chain of command, making him Germany's highest positioned spy anywhere within the U.S. Military.

Moore and his cover were beyond reproach. Born near Baltimore, of German immigrants, he, like millions of other U.S. citizens, happened to be of German descent. Unlike the vast majority of those U.S. citizens with German heritage, he idolized Adolph Hitler, and believed in Hitler's dream for a pure, Aryan nation, free from Jews and other 'impure' races. Moore knew his family lineage, and could trace his great-grandfather back to a small town in Central Germany where he'd been the Burgermeister, the town's mayor. He was as committed to the Vaterland as any other Nazi, and he was the only American Citizen with training and a full understanding of the Nazi's Enigma cipher machine, which was fading from daily, widespread use by Nazi spies.

Rumors had spread among the Nazi high command that Enigma had been compromised. The Germans kept their suspicions secret, and began transmitting false communiqués. But they had one more trick up their sleeves, new longwave radios, hidden in normal-looking shortwave radios, operated on frequencies not before believed possible. The portable devices, such as the one Mueller had used in Philadelphia, and that Moore was using, were two of three on American soil. The third Neue Langwellen (New Longwave) was hidden in a German P.O.W. camp in Myrtle Beach, South Carolina. The German engineers were so confident in the Langwellen's security that, other than passwords to identify the users, communications and conversations were simply spoken without need for elaborate codes.

Moore relayed the required password for the month of September; "Eins, zwei, null, eins, acht, acht, neun." It was the birth date of Adolf Hitler, April 20, 1889.

"Confirmed, Crossroads East," said the faraway voice. "Report."

"I have the coordinates for Operation Crossroads," said Moore. He read off a latitude and longitude, and the voice confirmed receipt.

"Arrival?" asked the voice.

"Weather may interfere," said Moore. "We may have to push earlier, or much later if we wait out the storm. Be advised a hurricane is rapidly approaching the Carolinas and mid-Atlantic coastline."

"Confirmed," said the voice. "When will you be able to advise on your rendezvous?"

"I should have a better estimate in six-to-eight hours."
"Confirmed. Anything else?"

"Yes the convoy will be made up of eight ships, plus the DE I'm aboard, nine in total; a destroyer, our destroyer escort, Merchant Marine cargo vessels, and a troop ship. I'll report again when I have certain timing."

A loud knock on Moore's door sent him scrambling to cover the shortwave.

"This is Captain Hammond. You there, XO?"

"Yes, Sir!" he yelled through the closed steel door. "Be right there." He looked to see that his radio was covered, and then unlocked the door.

"Moore," said the Captain, walking into his quarters. He looked suspiciously at the XO, sensing his general level of anxiety. "You have anything to tell me?"

Moore would have made a bad poker player. Even while staying relatively cool, his biggest tell was an inability to control his perspiration when he had to think fast. He wiped his brow with the sleeve of his shirt.

"No sir," he said. "I left the bridge a few minutes ago with instruction for the Chief of the Deck to report in."

"I called the bridge when I felt us go to full ahead," said the Captain, clearly displeased. "Did you think it important to notify me of a damned hurricane creeping up our backside?"

"No, Sir, I mean, yes, Sir. I was just waiting for another weather update."

"Any reason you're here listening to music instead of being where you belong on the bridge?"

"No sir. I'll head back up now."

"No need. I'm headed up," said the Captain. "Open, constant communication is expected from you, Moore. I don't like surprises and I don't like not knowing what's going on."

"Understood, Sir. It won't happen again," said Moore. Captain Hammond left the XO's quarters, and closed the hatch door behind him.

Moore sat, shaken from the close call. He wiped more perspiration from his forehead. Looking at the covered Langwellen, Moore was horrified to see he hadn't covered the antenna, sitting on top of his bunk. He wondered if the Captain had seen it, and if so, why he hadn't commented on it. When he reached for it, the ship, now cruising at close to 30 knots, listed violently to the starboard, throwing him against the bulkhead, and sending the unsecured radio crashing to the steel deck. Standing among its shattered pieces, he knew he'd probably made his last radio report to the Kriegsmarine.

"Scheisse…"

Chapter 28

Baltimore, Maryland
United States of America
3:57 p.m. September 10, 1943

In front of the Tastycake factory near Hamilton, a neighborhood on the Northeast side of Baltimore, Margaret slowed the car and found a parking place. Hank pawed at the dashboard nervously. She still didn't have a collar or leash for him, but he needed to get out of the car, quickly. After exiting from the driver's door, she circled to let Hank out on to the sidewalk, where he promptly peed on the nearest signpost.

"I think we lost them, Hank," said Margaret, scanning the streets for any sign of the black sedan. There were plenty of cars that might have matched the description, but her keen eye had watched for a broken hood ornament, making the vehicle easier to spot.

"Nope, don't see 'em." Pleased with herself, she continued her scan of the neighborhood and spotted just what she needed.

A Woolworth's stood nearby and would do nicely for her quick shopping trip and food purchase. She led Hank, who was reluctant to comply, back into the car by the scruff of his neck. He whimpered and watched anxiously as Margaret crossed the street.

"A leash, collar, dog food, water, a map, and a snack for the road," she repeated to herself, and Woolworth's delivered. She placed an order for a cheeseburger at the lunch counter, and while it was cooking she shopped for Hank. In a few moments she was back at her car with a few bags, a hot meal, a map out of the city, and was back on the road to Sugarland.

They sat in the car and shared a meal. Hank was far more interested in the cheeseburger, than the dry food she'd placed in a small pile on the floor of the car. She finally gave in and gave him half, and had to laugh at the ketchup mustache he'd given himself gulping down the burger in one bite.

After a quick review of the map, they were back on the road and within an hour had found the Gaithersburg Highway, a two-lane country road, that would lead them to Sugarland and, she hoped, a way to find Henry.

*****

"Stay low," said the Sheriff. "I can't afford for you two to be seen in my car."

Hitch and Henry scooted down in their seats the best they could, and were more eager than ever to get out of Southwood. They drove on for less than 10 minutes with no more conversation. When the car finally slowed and stopped, they saw the Sheriff retrieve his gun, check the cylinder, and place it in his shoulder holster. Ophelia didn't like guns, especially on the Lord's Day, so Sheriff Brooks had left his locked in his patrol car. Though he wasn't off duty any longer, he was committing so many capital crimes he'd lost count.

"Get out," said the Sheriff. The somewhat kinder tone in his voice from earlier had vanished. The men climbed out of the same rear door, and stood near the parked patrol car adjacent to a loading dock. They held the bundles Ophelia had prepared: food, water, and a blanket for each of them. Rollins stuffed his book, candle and matches in among the other items.

Nearly pitch black from a moonless night, only a dim glow from the patrol car's dashboard illuminated their faces. There was no one around, not a soul. When the Sheriff put his hand on his revolver Hitch and Henry felt uncomfortably vulnerable. When they heard an audible, soft metallic click, as he pulled back the gun's hammer, they stood in shock, unable to say anything. The Sheriff could solve his problems and remove his liability with two easily placed bullets. He could ditch the bodies in the back of an empty boxcar, or at the bottom of the Meherin River, and no one would ever know; not Ophelia, not Sheriff Overstreet from Emporia, not the C.B.I,, *not even Margaret,* Henry thought.

When a train whistle blew from a mile out around an unseen corner, and its headlight began to illuminate the tops of distant trees, the Sheriff checked his watch using the light from his patrol car.

"It's the 10:05," he said, not looking at the men. "She's seven minutes early." He released the hammer on his revolver, silently, and pulled the men deeper into the shadows of the loading dock as the train slowed and its engine rolled past them. "This train is never early," he said, as if detached from his surroundings. "Ain't that just somethin'" He almost sounded annoyed.

The rail yard was now well lit by the train's headlight, and they could see the depot was fairly large, but very quiet. A few figures emerged 100 yards west along the track. They pushed wheelbarrows and floor jacks with pallets of goods toward the train. Depot lights flickered to life as the train finally came to a full stop.

"This will be easy," said the Sheriff when one of 70 boxcars came to rest parallel to their position. Its sliding door was wide open, making entry as easy as walking in through any open door. Hitch and Rollins both wondered just what the Sheriff was referring to when he said 'easy.'

"Easy?" dared Rollins.

"Yes. I won't need to bother my man about this," answered the Sheriff. "What are you waiting for?"

The two men, still spooked by the Sheriff's odd demeanor, walked slowly across the darkened loading dock, toward the boxcar's open door. With their bundles in hand, and the Sheriff behind them, they felt more like prisoners being led down death row, than two outlaws making a clean escape.

Just before stepping from the concrete loading dock on to the wooden floor of the boxcar, the Sheriff pulled his revolver and pointed it at their backs. When a floodlight sizzled and flickered on behind them, they saw a shadow on the boxcar floor clearly silhouetting the Sheriff's outstretched arm and his pistol.

"Sheriff Brooks?" said a voice coming from back near the patrol car. "Is that you?"

The Sheriff holstered his weapon, but not before the men turned to catch him in the near act of their own execution. The Sheriff strained to see who was calling to him.

"Sheriff?" said the man again, getting closer, emerging from the shadows. The Sheriff turned in the direction of Hitch and Henry, but wouldn't look them in the eyes.

"Get in, you fools. Go!"

They wasted no time entering the boxcar, heading straight for a dark corner, where they might catch their breath and slow their hearts from beating out of their chests. They could hear the Sheriff making small talk with the man who'd quite probably and accidentally saved their lives. They couldn't hear what was being said, and didn't really care. When the train lurched a foot forward, and then began a painfully slow, steady increase in speed, they hoped they'd seen the last of Southwood.

Relaxing slightly as the train groaned along, a single gunshot added to the noise from the train's clattering metal and wood, ringing out in the empty boxcar. Hitch ran to the door, to peer around the corner, and saw Sheriff Brooks moving fast, almost at the boxcar's door. When he looked again he saw the crumpled body of a man lying in what looked like blood 20 yards behind the Sheriff.

"It ain't over yet, Henry," said Hitch, waiting by the door. "Stay back against the wall, behind me."

Just as the Sheriff, with his revolver in hand, made a running jump into the boxcar, only moving at 10 mph, Hitch kicked him squarely in the right knee, a snapping sound confirming a good placement. He simultaneously struck the

Sheriff's arm down, but not before Brooks got a round off. The noise of the gunshot inside the hollow train car was deafening, causing Henry to cover his ears and close his eyes. When he opened them he crawled on his knees to the side of the boxcar, where Hitch lay still, his right arm partially hanging outside. He pulled him fully in away from the open door and any prying eyes that might be looking their way from the busier end of the rail yard. He dared one last look outside to see the Sheriff looking at him, unable to stand, let alone give chase.

"We made it, Hitch!" yelled Henry, his ears still ringing from the gunshot. He hoped no one else heard or saw the commotion. Hitch didn't answer, and Henry shook his friend by the shoulder. "Hitch!" The train continued to accelerate. They were just clearing the train depot and the rail yard, almost back out into the countryside, headed west toward Lynchburg.

"Hitch!" Still no answer came. He lay slumped over on the floor of the boxcar. Henry tried to straighten out his injured friend's upper torso, and help him sit upright. He pulled back in shock and when he felt warm blood on his fingertips.

"No, Hitch. Come on." He shook his shoulder, trying to rouse him, but he lay motionless. "Hitch!" A shot through the center of the chest had cut his friend's journey short. Henry Rollins sat next to him, staring into the darkness, once again, alone.

*****

Two hours after leaving Baltimore, Margaret pulled off the main road in Sugarland, and drove up the stone driveway to the country house that had been in her family for 75 years. Always with a watchful eye, she was confident she'd ditched her F.B.I. tail. Of that small accomplishment, she took some pride, though any joy was tempered by the sickness in her heart. It had been a full week since she'd last heard from Henry. With each passing day she missed him more, but grew continually resolute in her will to find him.

Based on conversations she'd had with Henry after her own two-week odyssey, and after even more encouragement from Dr. Albert Einstein, she put all her hopes in the fact that Henry was somewhere in a land that she seemed able to access at will. Or at least she thought she could until, after an hour of failed tries, realized it might not be that easy.

After feeding Hank, and closing all the curtains, she wasted no time changing back into the same dress she'd worn in her other travels. Though her first disappearance had been close to a year earlier, and she had spent a lot of effort in blocking the memories, she allowed her mind to revisit the traumatic event. She remembered that she'd been wearing the same floor-length floral print dress, and that she bought it second hand just a few days before the vanishing.

She and Henry had only been married for a few months, and she worked when she could, around Henry's rigorous doctoral studies. They were usually counting pennies and stayed flat broke. When he returned home one evening after a late lecture, she modeled the dress for him and, instead of praising her beauty, he got mad.

"How can we afford new dresses?" he had yelled, immediately regretting it. "We can't afford food!"

When she told him she'd bought it at a church bizarre for $1, he felt guilty and was angry at himself for losing his temper, for yelling at the sweetest woman on Earth, and because he'd been unable to buy her the nice things she deserved. Though she cried that night over the silly fight, she now cherished the memory while reclining on the upstairs bed, luxuriating in the recollections. She closed her eyes.

"No!" she cried out loud, chastising herself, sitting bolt upright. "There's no time to wallow in memories, Margaret. Henry is out there." Suddenly energized and ready to get started, she literally ran down the stairs, almost tripping over Hank. Though she didn't have a plan, she had a place. She just wished, for starters, that it had a name.

"Hank," she said looking at a dog that sometimes seemed to understand every word being spoken to him, "I'm going away for a few days. You can't come with me." She filled three large bowls with water, and a Dutch oven with a week's worth of dry dog food, not realizing Hank would probably eat all in one sitting.

"I can't take you, Hank. It won't work, and besides, you drive me crazy!"

Hank was underfoot constantly. Everywhere Margaret went Hank would be two steps ahead. If she stayed still for a nanosecond, he would manage to stand, sit or lie down in front of her, touching her if possible. He became a constant, moveable canine obstacle course that was both endearing and maddening. She loved him for being so loyal and affectionate, but wished he could follow, instead of trying to lead. As she stood at the archway into the den, the point where all the traveling seemed to happen, she looked back at Hank who for once was actually behind her; there was something in the den he didn't like. She bent down to scratch behind his ears.

"Keep an eye on the place, will you?" She wondered about getting stuck, and how Hank might be locked in if something went wrong. *And what about doing his business?*

"Oh, this won't work," she said, walking to the backdoor, stopping by a kitchen drawer for a rubber band, which she placed around the door latch, allowing it to close without latching. *Family members take care of each other.*

"Okay boy, I hope to be home soon, and introduce you to somebody new, as soon as I possibly can. I think you're going to like him." This time Hank did really understand she was planning to leave, and he whimpered. Margaret faced east, pointed herself toward the far bookcase and took three long steps.

"Here goes…"

One of the two radio operators ran to the bridge of the Eldridge with a typed transcript of what had been a coded message. "Sir," he said, handing the order to Captain Hammond, who read it aloud.

"Weather deteriorating. Make port in Norfolk. Convoy delayed, returning to port."

Nearly at the rendezvous point, the sky over the Atlantic had turned dark gray. Even though they were further out to sea, the air actually got warmer as tropical moisture and wind shot up the Gulf Stream, curved slightly east at the Outer Banks, and made its way straight for the convoy.

The full contingent of officers was on duty at the bridge, staying in radio contact with other vessels, the Naval Weather Stations, and the ships of the convoy. All were reporting strong seas, but none felt them more than the Eldridge. Two additional DEs, all much faster than the large ocean-going vessels, stayed in port until the final call on the weather would be made. The largest ship in the convoy was five times the length and beam of the typical Destroyer Escort. For these big ships, swells of 10 to 15-feet were like a mosquito biting an elephant. The same swells sent the 300-ft Eldridge rocking, sometimes violently.

"What else can you tell me about this storm?" asked Hammond.

"She's a doozey sir. The wind field is maybe 400 miles in diameter, and there's a strong eye wall. Sir, they actually flew a plane over top of her and measured the eye and estimated the winds. They said the eye was about 25 miles wide and the strongest winds were probably around 150 mph."

"They flew a plane into that damned thing?" asked Hammond. "That's new."

"Yes, Sir," answered the operator, equally impressed with the new hurricane hunter crews just working out untested, new mission parameters. In an era before storms received proper names, it was simply called "H5," the fifth Atlantic hurricane of the season.

"Okay," said Hammond, considering the report and new orders. He was concerned, but not overly. He'd weathered bad storms before. "So, what's the good news?"

"There isn't any, Sir. She's coming, and coming fast. Moving about 18 knots, and she's so big there's just nowhere to hide."

"Get me a forecast plot of the strongest winds and highest seas on the double."

"Yes, Sir!" The operator left the bridge, leaving the officers to consider any and all moves.

Executive Officer Moore made an excuse to leave the bridge. "I'll make sure we're battened down from bow to stern, Captain." Hammond nodded, picking up binoculars, the same ones Henry Rollins had used to watch a battle unfold between the Eldridge and two Confederate Navy ships.

As Moore scampered down the stairs, the first raindrop he felt hit him in the eye, and it felt like a sucker punch. It was big and cold and came at him with the help of a 30 mph wind gust. Soon another followed, and then another, and then the heavens opened with a deluge of rain so heavy it reduced visibility to zero. The first rain band of Hurricane Five, was there to say hello, and give everyone a taste of what was to come.

Chapter 29

Though they'd only been friends for less than a week, Henry Rollins deeply mourned the loss of a funny, brave, resourceful and ultimately, selfless man. He turned toward the motionless figure on the boxcar floor.

"Wild Bill."

He pulled the lifeless body to the back of the boxcar, wrapped it in one of the large blankets Ophelia had given them, and thought about what to do next. *In an hour and a half we'll be in Lynchburg. When the train pulls into the rail yard, somebody is very likely going to find the body. Can't have that.*

The train chugged on through the night. With the doors wide open, the warm breezes felt good and helped soothe his overworked brain and frazzled emotions. Even though it had been September when he first boarded the USS Eldridge, it had become mid-August in an instant when the ship made its jump. He felt lucky for the warm weather, if for little else. It was still very much summer in this new world, and not the start of autumn, as it was back in Princeton. He loved fall in the college town, fresh faces, much like his own, eager to start their adult lives. He was missing all of it, and especially missing Margaret, more than ever.

"Maggs…" he whispered into the night air. He could almost hear her calling back 'Hank,' an affectionate name she used occasionally when she was feeling particularly playful. Henry wondered if they'd ever see one another again, let alone find new times together that might equal his sweet memories.

In the far back of the boxcar Rollins was hidden from sight, and out in the rural countryside he took a chance with his candle and book. He thought it might help pass the time and get his mind off of Margaret and Hitch, and postpone deciding what, if anything, he should do. Finding the least windy spot, he struck a match, lit the candle, leaned his back against the rattling steel, and opened the book.

"'The Rise and Fall of the United States of America,'" said Rollins. "This ought to be a real hoot." He read aloud, as if he were reading Hitch a bedtime story. "Chapter One: The Colonies." He skimmed the chapter and found the history to be pretty much the same as he expected it to be: details of the original 13 colonies, the British Lords Proprietors, the white-washed slaughter of Native Americans, the scourge of African slavery, the growth of towns and cities, and the more or less correct version of American history as he knew it. He fast-forwarded through to the U.S. Revolution and war with Great Britain. "That all makes sense," he said, pausing, glancing over occasionally at the lifeless form wrapped in a blanket.

"'Chapter Six: The Civil War.' Okay, now we're talking. States' Rights, articles of secession, the firing on Fort Sumter, General Lee, General Grant, that all looks right." He could find no great discrepancies with the book's accounting of history, as compared with his own remembrance, but then things got really interesting.

"The Battle of Gettysburg: The Strangers at Emmitsburg Road"

Henry, a bit of a history whiz in high school and college, had studied the U.S. Civil War, and had considered a history major before the math bug took hold. The book went on to describe a plot to trap the bulk of the Yankee Army, and ignite most of the C.S.A.'s battlefield munitions, wiping out as many enemy combatants as possible. "But there was no detonation at Gettysburg," he said to the empty boxcar. *This book presents this explosion as if it were a commonly known truth.* He read aloud.

> *"Two brave Confederate soldiers, in the face of chaos, developed and carried out the "Yankee Surprise" to destroy some 40 percent of General Meade's Army. Today, Crater Lake in the Gettysburg National Park, stands as a reminder and memorial to all who lost their lives."*

The boxcar shook so badly he was having a hard time concentrating and had to pause. He took the candle over to his friend, and looked at his face, eyes open, but lifeless.

"Hitch...I'm so sorry."

He studied the body, hoping he'd see some sign of life. Other than his parent's open casket funerals, he'd not seen a lifeless corpse before. He rested his hand on top of his friend's. He checked his wrist and his neck for a pulse. There was none. His ice-cold skin, the blood-soaked blanket and clearly visible bullet wound, convinced him that Hitch was really, truly, dead.

He carefully made his way back to the spot where he'd been reading. After retrieving a Mason jar filled with Iced Tea, he took a long swig, and opened the book, picking up where he'd left off.

Henry read about the Navies from both the U.S. and the Confederate sides and of burial at sea. The ancient practice had been carried out by seaman for as long as sailors have been going to sea and dying there. He thought of his friend Hitch, his love of the sea, and of his service in the Navy. He leaned back and dozed; he didn't know for how long. He was awakened when the train made a noticeable reduction in its speed. When the whistle blew, and the train slowed further, he knew there was either a crossing up ahead, or they were getting close to their next stop, Lynchburg.

Rollins got up, stretched his legs, and peeked outside, before sitting, taking in the view of the Blue Ridge Mountains out the open door. He could see a little better as the full moon had risen into the formerly inky black sky. Distant lights, he guessed four or five miles away, were expansive enough that they had to be coming from a city.

"Lynchburg, Virginia," he guessed, saying it aloud, saddened that his friend couldn't comment or corroborate.

He didn't know it was the James River, but Rollins saw wide water up ahead, and a long narrow trestle crossing the river. Through the rattle of steel wheels, and iron train tracks he heard a voice on the wind, as clear as if someone had been speaking to him in the boxcar. *Here, Henry. This is the place.*

He sat up, and, almost on a subconscious level, deciphered the message. "Here?" Rollins repeated out loud, waking himself from a sleep-deprived trance. "Here what?" he asked. He closed his eyes again and remembered the last passage in the book he'd been reading.

"A burial at sea?"

A cool breeze rushed into the boxcar as the train slowed further. Without over-thinking it, and before he changed his mind, he tended to Hitch's body. He removed Hitch's shoes, as well as his belt. In a corner of the boxcar Rollins spotted a partial pallet of bricks and spool of bailing twine. He wrapped Hitch's body including 15 bricks placed inside the blankets given to them by Ophelia. He buckled the belt securely around the body's arms at the waist, and used the bailing twine to tightly wrap around his legs, feet and head. He'd never prepared a body for burial at sea before, and though the St. James River wasn't the sea, he tried to convince himself he was doing the right thing. The train slowed further, as if it was preparing to stop.

"I'm sorry, Hitch," he said. "You deserve better." When the corpse, looking like a tightly wrapped mummy, was ready to go, he struggled to drag it, now heavy with bricks, toward the train car's open door. In the moonlight he caught a flicker of light coming from a metallic reflection on the floor of the boxcar.

"I'll be damned," he said. He'd found Hitch's murder weapon; Sheriff Brook's gun. He didn't know it had been sitting there in the dark. He looked at it, hated it and was tempted to kick it out the door when the voice returned. *No, you might need it.* He didn't know much about guns, but quickly figured out how to open the cylinder where he saw that one bullet was missing and five more were still in place. He slid it away from the door before rolling, sliding and maneuvering Hitch's body lengthwise to the boxcar's gaping entry. The long train slowed, and came to a full stop.

Looking over the edge of the boxcar, he could just see through the tracks and railroad ties to the wide river 50-feet below, the tips of its waves sparkling like small diamonds in the moonlight. He looked to see if he could manage the ghastly maneuver without being seen. In the dark of night he could spot no witnesses. He waited for the right moment, hoping he'd have the courage and strength to carry out his plan.

"Here goes."

He jumped down to the tracks, straddling the gaping spaces between the ties. He put his shoulder near to the boxcar door, positioning Hitch's heavy weight on his back. He struggled but managed to get the tightly wrapped body out of the boxcar and onto the tracks near the side of the trestle. He neither had the emotional strength or mental courage to offer a eulogy, as he unceremoniously let his friend's corpse drop from his shoulders off the side of the trestle. With little illumination from the moonlight, Rollins could just see the splash, and then the body, wrapped in brightly colored blankets, sink into the deep, black river.

*****

The storm eased slightly as the first rain band dissipated, but the seas had grown, and while the 12 – 15-foot swells were causing no imminent threat, they were throwing the Eldridge around more than the fresh crew was accustomed. They were cruising at maximum speed, and the weather was moving just as fast straight at them. If the storm grew much larger, they would run the risk of being overtaken and if the seas continued to grow, their speed would have to be reduced, creating even more risk.

"We simply can't go around it, Sir," said the navigator studying the latest charts and radar. "It's just too big. There's nowhere to go. Our current course toward Norfolk is about as good as any.

Captain Hammond nodded to the navigator that he'd understood. He wouldn't thank him, though. The Captain was not accustomed to thanking anyone who delivered bad news, whether it was their fault or not.

All eyes hovered on the radar screens. The brand new technology on board was the best the Navy had to offer. Hammond, his officers, and the crews of the ships in the convoy weren't the only ones in the North Atlantic watching the radar, however.

Under diesel power a new class of German U-boat, also loaded with the latest technology the Kriegsmarine could offer, was struggling through equally rough waters, headed toward the convoy from the south. Using encrypted intelligence from a Nazi operative, who'd mysteriously gone silent after saying he'd try to board the USS Eldridge, U-4713 had been ordered into very hostile territory. The weather was only part of their concern. Hedgehog mortars, and newer versions of depth charges had decimated the once proud U-boat fleet.

Another Nazi operative was working for the Kriegsmarine as well, and, working from the inside, was much closer to inflicting serious damage to the U.S. Navy. But turncoat Executive Officer Phillip Moore was not on a suicide mission; he dreamt of nothing but glory for himself and the Aryan race, with Adolf Hitler as the world's new ruler. Though radio contact was nearly impossible, he was working from two-day old orders that had him directing a sea battle between ships in the convoy and the most powerful U-boat ever created.

Moore was to abandon ship at night with an inflatable raft just before the reaching the Kreuzung, the German code word for 'crossroads.' Kreuzung referenced the plot point on the North Atlantic where the Convoy would meet the U-boat. Once he was in the water, and the convoy was destroyed and sunk, Moore would activate a flashing beacon and wait for pick-up by the U-boat crew. He would sail home to Germany as a naval hero, and settle in the town where he would best fit in, where his name matched that of hundreds of cousins, and was emblazoned on street signs, where he'd be a somebody. It was all he dreamt of, day and night. But the hurricane put everyone's plans in jeopardy.

Captain Zoeller's was no standard issue U-boat. Though the allies had advanced their own technology to eventually render the first classes of U-boat ineffective, this submarine was an experimental hybrid, the most advanced in the German Navy. Zoeller particularly liked it for the private quarters—most U-boats had the captain sleeping in a tiny birth, with just a curtain between his bunk and the rest of the crew. This ship featured the best of the older designs and the latest German advances in weaponry, radar, sonar, propulsion, and increased battery life. It could run five times longer underwater and hide without noisy engines giving away its position. Winston Churchill, the Prime Minister of the United Kingdom, had coined "Battle of the Atlantic," and said that he feared nothing in the war as much as the German U-boat.

"Okay, men," said Hammond, ready to give his pep talk to those on the bridge. "The Krauts are out there, we know that. This damned storm is out there. We sure as hell know that, but this is what we signed up for. As soon as this weather passes, our mission to protect 300 troops, and 27 tons of food, cargo and munitions, will be restarted. Right now, however, we're doing our best to get to port through this shitstorm outside. We've got a long six days ahead of us. I want everyone to stay sharp, follow the drills, remember your training, sleep when it's time to sleep—you're no use to me bleary-eyed—and stay focused when you're on duty. We can do this. I'm going below. Stay in touch. Got that Mr. Moore?"

"Yes, Skipper," answered Moore, a little embarrassed to be called out in front of the other men.

"Okay, then. You've got the Conn."

Chapter 30

Sugarland, Maryland
Federated States of America
7 p.m. August 22, 1943

When Margaret took her last of three long steps, she turned and, seeing Hank, assumed the travel trick was still not working. It wasn't until she glanced at the mantel over the fireplace to see the perplexing photographs that she knew it had indeed worked. *The dress has made the difference.*

"Hank, how did…" It hadn't dawned on her that a dog could travel at all, or at the same time, until she saw Hank wagging his tail, and sniffing the air like a bloodhound.

"Well, I'll be…," she mused, "I guess you *won't* be left behind?" She scratched his head and considered what to do. She peered through the curtain in the living room, hoping not to see the local police she'd ditched two days earlier. "I have a feeling they'll be watching for me, Hank."

She sat on the couch, her mind reeling. *If you're here, my love, then where exactly are you? Did you end up in Norfolk? Dr. Einstein seems to think maybe. How can I get to Norfolk? I'll need a car, but from where?* These and a dozen other questions raced around in her head, making it nearly impossible to focus. She did what she always did when she needed to calm down. *I'll listen to the radio.*

She found herself sneaking around, as if this wasn't her home. *It's not*, she told herself as she clicked on a floor model RCA radio that did not look all that familiar to her. The tuning was difficult; her favorite stations were not where they were supposed to be, but eventually she did manage to find some music. It was pleasant sounding, like old country gospel. It came in clearly, and the singers sounded sweet. Hank jumped up on the couch to sit next to her. It was then she noticed the front door was open. A light breeze was blowing it back and forth, unlatched. She got up to close the door just as a news report was beginning.

"Radio D.C. with your 7 p.m. Nightly News. Good evening. New struggles in Europe and tragic tales of wholesale Nazi executions continue to find their way through to news organizations as millions of refugees pour out of Europe to wherever they can find safety—the North African nations of Libya and Egypt along with Turkey and Syria have seen the greatest number of refugees. Many of the destitute are arriving in the C.S.A. from Florida to Virginia. New York is also receiving refugees by the boatload, some 35,000 this week alone, many of them women and children, and nearly all in rags and malnourished. A joint task force with representatives from both C.S.A and the Federated States of America will meet in Richmond next week to discuss the growing humanitarian crisis."

Margaret sat back down to listen, and to try to make sense of what she was hearing.

"The much maligned I.B.S., the International Border between the States, is back in the news as government-sponsored bounty hunters from the C.S.A., have stepped up their activity to curtail illegal border crossings, most of which take place as those in the C.S.A. seek to move north into the Federated States. Black marketers continue to move goods back and forth between the two nations, nearly unimpeded, creating chaos in both the C.S.A. and F.S.A. economies."

Margaret shifted, like she might get up, and Hank laid his paw across her knee, keeping her right where he wanted her; literally underfoot.

"A manhunt is underway in the C.S.A. for a suspected reunificationist, along with an accomplice. Reports of a shootout in central Virginia with the two suspected Fed-Stat fugitives have authorities across the region on high alert."

With no idea the news anchor had been giving details about the location of the very man she was looking for, Margaret reached for the dial, and swept through the frequencies desperate for some music, or even a little comedy—anything but the news.

"Abbot and Costello are always on at 7, Hank. Where are they? Why can't I find them?" Frustrated she shut the radio off, and leaned back into the couch cushions. "I wonder if my teaching job is still on hold?" she laughed. *Our lives have been turned upside down in the blink of an eye.*

"First things first," she said to the dog on her lap. "Finding Henry. Tomorrow we begin."

*****

As the train began to move again, Rollins hopped back in the boxcar that had provided him an escape. As it passed over the far side of the river, he caught glimpses of billboards in the growing urban landscape, advertising businesses of all sorts. *Definitely Lynchburg, I'm that much closer, Margaret.* Henry Rollins had never hopped a train before, and was about to find out that the Lynchburg Rail Yard was nothing like the one in Southwood. It was massive, with some 40 lines all converging in a complicated array of tracks, switches, and depots. One thing was missing, though, loading docks.

When the whistle blew and the train finally stopped, Rollins' boxcar, toward the rear of the long line of rail cars, was mercifully in the dark. Migratory workers carrying bindles appeared seemingly from out of nowhere, as soon as the train stopped. They walked quickly toward many of the empty boxcars and Henry scrambled out of his, not wanting any confrontations. He grabbed Ophelia's book, the matches, candle, a sandwich, and created a bindle of his own. He stuffed Sheriff Brooks' revolver in an extra cloth napkin, and placed it in the waist of his pants, hidden by the tail of his un-tucked shirt.

Two men in their 40s or 50s, it was hard for him to tell, jumped up into Henry's boxcar, just as he was jumping off. They were dirty, smelled like sour milk, wore tattered clothing, sported thick beards, and seemed otherwise uninterested in him.

"Excuse me, gentleman," said Rollins, poking his head back into the boxcar. "If you don't mind, how might I find transportation heading north, across the border?" He'd never spoken with real, live actual hobos before, and he overcompensated with politeness, hoping they would respond with helpful information.

The men looked at each other and chuckled. "Wantin' to go north?" one of them said. "I hope you can crap gold." Both men laughed. "It's going to take a bucket-load to get you there."

"No, no I don't have any money, but I need to get back to my family in Maryland."

"Get out of here!" the younger of the two vagrants yelled. "You'll get us all thrown in the hoosegow with crazy talk like that."

"Please, just tell me which train heads north," said Henry. "I'll give you a sandwich." He held up for display what would have been Hitch's paper-wrapped sandwich, fat with nearly a pound of chicken. The men's mouths watered.

"What's to keep us from knocking your teeth out and just taking it?" asked the older man.

Henry placed his hand behind his back, and turned to reveal the handle of the gun he was stowing in his waistband.

"Okay, okay, no trouble," promised the younger man. "We've got a deal, but the sandwich first."

"Half," said Henry. "You give me good information, and then I'll give you the other half." He held the thickest, most tempting half up into the boxcar, and the younger man, ravenous, snatched it out of his hand and finished it in two bites."

"Hey, you little bugger," said the older man to his companion, before turning to Henry. "Where's mine?"

"Where's the train?" he asked, bargaining.

The older man looked at Henry, and the other half of the chicken sandwich, and pointed. "You see the Southern Cross flag on that boxcar across the rail yard?"

Henry nodded.

"That's the C.S.A. Flyer. It's a passenger line. Usually has a few empty boxcars at the rear. It goes from Atlanta to Gettysburg."

"Gettysburg?" asked Rollins. "That's in Pennsylvania. That's north of the border," he said hopefully.

Once again the two men looked at one another, and then back at the odd young man who they were certain wasn't too bright.

"Not since about 1869," said the younger man. They shared another laugh.

"Gettysburg is in the…" Henry still had trouble getting the words to roll off his tongue, "…the Confederate States of America?"

"Where's my sandwich?" asked the older man. Rollins handed it to him. "Yeah it's in the C.S.A., and has been for the last 70 years."

Rollins didn't quite understand how any of this was possible. With so much of this place turned upside down, he still had to take what was told to him by everyone as fact, with no way to discern reality from hyperbole. He waited for the older man to finish his half-sandwich. He didn't have to wait long. The man licked greasy fingers, and spoke while still chewing.

"The Flyer stops in Leesburg and Frederick, too," he said. "But you better hurry, she leaves tonight, and pretty quick, and then not again until tomorrow night."

"Leesburg," said Henry to himself. He nodded his thanks, and he walked quickly toward the C.S.A. Flyer. "Leesburg is just 10 miles from Sugarland, on this side of the Potomac River. Perfect."

"I'm getting closer, Margaret," he continued, as he walked toward the depot, stepping carefully over a sea of a thousand iron tracks.

*****

The U.S. Navy's second biggest fear, behind the prowling Germans in their submersible wolf packs, had materialized in the form of a Category 4 hurricane. Not only had it grown in strength, it was now some 325 miles in diameter, and headed north-northwest at 22 knots, only slightly off parallel to the coast line. Virginia Beach to Norfolk and the Delmarva Peninsula seemed like the most probable target for landfall and her destructive fury.

Though it was called the "eye," both for its frightening clear view to the heavens, and for its shape and all-seeing spinning bands of destruction, it could just as easily be called the "mouth." Here, in their most terrible incarnations, the strongest winds circled the eye with tornadic speeds approaching 200 mph, seeking tasty tidbits of steel and flesh to pluck from the surface of the sea and devour whole, only to regurgitate as flotsam 100 miles away.

When the strongest of the rain bands reached them, 50 mph winds whipped through the rigging of the USS Eldridge, howling and unearthly.

"We ain't seen nothing yet," said the slack-jawed navigator, reading the latest weather bulletin. Just then the Eldridge listed 35 degrees when a 20-foot swell, 400 feet long, sideswiped her. The wave washed over the deck of the ship, and anything that hadn't been bolted down was washed overboard in a frothy, raging torrent of water.

"Sir, I think we need to head north-northeast," said the Navigator to Executive Officer Moore. "We'll at least be steering away from the center of this thing, while it goes north-northwest."

"No. We'll lose time reconnecting with the convoy. This is precious time the Allies don't have," said Moore. "Stay the course, helmsman."

Though it made no sense that the XO would purposely pilot the ship into the strongest northern wind bands, he followed orders. "Aye, aye, Sir."

Moore looked at his watch, and made a mental calculation: *11 hours and 14 minutes. You can make this happen.*

Below decks all hell had broken loose, not to mention every pot and pan in the galley. Captain Hammond sat at his desk and did his best to study the charts and the latest weather reports, and to consider his options. The noise generated by the onboard mayhem prompted him to make a personal visit to his immediate surroundings.

Outside his quarters, along the gangway, the Captain encountered sailors running back and forth, stopping to salute, running again, all while trying to manage the side-to-side, sometimes violent, rocking motion the ship was enduring. In light of the Eldridge's recent trip, courtesy of Albert Einstein, Hammond wondered just how much more battering his ship could take.

"Damn it," he said, when he was thrown against the bulkhead. "This can't go on." He made his way back to the bridge, to find four sailors, all looking paler than usual.

"Mr. Moore," said the Captain. "Can't you get us out of this mess?"

"The storm is just too big, Sir," said Moore, steadying himself with one hand, wiping his brow with the other.

The navigator, who knew of a way to lessen the impact, bit his tongue. He did roll his chair away from the front of the radar screen, and casually pointed to a clear mass, just 40 miles northeast of their current position.

"What say you, Navigator? Something on your mind?" asked the Captain.

"Well, Sir, if we shot northeast for a couple of hours, I think the worst of these rain bands and winds would swing west of us, at least for a little while, and give us a break. We could meet the convoy and then follow the storm to Europe, instead of trying to stay in front of it."

"Where's the convoy?

Moore spoke up. "They're all buckled in Norfolk, Sir, waiting for us."

"How long to Norfolk?"

"Just under 11 hours," advised the Navigator.

"And what's your opinion, Mr. Moore?" asked the Captain.

"I think we ride it out and make for Norfolk."

"You know how to pilot a DE in waves that could capsize us, Mr. Moore?"

"No, Sir. But you do. You've done it before."

Captain Hammond's reputation for weathering very bad weather was widely known in naval circles. In his last command he and a task force of four destroyers crossed the path of a storm in the Caribbean that recorded 135 mph winds and 60-foot seas, without losing anyone or sustaining any serious damage to his ship. Even as two other ships capsized, Hammond had the inspiration to fill some of his ship's empty fuel tanks with seawater, as ballast, making his ship less top-heavy and more stable in the high seas.

"Captain, I think the closer to shore the better. This thing could change direction. If we go northeast, we'd never outrun her. At least we stand a chance of it weakening as it gets closer to land."

"I don't relish the thought of being out there with this monster on top of us, I'll give you that Mr. Moore. But if we get hit broadside by the eye of this thing, it won't matter if we're 100 feet from shore. We could lose our rudders, capsize, or be crushed on the rocks. We can't out-power 150 mph winds." Hammond sighed and looked out the window at the chaos.

"At this point, it's too late to go back to Philadelphia. Dammit! We're at the mercy of this thing!"

No one said a word as the ship rocked from side to side and the wind howled through the antennae arrays. Everyone waited for Captain Hammond to make the final call.

"Ok, on to Norfolk. God help us all."

Chapter 31

"Der Radiomannsagt sie ist gross," said Albert Einstein to his secretary, assistant, and confidant, Helen Dukas. He had said to her 'the man on the radio said the storm is big.' When he and Helen were alone together they spoke in their native German. Einstein knew this annoyed, to no end, J. Edgar Hoover, who'd started surveillance two years earlier. Einstein turned off the large Philco, and twirled his mustache. He thought about the broadcasters' dire warnings of a large hurricane coming up the east coast.

"Yes, Herr Doctor. So they are saying," said Helen.

"Zhey're not expecting za storm to bring too much for us, zhough," he continued. "Zhey hope she'll turn und head out to sea."

"I guess that's good, right?"

"Gut for us, nicht so gut for za ships out zher."

Einstein turned his attention back to studying the Manhattan Project file laid out before him in preparation for more illegal meetings; one would come early the next morning.

"It's 11:30, Herr Doctor," said Helen. "You have an early start tomorrow."

"Yes, und I hate early starts. Vhy do you let me schedule 8:00 a.m. meetings?"

Helen ignored him. She could suggest his scheduling and appointments, but they were always ultimately up to him. Though he was just 64, his health had been on a continuous decline for decades, and late nights and early mornings took their toll. He sat thoughtfully and lit his pipe.

"You know it vill be 10 years exactly since together ve swore our oath on ze U.S. Constitution und became American citizens?" said Einstein. "Hard to believe. Ten years in October. If I had to do it all over again, I'd be a plumber."

She ignored his joke. "Yes, hard to believe. Ten years." Dukas had already folded the laundry, put away dinner dishes, and was tending to the last of the day's correspondence. She'd been his secretary first, and later also his housekeeper since the passing of his wife, Elsa, in 1936. Helen Dukas never married, and was one of a very small group of people Einstein trusted implicitly. Though she had her own apartment in Princeton, she didn't always use it. Perhaps this would be one of those evenings.

She'd noticed a pronounced melancholy hovering over Einstein like a gray cloud since his return from Philadelphia. She walked over to him and before resting her hand on his shoulder, she turned the radio back on and the volume up higher than normal. It was the way they sometimes blocked the F.B.I.'s listening devices. She leaned in close and spoke to him in a whisper.

"You're still upset over the Rollins' boy," she said.

"Ya, und his lovely, vife Margaret," he answered. "I feel so very responsible." He whispered back.

"This is not your fault," Helen told him. "You could not have predicted a Nazi saboteur would be working in the Philadelphia Navy Yard."

"No, but I led young Henry into the lion's den. I should never have put him in zhat position." She rubbed his shoulders gently as they listened to the Count Basie Orchestra perform "April in Paris."

"You know zhat boy reminds me so much of myself when I was his age," said Einstein. "He's a smart one. I believe his thinking on the Multiverse is more advanced, perhaps, than even my own. And you know zis Margaret Rollins may very well be a…an astronaut of sorts?"

Helen Dukas pretended to never understand any of his otherworldly musings, but she knew more than she let on.

"Astronaut?" she whispered, having never before heard the word.

"Vell, of sorts," he answered. "One who travels through space. Margaret claims to have traveled to a parallel universe, und based on za Eldridge's travels, she hopes zhat just maybe her Henry might be zhere, too."

He leaned back and re-lit his pipe. "I hope so too, and I'm not so sure she's wrong."

Helen stroked his neck and upper back, trying to get him to relax, but his mind never stopped moving. He sat up straight, picked up the Manhattan File project folder and looked at it with disdain, before letting it fall back to his desk.

"I vas hoping to get back out to za cottage in za Hamptons zis fall," he said, looking up at her, "do a little sailing. But, no, I guess zhat von't be possible. Not wis zhis damned war."

Helen had accompanied Einstein, his stepdaughter, and his wife, to the South Shore of Long Island on many occasions. She, too, enjoyed the sea breezes and calming effects of the salt air, but doting on her employer and friend was most important, no matter where they were, and neither could afford to stay lost in daydreams of seaside retreats.

Einstein spent the next 15 minutes looking over his own notes, and sketches of what Oppenheimer hoped would become the U.S. government's first atomic bomb, a project Einstein deplored. The only thing he hated more than the bomb, was the genocide of the Jews by Hitler's Nazi party. Still, as a pacifist, he was at odds with himself, at odds with his country, wrestling with a moral dilemma of unimaginable consequence.

"Enough of this!" he bellowed, closing the Project files, turning his attention to stacks of mail on his desk. A few pieces were laid out near the top. His celebrity had already long spread around the world and he received thousands of pieces of correspondence every year. Part of Helen Dukas' job was to sort the important government letters and telegrams from the even more important personal letters from children. Dukas, a former kindergarten teacher, had a soft spot for a juvenile's handwriting and their innocent, hopeful queries. She made sure Einstein saw those letters first.

He opened a letter, which turned out to be from a 10-year-old boy in Ohio. The child was upset, questioning why Einstein considered humans to also be animals, something the Doctor had said in many interviews. The concept was considered controversial and inflammatory in some circles. He spent 20 minutes crafting a thoughtful, caring response to the boy.

Next he came upon a letter from a schoolgirl in New Zealand. He decided to read it out loud to Helen.

"Auckland, New Zealand, 9 June, 1943. Dear Sir, I am a girl in grade 8, and so very interested in science, and especially in astronomy. Sometimes I wish I were not a girl because I hate dresses, and dances and all that rot. My friend Sarah and I sneak out of our rooms at night, past the prefects, to set up her telescope and look at what stars we might see. We have gotten in trouble so many times, we fear that the school may punish us harshly, should we get caught again. I have read about your curved space theories and that you believe space goes on forever. I don't really understand how this could be. But obviously you are the scientist, and who am I? I hope you are well, and do not mind that I am a girl, and that you will continue to make great scientific dis-coveries. Yours, Jane."

Einstein chuckled. "Oh, zhat's a good vun. I love zhese." He took out a fresh sheet of stationary and crafted a response.

"Princeton, New Jersey, 11 September, 1943. Dear Jane, Thank you for your letter of June 9th. Be not worried about "curved space," nor about being a girl. I do not mind, but it is more important that you do not mind. Regarding the infinite and space, you will understand at a later time, and "curved," in this context, is different from the meaning in everyday language. I hope yours and Sarah's future

204

astronomical investigations will not again be discovered by the eyes and ears of your school government. This is the attitude taken by most good citizens toward their government, and I think rightly so. Stay curious. What we see depends on what we look for. Yours sincerely, Albert Einstein."

The radio announcer played the 1:00 a.m. chime and started Count Basie's "One O'clock Jump."

"Bitte mit mir tanzen? Care to dance, Helen?" he asked, with a twinkle in his eye.

"It's late, Albert," she said. "Let's retire."

"Ja, mein Liebe," he answered. "Lets."

*****

In rapidly deteriorating weather, just 20 miles due east of Kitty Hawk, North Carolina, Kriegsmarine Captain Walther Zoeller ordered his U-boat to dive. Within three minutes of the dive there was little to indicate that a raging hurricane spun at the ocean's surface. The sea's remarkable ability to carry on as usual just a few meters below the tempest made submarines and submersibles some of the safest bad weather vessels to be aboard. Zoeller and his crew were relieved to be out of the 30-foot swells and battering winds.

H5, a monster storm, had developed from a minor tropical depression into a full-blown Category 4 hurricane in less than 36 hours. Instead of the storm following the forecasts, gradually turning east, away from the Mid Atlantic coastline, it was making a slow turn to the west, catching dozens of ships unaware in its 100,000 square miles of spinning chaos, the worst of it now headed straight for Norfolk.

At 100 meters in depth, still safely well above the 280-meter danger zone called the "collapse depth," U-4713 cruised at a painfully slow 7 knots, around 8 MPH. The best guess was that the storm was traveling at around 20 MPH, and it was hoped that it would overtake them, and be well on its way by the time the U-boat would be forced to surface for fresh air, run its diesel engines, and recharge its 50-tons of batteries.

"Fifteen hours," said Zoeller to himself, lying on his bunk dreaming of Austria. He knew they'd have to surface, regardless of what was happening in the skies above. He also knew that he had to find the Eldridge before he could even think of heading back to port in France; orders were orders. He'd had enough of this war. He knew all too well that the odds of survival were stacked against him. He also knew the age of U-boat dominance was coming to a close, and that, for the first time since the War started, Germany was in jeopardy of losing. He'd heard the rumors and knew that the allies were making ships and planes faster than Germany could take them out, and that the U.S. and Canada, among many other nations, were fully committed and functioning as England's allies against the Third Reich.

"If only there was some way out…" He drifted off into a fitful sleep, one ear waiting for the Radio Officer to knock.

U-4713, towing an antennae buoy with some difficulty, was on alert for Kreigsmarine Kommand to update Zoeller's orders, but for three full hours no call came. The standing directive was to intercept the USS Eldridge, get a visual, disable her, board her if possible, sink her if necessary, and attempt to find out what assistance Albert Einstein was offering the U.S. government.

Zoeller didn't know that the convoy was tucked safely well up the James River, in Norfolk. But he'd heard reports from spotters that the Eldridge, racing south just off the Delmarva Peninsula, was likely headed to Norfolk, herself.

Captain Hammond hoped to beat the storm and find some safety in the protected waters, and Zoeller was hoping to catch them as the weather cleared and the convoy set sail for England. The storm had grounded air patrols, which worked in the Nazi's favor. With no air reconnaissance it would be harder to detect the U-boat, especially while submerged.

U-4713 would be ready with 19 torpedoes to disable or destroy the Eldridge, try to determine her mission, discover her secrets, and take out as many ships in the convoy as it could. The mission for twentieth torpedo, G7e-UP1, still was yet to be determined, awaiting the name of a target.

Resting on his bunk, Junior Lieutenant Luca Adams closed his eyes while considering all the targeting possibilities for the deadliest weapon yet created in human history. With U-4713's proximity to the Chesapeake Bay, an idea was forming, one with global consequences.

*****

The train yard was poorly lit in its southeast sector where Henry Rollins, keeping his head low, crept along toward the main depot. Confederate flags flew everywhere, and Southern Cross bunting, left over from the Confederate Armistice Day celebration, hung over the largest stone archways. He scanned the crowd nervously, not knowing what, if anything, the Sheriff in Southwood might have told any officials. The Sheriff was left with a missing gun, a broken leg and a dead railroad worker's body to somehow explain.

The ever-present possibility of getting nabbed was never too far from his mind. Though the fear of being hunted was taxing, getting home to Maryland, or New Jersey, or even a bit closer was his priority. With no cash, no I.D. and with the place probably crawling with cops, finding the right train, and getting on board would be Henry Rollins' next great challenge.

As he carefully scanned the crowd, he noticed that the clothing given him by Ophelia's family couldn't possibly have been any better suited to helping him fit in. A loose fitting, long sleeve, brown, workman's shirt, slightly worn khaki pants, and even a pair of work shoes all helped Henry Rollins present a working man's demeanor; not too rich or poor, but somewhere comfortably in the middle class. He looked just about like every other young man at the station.

"Thanks Ophelia," he whispered to the wind. "And thanks Hitch, for getting me this far."

He stuck to the shadows among a not too large crowd, busy with destinations and dreams of their own. Without a ticket or any money to buy one, he was unsure how best to proceed to find the train headed north toward the border. Mounted to the wall just ahead of him he spotted a sign: "Ticketing and Information."

The line was short. Rollins made it to the counter in less than a minute.

"Next," said the ticketing agent in a flat monotone without even looking up. Henry moved to the window.

"Yes, I'm headed north. What are my options?"

The agent stopped scribbling in a ledger and looked up, eyeing the young man.

"North?" he asked. "Can you be more specific?"

Henry paused. "The last station before hitting the, umm… border."

"The end of the line, then?"

"Ahh…yes, please."

"That'll be $12. Track 14. Train leaves in…" The agent glanced at the clock in his booth. "…about 11 minutes."

"Thank you," said Rollins smiling. "I'll be back with my wife in a minute; she has all the money." The agent looked annoyed.

"Next!"

Rollins moved quickly, almost forgetting to look out for anyone who might be looking for him. He spun, trying to make out the confusing signs in the midst of rushing crowds, and spotted an arrow sitting atop a carefully hand-painted sign that read: "Tracks 1 – 15."

"Eleven minutes," he said. "Okay, I can do this."

He moved quickly in the arrow's direction, his heart beating faster. He spotted a large pedestrian tunnel, with "Track 14" emblazoned above its arch. As he moved closer he spotted two Lynchburg Police officers casually eyeing the crowd. They didn't look like they were too interested or involved in a manhunt, and with their muted laughter he figured they must have been sharing a private joke. He straightened his back, breathed deeply, and tried his best not to look terrified as he walked by them. It worked, as the cops paid him no attention.

A ticket taker stood by the steps leading into the train. Getting past him would be impossible. Rollins stopped, and leaned back against a stone support beam. He turned to look at the back of the train, to see about hopping on board. *I've done it before. Why not again?* As he walked casually away from the train's engine, he saw that all the cars were passenger cars, except for the caboose, which was active with children shouting and pointing as they looked out over the train yard. Rollins stood at the end of the platform and glanced toward the growing crowd. What he saw made him shudder.

Two plainclothes agents passed out flyers and engaged the two Lynchburg cops. Rollins could see that they'd answered the agent's questions with a "no," both shaking their heads. He stepped back into the shadow as the agents turned to leave. Just before they exited back toward the center hub of the train station, they turned in Henry's direction and began slowly walking toward him, looking hard at every man and woman they came across.

Rollins, at the end of the platform, had nowhere to go. His heart raced as he slipped to the far side of the large support beam. It would hide him, but only as long as the agents didn't come that far.

"Please turn around and go the other way," he said quietly.

He dared to peer around the corner and saw the agents talking to a man about his age. They looked at his I.D., and showed him the flyer, which Henry could now see had a photo of Hitch and a not too bad sketch of himself. He ducked back behind the stone beam, and closed his eyes tightly.

"This is it," he said. "I'm done."

A sudden strong breeze swirled throughout the station through the open end of the platform, alternating warm and cool. The wind howled singing an angry song.

"You're not done yet, Henry." The voice of Hitch, imagined or real, spoke to him as clearly as if he'd been standing by his side. Then came another voice, softer, one that melted his heart. *"Come on, Henry. Don't give up."* As these voices called to him through the fading echoes of the wind's song, he found new courage.

The agents, one of whom had to chase a black fedora blown from his head, had momentarily stopped, but they were clearly intent upon finishing their search of the Track 14 platform.

Okay, here goes.

Staying as hidden as possible, Henry ran to the end of the platform and jumped some four feet down to the gravel of the rail yard. As he ran toward the caboose, the kids, three young teenagers and a boy, no more than five or six, yelled and pointed. Henry briefly turned to them and put a finger to his lips in the universal "Shhh" sign. He added a "please" and the boys stopped their yelling. But it was too late.

The agents, having heard the commotion from the caboose, turned just in time to see Henry disappear around the back of the train car. They ran to follow, jumping down at the same spot Henry had used seconds earlier. The boys watched Henry jumping tracks and running left and right into a sea of train cars. In the dark the agents were unsure which way the runner was headed. When they reached the caboose one of the agents yelled up toward the youths.

"Which way?"

The older boys stood stoically, not saying a word.

"Come on you little bastards. We know you saw him. Which way?"

The teens shrugged their shoulders in continued defiance.

"We will board this train, and have every last one of you removed and thrown in prison for obstructing justice. Last time we ask. Which…way?"

The train whistle blew and a second later the locomotive lurched forward with its first slow roll out of the station. The agents stared hard at the teens as the train pulled away. A small face peered through the iron rails. It belonged to the boy, who, with the others, had watched Henry's escape. The child stuck his tiny hand through the iron rail and pointed to the left, the direction of Rollins' disappearance into the dark.

Chapter 32

Margaret Rollins hadn't been able to get comfortable in a bed she felt was a stranger's, even though she knew the linens, and even a quilt made by her grandmother. Unable to sleep, she went downstairs into the living room where she and Hank bedded down on the couch with the radio playing softly. Hours later, the early morning sun blasted through a small part in the living room curtains. Its warm, golden light fell across her face. She sat up and found she couldn't move her feet. Hank was sprawled across her legs, and to the best of her knowledge he hadn't moved all night.

"Come on boy," she said, wiggling her toes. Hank yawned. A short whine escaped his throat just before he turned his head to look at her. Eventually they both sat fully up, at least one of them eager to get moving. Margaret was nervous in this place, and felt like the authorities could show up at any minute. She hated the feeling of being wanted by the law, and tried not to dwell on it. Though her nerves were rattled, Henry's predicament competed for space in her mind. She had no idea what he was enduring, but somehow she knew he was alive. She couldn't explain how she knew, but she knew.

Starting a new day in a parallel universe was something that would take getting used to. For starters, it was August, not September. Everything else was just peculiar enough to throw her completely off kilter. The kitchen was where it was supposed to be, but the dishes weren't. And where were the occupants of this house? Who was paying the electric bill? Who mowed the lawn? It was all very unsettling. She found canned and dried goods: flour, coffee, powdered eggs, and enough to feed herself and Hank, but the brands were completely

210

unfamiliar. The refrigerator was running, but nearly empty, except for a jar of English Devon Cream, something both Henry and Margaret loved. These details of the household's operation confused her and muddled her already stressed sense of clarity, threatening to derail her from the task at hand—finding Henry.

"We don't have a car, Hank. We don't have any money that will work here, or a way across this border they're talking about. How do we get to Norfolk, Virginia? Is Norfolk even still there?" Hank wagged his tail, and twitched his expressive eyebrows, but did not answer. They dared to go outside and felt comfortable on the porch, as the long driveway would give them enough warning should someone, the detectives or anyone else, decide to pay a visit.

Though she couldn't see it through the trees, she heard the sounds of construction and hydraulic post setting machinery working on the creation of an insurmountable border fence between North and South, one that might finally and irreparably separate North and South, Yankee and Confederate.

The house was just a couple of miles from the Potomac River and the site of the federally funded I.B.B., the International Border between the States, construction project. She didn't yet know how, but that was the direction she'd have to go.

"Let's explore, Hank."

With a cup of coffee in hand, Margaret and Hank surveyed the property. It was very much, though not exactly, like the house and yard she'd known and loved since she was a girl. When they reached the closed barn door, and swung it to the side, a few birds screamed, dove at them and flew out, prompting Hank to bark.

"Well look at that, Boy," said Margaret, walking toward a vehicle she'd never seen before. "Maybe we found a car, after all?"

The large, jet-black two-door sedan had been backed into the barn, and was the size of a tank. It carried the Marathon Motorworks emblem and matching hood ornament. She opened the dusty door, and her heart sank as she realized the car had been sitting for a while. A glimmer of hope returned as she noticed a small interior light glowing a dim yellow.

"Keys," she said, running to the house and looking in the drawer where she and Henry always threw their own keys and miscellaneous bric-a-brac. "Yes!" A large leather MMW key fob stared back at her and she ran with it back to the barn. Depressing the clutch and pumping the gas pedal a few times she turned the key, heard one revolution of the large V-12 motor, and then nothing. She slumped back in the seat.

"Now what…?

As she let her foot off the clutch, she remembered a trick her father taught her when she was first learning to drive at age 15. She could almost hear his voice. *Listen to me, honey, if your battery goes dead, and you're near a hill, and you can get the car rolling, even just five miles per hour, put it in second gear, turn the key on and pop the clutch. It's called a "push start. Once the engine's running, it will recharge the battery. It might come in handy one day…"*

"Can I do that?" she asked Hank, who wagged an enthusiastic "yes."

"Well then, okay. Hank, get in. Here goes nothing." Hank hopped in, jumping over her, sitting as co-pilot in the passenger's seat, eager to begin another flying session.

"Turn the key on," she said, repeating the steps out loud. "Depress the clutch, put it in second gear, and...now what?" The large car didn't move on the flat grade of the barn's hard, gravel floor.

"A-ha!" She released the emergency brake and the car inched forward, but stopped without nearly enough momentum to send them out of the barn and down the driveway.

"Crap, Hank."

She got out of the car and immediately saw the problem. A small ridge of concrete, less than an inch high, stopped the front wheels from moving any further. She pushed on the car's doorframe. The big vehicle budged, but not quite enough to clear the mini speed bump on the barn's floor. She got out and walked around the hulking vehicle, thinking about what she might do.

At the back of the car, the rear bumper was just two feet from a large, sturdy workbench, bolted to the floor. She wedged herself between the bench and the rear bumper, realizing she might have enough strength in her legs to push the car from behind, over the concrete ridge. *Put the car in neutral, leave the door open, push it over the ridge, and then run like hell to hop in?* The prospect of this maneuver, while seeming plausible, was frightening.

"Hank," she yelled, "Come on, get out. I don't want you inside that car if this goes wonky." He reluctantly got out and watched helplessly as Margaret put the car in neutral, made sure the wheel was straight, turned the key on, and got ready to try something she'd never imagined herself doing.

"Ready, Hank?"

She wedged herself between the workbench and the huge, chrome rear bumper, and slowly pushed the car by straightening her legs. The big car crept forward, almost cresting the ridge, and she ran out of steam, yelling out loud as it rolled back the few inches she'd just gained.

"Come on! I almost had it!"

Hank barked, mimicking her agitation.

"Okay, this time."

She took a deep breath and pushed harder and a little faster. On this effort the front wheels made it over the hump, and the car began slowly rolling out of the barn.

"Oh wow...it's going! Hank! Come on!"

She and Hank squeezed past the barn's doorframe, and the moving car, which was picking up speed as it was now fully out of the barn and headed down the gravel driveway. Margaret ran to the cracked open driver's door, while Hank followed on her heels, barking madly. She was running now as the car had picked up more steam than she had anticipated. It veered to the left, and was half on the grass and half on the driveway, headed downhill more or less toward the road. She threw herself into the front seat, grabbed the wheel, straightening out the steering, just before the car would have rolled down an embankment. Like she'd done it a thousand times before, she braked slightly, pushed the clutch in, shifted into second gear and popped the clutch. The big V-12 motor sputtered, popped, backfired and then roared to life. She screamed with delight, to the amusement of Hank just outside the car's door, still barking.

When she braked to a stop near the front of the house, the Marathon threatened to stall, but she knew to give it gas for a minute while it warmed up. Within 90-seconds it idled peacefully, purring like a motorboat.

"Thanks, dad," she whispered. "Well, we did it, Hank. We've got a car. But now what?"

The house was as closed up as it needed to be, so she opened the car door and let a very relieved Golden Retriever in to take his rightful place in the passenger seat. The car was twice the size of the one she'd been used to driving. But if she could push start it by popping the clutch, and then hop into it while it was moving, she could do anything.

Margaret Rollins knew the roads around Sugarland, and even those out of town. Though she hadn't been South in a while, generally she knew the way toward Richmond, Virginia, and then to the coast toward Norfolk. The day was bright and sunny and helped restore her spirit, if only a little.

"Whoever left us this car, left a full tank of gas, Hank." With the Marathon still idling in the driveway, she opened the glove compartment and rummaged through some papers. The registration read "Henry Rollins," and the sight of his name brought tears to her eyes.

"My Henry," she said staring out the window, looking over the rural landscape. "Where are you?"

*****

Some nine hours before Margaret Rollins awakened in his world, Henry Rollins, south of the I.B.S. border, had never run faster in his life. He dodged obstacles and hopped over train tracks like an Olympic athlete. On his tail were two Con-Fed agents, not certain of his identity, but highly suspicious, and motivated. When they spotted a flash in the darkness, and the silhouette of a man running along the tracks, they set out to close the gap.

Henry lost out on the opportunity to take the train north toward the border, but knew he had to go somewhere fast. He hadn't seen the men for a few seconds, but he thought he heard the sound of running and feet pounding the gravel not too far behind him.

Lost in a maze of tracks and trains, he was able to avoid direct detection for another minute, but when he heard the two men shouting to one another, he could hear that they were close. When a freight train lurched forward, and let out a metallic scream as steel braking mechanisms were released, Henry spotted the open door of a boxcar. He ran for the moving train car and hopped up and in, just as agents appeared behind an adjacent train. Rollins saw them with their guns drawn, but he wasn't sure if they'd seen him. He checked his pistol, which had been stuffed in the back of his pants.

"Five bullets left," he said to himself. "If they know I'm in here, it's all over. There's no way out."

The train picked up only a little speed as it made its painfully slow departure out of the rail yard for some unknown destination. It crawled along at a pace slower than an old man might walk a dog. Henry cursed the train, and pleaded with it to go faster.

The agents outside walked along with the moving train, getting closer to the open door. Henry could hear bits of conversation and knew they were close, very close. He spotted a rock on the floor of the boxcar, about the size of a large marble. He threw it up and out of the open train car, so that it cleared the cars in the next adjacent track and landed with a loud bang hitting a train car two tracks over. The agents reacted, yelling at one another. Henry finally exhaled and took a deep breath when he heard their fading conversation as they went to investigate.

"They didn't see me," he said with shock and relief to the darkened boxcar's walls. He'd never felt more relieved and more alone.

Hungry, dehydrated, and with a body coursing with anxiety, he became light-headed, and tried to steady himself against the side wall of the boxcar. When the train, clearing the busiest part of the rail yard, picked up speed with a hard heave forward, Henry lost his balance and began to fall backward. As if in slow motion he ran in reverse, trying to catch himself in the pitch-black boxcar. Now falling and back-pedaling at the same time, his already bruised and concussed head hit the back of the boxcar, taking the full force of his momentum. He was out cold, and lay on the floor as the train picked up speed, chugging on into the night.

*****

On an interdimensional plane, more or less parallel to the world as it is known to the humanity of one version of planet Earth, a manhunt was underway. On this particular plane sat an Earth-like world, and in fact its inhabitants even called it 'Earth" and it was one of perhaps an infinite number. On a continent in the Northern hemisphere of this similar, but alternate Earth, sat a jurisdiction called "Virginia."

Within this place called "Virginia," located in a nation-state known as the "Confederate States of America," the authorities sought two fugitives— a Henry Rollins and Bill "Hitch" Hickok wanted for escape from prison. Additionally the two are also wanted for an assault and murder they did not commit. Sheriff Brooks of Southwood, Virginia, phoned the State Police informing them of the near capture of the pair. He told anyone who would listen, the tale of his heroics and of the shooting that killed a railroad employee, and left him with a broken leg. In the previous 24-hours the authorities added a person-of-interest to their search—Margaret Rollins.

Not terribly unlike the world Henry Rollins had left, not by his own choice, the people of this place called the year "1943." But in this alternate world in which he found himself, no hurricane loomed just off the coast. On this morning the summer weather was hot, clear, typical and pleasant. A pair of plainclothes Confederate Bureau of Investigation agents left Richmond, Virginia, the C.S.A. Capitol. They traveled by car and were on a mission to find a woman this woman initially known only as "Margaret," but later determined to be the wife of one of the fugitives. They concluded that their suspect may be living in, or had once lived in, or visited, a town called Sugarland, Maryland—it was there that they were to start their search.

Once on their way, driving north, lead Special Agent Douglas Cornell, a man of small stature, but a powerful, no-nonsense, ex-C.S.A. Marine-turned C.B.I. operative, spoke.

"Did you call the boys at The Cottage?"

"Yep," answered his partner, Special Agent Ben Travers, also ex-military, and like Cornell, now happily in the spy business. "They said they're on it."

The Cottage was code name for a rural C.S.A. undercover sanctuary. It was located in Rockville, Maryland, right under the noses of the Washington D.C. Federals. The Agents stationed at The Cottage had already told Travers that they knew of Sugarland, Maryland, and after a little digging, they even unearthed intel on Margaret and Henry Rollins. They offered what they knew about the couple, none of which made much sense.

"The boys said that the Rollins couple are "Missing Persons," said Travers. He flipped open a small notebook and referred to a mass of scribbled entries. "Seems Henry Rollins worked at the local Post Office. He's been missing for about 10 days. Apparently he just didn't show up for work one day. His wife, the one we're after in Sugarland, is a schoolteacher. She's been missing for almost a year."

"Huh. Ain't that something strange?" asked Agent Cornell.

"Yeah, and no record of them ever being in Princeton, New Jersey."

"Okay, well then we'll scrap New Jersey, and focus on Sugarland. You got the crossing worked out?"

"Yeah, no problem," said Agent Travers. "The border is still wide open…if you know where to go."

"And you know where to go, I suppose?"

"'Course, I do."

"That's what I like to hear."

"We'll go a little west, through Culpepper and Manassas, before cutting back east. We're looking at about four hours 'till we get near Sugarland." Agent Travers yawned and leaned back in the couch-like, passenger seat of a large Marathon, the nationalized car of the C.S.A.

"Listen," he said, holding back another yawn. "I'm gonna catch some sleep."

"The hell you are," spit Cornell. "You're going to stay awake and keep me company."

"Then you better pull off and find some strong Joe."

"You and your coffee."

"Makes the world a happier place," said Travers.

"So does Extra C Coke," said Cornell.

"Nah, can't stand all that cocaine crap," said Travers. "Messes with my belly. I'll stick to coffee. I know a spot on Route 3 halfway to Culpepper. The Fuel and Drool. Has gas, decent food and good Joe. I can wait that long."

"Fuel & Drool it is then."

Chapter 33

As time, space, and gravity bend and twist, the fabric of one universe keeps a respectful distance from its nearest neighbor. This leaves most sentient beings blissfully unaware that they are sharing space in an infinite, multi-dimensional environment. Only those who might know the shortcuts between the worlds could contrast and compare life on neighboring worlds. Margaret Rollins, who'd learned she could travel between Earths at will, had not yet fully comprehended what that might mean.

While Henry and Margaret Rollins were visitors in a universe much like their own, but not their own, neither knew that on their home Earth, a monstrous, rotating storm, hundreds of miles wide, was consuming the attention of nearly everyone from the mid-Atlantic to New England.

One hundred miles off the Outer Banks of North Carolina, the wind whipped with such a fury that high-tide storm surges were already reshaping the North Carolina coastline, even before the strongest winds and the storm surge made it ashore.

From Virginia Beach to Boston, preparations were underway to try to protect life and property from what some feared could be the largest hurricane to ever threaten the region. Near the storm's center and along its northern wind and rain bands, the surface of the sea tumbled, roiled, and rolled like liquid mountains. Sixty-foot waves rose up, crashing in on themselves, only to rise again to be ripped apart by 150-mph winds. Fierce lightening and towering waterspouts spun up, accompanying the storm like furious canine henchmen, frothing and snapping at the ends of multiple leashes.

At 300-feet below the surface, U-boat 4713 endured only the occasional five-degree roll, and heard none of the raging storm overhead.

"We had to retrieve the radio buoy, Sir," reported a junior officer to U-boat Captain Walther Zoeller. "The waves up top were about to snap the cable. We did receive one last transmission before we went dark, however."

Zoeller looked annoyed, wishing they'd gotten to that part of the report a bit sooner.

"Well?" he asked.

"It only says "To Captain Zoeller. Lieutenant Luca Adams— Priority Code Angriffsziel Omega.""

The stoic Captain revealed no emotion about receiving the highest-level code, one that meant 'Attack Objective End,' but nodded that he understood. Of all the Third Reich military plans underway in Europe, in North Africa, and on the Russian Front, this Angriffsziel Omega told Captain Zoeller, that at the moment, his mission was of the highest priority. It had been developed in secret, and had been approved by Chancellor Adolf Hitler.

He ordered the Ensign to summon Lieutenant Luca Adams, the new officer aboard. Zoeller looked at his watch and knew they'd been below the surface and running on batteries for four hours.

Four down, eleven to go.

The U-boat moved much more slowly when submerged, slower than the raging storm's forward progression above them. Zoeller's best guess was for arrival near Norfolk in eight hours. At last calculations H5, if it maintained its speed, would have already moved through the Norfolk area some six hours earlier before their need to surface. His order to intercept and sink a modified experimental Destroyer Escort, the USS Eldridge, was still fully in force, though the newly received Omega Code meant anything was possible.

"This damn storm might just be the perfect cover for whatever else they have in mind. Angriffsziel Omega. I'll be damned…" he said, before closing his eyes.

******

International Border between the States
Rural Maryland
Federated States of America
10:51 a.m. August 23, 1943

As Margaret Rollins neared the Maryland-Virginia border she noticed a pronounced increase in military vehicle traffic. The small trucks didn't carry the U.S.A. emblem or an American flag as she'd expected, but rather the unfamiliar F.S.A. insignia. If she hadn't blocked most of her memories of the traumatic two weeks she'd spent in the Federated States of America 10 months earlier, she might have remembered seeing it.

The military personnel didn't pay much attention as they passed by, but when she reached the turn she needed to take, toward Richmond and Norfolk, the road was blocked. A fully operational and well-guarded checkpoint was in place just a half-mile ahead.

"Not going to mess with them, Hank," she said, turning, heading northwest along the Potomac River instead of southeast, the direction she needed to go.

When she rounded a bend in the road she came face-to-face with a massive, ominous, 100-foot tall border fence and crews of construction workers setting posts, pouring concrete and installing razor wire. At first she thought someone was building a prison, not realizing she was looking at a steel curtain separating North from South.

A few miles further into the countryside, the military traffic all but disappeared. She slowed the car to pull off the road where she hoped to consult a map and consider an alternate route.

In another Marathon, traveling at a high rate of speed, two teens laughed and argued about anything and everything—girls, music, and cars, mostly.

"Lemme bum a cigarette," demanded George Dietz, the freckle-faced, redheaded driver, who at 15, was just old enough to be behind the wheel without the authorities bothering him.

"Man, I'm getting tired of supplying you with cigarettes all the time," said the passenger, his best friend, who never got to drive the company car. "We got all the money we could ever want, and yet you never have smokes?"

"Don't blow your fuse, Applesauce," said the driver.

"Fine," said the other, knowing he'd never win an argument with the boss's son." From his shirt pocket he pulled out a pack of Stonewalls, named for the great Confederate General of the C.S.A. He slipped two cigarettes from the half-empty pack, lit them both and handed one to the driver.

At the same moment Dietz went to grab the burning cigarette, the speed of the giant automobile didn't line up with the curve in the road, and they fumbled the hand-off. The lit cigarette bounced off the dashboard in a sea of sparks, dropping on the seat. In the mayhem and screaming they never saw the oncoming car, or that they were in the wrong lane.

As Margaret Rollins turned left to cross the road, a car, not much smaller than her own, careened around the corner. The driver, moving much too fast, slammed on his brakes, but was unable to avoid a collision. With a great crash, the two cars, both Marathons, met side-to-side, and spun in a dance of dust and squealing tires, before coming to rest on the wide shoulder.

Margaret and Hank were fine, but shaken. Two stunned teenagers got out of the offending vehicle and walked to Margaret's door, which she was just opening.

"Are you all right?" said the red-haired lad, flush from the collision he knew he'd caused.

"Yes. I think so," answered Margaret. She looked at Hank, who seemed nervous but okay.

"I'm really sorry, Ma'am," said the boy, removing a worn brown Fedora, two sizes too big. Margaret tried not to smile. The other boy circled both cars, surveying the damage.

"Man, we're going to get it but good," he said, on the verge of tears.

Margaret looked at the passenger side of the car, which had seen all the action, and found it scraped up and dented pretty badly. She sensed an opportunity.

"You're not kidding. You *are* going to get it," she said, acting angrier than she really was. "You're lucky you didn't kill us all. Who's going to pay for this?"

Dietz turned on his swagger.

"I think we can take care of this, Ma'am," he said, putting on a show of bravado and maturity that almost made Margaret laugh out loud. She paid closer attention when he pulled out a bankroll of bills, gathered with a rubber band and flashed it at her.

"I see," she said. "You're going to try to buy me off?"

"Money talks, don't it?" said Dietz. "But not here. We need to get off the road. Follow us. We'll take care of you."

Margaret should have been concerned for her safety, but the boys seemed so young, and with Hank by her side, she decided to take her chances. As they drove away slowly, she spoke to Hank. "You got any better ideas?" Not quite convinced, Hank whimpered and stared nervously out the window.

Less than a quarter-mile up the road, the boys turned their car into a driveway leading to a small farmhouse with a well-kept barn sitting up against the side of a large long, high ridge.

They all got out and met under the shade of a massive oak.

"So, how much to take care of this?" asked Dietz, getting a good look at the damage.

Margaret had no idea how much to ask for. "You tell me," she said. "What's your offer?"

"How 'bout $500?"

That sounded like a lot of money, and would more than fix the fender, she thought, though she wasn't worried about bodywork. "I think that might do," she said. "I'm headed to Norfolk, so I'll need another tankful of gas, and some food…plus the money to fix—"

The boys looked at one another. "Did you say Norfolk? As in Norfolk, Virginia?"

"I did."

"So…you mean to cross the border?"

"I do."

"Maybe it's none of our business, Ma'am, but do you have papers to cross?"

Margaret hesitated. The boys clearly knew more about operating in this place than did she. "Well, no."

The teens shared another awkward glance.

"You won't be able to cross the border without papers. It's illegal."

Margaret almost cried, but held it together. "I'm trying to find my husband," she said, choking back real emotion. "I'm not sure, but I think he might be there…I just don't know."

"You have the right car for the trip," said the quieter boy, trying to encourage her. "Not many Yankees drive Marathons, but getting across the border is tricky."

"But not impossible. I think we can help you," said the red-haired teen.

"George!" yelled his friend, sensing where this was headed. "You are going to get us both whipped."

Margaret looked puzzled, but the redheaded boy had obviously taken a liking to her, and wanted to show off, on top of feeling responsible for the accident.

"It'll be alright," said Dietz to his friend. "I got a good feeling about her."

Margaret looked at them both and decided she needed answers. "What are you two talking about?"

"Look, Ma'am," he said. "I feel real bad about what happened, but we can get you across the border, and even back, if you want."

"How?" asked Margaret, confused, but encouraged.

"We're black market boys," said Dietz. "We're runners. We make the trip 10 times a day some days. We're in the….ahh…delivery business, let's say."

"Oh, I see," said Margaret, with a hint of condescension. "Black market boys?" She had only a guess at what that actually meant.

"We sure are. And right behind that barn door is clear sailing to Virginia. There's a tunnel. An old train tunnel they missed when—"

"George! Shut your stupid mouth," said the other teen, angry at his friend's free flowing stream of information.

"What's eating you? Calm down," said Dietz, who turned back to Margaret. "We live in Con-Fed. We've got Con-Fed cash to give you, too. All you want." The lad was so excited to be offering these services to a pretty, young woman that Margaret had to smile, and finally just thank them.

"Let's go," she said.

The other boy, still not sure they were doing the right thing, shook his head, cursing under his breath.

"You're stuck on her," he whispered, elbowing Dietz in the ribs.

"Am not," he protested, checking to see that Margaret was still behind them, arriving at the barn door, swinging it wide open.

"One and a half miles through the mountain, you'll find another barn, just like this one," said Dietz, "and you'll be on your way. Follow us. When we get there I'll get you some cash. We print our own! Got all you want!"

"George!" yelled the other boy. "My god, shut up already!"

"Don't mind him," said Dietz. The two boys got in their car and led the way. Once inside the barn, they closed the barn's front doors, and swung another door at the back of the barn open, revealing the entrance to the repurposed, abandoned train tunnel.

Margaret and Hank followed, with only their headlights illuminating the otherwise pitch-black tunnel. Three minutes later, the boys in the lead car honked their horn, and a wide, wooden door swung open letting them through into another country.

After some discussion with another teen, who did not look at all happy with young George Dietz, Margaret's car was given a quick once over, a set of C.S.A. Virginia license plates, and $500 in freshly minted Con-Fed cash.

"This kind of money could come in handy," she said to Hank.

"Fellas, I have a question for you." The boys walked to her open window. "How good, how passable is this funny money?"

"Don't run it through the wash, or nothin' but it's pert damned near perfect, from what we been told. We don't hardly ever get to spend it, though. Got piles of it."

"How much might you be willing to loan me?"

"How much you want?"

Margaret thought for a moment. *Might as well shoot high.* "How about $50,000?"

Dietz laughed at the sum. It was more money than he'd ever assembled before.

"If it's too difficult..." Margaret started.

Dietz thought for a moment. "You say you're comin' back through, to head north?"

"I certainly hope so."

"We'll give you the money in trade for your car when you come back."

"Deal," she said. "You can really get that kind of cash?"

"It's no problem," answered Dietz. "That's 1000 $50 bills. We keep 'em bundled up."

"You're good at math. I'm sure your teachers love you," she said, making the youth blush.

Young George Dietz was in charge of the operations while his father was away on business. Junior was not always the best at making smart deals, but he advised his friend to retrieve 40 stacks banded with 25 bills each, which were stuffed into various locations throughout the car. Half the money, some $25,000 was wrapped in thin, watertight canvas bags and wedged into a space behind the damaged fender well. The rest was placed under the seats, with a few thousand dollars making it into the glove compartment.

After being led out of the barn, she leaned out of the window and looked back at the boys, one of whom seemed very sad to see her go.

"Thank you, young man," she said waving him toward her. "I'll find a way to make this up to you." He walked to the window, and she pulled his head down and she kissed him on the cheek. His face turned as red as his hair and he grinned from ear to ear.

"I hope to see you boys again," she said, waving. She turned to look at Hank, who was only too eager to get going. "Ready?" She pulled to the end of the driveway leading to the road toward Richmond, the C.S.A. capitol. She leaned out of the window again, and looked back toward the farm.

"I never got your names!"

"They call me Georgie! This is Buddy!"

"Okay, I'm…" She hated lying, already having grown fond of them in their short time together. "…I'm Delores. Thank you! You boys be careful, and don't drive so fast. I'll be back with your car, I hope."

"You better be!" yelled Dietz. "We just paid you $50,000!" They continued to wave as Margaret pulled out on a backwater Virginia state road, along the border of the Confederate States of America.

Chapter 34

Atlantic Ocean
United States of America Coastal Waters
September 10, 4 p.m. 1943

Headed south, six miles west of Assateague Island, just off the Delmarva Peninsula, the USS Eldridge was bearing the brunt of H5's northernmost outer bands. For Captain Hammond it was a toss-up between backtracking to the safety of the Delaware River and Philadelphia to the north, or steaming ahead past Cape Charles and to the protected port of the Norfolk Naval Base, trying to get there before H5 capsized them.

Executive Officer Moore, who was literally green from seasickness, had been unceremoniously sent to his quarters. He was of no use to Captain Hammond on the Bridge.

"At this speed we're three to four hours before hitting Cape Charles," said the navigator, white knuckled from gripping his console so tightly.

"Try not to use that exact terminology, Ensign," said Hammond. I'd prefer not to 'hit' anything."

"No, Sir. Me neither."

Another swell, a 20-footer, broadsided the Eldridge sending spray and tons of seawater up and over the length of the 300-foot ship, easily reaching the tower of the flying bridge some 40 feet in the air. The subsequent 15-degree starboard list was particularly pronounced and violent at the top of the ship. Every one-foot movement at the waterline was magnified, translating to 10 lateral feet at the bridge.

"Damn it!" yelled the Captain, to no one in particular. "These swells are coming at as from the east now?"

"Yes, Sir," answered the Ensign. "It's the outer bands. I'm afraid we're headed about straight into the belly of the beast."

"There is just nowhere to go," said the frustrated Captain. "How far back to Ocean City? Couldn't we ride out this bitch in the West Bay?"

"I don't know, Sir. After we turn around, which wouldn't be too easy in this stuff, probably two hours."

"We're betwixt the Devil and the deep, blue sea."

The wind, gusting to 70 mph. whistled through the rigging, and sent a tortured wail throughout the ship. It was the same moaning Captain Hammond heard a week earlier when his ship was being stressed and tossed through time and space in a hurricane of a different sort. He felt just as helpless in this storm as he did watching his ship levitate, disappear, only to later reappear at the Philadelphia Naval Yard.

"We could try for Hog Island Bay or Cobb Bay, but the shoals there…it's just too shallow. I don't recommend it."

"What's the latest from the Weather Service?" asked the Captain.

"Not much change from 30 minutes ago, although they think the storm's forward movement may be slowing down some. It was originally tracking around 18 knots, then they said 12-15 knots, and now they're guessing it's about 9 – 12."

"Can we get any more speed?" asked the Captain.

"Yes, but we risk being unable to correct from a side hit," answered the helmsman. "The faster we go, the more unstable we are."

"Thank you, Helmsman. I am well aware of how the ship handles in a storm. Full ahead!"

"Full ahead!" answered the Helmsman, sending the signal to the engine room through the ship's telegraph.

When the first lightning strike hit the antennae array amidships, the crack was deafening. There was no significant damage done, but it rattled the nerves of every man on board, especially XO Phillip Moore. With the boom and shaking below deck, reverberating through the steel hull, it sounded as if the ship was under attack, which, in many ways, it was. Though vomiting into a bucket every few minutes, Moore managed to reassemble his damaged Kriegsmarine Langwellen radio. In what felt like a futile effort, he broadcast to the last known German-monitored channels.

He spoke in German. "Kriegsmarine, Crossroads East. USS Eldridge in trouble. High seas. Headed for Norfolk Navy Yard. Two and a half hours, ETA, 6 p.m. Eastern Standard Time, if we survive the storm." He could barely get the words out through the retching. Weak, dehydrated, and still very sick, he repeated the report five more times, on four additional frequencies before fainting and collapsing to the floor of his quarters where he lay unconscious.

Rural Virginia
Confederate States of America
6:39 a.m. August 23, 1943

Henry Rollins awakened crumpled on the floor of a fast-moving train car. He first fluttered his eyes as a warm breeze blew dust and debris around his face. Only the faintest hint of dawn showed itself out of the open door of the boxcar. It was the second boxcar in which he'd hitched a ride in less than 24 hours.

"Ohh…" he moaned as he struggled to sit up, blood pumping freshly through his veins. His head ached and throbbed, courtesy of the third traumatic blow to his skull in less than two weeks. He put his hand to the back of his head and felt a goose egg, but no evidence of blood. Scooting toward the open door, he saw more stars in the sky, the occasional light from a distant house or farm, but nothing to give him a clue as to where he was going.

"I hope to God I'm headed North," he said to the breeze as the train chugged along. Desperately thirsty and moderately hungry, he wished he was anywhere else but on this train headed full speed into the unknown.

"You ain't, you know? No, Sir, you ain't," said a disembodied, gravelly voice from out of the shadows. The voice seemed to originate from the far side of the boxcar, and it shook him. *Am I dreaming?* Rollins waited to see if what he'd heard was a trick of his mind, or of the wind. A few seconds went by, and he relaxed.

"Nope, you are not headed north. No, Sir."

This time the man's voice was clear as a bell, and Henry realized he was definitely not alone.

"Who's there?" asked Rollins, struggling but unable to see.

"Just me," answered the voice. "They call me Moondawg."

"Moondawg?"

"Yeah, on account of I sometimes howl at the moon."

Rollins couldn't see him, but heard the man making his way in the blackened boxcar. When the stranger shuffled toward the door, the train rounded a bend allowing the fading moonlight into the car. He could see the man dressed in layers of rags. He looked a medieval prisoner of war, except that he was rotund to the point of being obese. How, Henry wondered, would a man living as a hobo manage to get that large? Upon seeing the moon, true to form, Moondawg howled like a lycanthrope out the open door into the vanishing night. Henry felt for his pistol, still lodged in the back of his trousers.

"So," began Rollins, after the howling ceased, and still unsure if the man was insane or dangerous, "if not north, then where are we headed?"

"Can't you smell it?" asked Moondawg, whispering.

"Smell what?"

Moondawg took a deep breath through his nose, closed his eyes and smiled. "Our dear mother," he answered. "That's salt air. We're right close now. The Chesapeake is welcoming us."

"The Chesapeake, as in Chesapeake Bay?"

"Is there another? Yes, the Chesapeake Bay and the wonderful city of Norfolk, Virginia."

"No!" said Rollins in disbelief. "Not Norfolk!" The shouting caused him great pain, and though heartfelt, he regretted it.

Moondawg ignored him. "We've been running for hours," he said. "We made a stop in Emporia at the Southwood Station—that took forever—and then moved on."

Henry didn't like hearing about Southwood, which reminded him of the monster of a sheriff who killed his only friend in that place. He forced away the awful memory, focusing on his immediate predicament.

"Norfolk? Why didn't you wake me?" The question was born out of frustration, not logic.

"You had your 'Do Not Disturb' card displayed," said the hobo, who, with some difficulty, managed to take a seat on the floor of the boxcar, closer than Rollins would have liked. In spite of the fresh air blowing through the train car, Moondawg's stench was almost overwhelming. "Did you expect turndown service, too?"

Henry was silent, processing the news of Norfolk as an unwelcome bit of information.

"Is there a place to hop off early, before we arrive at the rail yard?" he asked?

"I expect so," answered Moondawg. "Maybe there's someone in Norfolk you don't particularly want to see?"

"You could say that."

"This train slows way down as it rounds a pretty good curve, coming up. If my recollection is good, that's about two miles before she finally comes to a full stop. But we're in damn near the last car of this train. Unless somebody's lookin' hard for you, I wouldn't worry about it. Nobody gonna bother us."

Moondawg took a moment to size up his traveling companion. "You don't 'zactly look like us," he said. "You got a clean-shaven baby face, a suit, dress shirt, nice shoes…you don't really fit the mold. What the hell are you doin' hoppin' a train?"

"Didn't mean to be on this one, that's for sure," answered Rollins, evading the question. Moondawg didn't press him. Men hopping trains did so for an unending variety of reasons, and the rule of the rail was 'to each his own.'

"Well it's comin' up. I rode this so many times I know the route by heart. Less'n five minutes, I reckon." He breathed in deeply through his nose. "Hello Mother Ocean."

*****

At the Fuel & Drool, a popular truck stop not too far from the International Border, you'd find gas, diesel fuel, a hot meal, and a sea of travelers. As C.B.I. Special Agents Cornell and Travers rolled into the parking lot, the activity was frenetic. Cars and military vehicles of all types and sizes, filled the parking lot, weaving in and out of the fueling lanes. The agents parked and walked to the front door.

"Hey, look at this," said Cornell, pointing to a Wanted Poster with a grainy photograph of "Wild" Bill Hickok and a pencil sketch of Henry Rollins, the C.S.A.'s two Most Wanted.

"Somebody was doing their job, I guess," said Travers. Cornell rolled his eyes. The reputation of the Norfolk P.D., who'd let the two fugitives slip through their fingers, was not currently held in the highest regard, and now the C.B.I. agents were called in to clean up the mess.

"Needs to be updated with the picture of the Rollins woman, too," said Travers.

They took a seat in a booth at the back of the dining room. A row of specially designated high-backed booths each had a private payphone attached to the wall, just under the windows. When the waitress finally came by, each ordered coffee and a scrambled egg breakfast. By the time the food came and they'd finished up, an hour had gone by, giving lead agent Cornell a chance to think about the day's mission.

"Call your boys at the Cottage, would ya? I want to find out if they've heard anything."

Travers reached into his pocket for change and finding none, motioned to his boss with an outstretched hand. After slipping a dollar's worth of coins into the phone, Travers dialed a series of two-digit codes, and read a password to an operator. He was put through using a secure line across the international border to make a call that was prohibited for almost anyone else.

After a few static-laden switches and loud clicks, a surprisingly clear voice answered.

"Cottage."

"Yeah, Travers here. Special Agent Cornell and I are near the border. Coming over in an hour or so. You guys have any luck with the Rollins case?"

"Yes and no. We confirmed the Sugarland dame from your picture is Margaret Rollins, the wife of your fugitive. They both live, or I should say, once lived, in a place called Sugarland, a little burg in the sticks of Maryland."

"Whaddyamean 'once lived?'"

"Well—and this gets pretty weird—this Margaret Rollins has been a missing person for almost a year. A few kooks said she just vanished one day. The Henry Rollins you're so hot for was the postmaster of this little town. A few more kooks say he vanished, too, about 10 days ago. So we tracked the Rollins couple, married for about two years, down to this house in Sugarland, nice little place,

228

and we poke around. No sign of anybody, but we find women's clothes scattered around the bedroom, a couch that had just been slept on, and dirty dishes in the sink, and maybe a dog bowl with water and some kibble scattered on the floor. The coffee pot was still warm. We just missed whoever it was. And we find a scribbled note. Has the name 'Henry' re-written in patterns, and then 'Norfolk,' big and bold, and underlined."

"Okay, that is weird," said Travers, glancing at Agent Cornell, who, hearing only his partner's voice, desperately wanted in on the entire conversation.

"Not much more to tell, really," continued the agent at The Cottage, "only that when we flashed our phony Fed-Stat Federal badges around the local P.D., these two cops overhear us asking about this Margaret Rollins. They get real interested and follow us out to our car, and when we're all out of earshot of the headquarters, the floodgates open. They swear us to secrecy and tell us they'd never admit it publicly, but they saw this Margaret dame supposedly vanish before their eyes—they used those exact words. She was there one minute talking to them, and gone the next. They can't explain it, but they both saw it and both swear to it. They were pretty shook up. It's kinda spooky."

"Yeah, spooky," repeated Travers. Agent Cornell raised a skeptical eyebrow as he tried to piece together what kind of odd conversation was taking place.

"You guys can come on up if you want, but you ain't gonna find 'em here," concluded the operative at the Cottage. "They're gone."

"Okay," said Travers, "hang tight and we'll let you know what we plan to do." He hung up the phone and looked at Cornell.

"Weird," said Travers, trying to figure out how best to retell the story. "Spooky, like, kinda."

"Look, Travers," said Cornell, frustrated and losing patience. "I have to check in with Richmond and the Command Center in Norfolk. 'Spooky,' and 'weird,' ain't gonna cut it with them. What the hell did they say is going on up there?"

Travers recounted the odd tale while Agent Cornell reclined against the booth seatback, listening, considering the possibilities. They ordered more coffee and two powdered donuts. Another hour passed before Cornell finally called off what would be a tricky border crossing.

"Well, no sense going to Maryland. Let's head back to Norfolk and report in. They're not going to believe this, but with all the talk of the Gosport Ghost Ship, I know one Admiral who'll try to connect the dots."

The two agents paid for their meal and made their way out into the Fuel & Drool parking lot. As they pulled out, headed back to Norfolk, a Nashville Marathon with a freshly dented fender pulled up to the gas pumps. A striking young woman, who was not alone, wheeled the big car around to the far set of pumps. Riding shotgun, a Golden Retriever with his nose stuck out the window, sniffed the essence of sausage gravy wafting out of the diner's kitchen vents.

"Ready for a break, Hank?" asked the young woman. The dog wagged his tail and licked his lips.

Chapter 35

U-4713 ran so quietly on its bank of electric batteries, that the ship was nearly silent, allowing Captain Walther Zoeller a moment to lose himself in a recurring fantasy. He should have been in the control room with his officers, but he was losing confidence in the War, and the Kriegsmarine. The cramped quarters, the awful smell of 50 men who hadn't bathed or changed their clothes in two months, and this suicide mission, were wearing thin. He'd been a good, loyal German sailor and an upstanding member of the Nazi party, but even good sailors get war-weary. He dreamt of the bright blue Mediterranean Sea, a little villa by the water's edge, and abundant fresh air and sunshine.

Six months earlier, after he had torpedoed a ship just off Melilla, Morocco, carrying 221 European refugees, he went topside. He surveyed the smoldering wreckage and the fire-blackened bodies floating in the azure waters of the Mediterranean. After ordering his machine gunners to mow down any survivors where they floated and begged for mercy—men, women and children—he noted how beautiful the sea and landscape were. He wondered how lovely the Spanish city would be as a place for second home. This was his favorite mental getaway and he was enjoying luxuriating in the particularly vivid fantasy until he was shaken by a loud knock at the door.

"Captain!" yelled First Watch Officer Oberleutnant Dengler through the closed door.

"Ja, Dengler, come in," he said, disgusted with the interruption.

"Sir, you're not going to believe this," said the Officer excitedly as he stepped into the Captain's quarters, "but we received a transmission from …from the USS Eldridge."

"How? The American warship?"

"Yes, Sir!"

"But our antennae buoy is retrieved, correct?"

"Yes, but we keep the Langwellen on and the transmission came in faintly. We verified the codes. Apparently we have a man on board the Eldridge."

Zoeller sat up, fully awakened from his daydream. "Ja, and just what did this man have to report?"

Before Dengler could read the transmission, Lieutenant Luca Adams tapped on the doorframe.

"Sir, Adams reporting."

"Okay, Dengler, Adams. Come inside, close the door." The three men found space to sit in the cramped quarters. "So, Lieutenant Adams, welcome aboard." The Captain did not appear to be all that happy to see him.

"Thank you, Sir."

Zoeller faked a smile. "I received your Omega clearance, Adams," he said. Adams knew the Captain was breaking protocol in sharing that information in front of the First Watch Officer; Omega Clearance was the most confidential order that could be given to a German ship's captain. It was supposed to be known only to the captain and one other referenced individual, in this case the spy Luca Adams. He looked at the floor, stumbling for a response.

"Come now, Adams," said Zoeller. "Now that you have authority over all my weapons, why don't you tell us what you would like to target with your little experimental torpedo?" Adams remained silent.

"You're worried about Officer Dengler?" asked Zoeller. "Don't be. In fact he was just about to share a message from one of your colleagues aboard the USS Eldridge. You spies are getting sloppy."

Adams raised an eyebrow, but was too well trained to be rattled by an arrogant and angry ship captain.

"Go ahead Dengler. You were saying?"

"Yes, Sir," said Dengler, confused, having never heard of the Omega Clearance. He'd been a recipient of the Captain's sarcasm and displeasure too many times to count, and recognized that Adam's was the Captain's new target. "Here it is word for word, Sir. The sender repeated it four times, so we're quite certain." Dengler cleared his throat.

"Kriegsmarine, Crossroads East. USS Eldridge in trouble. High seas. Headed for Norfolk Navy Yard. Two and a half hours, ETA, 6 p.m. Eastern Standard Time, if we survive the storm."

"And that was it."

"What do you think, Adams?" asked Zoeller. "Apparently the Kriegsmarine has a lot of faith in you. By the way, did you enjoy your stay in Myrtle Beach? You look quite relaxed and like you've had plenty of fresh air and sunshine."

Adams ignored the derision. He understood the Captain's sensitivity regarding the Omega Clearance, which essentially relieved Zoeller of his primary function as gunner-in-chief, reducing the Captain to little more than an Operations Officer and chauffeur.

"If it makes you feel any better, Captain Zoeller, no, I did not particularly enjoy laboring in the fields and the malaria-filled swamps and backwaters of

South Carolina. And, further, I am interested in firing only one weapon, the G7e-UP1, which you so kindly took into possession a few hours ago. You may do what you wish with the other 19 torpedoes."

"Thank you so very much, Adams," said the Captain, still annoyed. "I ask again, do you have a target in mind?"

"I do now," said Adams. "We will sail into the Chesapeake Bay, then up the Potomac River, and launch the weapon at the Jefferson Davis Highway."

The reality of Adams' statement set in, as Zoeller looked at an unfurled nautical chart on his desk. Using his index finger he traced the Potomac River inland. "You mean to—"

"Yes. Hit Washington, the capitol of the United States of America. Specifically, The Pentagon, and with any luck, we take the Weiss Haus with it."

Zoeller stood, and took a step toward Adams. "And do you think they will throw a parade for us, allowing us to sail up to their front door?"

"No," said Adams coolly, "but the storm will buy us cover, and buy us time."

Zoeller looked at him like he was mad, even though some of what he said made sense.

"Captain Zoller, we can detonate this weapon within 1000 feet of the Pentagon, which is conveniently less than two miles from the Capitol building. We can launch, and be safely out of harm's way 20 minutes later, without ever surfacing. If all goes well, they'll never know we were there until a good portion of Washington D.C. is leveled. Even then, those that survive won't know what hit them. This is the weapon that will change the course of history."

"Excuse me, Sir," said Dengler, daring to ask. "What weapon?"

Adams smiled, knowing it was pointless to bother with protocols any longer. He'd shared a few meals with Dengler and liked and trusted him. "Oberleutnant, we have a nuclear weapon on board; an A-bomb, which has been loaded in aft torpedo tube three. We are going to win this war with one massive strike at the heart and brain of the enemy."

Zoeller, warming to the idea of ending the war, wouldn't show his growing delight at the prospect of launching a nuclear weapon. He opened the door, signaling the end of the meeting. He was, after all, still Captain.

Adams looked at the First Watch Officer. "Oberleutnant Dengler. I don't need to tell you how sensitive this information is, and I trust what you've heard here will not leave this room?"

Dengler nodded.

"1800 hours," said Zoeller, looking at his watch, while making mental calculations. "Ready all the torpedo tubes and sound Gefechtsstatione. I want Combat Stations fully operational by 1700. With any luck we should beat the Eldridge to Norfolk, take care of her, and then on to more pressing matters. I'll be in the control room in a moment. Tell the Navigator to set a course for…" he looked at the chart, "37.09 North by 75.98 West. We'll pray for calm seas when we reach those coordinates. We will have to surface at some point sooner, rather than later."

"Yes, Captain!" said Dengler, who moved to ready a crew for a likely battle less than three hours away. He left with a sense of excitement and dread at the coming hours, wondering just exactly what a nuclear weapon might do to a city such as Washington, D.C. He shuddered at the prospect.

*****

When a second bolt of lightning struck the Eldridge, the already rattled crew jumped, including the five officers on the bridge. Sustained winds of 40 mph with gusts up to 75 mph were far more than the ship was designed to sustain for long periods of time.

The ship cruised 20 miles off the Delmarva Peninsula, to avoid shoals and shallow water. The open seas of the Atlantic roiled and heaved with mountainous swells like no one on board had ever witnessed, except for Captain Marcus Hammond. The seasoned Captain outwardly remained cool, but knew the dangers of capsizing were all too real.

"How long before we can make our turn, Navigator?" asked Hammond.

"Dead reckoning says we should clear the shoals off Cape Charles in about 90 minutes, Captain."

"I'm not sure we can stand 90 more minutes of this," said Hammond, under his breath, but loud enough to be heard by his officers. He was sorry for saying it. "Okay, look, this is bad, but I've been through worse. Once we make the turn and head into Norfolk, we're protected, and we'll be fine. Officer of the Deck, you have the Conn. I'm going below to check on our Exec, who seems to have forgotten to take his happy pills."

Hammond left through the companionway, an interior hatch that snaked down some 40 feet to the decks below and the officers' quarters. He knocked on Executive Officer Moore's door.

"Moore!" he yelled. No answer. He knocked again. "Moore! This is Captain Hammond." He tried the door latch and found it to be locked. Reaching into his pocket, he produced a master key, one of only three on board the ship. It would open every lockable door from bow to stern. When he made his way into Moore's quarters, he found the officer unconscious, sprawled out on the floor.

"Moore!" yelled Hammond, reaching down to take the XO's pulse. When he picked up the officer's limp arm, a hand-held transmitter microphone fell from the unconscious man's hand to the floor. Hammond followed the cord to a small, patched-together radio covered with German language settings.

"No..." said Hammond, in disbelief, trying to deny what his eyes were telling him. He slapped Moore on the face in an attempt to awaken him, "Moore! Come on! Wake up!"

The XO's eyes fluttered open to see his Captain just a foot away. Hammond, cradling the ill man's head, helped him sit up. He was able to maneuver the Exec to a chair, then pour him a glass of water from a steel sink.

"Drink this," he said. "You're dehydrated. It smells like you puked up the last three weeks of meals in here." Hammond heard voices in the gangway, and called out.

"Get me a medic, on the double!" he yelled.

Moore, coming around, spotted the radio on his bunk, and the handset still on the floor. He struggled to come up with an explanation.

"My hobby," said Moore, nodding toward the German shortwave. "I like radios. I was trying to pick up some music."

"I see," said Hammond, not yet willing to confront the officer with his suspicions. "Any luck?"

Moore looked at him, not understanding.

"Any luck reaching anyone?" said Hammond. "You must have been trying to make a request? You were still holding the handset when I found you lying here on the floor."

Moore wouldn't make eye contact with his superior. "No, Sir. No luck."

A medic and a crewman stuck their heads in the door to find Moore sitting, weak and unmoving, while the Captain stood sizing up his XO, a man about whom he knew very little.

"Take Officer Moore to sickbay," said Captain Hammond. As the seamen were helping the wobbly officer out into the gangway, Hammond spoke again.

"Put three guards on him, and as soon as he's medically cleared throw him in the brig."

*****

As Moondawg predicted, the train heading into Norfolk did slow as it came toward the rail yard, and rounded a 60-degree curve. Henry Rollins could clearly see the lights of the City, and of the Navy Yard along the waterfront. The one place from which he'd worked so hard to distance himself was suddenly coming back into sharp focus.

"Well, Moondawg," said Rollins. "It's been a pleasure, but here's where I make my exit."

"Okay, young man," said the traveler. "Best of luck. Where you headed, anyway?"

Rollins considered what, if anything, he might tell him; he wasn't sure why, but he trusted him. The problem was he was having trouble answering the question for himself.

"I'm trying to get back to a girl I miss very much," said Rollins, finally. "My wife, to be more specific." He stood by the open boxcar door, waiting for the train to slow a little.

"Oh, a girl," said Moondawg. "Well, now that makes sense." He chuckled. "I had me a girl once. I'da jumped trains fer her, too."

Rollins smiled as he thought about the last 10 days and all he'd survived. He knew that as hard as it was on him, it would have been just as hard, or harder, on his beloved.

As the train slowed again and the edge of the rail yard was in sight, he made his move, hoping for the softest landing he might manage.

"Good luck, Moondawg," said Rollins as he jumped from the slowing train, hitting the ground, curling into a roll. Moondawg howled and waved, as the train rumbled on ahead.

When the dust settled, Henry stood, brushed himself off, and considered what his next move might be. *Now what, Margaret?* Not quite knowing what else to do he walked slowly, almost aimlessly toward the City. A road running parallel to the tracks seemed as good a place as any to put one foot in front of another. A half-mile down the road he had a much clearer view of the train depot. When he heard distant shouting he lay prone to peer through the tall weeds.

"Dammit," he said, as he saw a small army of uniformed and plainclothes deputies with flashlights searching boxcars, and even stopping passengers getting off the trains. They were clearly on a manhunt, and he had a hunch for whom they might be searching. *I guess hitching another train is out of the question.'* He sat and put his head in his hands.

"Okay, Margaret. You were always the practical one. Now what?" A light wind blew carrying the strong aroma of the sea, triggering memories about his time both on and off the Eldridge.

"You hate boats, Henry," said Margaret's voice as his mind flashed to their last night together in Princeton. He had so nonchalantly kissed her, and hurried out the door their last moment together. He now regretted their speedy goodbye. He'd been so excited at the thought of working with his hero, Einstein, he'd barely noticed the beautiful woman who had to stop herself from begging him not to go.

"I'm so sorry, Margaret," he said, holding back tears for them both as the hopelessness he was feeling threatened to overwhelm him as his wretched journey dragged on. After all he'd been through, he was still not one step closer to wherever it was he was trying to go.

"Be strong, my love," she said loud and clear through the vastness of time and space, her whisper carried on a salty breeze.

"I do hate boats. You were right about that," he said, the germ of an idea forming. "Maybe now more than ever. If a train is out of the question, maybe…maybe I could try stowing away? Head up the Chesapeake Bay toward Baltimore? There must be boats headed north?" He detested the plan even as he said it aloud. He'd hoped to never see another boat as long as he lived, but in light of the searches taking place on land, he thought he'd give the sea one more chance to redeem itself.

I came here by boat, maybe I can go home by boat? "Okay, Henry, your sea legs ready?"

The early morning hours were warm and clear, with only a gentle breeze occasionally moving the scent of jasmine down the dusty road toward town. When he looked up at the fading sea of stars nestled in the deep purple blanket of the early morning sky, he thought about Hitch pointing out Polaris, teaching him about navigation. He had in turn taught Hitch about the Underground Railroad, which started before the Civil War, and how the abolitionists used the same constellation to guide their formerly enslaved African charges to freedom.

The vision was so lovely, and he was so exhausted, he lay in the tall grass and slept.

Chapter 36

In another universe, one not too far away from Henry Rollins, the sky was not clear at all. The home to which Henry Rollins was so desperately trying to return, was under attack from the Germans and the Japanese, mostly on foreign soil. For the first time months, something other than World War II took the top headlines in the Nation's newspapers. A potentially vicious attack on the homeland, one from the elements, had the Nation's attention.

H5, the fifth storm of the Atlantic hurricane season, raged in Rollins' home universe, and covered some 400 square miles of sea. Its great eye was moving toward landfall, unwavering, with Norfolk as its target. The storm had wobbled east and west, and slowed down and sped up, but for the previous three hours its line of trajectory was straight toward the busiest Naval port in the world.

Captain Hammond, below deck on the USS Eldridge, sat at Executive Officer Moore's desk, looking at the German shortwave and wondering just who his new XO really was. The radio was turned on with the volume quite low, but loud enough so that he heard occasional squawking and static and even a few random German words. He fumbled with a few knobs and managed to increase the volume, just as his third in command, stuck his head in the door.

"We're between rain and wind bands, thankfully," said the Officer. "But who knows for how long?" The officer took a few steps into the XO's quarters. "Umm, Sir. I hear you're going to throw our Exec into the brig once the Doc clears him?"

"I'm afraid so," said Hammond. "Found him passed out from sea-sickness with this goddamned German transmitter still in his hand. Who the hell knows who he was trying to reach and what he was transmitting? Anybody on board speak German?"

The Officer thought for a moment and shook his head. "Beats me," he said while holding on tightly to the bulkhead as another large swell tipped the boat

20 degrees. "Those mountains of water out there are killing us. A full third of the crew is just as green as Moore. If we had to sound General Quarters, we'd be in trouble."

Hammond dialed the shortwave's tuner hoping to find something other than static, but had no luck. He unplugged it from the wall, wrapped the cord around it and gathered up the small, portable antennae.

"Take this to the radio room and let them have a look," he said dumping it in the Officer's hands. "I probably won't be able to get anything out of Moore. He was barely conscious when they dragged him out of here. He's a damned Kraut spy, you know? I had my suspicions early on, but decided I had to be wrong. I hope the bastard never wakes up."

"I'll get the boys to look at this and see you back on the bridge?"

"Yes, after I check on our guest."

*****

Norfolk, Virginia
Confederate States of America
3:15 p.m. August 23, 1943

The C.S.A.'s Norfolk Command Center was buzzing with new information coming in from around the State of Virginia. Agents in Lynchburg reported just missing their mark, suspecting Rollins had hopped a train toward Norfolk. Agents Travers and Cornell reported in as C.S.A. General Hannaford finished up a phone call to Richmond.

"Yes, Sir. I understand," said Hannaford, phone cradled under his chin. He was speaking to the C.S.A Attorney General. "We're working around the clock. We'll find them. Yes, Sir. We'll talk as soon as I have new information. Goodbye."

"The Sugarland, Maryland, lead was a dead end," said Cornell, walking toward the General and a few of the staff, "except for the undercover Maryland operatives finding a scribbled note that read 'Henry' and 'Norfolk?' in the couple's home. They verified the woman in the photograph as Margaret Rollins. Here's where it gets really weird. This Margaret Rollins has been listed as a Missing Person for around 11 months, and Henry Rollins for 8 days."

"That's not all," said Travers to General Hannaford. "Local P.D. in Maryland swears they saw this Rollins woman disappear into thin air."

"You're not going to start with the ghost stories, are you?" asked Hannaford, sitting, exhausted.

"Others in town saw this Henry Rollins vanish, too," continued Travers. "Rollins is, or was, the Post Master of a tiny little three-man Post Office in Sugarland."

238

"What about Princeton?" asked the General, head in his hands. "Rollins I.D.s all had him from Princeton, New Jersey."

"There's no connection to Princeton, New Jersey, from either of them."

"Disappeared, huh?" asked the General. "Right before their eyes?"

"That's what they said."

"I know a particular Admiral who'd be eager to hear those details," said Hannaford in reference to Admiral Josiah Brown III. The decorated Confederate Navy Admiral had been telling anyone who'd listen about the vanishing Gosport Ghost Ship, his great-grandfather and the mysterious man who'd vanished in the sea a week earlier.

Hannaford sighed, again.

"It's tough enough to mount a serious manhunt without adding in a magic show. Look, I am *not* losing Rollins—who the hell knows what happened to Hickok—especially if he's headed back here. I want you two to head up an undercover unit to canvas the streets here in Norfolk. I want 10 men on it. Keep an eye out for either of the Rollins pair, Henry or Margaret—and for Hickok, too. Put a bounty on them all, $5,000 a head."

In a day where the average annual salary for an agent was $3,500, the bounty was impressive.

"Yes, Sir," said Travers, who would set about recruiting a handful of Norfolk P.D. detectives into covert service.

Travers looked around the room, sizing up the handful of local cops wandering in and out. A tall, thin plainclothes detective stood near the coffee pot and was mid sip when he felt a tap on his shoulder.

"You're working for the Southern Cross now," said Travers instantly deputizing a surprised detective who made the mistake of standing still just a moment too long. "Find me eight more good men with unmarked cars and we'll get this show on the road."

*****

After a long, late lunch at the Fuel & Drool, paid for with counterfeit C.S.A. money, Margaret and Hank set back out on the road headed to Norfolk. Margaret found curious differences in the lay of the land and the general attitude of the place. She felt as if she were in a foreign land, which she realized, she was. Though mostly unfamiliar with the drive toward Norfolk, even in her own world, she noted more signs of poverty here than she expected. Confederate flags flew everywhere, the roads were in bad shape, and the people and places she could see as they sped down the road looked like pictures she'd seen from the 1920s and the Great Depression.

After a few pit stops for both her and Hank, they hit the outskirts of Norfolk in the early evening. The city had energy, and had plenty of humanity moving to and fro, but it looked chaotic, unkempt, as if something of great importance was happening.

"This doesn't look too good, Hank," said Margaret, spotting flashing police lights, and a roadblock ahead. "Keep cool, Dog," she said, scratching Hank behind the ears in what was really a move to calm her own nerves. She slowed the car, took a deep breath, and rolled down the window. Two officers with flashlights came to either side of her Marathon.

"Yes, officer?" she said flashing a pretty smile and adding a hint of a southern accent.

"Good evening, Ma'am," said the Virginia State Trooper standing by the driver's side of the car. "Traveling alone?"

"Well," she smiled, "not quite. I have a good friend with me." She nodded toward Hank, who looked agitated.

"Where are you headed?"

"To see my Aunt in Norfolk," said Margaret. "What's going on? Any trouble ahead?"

"Where are you coming from, Ma'am?"

"Oh, I live in the northern part of the State."

"Yeah? Where exactly?"

Margaret panicked, but didn't show it. "Oh it's a little backwoods four corners you've never heard of."

"Try me," said the Trooper.

"It's called Barn Swallow Gulch. Not too far from the border."

"Do you have any I.D.?"

Margaret smiled, and contrived embarrassment. "I don't. I left my purse at my Aunt's house. That's why I'm headed back here."

The Trooper shined his flashlight around the car's interior, and then back in Margaret's face.

"Have you seen any hitchhikers or a pair of men walking along the road?"

"Why, no. I haven't."

The officer pulled a worn, folded sheet of paper from his pocket. He opened it and handed it to her, shining his light so she might see it clearly.

"These are the two men we're looking for. If you see either of them, report it immediately to any law enforcement officer."

Margaret stared in shock at a pencil sketch of her husband, whose name 'Henry Rollins' was neatly typeset in bold, black letters underneath his likeness. Shock turned to indescribable joy as she realized that she and Dr. Einstein had been correct to follow their hunches. It was the first indication in more than a week that her husband might still be alive and might be nearby. She fought back tears and emotions, handing the wanted flyer back to the trooper.

"I will do that," she said. "What did they do, anyway?"

"Don't worry about that, Ma'am. Just know that they're Con-Fed's Most Wanted. Be careful. Move along."

"Thank you, Officer," said Margaret, fighting tears that would seem out of place had the trooper seen them. She rolled up the window and eased the car forward. Her hands trembled on the wheel as she looked in her rearview mirror to see the Troopers stopping the next car in line. She glanced over at her co-pilot and gently grabbed a hunk of his beautifully soft mane.

"Hank, I think we've found your daddy."

*****

Atlantic Ocean
Coastal Waters Delmarva Peninsula
United States of America
5:30 p.m. September 10, 1943

Only U-Boat Captain Walther Zoeller, a few Nazi officers, and German Spy Phillip Moore knew of the potential meeting between the German Kriegsmarine and the U.S. Navy, now less than an hour away. The Eldridge's Captain, Marcus Hammond, having found the portable German Langwellen longwave radio, suspected something was afoot, but had little to go on. He hoped his barely conscious Executive Officer, Moore, might help shed some light on any potentially unpleasant missions underway.

"Moore," yelled Hammond, shaking the handcuffed and prone body of a man he now fully suspected was a German spy. Moore groaned and kept his eyes closed.

"How is he, Doc?" asked Hammond, turning to his Chief Medical Officer who was busy tending to an unending parade of seasick and, temporarily, worthless sailors.

"How does he look?" answered the Doctor with a sarcastic snarl. "This goddamned storm you're driving us through has most of the ship green and puking, including Mr. Moore."

Hammond ignored the sarcasm. He had been used to it coming from high-ranking officers in high stress situations; he was guilty of it himself. It was the thing he liked most about the U.S. Navy, it had a sense of humor, though he wasn't in a laughing mood.

"Come on, sit up!" yelled Hammond, prodding the sick officer, who was trying to will away consciousness. Hammond propped him up in the bunk and slapped him in the face hard enough to get his attention.

"Moore! Wake up!"

"Fich dich," mumbled Moore, eyes still closed.

"What was that?" asked Hammond.

"Fuck you, Sir," answered Moore, opening his eyes and looking at his handcuffed wrists.

"Oh, I see," said Hammond. "Now that you're found out, you're a little upset?"

"Essen scheisse!" said Moore, coughing.

"Sorry," said Hammond. "I don't speak Kraut."

Without a hint of a German accent, Moore looked at the Captain and translated. "It means 'eat shit.'"

Hammond turned red with anger and would have landed a punch square in the center of Moore's blue-eyed, Aryan face had the Doctor not shook his head, reminding him to stay calm.

"I hope we survive this storm," said Hammond, "because if we do, I will personally attend your hanging, and then celebrate the date each year as a kind of holiday, as I live out my long, happy life with my family and friends."

"Ich ficke deine mutter."

Hammond didn't need a translation. "You know, Moore, I might persuade a military tribunal to give you life in prison, if you tell me who you were talking to, and what you told them."

This time Moore was either out of insults or overcome by a fresh wave of nausea. He said nothing, but closed his eyes, and began mumbling incoherently.

"Kriegsmarine..." he whispered. "The Kriegsmarine will come and..."

"And what?"

"...und spule deine verdammten boot auf den grund, dann meer. Sie warten auf sie sebst, wie wir sprechen. 1800 stunden!"

Moore collapsed, crumpling into the bunk.

"Moore!" yelled Hammond, but he could not be roused.

"What the hell did he just say?" asked the Captain, looking around sickbay for someone, anyone, with a clue.

A loud thump, followed by the sound of bending metal, reverberated through the ship as the power and lights in the sickbay flickered on and off. The entire 300-foot length of the ship rose into the air riding a 40-foot swell, then listed 90-degrees to port, and slammed back down into the angry Atlantic. As the ship twisted and turned like a bathtub toy, medical supplies, sick sailors, the Doctor, and even the Captain himself crashed into one another in a great pile of humanity and medical debris against the bulkhead.

When the ship righted itself, the power and lights flickered, then went permanently off. In the pitch black, a medic with enough brains and strength left in him, found an emergency light and illuminated the sick bay. Those who could, got up from the deck and tried to get their bearings; others lay on the floor, crying out, unable to stand. The medic with the flashlight came to Captain Hammond's side.

"Sir, are you okay?"

"I've been better, Sailor."

The seaman helped Hammond to his feet. "Ah, Sir. I studied a little German in school. What I think the Exec said was something like "we're going to send

242

your goddamned boat to the bottom of the sea. They're waiting for us, even as we speak." I think he also said something about '1800 hours.'"

The lights of the sickbay fluttered and then blinked back to life. The sickbay looked as though a Kansas twister had come through. At the bottom of two overturned gurneys the lifeless body of Executive Officer Moore lie contorted and unmoving. Blood ran from his nostrils, black against his almost white face. The fall had killed him when his head struck the bulkhead, and Captain Hammond was glad of it. He looked at his watch. It read 5:35.

"1800 hours is 25 minutes away," he spoke aloud, helping a few of his battered crew back to their feet.

After Moore's arrest and death, the Eldridge's Lieutenant Commander, Alexander Atkins, became the acting XO. When Atkins flew into sickbay, he saw the same kind of chaos he'd seen elsewhere on the ship.

"My God, Captain Hammond!" he yelled, moving to help steady the still wobbly ship's Captain. "Are you okay?"

"Everyone keeps asking me that," said Hammond, shaking off the unsteadiness and clearing the fuzz from his head. "Yes, I'm fine Atkins. How's my ship and crew? You're acting XO, by the way."

"I heard you had Mr. Moore in the brig, so I assumed…"

Hammond glanced down toward the body of Moore, and shook his head.

"What the hell happened?" asked Atkins, seeing Moore's lifeless form.

"The storm is what happened and is still happening," said Hammond.

"That's not good," said Atkins, still looking at Moore's body.

"Don't feel sorry for him," snapped Hammond. "He was a damned spy. Sold us out, too."

Atkins, shocked, remembered he had a message. "About that…Sir, I came from the radio room, and just before that wave hit, the boys had a signal on that Kraut radio you gave me. It was all in German, but it appeared to be East Coast weather reports repeating themselves. Then we heard talk between…" he dared not say it aloud.

"Spit it out, Atkins," said Hammond.

"We think it was between two U-boats, and at least one of them is apparently headed for Norfolk. Then all hell broke loose, the radio flew off the table and smashed against the bulkhead. It's beyond the Radio Room's ability to repair it. They said it's like nothing they've ever seen. Some sort of new technology, and it's done. Toast."

The Lieutenant's report confirmed it. Hammond suddenly had more than just the storm on his mind.

"Atkins," he said calmly. "Sound General Quarters. I'll be on the Bridge in 10 minutes. I'm going to see for myself what's left of my ship and crew."

"Aye, aye, Sir!" said the Lieutenant, stepping over bodies and rubble on the sickbay deck. The Boatswain's whistle sounded throughout the ship preceding the call to General Quarters, preparation for imminent battle. Those men who could still stand, or in some cases crawl, headed for their battle stations.

Chapter 37

Norfolk, Virginia
7:15 p.m. August 23, 1943

The C.S.A.'s Navy Yard at Norfolk buzzed with energy. Some 8,500 Con-Fed Sailors called Norfolk home. The City itself was alive with activity and non-military commerce, too. On a Saturday evening every illegal speakeasy in town would be filled with locals and the few sailors that weren't on duty.

Prohibition may have been the law of the land in the C.S.A., but it was the least enforced of all the bad legislation the country had dreamed up since 1866 when it drafted a new constitution. This purposeful lack of enforcement prevented the kind of trouble known elsewhere in the Multiverse where governments failed miserably in their attempts at prohibition. In the C.S.A., temperance was all but ignored, and the bar business flourished in a 'don't ask and don't tell' atmosphere.

After a brisk 30-minute walk, Henry Rollins managed to hide among the crowds and make it into the town center, nearing the waterfront and the commercial wharf just 20 blocks further. He rounded the corner of a busy street, and, quite by accident, found himself nearly on the front steps of the main headquarters of the Norfolk City Police Department & Detention Center. When he saw an 'out of order sign' on the pay telephone near its front entrance, he crossed the road as quickly as he could. He made another quick turn and found a quieter street that seemed to be headed toward the waterfront.

"Excuse me?" The young man's voice coming from behind startled him, and he dared not look.

"Excuse me, I'm just after a light," said the voice again. This time Henry slowed his pace and glanced over his shoulder, without really seeing the man.

"Sorry, don't smoke."

"You don't smoke?" asked the man disbelieving. "Who doesn't smoke? Everybody smokes." It was true. Most of the C.S.A.'s population of males over the age of 14 smoked. Tobacco and cotton were the C.S.A.'s biggest crops, and cigarettes, Tennessee whiskey, and Kentucky bourbon, its biggest vices. "Ok, then," said the man, giving in. Both men continued to walk, the stranger a few paces behind. "You a G-man? A Navy man?" he asked, picking up his pace.

Henry tried his best to ignore him. "Nope, just a…just a civilian." He could hear the man behind him run a few steps to catch up. He walked, uninvited, directly beside him.

"What are you doing down here?" said the stranger, as Henry finally got a look at him. He was tall, but no more than a teenager, his face stuck somewhere between 16 and 25; it was hard to tell as he looked a little underweight, and not terribly well. Though Henry felt sorry for him, it put him at ease to see youth, and that his clothes were threadbare. This was not a cop, or anyone who cared about anything other than, at the moment, getting a light.

"Just wandering around," said Henry.

"Me, too," said the boy. They walked together in awkward silence for 10 paces. "You got any money?"

"I don't." Henry caught on that the kid was just hustling. Cigarettes, booze, spare change, a light, he had nothing and therefore was after anything.

"I'm trying to get the hell out of Norfolk, to be honest with you," said Henry, and he wasn't lying.

"That'd be nice," said the boy as they approached the Wharf District. "You gonna swim?" he asked.

"Hope not. Tried that once. I'd like to find a boat out of here. Any ideas?"

"Ha," said the youth. "I tried that once myself. Got caught and spent three months in Juvy."

"Juvy?" asked Henry.

"Juvenile Detention."

"Whaddya mean 'got caught?'"

"Stowing away. Trying to get to Philadelphia."

"Philadelphia?" Henry stopped walking and turned to face the youth. "That's exactly where I'm headed," said Henry, "or at least that's where I'd like to be headed."

"Well, good goddamn luck," said the boy. "Those big freighters are locked up tight as a dicks' hatband."

"Good one," Henry said, containing a chuckle. They eyed one another for a moment and the boy broke the silence.

"You know you're gonna get your ass whooped out here? The wharf is dangerous at night. Name's Jacob. Friends call me Jack."

"Henry," answered Rollins, extending his hand. "My friends call me…well, they call me 'Henry.' It's kind of funny, but my wife started calling me 'Hank' right after we got married and I told her it wasn't dignified enough for a college professor, and talked her out of it. Secretly, I used to like hearing her say it."

245

He found himself completely at ease with this stranger, in the same way he'd been with Hitch, and with Cecil in Southwood. His friends from Princeton and those he knew in New York were never that comfortable with strangers. He liked that about these Southerners.

"I'm Henry." They both shared a smile. "What are you doing out here if it's so dangerous, Jack?" asked Rollins.

"I dunno. Trying to get something to eat. You looked about my age, a little older, seemed safe enough. I was hoping you had a couple of dollars. Anyway, two is better than one out here, that's for sure."

"So, ships go up North from here? What about the border?"

"Sure. All the time. Philly, New York. Them Yankees love our T&B."

"T&B?" asked Rollins. The youth looked at him strangely, as if it was something he should have known.

"Tobacco and booze," said Jack. Whiskey to be more specific. And we love their money."

"Anybody hire out ship's hands that you know of?"

"Yeah," said Jack. "On the wharf, but you gotta know your stuff. They don't hire no landlubbin' greenies, and you're not exactly a big fella."

A loud conversation caught their attention. It was coming from down the block, on a side street adjacent to the darkened wharf. A group of men, dockers, were arguing by the front door of the Rum Runner's Tap House, a bar whose entrance was lit by a single yellow lamp. Henry and Jack stayed in the shadows.

"The Wharf Rats are at it again," said Jack. "All they do is get drunk, fight, go to work, get drunk, fight – it never ends with them."

"Sounds like you know these guys' habits pretty well?"

"You could say that. The big ugly one with the beard – that's my ol' man."

A warm breeze blew a foul-smelling stench down the street. It came from centuries of seafood processed on the water's edge. Two trawlers steamed into port setting the local seagulls into a frenzy of screaming as they dove for scraps.

"Maybe a fishing boat is more my speed?" asked Henry, watching the lights of the two boats maneuver to the dockside.

"Maybe," answered Jack courteously, not believing for a minute that this obvious city slicker could work his way around a fishing trawler.

"I think I could pilot that boat," said Henry.

"You?" Jack's doubt in his companion's maritime skills was now clearly evident. "You ever piloted a boat before in your life?" he added with a condescending laugh.

"Yes, actually. Quite a big boat, to be truthful."

The two men stayed away from the nearby ruckus and looked out over the relative quiet of the wharf at night. The black ocean, just beyond, beckoned to them both; it called to Henry Rollins, whispering of home and of his Margaret. Jack, too, heard its voice and promises of escape to a better life.

Special Agents Travers and Cornell met with eight fresh recruits in a small room just down the hall from the Command Center. The eight recruits would team up and disperse, hitting the streets of Norfolk to see what or who they could find. It was summer, but each of the detectives wore a light jacket to conceal their handguns and shoulder holsters. They tried not to look like cops, but the effort was mostly futile.

"We're looking for any one of three," said Cornell. "Henry Rollins and Wild Bill Hickok, who you already know about, and as of this morning, Margaret Rollins, who we believe may be on her way to Norfolk. She may already be here."

He tacked updated facsimiles of the three C.S.A.'s Most Wanted on the wall, and then handed them each a single composite that they could carry with them for reference. Margaret's picture had been added, though the enlarged photo was not clear. At the bottom of each handbill, in big bold letters, an ominous offer reinforced the C.S.A.'s intentions and growing frustrations: "Wanted: Dead or Alive $5,000 each."

"Agent Travers and I will take the waterfront from the wharf to the Park," said Cornell. "The rest of you split up. Start on the outskirts of town, and work your way back to the center. We'll meet back here in three hours. Remember, ideally we want them alive for questioning, but do not let them slip away. Shoot to kill if you must."

Less than a mile from the Police Headquarters, Margaret and Hank wove their way through the busy cityscape looking for Henry, while trying to keep a low profile. It wasn't easy. Pedestrians and other drivers looked at the lone woman driving a car, which was not unheard of, but was still far from the norm. Most in the C.S.A. could not afford a car, and it was even more unusual to see a woman alone, at night, behind the wheel.

"I think they're looking at us, Hank," said Margaret, tipping her head low. "Maybe we should ditch the car. Can't afford to be too obvious." Hank wagged his tail, eager to get out and explore this new place filled with exotic smells and sounds.

She wheeled the big Marathon down a darkened side street, and fished Hank's leash from the backseat. After clipping him in, she opened her handbag, and recounted the handful of counterfeit bills.

"Two hundred dollars."

Hank sniffed at her open handbag paying close attention to a handkerchief crumpled at the bottom. When they exited the car, she locked it and placed the keys inside the purse. They stood together on the sidewalk. She was suddenly very glad to have Hank with her. Hank sniffed at each passing breeze. Beyond any human's ability to detect, but easy for the dog with his 300 million olfactory sensors, the breeze carried the scent of some delightfully rotting seafood and the hint of something or someone else. This second scent in the air was familiar; a scent with which he'd just been recently acquainted.

"Ready? Let's go find daddy."

*****

When the dockers finished their argument and went back inside Rum Runner's, Jack and Henry continued down the darkened street. Henry had no idea why Jack was so intent on avoiding his father, but observing the man's demeanor, even from a distance, he began to understand.

"You really gonna try for a job on a fishing boat?" asked Jack.

"Something like that," said Henry, still not sure what he was planning. "Look, Jack. It's not safe for you to be seen with me," he cautioned using a fatherly tone. "I appreciate the company and the good advice, but this could all go wonky at any moment, and I'd rather not involve you, if possible." They walked a bit further and stood in the shadows not far from the entrance to the tavern.

"You on the run?" asked Jack.

"Something like that." He found he was saying that a lot in this place.

"You kill somebody?"

"Not that I know of." The boy looked a little disappointed in Rollins' answer. "Let's just say the C.S.A. has been looking for me and there've been a few close calls."

"Okay. I get it." Jack was used to being dismissed. "You should know the boats are in for the night. They won't go out again until just before daybreak. If I were you, I'd—"

Jack's comment was cut short when a fresh brawl spilled out of Rum Runner's practically at their feet. In a frenzy of yelling, cursing and even some laughter, Jack watched his father, a six-foot, five-inch, 300-lb brute-of-a man, nearly knock a much smaller man's head from his shoulders with a particularly violent punch. When the victim fell to the pavement unconscious, or possibly even dead, his assailant stood over him, staggering from intoxication, and raised his booted heel two feet over the prone man's head, ready to administer a final, execution-style blow.

"No! Pop!" yelled Jack from the shadows, running to the middle of the street. The kid managed to save the docker's life, and save his father from the gallows. Henry took the opportunity to slip unseen from the alley, leaving the familial and social strife to those hardscrabble individuals who lived and worked along the wharf.

As Henry neared the docks, he gazed across the bay to the Navy Yard and Naval Base where he could just see the C.S.N. and its armada of warships. It was a sizeable fleet, some 20 ships he guessed, and probably that many more out to sea.

"A modern Confederate Navy…"

Pondering the 'what-ifs' was more than his brain could handle. At the moment he was glad to be on the other side of the tracks with the fishermen and the dockers, away from a Navy too happy to blow him to bits without so much as a how-do-you-do.

Henry Rollins hated boats. But, for whatever reasons, the universe had conspired against him, presenting boats, or ships, as a means of employment and interdimensional travel whether he hated them or not. He found himself surrounded by vessels of all types and sizes and thought about his half-baked plan to sail to Philadelphia. *I can't get a job on a fishing boat. They'd spot me as a fraud before I opened my mouth.* "But that doesn't mean I couldn't borrow a boat for a few hours," he whispered aloud.

Sticking to the shadows, Henry watched for 30-minutes as the two 45-foot trawlers finished their business, secured their lines. He waited until it seemed that their small crews left for the night. The boats were not particularly safe from vandals and thieves, but thefts were rare and severely punished, so boat owners gave security little thought. When all activity had ceased beyond question, he made his move

Slipping unseen to the nearest of the two boats, Henry climbed aboard and did his best in the dark to look around and size up his potential for actually stealing a boat.

"Keys?" he asked to the air. After searching for 10 minutes, checking ashtrays, and everywhere obvious he gave up. *This is a simple electrical circuit. How hard could a hotwire be?*

With a found flashlight and pair of pliers, Henry Rollins, boat thief, bypassed the ignition switch, twisted two wires together, pressed the red "Start" button, and had the trawler rumbling and gurgling where it sat.

A transmission with a 'Forward.' 'Neutral,' and 'Reverse' setting, too seemed obvious, as did the function of the steering wheel. Operating the boat, he thought, seemed simple enough. A dozen additional levers, switches and gauges operated swing arm hoists, nets, bilge pumps and other non-travel essentials. He wouldn't be doing much fishing, so he didn't concern himself with anything but the basics. The fuel gauge read "3/4," which would have to do. His spirit was bolstered. *If I can manage to get out of port and stay close to shore, I could be in Philly before they know their boat is missing.*

"This will never work," he said a moment later, resting his forehead on his wrist, "I won't know where the hell I'm going, but what else am I going to do? Any ideas, Margaret?"

Chapter 38

Atlantic Ocean
Coastal Waters United States of America
6:01 p.m. September 10, 1943

With nearly half of his crew too sick to perform their duties, and another 25 percent crippled and barely capable, General Quarters aboard the beaten and battered USS Eldridge did not pass muster.

"Damn it," said Captain Hammond to acting XO Atkins, both standing on the bridge. "I've got Kraut U-boats out there, no communications, less than half a crew, and a storm that's getting worse by the minute. Now you're telling me we're not even close to battle ready?"

"You said it yourself, Skipper!" yelled Atkins, screaming to be heard over the howling wind. "Half a crew. That's our biggest problem! We've got gunners missing their loaders, loaders missing their gunners. There're only two engineers out of eight keeping this ship running! We're in a pickle, Sir!"

Hammond closed his eyes and took a breath before he spoke. "Does anybody have any good news?"

The 21-year-old Navigator dared to turn his face away from the radar screen and stuck his pencil in the air, as if to ask permission to speak. "We've just passed the last of the shoals south of the Delmarva Peninsula. I think we can make our easterly turn into Norfolk."

The wild-eyed Captain beamed at his Navigator, a big kid fresh off the farm, who cowered in fear as the Captain ran to him. "You big, beautiful idiot!" screamed Captain Hammond, delighted with the news. "That's the best thing I've heard in weeks!" He slapped the Navigator hard on the shoulder and shouted new orders.

"What are you waiting for? Get us the hell out of here!" The men on the bridge laughed and hurrahed at the news as the helmsman began turning the ship toward the relative safety of the Norfolk Naval Shipyard.

*****

Out in the Atlantic, fifteen miles east/northeast of Virginia Beach, and just

10 miles south of the Delmarva Peninsula, U-4713 was out of time. With its banks of batteries nearly depleted, the craft was slowing. Oxygen levels were falling and it was time to rise to the surface, regardless of what wind-blown fate awaited. The ship had remained submerged some 14 hours, a bit beyond the recommended maximum. Only by running the massive diesel engines could the batteries be recharged, and only by surfacing could fresh air replace the stale, CO_2 laden air the crew of 57 had been breathing for the better part of a day. On the surface H5 awaited the Germans and would test the valor of every man aboard.

The hurricane, which had not passed over them as hoped, sat nearly idle in its forward movement, its massive eye hanging 90 miles due east of Virginia Beach. Sustained 80 Mph winds and gusts over 120 Mph had turned the seas to rolling hills with waves of 50-feet and occasionally higher. Even between wind and rain bands the seas were so agitated that they continued to roil and roll unabated.

Captain Walther Zoeller readied his ship and crew for surface conditions they all knew would be life threatening at worst, and miserable at best. Two crewman operated valves that sent compressed air into the water-filled ballast tanks, changing the submersible ship's neutral buoyancy to one whose natural inclination was to rise slowly to the surface.

With each 20-foot incremental reduction of the ship's depth the effects of H5 became more pronounced, rocking the ship with currents so strong they threatened to roll her. Captain Zoeller may have had his orders to engage the Eldridge, and then turn his weapons over in the Angriffsziel Omega mission to follow, but at that moment his only concerns were getting to the surface, getting fresh air, and running the diesels. If the Eldridge happened to be in the neighborhood, which he had every reason to believe was possible, he'd be happy to launch a torpedo or two while he was at it, but saving his ship and crew would come first.

*****

Norfolk, Virginia
Confederate States of America
Waterfront
9:12 p.m. August 23, 1943

Because Albert Einstein proved that 'time is relative' it is not too big a stretch to consider that events occurring on August 23, 1943 in one world, could happen at the same 'time' as events of September 10, 1943 on another world. "Time is an illusion," said Einstein, and nobody knew that better than Henry and Margaret Rollins.

251

A universe away, at a corresponding point on the nautical map, a steady, light breeze blew on an otherwise quiet Atlantic Ocean. The mysterious breeze was not driven by any particular atmospheric conditions; the winds were metaphysical sympathy pangs for what was happening in a nearby dimension, blowing through an unstable vortex at the mouth of the Chesapeake Bay. These vortices were known to theoretical physicists as an Einstein-Rosen Bridge. The rest of science called them wormholes.

Short of supernova, supervolcano eruptions, and asteroid collisions, hurricanes are the universes' most violent planetary acts. The massive energy created and released, and their reverberations, can travel in unexpected ways and to unexpected places.

An odd, cooler breeze blew across Henry Rollins' face and he welcomed it. The air somehow smelled different—it reminded him of home, though he didn't know why. He breathed it in deeply as he mentally rehearsed his next moves. *Untie the bow and stern lines, ease her into reverse away from the other boat, then into forward. Just like pulling my car off the street and into traffic. Right.* It sounded easy enough, but to do so under the nose of the Police, the Harbor Master, The C.B.I., and the entire Confederate Navy would require a miracle. *Or a distraction*, he thought.

"How can I divert attention away from the dock?"

"I could help you, but you've got to take me with you," said Jack, who'd appeared from the shadows.

Rollins jumped. "Jack! You scared the...well, I'm surprised to see you."

"I figured I'd find you here," he said. The youth took two steps forward and Henry could see his swollen face, bloodied and bruised, with his right eye almost closed.

"Lemme guess...your ol' man?"

"The hell with him," said Jack. "I want nothing to do with him *or* this goddamn place. I don't care where you're going or how you plan to get there, but I'm going with you."

Henry helped Jack on board and they sat, resting against the gunwales of the wooden boat. Henry wanted to help, but had no idea how. He couldn't exactly tell him he was an interdimensional traveler hoping to find a portal back to his home universe. But, when he considered the life the kid was leading on the streets of Norfolk, begging for cigarettes and money, and getting beaten by his drunkard father, how could anything he might get him involved in be any worse.

"We could get caught," said Henry, "both be executed."

"Yeah, so?" asked Jack, without a hint of sarcasm.

"Okay, then," said Henry, finally. "I guess you heard me thinking out loud. I'm going to steal the boat, but need a distraction away from the wharf, maybe even in the heart of the city, something that will draw all the attention away from me."

"You mean, 'us.' Away from us."

"Yes, sorry. Us."

"How about a fire?" asked Jack.

"That could work, but it might only draw the Fire Department. We need something big that would get law enforcement involved, even the Navy if possible."

Jack thought for a moment. "About 10 blocks from here The Office of the Navy sits on top of the tallest building in the city. On the ground floor is the NBC."

"NBC?" asked Rollins.

"The National Bank of the Confederacy. It's got a big plate glass window on the street and its wired to the alarms, or at least I think it almost has to be. A well-placed rock heaved through the glass should set it off. It's a damned important building. That would draw all kinds of attention."

"You could do that?"

"I throw a mean fastball. I was scouted in the 10th grade as a pitcher before my ol' man dragged me out of school." Jack's mind drifted. "The bastard said 'school is a waste of time.' Really he didn't like me bein' smarter than him, and he decided to put an end to any education or talk of college baseball, scholarship or not."

That part of Jack's story resonated with the burgeoning educator buried deep within Professor Henry Rollins, and it infuriated him. "That bastard," he said.

"Tell me about it," agreed Jack, touching his swollen and tender cheek.

"Are you alright?" asked Rollins, getting a good look at the young man's recent battle scars.

"Yeah, this is nothing. I've had much worse."

"Okay, then Jack. We've got a plan. How fast can you get back here after you throw the rock?"

"Three-four minutes, tops. I know a shortcut."

Henry looked out into the Bay and thought for a moment. "I'll keep the boat running, and ready to go," he said. "As soon as you jump on board, we make for the open sea, and hope for the best."

Jack nodded.

"You know this will never work and we'll be dead or in custody before midnight?" suggested Rollins with a grin.

"No doubt about it," agreed Jack.

*****

Norfolk, Virginia
Confederate States of America
9:22 p.m. August, 23 1943

"I know he's here, Hank," whispered Margaret into the dog's ear. He drank from a leaking fire hydrant, then lifted his muzzle and sniffed the air, agreeing.

When the two accidentally found themselves walking by the Norfolk City PD, Margaret led them in a 180-degree turn, and then down a side street. When she passed a boarded-up building plastered with posts bearing her likeness, and offering $5,000 for her capture, she really began to get nervous. She tore one off the wall and folded it in her hand.

"I don't like this, Hank," she said. "Too many people are looking for us." They walked a bit further while she tried to reconcile how she could look for Henry and avoid being spotted herself. No solution came to mind, so they kept walking. On a quieter street, one filled with government office buildings, she and Hank found a bench on which they could rest. The emotion and stress generated during the previous 10 days was again catching up with her and she began to cry. Hank jumped up on the bench and licked her face, sensing her distress. With her head in her hands she didn't see the youth just a few yards behind her, though Hank spotted him and sniffed the air suspiciously. The kid had something in his right hand, about the size of a baseball.

The sound of breaking glass and the piercing alarm that immediately followed, shook her from her trance. She stood quickly, looking desperately left and right, as a crowd began to gather. Hank saw the boy who'd thrown the rock that broke the window of the National Bank of the Confederacy, and barked wildly. He'd been less than 10 feet away, and when he saw the obsessed dog break free from its owner's grip on his leash, he took off. When he did, Hank gave chase of the vandal who was now running as fast as the wind.

"Hank!" screamed Margaret, dropping her handkerchief and the folded wanted poster. She took off after her dog who was chasing this stranger. They wound through alleys and side streets toward the waterfront. They'd pass people moving in the other direction as sirens wailed, and military vehicles and personnel all seemed to be headed toward the center of the commotion. When the wailing of the sirens slowed for moment, she could hear Hank, well out of sight, barking and followed his call. She was two or three blocks behind them, but, thanks to Hank, was keeping tabs on their general location.

She caught a glimpse of the vandal and Hank as they rounded the corner of a dark street on the wharf. When she finally made it to the corner of the two streets she saw the boy in the distance jump aboard a boat, with Hank at his heels, standing on the dock, barking wildly. In the commotion, which was the last things the thieves wanted, the boat made haste away from its mooring, while Margaret called out.

"Hank!"

The dog turned to look at her but wouldn't stop barking, at whoever was on the boat. Margaret, exhausted, moved as quickly as she could toward Hank, who had run the full length of the quarter-mile dock, and could go no further. The boat picked up speed maneuvering out into the harbor, and Margaret's greatest fear was that Hank would jump in the water to try to follow.

"I'm not going to lose you both," she said, wiping away fresh tears, resolute to get him before he did something stupid. "Hank!"

Aboard a 45-foot fishing trawler named, ironically, the *"Almost Home,"* Henry Rollins and his young accomplice, pushed the single diesel motor to its limits helping distance themselves from a crazed Golden Retriever, who'd threatened what was already a risky plan for escape.

"I heard the sirens, and knew you'd hit your target, Jack," said Henry. "Well done!"

Still catching his breath, Jack had trouble responding. "That dog and woman chasing me," he sputtered, "they helped motivate me." He looked behind him and could see the woman and dog still at the edge of the wharf, a quarter mile in the distance.

"Yeah, that dog," agreed Henry. "I didn't see that coming." Henry looked left and right for any signs of the Harbormaster or any other marine law enforcement or C.S.N. activity. *All clear*. With the running lights purposely off, he steered straight for the center of the channel, which would give way to the open sea. When he finally eased up on the throttle, the boat planed, and the motor quieted. An onshore breeze carried the sound of a distant alarm, and then a dog's bark. He turned to look and in a dim light saw a silhouette of what appeared to be a young woman, standing next to the same dog who'd been carrying on. The breeze picked up, gusting, carrying more sound across the flat water. When he heard the woman yell 'Hank' he felt his heart skip a beat, then stop. He throttled the boat to idle and put the transmission into neutral, running to the stern, straining to see.

"It can't be. It can't be…" He strained to look at the small, dimly lit figure. "Margaret?" he asked quietly into the salty breeze.

He ran back to the pilot's seat, found the flashlight and searched for binoculars.

"Come on! Every boat has a pair! Help me look! Jack! Binoculars!"

The two opened every cabinet and possible place on board to stow a pair of binoculars, while the boat drifted further out into the harbor, partly from its own forward momentum aided by the odd, gusting breezes that had been picking up.

"Here! Henry!" yelled Jack, still not sure why his friend was so wildly intent on suddenly finding binoculars. Henry grabbed the pair of beat up, fish-gut-stained binoculars from the boy's hands. He ran back to the transom of the *Almost Home*, focusing on the image. The woman, with the dog who was now secured by a leash, had turned to walk back down the long concrete wharf while Henry struggled to focus.

He recognized the woman as having the same build as his wife. Her hair, her curves, her height. He knew every inch of her body, and thought he even recognized the dress she was wearing, but unless she turned around, he couldn't know for sure. "Come on," he said quietly. "Turn around, please." The woman and dog continued to walk slowly away.

"Jack, throttle up and turn the boat around. We're going back," said Henry, not daring to take his eyes off the departing woman.

"What?" yelled Jack, disbelieving. "Are you crazy? We're free, Henry. We've made it. It's just four hours to Philadelphia!"

Henry put the binoculars down for a second, put his hands around his mouth to create a makeshift megaphone. When the odd wind momentarily quieted, he yelled.

"Margaret!"

Chapter 39

Atlantic Ocean
Chesapeake Bay
United States of America
7:50 p.m. September 10, 1943

When U-4713 broke the surface of the sea for the first time in almost 15 hours, the ship, like Noah's Ark, sat momentarily atop a Mt. Ararat of water, at the peak of a 35-foot swell. Within seconds the 250-foot long U-boat surfed down the face of a mountain of seawater, diving back underwater 25 feet, before rising again. The officers and crew could do little more than hang on.

The U-boat's radar and sonar was all but useless in the storm, and trying to maneuver in the hurricane-ravaged seas was nearly impossible. When the boat resurfaced a second time, Captain Zoeller had a spilt second to see land. Though unfamiliar to him as a landmark, he assumed, correctly, that they were just south of the Delmarva Peninsula, and were possibly at the mouth of the bay leading into Newport News and the Norfolk Navy Yard, the heart and soul of the U.S. Navy and the entire Atlantic Fleet. At just 175 miles to the U.S. Capitol they were closer than any foreign warship had been since the U.S. Civil War.

Within a few minutes the seas calmed to more manageable 15 – 25-foot swells. Zoeller ordered air intakes opened and the diesel engines to be started. Continued forward movement was vital in keeping the boat stable and steerable. With surface sight somewhat restored, they could catch glimpses of land between clouds, rain and wind. They scrambled to their charts pointing out landmarks. The navigator, pale with the realization of just where they were, shook his head in the affirmative.

"Chesapeake Bay, Cape Charles on our starboard, Cape Henry to port, Norfolk, straight ahead, Sir."

Zoeller had to contain his laughter. Here they were within striking distance of convoys, warships, and the very headquarters of the Atlantic Fleet, with Washington, D.C. just a bit further.

"*Just maybe...*" he thought. "If the damned thing really works we could end this war today."

No one on the bridge responded, as they weren't sure they knew exactly to what the Captain was referring. Though it was common knowledge among rank & file that Hitler and his scientists were constantly working on bigger and better weapons of war, few ever knew about actual prototypes or finished weapons until they were being used. Talk of a nuclear weapon had been whispered about years earlier. It was mostly seen as a fantasy, but now the reality was loaded in an aft torpedo bay, that fact only known to three men on board.

As the ship dared to move slowly into the abandoned channel, the waves calmed long enough for the navigator to attempt to calibrate radar and other long-range sensing devices. If there were ships moving in the area, or airplanes overhead, they'd see them. He also knew that if his radar was working, so too would be his enemy's.

"Achtung! Make torpedoes ready! Gunners to their posts! We are in the belly of the beast!"

*****

Almost as soon as the USS Eldridge turned toward shore, the largest and most crippling swells began to shrink. The ship was still taking a pounding, but it was experiencing fewer broadside hits, the kind that could capsize even 300-foot steel warships.

"Our primary radar and sonar are inoperable, Captain," said the Ensign, coming up from the radio room one deck below the bridge. "I think it was that last lightning strike. It knocked out a bunch of our instruments. Radios aren't working either. We're kind of blind at the moment."

"Do what you can," said Captain Hammond, "and report back. If it's safe, send a man up the tower to assess lightning damage and start repairs. The weather appears to be giving us a bit of a break."

The Captain turned as the Ensign left the bridge. "How about you, Navigator? Is your equipment functional?"

"Radar and Sonar are out. We do have a visual out the window, Sir." The Bridge erupted in laughter.

"Thank you for your excellent grasp of the obvious, Navigator. Just exactly where do your eyes tell you we are?"

"Well, Sir. Best guess, we're about four nautical miles southwest of Cape Charles, in the mouth of the Chesapeake Bay. About 10 miles farther into the harbor and we're in Norfolk. At this speed, I'd say we're 20 to 30 minutes out from the Navy Yard."

"Finally," said Hammond, with a grateful sigh. "I think we're out of the woods."

Norfolk, Virginia
Confederate States of America
9:35 p.m., August 23, 1943

Margaret Rollins never heard her husband's call from the boat, a full half-mile out into the mouth of the Bay, but Hank had. He struggled against the leash, barked and urged her to turn. When she did, she scanned the dark water. Her eyes spotted a pinprick of light, a flashlight perhaps, swinging around in the darkness on the edge of the visible horizon of black sea. She focused again and saw the trawler more clearly—it was the only boat on the water. Then she saw the tiny form of a man, standing on the boat's transom.

Something beyond the insistence of her dog urged her back toward the end of the dock. She dared not think it possible. *No...Henry, you hate boats*. On autopilot she and Hank picked up their pace, and she finally gave herself over to the wonderful possibility.

"Henry?"

Now standing at the end of the long wharf, she remembered the lost-and-found opera glasses she'd used in Philadelphia. She dug through her purse, found them, and quickly focused. It was dark, but she could just make out the man waving his arms wildly in the air, jumping. It looked like he was yelling something. She couldn't hear anything over the sirens some 15 blocks away toward the city's center.

Though the figure was dark, and tiny, somehow she was certain. "Henry."

From the boat, with tears in both eyes, Henry yelled her name. "Margaret!"

Rollins turned to look at the confused youth. "It's her, Jack. It's my Margaret!" He waved wildly and jumped again, nearly slipping off the wide transom at the stern of the boat. He double checked the image through the binoculars and then he too was certain. "It's my Margaret!"

Clueless as to just who 'Margaret' was, Jack said nothing and watched as his partner in crime seemed to unravel, along with their plans to escape.

"Jack, it's okay!" said Henry, smiling, and grabbing his friend by the shoulders, shaking him. "It's my wife. We're going back." Henry ran to the console, threw the transmission into Forward, eased the throttle to three-quarter speed, and whipped the steering wheel hard to port. The big trawler made a wide, left-hand turn, passing into the center of the channel, just as the strange breezes picked back up.

"I'm coming to you," Henry said, steering the boat while straining his neck backward to make sure she hadn't left the dock.

With their 180-degree turn nearly completed, the *Almost Home* unexpectedly crashed through what could have best been described as a brick wall; a brick wall made of seawater some 15-feet high. The once blackened night sky flashed, turning lighter, into a dark shade of gray. The winds, like that of prop wash from a giant airplane, buffeted the 45-foot boat. Henry's gut clenched as he fought off suspicions about what was happening. *No, it can't be. Not again.*

Jack stood frozen; terrified with the sudden and dramatic changes they were experiencing. "What the hell? Henry! What's going on?" he said, finally.

Rollins struggled to keep the boat perpendicular to the giant swells; that bit of nautical knowledge came instinctively. At the top of a particularly large mountain of seawater, he caught a birds-eye view of the wharf. Not a single boat could be seen anywhere in the harbor, and giant waves crashed over the concrete structure, sending spray high into the air. When the over wash settled, Henry could see that Margaret and the dog were gone.

"No, no, no! So close. Margaret!"

*****

Chesapeake Bay
United States of America
8:11 p.m. September 10, 1943

"Wind is picking up again, Sir," said a rain-soaked sailor reporting in to Captain Hammond. He had attempted to repair the antennae array, when a strong gust nearly knocked him into the sea.

"I can see that, Sailor," said Hammond. "The swells are back, too." Almost before the words left his mouth a monstrous wall of water flanked the Eldridge on her port side, sending the ship listing 35-degrees. Whatever respite they'd been given was clearly over.

Hammond struggled to see out of the bridge's windows. Heavy, blowing rain had strengthened, reducing any visibility to zero.

"Damn it," said Hammond. He looked around the bridge as his officers gathered themselves, several having been knocked off their feet to the deck.

"I want fresh damage and crew readiness reports. You have five minutes. Go! Be careful." Three officers tightened their rain gear and hurried off the bridge.

He turned to his helmsman. "Can we maintain this course?"

"We can try, Sir, but we need to hit these swells as straight on as possible, or they'll capsize us."

"Do what you have to do. Just do your best to stay the course to Norfolk."
"Aye, aye, Skipper."

Breathing fresh air for the first time in almost 15 hours helped partially revive the crew of U-4713, though the surface conditions at the mouth of the Bay took a toll not only on their health, but on the Unterseeboot, as well.

"Sir, we've lost both gunners," said an out-of-breath Junior Officer.

"What?" said Captain Zoeller. "Lost them?"

"Yes, Sir. Overboard."

"Overboard? Weren't their safety harnesses attached?"

"Seems so, Sir. They snapped in two. The wind. The waves."

"Slow as much as you dare, Helmsman. I need two volunteers to the deck with binoculars. I want those gunners found." He was less concerned about saving their lives as he was being down two crewmen. There were no redundancies aboard a U-boat. Every man was needed.

The foul weather that U-4713 was experiencing was exactly why U-boats were designed as semi-submersibles. Unlike less fortunate craft, they could dive below the surface and ride out bad weather, but Captain Zoeller did not have that luxury. He'd be forced to stay on the surface for at least another hour to get any kind of usable charge on the batteries. If he submerged again, he knew he'd lose power and maneuverability, and would be at the mercy of the currents, not a risk he could take.

*****

Chesapeake Bay
United States of America
8:21 p.m. September 10, 1943

When the wind gusts, now peaking at 75 Mph, battered the fishing trawler, it was all Henry Rollins and young Jack could do to keep from being blown off the deck of the boat.

"Jack, go below. Find two life jackets!" yelled Henry, who struggled to keep the boat headed for whatever protection the harbor might offer. In the open Bay, they were being tossed around like a child's toy.

Jack quickly found two life vests and the men were secured in a matter of seconds.

"Where did all this come from, Henry?" asked Jack, still visibly terrified. "And why is it so light? Is it daytime? How could it be?"

Henry couldn't take the time to explain relativity, theoretical physics, and quantum mechanics at that particular moment. The largest swell they'd seen yet, combined with the strongest wind gust, had reduced them to holding on and praying for their salvation.

They rode the giant wave up, up, up, seemingly straight into the gray sky, when another powerful gust spun them like a top, 180-degrees. The boat was forcibly turned as they skidded back down the swell away from port, into the mouth of the Bay. At the bottom of the trough all they could see was wind-whipped water and rolling hills and valleys of sea-green. At the top of the next swell, Jack's already pale face went whiter still. He had trouble getting the words out.

"Henry…" Rollins didn't answer as he was fumbling with a loose buckle on his life jacket. "Henry! What's…what's that?"

Rollins looked up, and through the thick rain bands saw what had his companion so agitated.

"Oh my, Lord," said Henry. The wind howled so loudly Jack couldn't hear him.

"What?" Jack yelled, unable to understand.

Henry looked again and focused on the all-too familiar painted call sign: '173 USS Eldridge.' Not unlike the *Almost Home*, the Eldridge, too, rode the cresting waves, its great bow slicing through the smaller ones. Just 1,500 feet ahead, on a direct collision course, steamed a ship Henry Rollins thought he'd never see again.

"It's the Eldridge, Jack! I don't think we're in Kansas anymore!"

Henry let out a grunt as he instinctively wheeled the *Almost Home* hard to starboard. An unrelenting wind blowing from the south kept the trawler from making any real progress away from the oncoming ship. He spun the wheel to its maximum position and pushed the throttle to full. The great diesel engine whined and spewed black smoke, struggling against the tempest.

"I'm sorry, Jack. I don't think we're going to make it," said Henry, sober and defeated as the Eldridge drew nearer by the second.

"Shit, Sir!" yelled the Eldridge's Helmsman, pointing out the window. "Sorry, but I saw something 1200 feet ahead, dead on. It looked like a…like a fishing boat!"

"Full stop!" ordered Captain Hammond. "Hard to port!"

"Full stop! Hard to port!" repeated the Helmsman, sending the orders through the ship's telegraph to the engine room. He spun the large wheel, hand over hand, until it stopped.

Hammond struggled to see through the torrent of sideways rain. No sign of any boat.

"Are you sure, Helmsman?"

"Positive! No question, Sir. There's a small fishing boat dead ahead."

The Eldridge slowed, and began making its turn, when the visibility improved just enough for all on the bridge to see it for themselves.

"Damn it!" yelled Hammond. "I see them! Why don't they turn? We're going to hit!" The Captain reached for a switch to engage a loud horn, though it had been rendered useless, silenced by lightening or rain, or both.

"Damn it! Does anything still work on this tub?"

"I can't seem to get out of its path!" yelled Henry, their boat now less than 1,000 feet from the front right quarter of the Eldridge, which was six times the trawler's length, and three times its beam.

"I can't believe I'm saying this! But I think we may have to go overboard! It's safer than crashing. I'm sorry!"

Jack was unable to speak, but he'd heard Henry and nodded, agreeing that they were safer taking their chances in the water rather than splintering in the unavoidable collision with the huge hull of the Eldridge.

"Here I go again," said Henry, with a sigh, tightening his life vest. "Ready, Jack?"

Jack nodded and the two men climbed up on the wide transom. "Now!" yelled Henry as they jumped from the far side of the *Almost Home*, as far out, and away from the impending crash as they could manage.

*****

"We've got them!" yelled the radar operator aboard U-4713. "It must be the Eldridge, Sir. The signatures match a Destroyer Escort."

Captain Zoeller looked over the shoulder of the navigator at the brightly lit green screen and watched the ping indicate a large ship just ahead by 2,400 feet.

With the U-boat bouncing on top of the heavy surf, firing conditions were far less than ideal, and though they couldn't see the Eldridge, the radar said she was there.

"I need firing solutions, now! Launch forward torpedoes 1 & 2," said Zoeller, with a menacing calm, in his voice. More than any other type of ship in the Battle of the Atlantic, the Destroyer Escort was the most hated by U-boat captains. Almost single handedly the agile American ships, which were built faster, bigger and deadlier, had ended the domination the Wolf Pack German U-boats enjoyed during the first half of the War. Now it was time for a little Nazi revenge.

Though the Eldridge was not positioned ideally broadside, where a hit was more likely, Zoeller felt he couldn't lose the chance to fire. Once the Eldridge spotted them the real battle would begin. It was a risky but calculated move. The G7e/T3 torpedoes were each 23-feet long, 2-feet wide and were propelled by a 100 hp electric motor. They used a magnetic sensing device designed to detonate their 280kg warheads underneath the keel of their targets. When they worked, the concussion they caused at the keel or amidships could split a large vessel in two, sending it to the ocean floor with just one hit. As much as the U-boats

263

feared the Destroyer Escort class, merchant ships and warships alike feared the Kriegsmarine U-boats. The Battle of the Atlantic, the longest naval battle in the history of the modern world, raged on.

"Torpedoes away!" came the call from a small speaker on the bridge. The U-boat rocked from another swell, though the ocean had calmed a little. There was no telling how a hurricane might affect the operation of the torpedoes; underwater currents could play havoc with their trajectory. Regardless, the torpedoes were off at some 30 knots, just below the surface of the water, headed straight for the unsuspecting Eldridge, which still had no idea U-4713 was on their tail.

Zoeller was well aware of the high failure rate of German torpedoes; around 30 percent, still they had performed well enough to sink thousands of ships around the globe, many at his own hand. He knew the strong likelihood that one or more of the torpedoes he'd just launched wouldn't detonate, but yet it was his best and only hope for sinking the Eldridge. As is true with most statistics, the probability of success would grow exponentially with greater deployment, and Zoeller was ready to unleash his entire arsenal if need be.

When the outer hatch opened, the howling wind blew through the control room of the U-boat as two volunteers made their way back inside.

"Well?" asked Captain Zoeller. "Any sign of them?" The two men shook their heads, 'no.' "Keep searching, then!" He pointed and the two men went topside once again, facing the raging seas, rain, and hurricane force winds.

Chapter 40

Norfolk, Virginia
Confederate States of America
Waterfront
9:41 p.m. August 23, 1943

Margaret gasped when she saw the small boat vanish before her eyes. While she couldn't be completely certain, she had convinced herself that Henry had been aboard the fishing boat, that he had seen her, and that he was turning back, and then...nothing. She felt like crying, but nearly out of tears, she was beginning to see it as useless, and a waste of valuable energy. The frustration of not knowing what to do, however, was driving her mad. She tried not to, but she couldn't help cursing Albert Einstein, and his meddling with wormholes and things in which humankind shouldn't be involving themselves.

Hank whimpered at her side, searching the horizon for the boat. He didn't need convincing, he was certain that the man aboard the distant boat belonged to Margaret. He'd first picked up Henry's scent from a handkerchief soaked in his dried perspiration from 10 days earlier. It had been stuffed in the bottom of Margaret's purse, and introduced to him when Margaret used it herself. He picked up the scent again on the streets of Norfolk, first in the breeze, and then stronger as they neared the wharf. When a young man, hell bent on breaking a bank's window, stood close behind them in the Park, Hank picked up the scent one more time. Acting more like a bloodhound than a retriever, Hank tried his best to be both. Pleasing Margaret, the giver of food, shelter, water, and love, was his greatest mission in life, and he hated to disappoint.

In utter frustration, Margaret sat on the wharf. It was quiet there; she had time to think. Hank sat beside her, alert, but with his muzzle in her lap, while she stroked his head.

"If it really was Henry, and he saw me, he'll try to get back here. Won't he? He's gone through one of those nasty vortexes, or wormholes, or whatever Einstein called them. I know he has. I've seen it before, Hank." She looked at the dog, who twitched his expressive eyebrows, and wagged his tail. It wasn't much to go on, but she was reluctant to leave the last place she'd seen her husband.

"Come on Henry. Come back to me; you can do it."

*****

Chesapeake Bay
Confederate States of America
9:59 p.m. August 23, 1864

Mid jump, before even hitting the surface of the water, the sky flashed dark again, and Henry and Jack both landed with a splash into a jet-black, calm sea, No wind, no rain, no fading daylight, and no sign of the Eldridge or the *Almost Home* anywhere.

"What in hell is happening?" sputtered Jack, as they both bobbed on the surface. Distant yellowish lights flickered on shore. Gone was the glow coming from the nearby cities.

Henry looked to the wharf, which was no longer a concrete ribbon, but had been replaced by wooden docks.

"We've time jumped," he said.

"What?" asked Jack, still coughing out sea water.

Henry didn't answer him. When he focused his eyes he saw the tall masts of sailing ships, and formed a new hunch about where they'd landed. His head spun with the apparent likelihood of yet another trip through time and space. Even with a million worries flooding his brain, he knew getting out of the water had to be their first priority.

"I recommend we try the back float," said Henry, re-tightening his life vest. "Start kicking toward shore. By the way, we're still in the Confederacy, only it's a bit earlier than when we left, like by about 80 years or so."

Jack was as confused as any human being has ever been in the history of humankind. As they floated, and with nothing better to do, Dr. Rollins did his best to explain rudimentary interdimensional travel, wormholes and alternate universes, adding in the possibility of skewing timelines.

"Yeah, okay," said Jack, not buying much of it.

"You have any better explanation?" asked Henry, sensing his disbelief. The young man was silent. All that could be heard was the rhythmic kicking of their feet in the calm ocean water.

When a large fish jumped, just a few feet behind them, both men, startled, stopped their kicking and remained still.

"Whoa! That kind of surprised me," said Henry.

"Yeah, me too. Let's get out of here," offered Jack.

They resumed their kicking with a newfound energy. They'd made a few more feet of progress when Jack yelled. "What was that?"

"What was what?" asked Henry, alarmed.

"Something swam by me. Something big."

With only a half-moon lighting a muggy sky, it was difficult to see much of anything. Henry's jaw dropped when a dorsal fin broke the surface of the water directly behind them.

"Jack! Stop kicking! Don't move a muscle."

He didn't have to be told twice. Both men froze as a lone 10-foot Tiger shark circled slowly. Once again Henry Rollins felt himself on the verge of laughter, the kind that comes just before a full psychotic break.

"Oh come on…" he dared to say out loud. "What's next? I mean really…?" Then he raised his voice as the good humor he momentarily enjoyed turned to anger. "Is this the best you can do, God? Sharks? Really?"

Rollins cursed his luck, nearly given over to tears with the fading memory of his Margaret on the wharf.

"What's next…?

As if on cue, the sky flashed again, and the two men found themselves back in September, 1943, in the midst the raging tempest. The dark, quiet night, with tranquil seas, even with its sharks, had given way to something potentially far more dangerous; a hurricane.

As a 20-foot wave crashed over top of both men, the force of the water sent them rolling, unable to stay at the surface. When they both popped up within seconds of one another, Jack coughed out a lung full of seawater. Henry Rollins willed himself through the water to aid him, helping bolster his head above the sea, even as the wind howled and taunted.

Floating 1,500-feet to the port side of the Eldridge, which was slowly making forward progress, the two men did their best to literally keep their heads above water. Henry saw Jack's expression turn to panic as they again saw the warship.

What was left of the *Almost Home* could be seen smoldering in bits and pieces as flotsam on the surface of the sea. The crash, which Henry and Jack did not witness, had been enough to destroy the wooden trawler, but only dent the starboard side of the bow of the Eldridge, leaving a black smudge from the ignition of diesel fuel. The collision popped a few rivets but didn't do any irreparable or serious damage.

"Jack, they're friendly!" yelled Rollins nodding toward the Eldridge. "In fact, I think I may know the Captain! Wave your arms if you can, but don't bother shouting, they'll never hear us!"

As another swell lifted the men into the air, a new threat presented itself in the form of two Nazi torpedoes. Rollins and Jack witnessed both torpedoes shoot straight out of the side of a nearby 25-foot mountain of water, passing them, headed straight for the Eldridge. As the mountains of water rose and fell, they spotted something more ominous, the birth mother of the torpedoes, U-4713 with the Kreigsmarine emblem on its hull.

"My God," said Rollins, half to himself. "That's a damned Nazi U-boat." Jack knew of the Nazis. They'd ruled much of Central Europe for a decade, and were now fighting for the rest of the continent, but in Jack's world there'd been no involvement in the war from the C.S.A. or Federated States, and consequently, U-boats hadn't been in the headlines. Yet the frightening Nazi war machine was there before them in the Chesapeake Bay showing itself between rain bands and rolling peaks and valleys of water.

Between the wind and the chaotic movement of millions of gallons of wind-whipped seawater, both torpedoes missed their mark. The deadly weapons zoomed by the Eldridge, their magnetic detonators unable to lock onto its massive metal hull. The sharp eyes of the Eldridge's helmsman spotted the errant weapons skipping in and out of the water at 30 knots, having just passed by them.

"Captain! We've been fired upon!" The helmsman grabbed a pair of binoculars and scoured the water, homing in on the unmistakable propeller trail headed out past the bow of the ship. "It looks like two U-boat torpedoes just missed us."

"What the hell?" questioned Hammond, grabbing the binoculars. He and his officers were still trying to make sense of the trawler impact. He'd sent a recovery team outside to scan the water for survivors. From the bridge he saw for himself the torpedoes just before they disappeared underwater. "Sonofabitch. Nazis? Here? At the mouth of the Chesapeake Bay? Can't be."

The cold wind and rain blasted through the bridge's hatch door as an out-of-breath officer stood before them.

"U-boat, Sir! To our rear, 1800-feet! I ordered countermeasures and depth charges! But General Quarters has been a joke. We've only got half the men needed to man the battle stations. I pulled men off the toilets and out of sick bay to assist, Sir. Communication seems to be out. I tried to radio you from the deck, but only got static."

"Thank you, good job," said Hammond. "Yeah, we just saw two torpedoes. Way too close for comfort. I want gunners on those .50 cals. If you can see that damned U-boat, you can shoot at it!"

"Already on it, Sir. It looked like the U-boat was struggling in the swells. I'll bet she's preparing to dive again."

"Hit her with the cannons, dump half the depth charges, and don't let up."

Hammond attempted to reach the radio room, but the electronics were still out. He turned to Atkins, just arriving on the bridge. "Any signs of survivors from the damn fishing boat suicide squad?"

"No, Sir. Not yet. We're still looking."

"A U-boat?. How the hell did they even know we'd be here...and in the middle of a hurricane?" asked Hammond of anyone who'd listen. Visions of a German radio and the former Executive Officer flashed into his head. "Moore, the sonofabitch..."

Just how close the torpedoes had been was something the Captain couldn't know. If the torpedo closest to the ship had been four feet nearer to the hull, it would have triggered the detonator and they'd be having a very different conversation.

*****

Like riding the inside of a tin can on a waterfall, the ordnance crew of U-4713 struggled to ready two additional torpedoes. They had them nearly loaded in the tubes when a large shell launched from a big gun on the rear deck of the Eldridge rocked the U-boat so hard, it stopped the men in their tracks. Additionally, bullets from the Eldridge's .50 caliber machine guns rattled the steel shell of the U-boat, a few nearly penetrating the hull.

"Alarm! Planesman! Crash Dive! Sixty meters! Hard to starboard!" screamed Captain Zoeller, knowing that it would take 45-seconds to shut the diesels down and secure the air intakes. His calculated risk had failed. He initially had the element of surprise and a reasonable shot at sinking the Eldridge. Now the Americans knew he was there. With his batteries at less than 10-percent, he'd have limited propulsion, but he couldn't stay surfaced and hope to survive additional counter attacks. It was only slightly less dangerous below the surface.

The U-boat's Radioman tried in vain to listen through the Gruppenhorchgerät, a hydrophone, for the telltale splashes made by depth charges, but the storm made that nearly impossible. He missed hearing four depth charges deployed as soon as the U-boat slipped beneath the sea. One charge lunched from a K-Gun hit the water 15 feet from U-4713.

Captain Zoeller paused, fighting to stay focused. He feared the end of his mission, and on a greater scale, the lingering suspicions and very real possibility that Germany would lose the war. Just a year earlier the U-boat Wolf Packs had sunk 1,000 Allied ships in the Atlantic, and enjoyed nearly total domination of both the Atlantic and the Mediterranean Sea. But with increased American involvement, the deployments of some 50 additional Destroyer Escorts given to Great Britain by the U.S., along with better anti-sub technologies, those heady

269

days of 1942 were all but a distant memory. The Allies were winning the Battle of the Atlantic. The world sensed it and Zoeller feared it.

A particularly strong wind-driven current calved a giant swell, some 35 feet tall, which carried in its belly an unexploded ordnance from the Eldridge, an MK6 depth charge, equipped with a magnetic detonator. Depth charges could be set to detonate by water pressure at calculated depths, or by magnetic proximity, looking for anything big and metal. Having initially missed U-4713 upon entry into the violently rolling seas, the MK6 was given a second chance to fulfill its mission while riding high like a fishing bobber, just close enough to U-4713 to trigger its magnetic detonator.

The surface explosion caused by the MK6's 300 lbs of TNT sent shrapnel from its steel casing 1,200-feet to the rear deck of the Eldridge, forcing the gunners to duck. Though close to the U-boat when detonated, U-4713 narrowly missed a hull breech as the huge swell shifted the vessel out of reach from the most damaging force of the concussion. Immediately an orange fireball mixed with 1000 cubic feet of seawater stood in stark contrast to the darkening gray skies, painting a nightmarish picture for all who were watching.

"Damn…" proclaimed Jack, having never seen anything like it. This was all new to him; the USS Eldridge, U-4713, and an explosion from a 300 lbs of TNT, were not things men of his world and time were likely to ever see. Additionally there was this confusing issue of the United States of America. Before he'd quit school, he'd learned that the U.S.A. had dissolved after the Yankee surrender, yet before him was an American warship, flying a tattered U.S. flag. Reconciling the irreconcilable would have to wait. Survival was taking priority. When a crewman aboard the Eldridge spotted Rollins and his companion floating in the Bay, he ran to the bridge.

"Sir, two men overboard!" shouted the sailor, pointing out into the sea.

"I don't see them," said Hammond, scanning the floodlight-lit water for any signs. Between waves he caught a glimpse of their life vests. "Gottem!" he said. "They might be Krauts. Those life vests are not ours."

"Or the fisherman?" added XO Lieutenant Atkins.

"Either way, we can't leave them out there in this crap. Let's fish 'em out, and we'll know for sure."

"They're about 800 feet to our port, and we're pulling away steadily," said the helmsman.

"It's too rough to man a lifeboat," said Hammond. "And lets not forget the damned U-boat is still out there, though between the .50 cal, depth charges and these seas, I'd be surprised if they're not in pieces on the seafloor. This is one helluva mess."

The Captain thought about his options for a moment, and then acted decisively. "Helmsman, hard to port. As soon as we're in range I want the hedgehogs launched 1000 feet west of the last known position of the U-boat. Atkins, have engineering run a 500-foot line with two life rings from the rear deck. Use the electric winch. Let's go fishing, boys."

Again, Hammond's disciplined officers and crew scrambled to carry out the orders. The Eldridge was still vulnerable to the elements, as well as its position relative to the U-boat. As they circled wide, if the Nazis saw the Eldridge's perpendicular placement, they'd almost surely attempt another torpedo launch.

"I'm not leaving those men in the water," said Hammond quietly as he considered the jeopardy under which he was putting his ship and crew.

"What's that, Sir," repeated Atkins.

"Nothing, Atkins," said Hammond. "Just thinking out loud."

Hammond's confidence in the anti-submarine ordnance was well deserved. He was personally responsible for the sinking or disabling of 11 U-boats in the past 10 months. The U.S. had been winning the Battle of the Atlantic thanks to improved Destroyer design, more versatile depth charges, and the addition of the British-designed Hedgehog weapon.

When in ready mode, a battery of 24 spigot mortar Hedgehogs looked like the back of the small animal for which it was named. The weapon had become a deadly anti-sub ordnance in the previous 10 months of their widespread use. Any remaining U-boats patrolling the Atlantic did so in constant fear. With depth charges to the rear, and Hedgehogs forward, the U-boats domination of the seas was all but over, but they were still dangerous, and there was one particularly dangerous U-boat in the Chesapeake Bay, just 200 miles from the Nation's capital.

"Get me the Communications Officer up here on the double," yelled Hammond, frustrated that he had no way to communicate with onshore command, or anyone else, for that matter.

"Yes, Sir," said Atkins, disappearing down the interior hatch to the Radio Room, one deck below. When the young Communications officer appeared on the bridge a moment later, he knew he was in for a good grilling.

"Sir, we're doing everything possible," said the shaken officer, a bit green from seasickness.

"Are you alright?" asked the Captain.

"I've been better," he answered, "but I haven't puked in..." he looked at his watch, "10 minutes."

"What seems to be the problem with my communications? We're 20 minutes from shore and I can't speak to or hear from anyone? This is a real problem, Mister."

"I know, Sir, and I'm sorry. Lightning fried everything, and the antennae arrays are barely hanging on in this wind. That's the bad news. The good news is; I think we should have some rudimentary communications up in 15 minutes or so."

"We may not have 15 minutes. Can you make it 5?" asked Hammond.

"We'll try, Sir."

"Good man, now do it!"

With the ship now 45 degrees into its 90-degree maneuver, the Hedgehogs were in firing position. The ordnance officer calculated the last sighting of U-

271

4713, and guessed at where is might be now, some six minutes after its torpedo attack.

The spotter saw two men still floating in the sea, waving their arms, as the Eldridge came around. The helpless men were far enough away from the projected Hedgehog entry patterns that the order was given to launch.

When deployed, like 24 giant lawn darts, their pattern spread in a 100-foot diameter circle in a loose shotgun pattern. They hit the surface of the water with a minimal hydrodynamic splash, diving down in search of anything solid. The men on board the Eldridge waited and prayed they'd hear and see a detonation. Five seconds later, nothing. None of the 24 mortars found a target.

"Reload!" came the order and the Hedgehog was loaded with its next deadly round.

At the other end of the ship the engineers had done as the captain ordered, with 500-feet of line almost fully deployed. When the ship finished its turn, the line and life rings would come in contact with the two men afloat in the still raging sea. The success of their rescue was not certain, but the men respected the Captain for making the effort; it had been the rule of honorable navy men for centuries.

"I think they mean to help us!" yelled Henry Rollins over the continued raging currents of air. Each drop of wind-driven water stung his face like the tail end of a hornet. Jack was still too confused to respond. "We're going to be alright! Hang on, Jack!" The young man managed to nod.

As the Eldridge had now completed its dangerous turn, Henry spotted the bright white rope strung from the stern of the warship, and saw two life rings, buoyant on the surface of the swells, which had once again picked up.

"Look, Jack! Those are life rings on the end of that line!"

Shielding his face from the stinging salt spray, Jack turned to see what Rollins was yelling about. He allowed himself a bit of hope in an upside-down world. When the line passed by them, Rollins grabbed hold.

"Grab onto my life jacket and hold tight!" yelled Rollins.

Hand over hand, Rollins pulled his way down the line toward the two life rings, with Jack grabbing tight, but running out of strength. Aboard the Eldridge another round of Hedgehogs was deployed as the ship began to turn again, back toward port. Sailors working the winch, reversed the motor and slowly wound the 500-foot line back onto its spool, pulling the two men along with it.

Six spotters scoured the surface of the sea looking for the brazen U-boat that dared engage a U.S. warship just eight nautical miles from one of the largest naval bases in the world. The German vessel had gone below the surface and was nowhere to be seen. With no floating debris telling the Eldridge that they'd hit her, they had to assume the U-boat was still a threat. That assumption was correct.

Chapter 41

"They're turning again!" yelled a German submariner, eyes glued to the sonar screen.

"Kapitän, we have a firing solution, launch now, while they're broadside!" pleaded U-4713's overeager Oberleutnant Dengler.

The prideful U-boat Captain Walther Zoeller, turned, displeased with the lack of protocol and impertinence from his second in command.

"Given the chance to speak for myself," said Zoeller sarcastically, "we will launch when I say, not when you say."

"Of course, Sir. Sorry, I just thought…"

"Halt die klappe, Dengler. Launch the damned eels."

As the Eldridge did its best to maneuver in the hurricane ravaged waters of the Bay, U-4713, down to 4-percent battery power launched two more torpedoes. Almost simultaneously, depth charges had been released from the Eldridge and were slowly falling toward the seabed. When one of them struck the oncoming German torpedo in a one-in-a-million chance meeting, the resulting explosion, just 10 feet below the surface of the water lit up the sky with the force of 500 lbs of TNT. Not only did the concussion skew the trajectory of the second torpedo, U-4713 was slammed so hard by the detonation, a hull breech in the engine room triggered alarms sending the crew into the chaos of incoming seawater, short-circuiting electrical motors, and the most feared event aboard any ship, but especially a submersible, fire.

"Kapitän!" shouted an ensign just arriving from the rear of the U-boat, where the worst of the damage was centered. "Fire!"

"Suppress it! Don't tell me about it. Put it out, man!" screamed Captain Zoeller. "What about the G7e-UP1?"

"Sir"? asked the confused man.

"The new ordnance!"

"Undamaged, Sir, and operational, for now. But we're taking on wasser!"

"Where's Lieutenant Adams?"

"Dead, Sir. In the fire."

Zoeller looked to Dengler who stood next to the planesman, as they both studied the depth gauges.

"Twenty meters, twenty five," said Dengler. A few seconds later he spoke again. "Thirty meters. Kapitän, were sinking fast."

"Blow the ballast tanks! Rise! Rise!" ordered Zoeller. "Helmsman, point our bow due east!" The U-boat captain had one chance to launch the nuclear ordnance from the aft torpedo tubes, requiring a 180-degree turn. Even though they were short of their Washington, D.C., target, the Norfolk Navy Yard would do. Floating dead in the water next to the American warship was the last place Zoeller wanted to be, but Fate had forced his hand. What awaited U-4713 on the surface, far from the crew's homeland, and what awaited Norfolk, could not be imagined.

*****

Norfolk, Virginia
Gosport Navy Yard
11:16 p.m. August 23, 1864

"Do you see that?" asked a young Confederate Marine on watch near the wharf at the mouth of the Chesapeake Bay. His watch partner, a man of some 60 years, had been dozing.

"What? See what?" answered the older man through a yawn.

"Those flashes of light out yonder, in the middle of the Bay."

"Probably just lightning."

"It's a crystal clear night. Look," he said pointing skyward. "There's the moon, and look at all the stars. It ain't lightning, I tell 'ya. I saw an orange fireball a minute ago. Mighty peculiar."

"You're drunker than Cooter Brown," said the sleepy Marine, rubbing his eyes. When he finally fixed his gaze outward, using the binoculars that hung around his neck, he saw what had his partner so agitated.

"Well I'll be..." agreed the once skeptical Marine. "I ain't never seen anything like—"

Another fireball lit up the sky and was accompanied by a shower of seawater and wind that literally appeared from nowhere and rained down water in a 100-foot circle on the still, black surface of the Bay.

Both men were silent for a moment, trying to grasp what they'd just seen. "We gotta report this," said the older man.

"You don't suppose it's—"

The seasoned Marine interrupted his younger watch partner whose eyes were still glued to the sea. "I know what you're fixin' to say, and no it ain't the

274

goddamn Gosport Ghost Ship. You lost your marbles? Let's just tell 'em we're seein' lights we cain't explain, and leave it at that."

The two men hurried from their post and moved on the double-quick toward the Sentry's guardhouse. They were met by two more Marines and a handful of Navy men coming their way.

"You seen it, too?" asked a Confederate Naval officer, who had come from the tower in the middle of town at the Naval HQ.

"Yeah, we seen it, Sir," said the younger Marine who'd first witnessed the strange lights. "Never seen nothin' like it before."

"I reckon they sendin' out the Ironclad, the Virginia?" asked the sailor.

"Yes. Cap'n Brown thinks it's more of that craziness from last week. Said he wants to see the monster again."

The Marine elbowed his partner in the ribs, satisfied that the incident was connected to the strange events of a week earlier.

Though the fireballs had ceased for the moment, the spot in the middle of the main channel was still oddly illuminated. Like a faint hole in the black sky, the star field vanished behind it. The area flashed gray, with what looked like intermittent bands of rainwater falling seemingly from nowhere, just above the surface of the still sea.

As the men turned and hurried toward the end of the wharf, the 275-foot mighty CSS Virginia, fully repaired, steamed past them, with its great stack bellowing black smoke and sparks into the night sky. Behind the Virginia three more ships of the C.S.N. followed, fully manned and ready to meet the beast that Captain Brown was sure they'd find. The CSN's submersible, the David, was back in action, too, ready for another attempt at whatever was threatening the heart of the Confederate Navy.

Through the anomaly of light, wind and rain, unseen to the men of 1864, a naval battle and rescue were taking place, just beyond a very thin veil of spacetime.

*****

Chesapeake Bay
United States of America
8:59 p.m. September 10, 1943

"Slow the winch!" screamed the senior Eldridge engineer, seeing that the two men being assisted were at the end of the line and had secured themselves in the life rings. When one of the men bobbing in the rolling swells waved, and flashed the 'OK' sign, the engineer gave the signal to begin hauling them in inch-by-inch, foot-by-foot, closer to the Eldridge and out of the raging seas.

In the dark, with no working sonar, no radar, and only limited radio communications, Captain Hammond feared the unknown, and unknowable.

"Any sign of the Krauts?" he asked his First Officer, arriving on the bridge, dripping seawater. Outside the wind howled anew as gusts picked back up. The storm was far from over.

"Not yet, Sir, but we're looking, and the gunners are positioned."

The officer's face was bright red from having been stung by wind-driven droplets of salt water. Just as he made his report to the Captain, and unseen to those on the bridge, U-4713 popped up out of the water, bow first, slicing through the wave like an arrow shot from the quiver of Neptune himself.

With the Nazi Kriegsmarine swastika insignia proudly displayed on its hull, the crippled, but still dangerous, U-boat was in clear view of the Eldridge, positioned 1000 feet off her stern. The Eldridge's spotters tried radioing the bridge, but were only able to transmit and receive static.

The gunners had their standing orders and began to fire at the U-boat, just as two German sailors appeared through the hatch, scrambling to take position on the U-boat's deck to fire back.

"She's running!" yelled one of the gunners, seeing U-4713 moving away from them with what little power they still had.

"They'll fire aft torpedoes, if they haven't already!" said the gunner's mate. They fired, killing one of the German machine gunners. He was quickly replaced by another, who wasted no time firing back at the Eldridge.

Located precariously in between the two warships firing upon one another, Henry Rollins and a boy named Jack were at the mercy of the wind, waves and the winch. Jack, who was in shock, hadn't said more than three words since they'd traveled through the portal and abandoned their trawler, the *Almost Home*. Rollins, though beaten and battered, had retained most of his wits, and was feeling freshly revived. After having seen Margaret, he was more motivated than ever to survive whatever the universe or universes would throw his way.

"Keep your head down, Jack!" yelled Rollins, even though he and his young friend were already 90-percent submerged. Jack closed his eyes while his brain tried to catch up with events of the previous 20 minutes.

Though the Eldridge and the U-boat were firing at one another, trying first to take out each other's guns, the motion of the waves made accuracy from either ship nearly impossible, and put the two men still in the sea in life-threatening jeopardy. If the U-boat decided to fire directly upon them, their odds of survival would further diminish. As it was, dozens of rapid-fire shells, some friendly, some German, whizzed by them, landing in the sea as close as a few feet away.

Boom! Boom! When the Eldridge's great rear-mounted cannons fired, Rollins and Jack could feel the concussion and the heat on their faces. Both shells missed their target. With the American and German ships rolling in the waves, it was just as impossible for the big guns to maintain accurate targeting. One of the shells punched into a wave and dove deep into the bay, but the other skipped across the surface of the water at 1,500 feet per second, making landfall a mile-and-a half out, detonating on the dunes of Fisherman's Island. Though the big guns had missed U-4713, they would try again.

With a little less than 300 feet remaining on the life line, the men could feel the heavy rope stretching and tightening as it was just starting to add lift to what had been only drag.

"Hang on Jack, this won't be much fun, but they're going to hoist us on board!" said Rollins. When a large swell lifted them high in the air, a small caliber shell grazed Rollin's life ring as it shot past them. More shells peppered the water around them as the U-boat gunners seemed to finally take the men in their sights.

Helpless to do much of anything, Henry and Jack hung on and tried to keep as much of themselves underwater as possible. It was their only protection from the machine gun fire.

"They don't seem to want us to make it out of the water, Jack!" said Henry. "Sorry I got you into this!"

This time Jack nodded, though he still had nothing to say.

Boom! Boom! The Eldridge's twin cannons fired again. One shell missed the top deck by four feet, shooting rocket-like out into the Bay, but the other was as close to a direct hit as they'd managed. The shell took out the U-boat machine gun nest and the two German gunners in a gruesome, fiery instant. Henry and Jack were close enough now to the Eldridge to hear the men on board shouting with joy at the hit. For the moment U-4713 was not answering the fire, nor taking any evasive action.

Lightning flashed as two mighty bolts struck nearby on Fisherman's Island. A new particularly active band of weather was bearing down on them. Henry and Jack watched the rain and wind bands move across the Bay, as the seas grew.

Captain Hammond was torn between guiding his battered ship toward the relative safety of port, and turning to re-engage the U-Boat. Though he could see the channel markers and wharf just ahead, the Captain decided to see this thing to its conclusion.

"Helmsman! Hard to starboard!"

"Aye, aye Captain. Hard to starboard!" yelled the sailor, who spun the great, brass wheel four full generations before it would go no further.

The ship began its turn just as a junior officer arrived on the bridge to relay the news of the fresh sighting of the U-boat, of their direct hit, and of the imminent arrival of two very fortunate sailors.

At the stern of the ship, activity was frenzied. Dripping from salt spray, the Eldridge's gunner turned his gaze from another lightning strike, now just a mile away, toward the crippled, but still menacing, metal snake slithering through the swells behind them.

"I think they're done, maybe?" asked the hopeful gunner, hoisting another 40 lb. shell into place.

"Don't count the Krauts out yet," said an officer. "Hurry with that reload!"

277

More lightning crackled in the air. The sky, which had been showing signs of getting brighter, again turned dark gray and black as 12-mile high thunderheads blotted out the sun.

On board U-4713 the almost anarchic activity stood in stark contrast to what the crew had been experiencing for the 40 days prior. Such was life on a U-boat. Days, weeks, even months of inactivity and tedium could turn into a literal life and death struggle in a matter of minutes. This was one such struggle.

When the machine gun turret was ripped from her deck the entire vessel shuddered and cried out, as if the ship had felt one of its limbs being torn off. The damage, as bad as it was, hadn't caused any significant structural integrity issues, not that the U-boat was in much of a position to dive, maneuver, or do anything at all. The fire was out in engineering, and now that they'd been forced to the surface, Captain Zoeller ordered the diesel engines to be restarted.

"We have one chance left before the American pigs finish us off," said Zoeller to his First Watch Officer, Dengler. "How long before we can launch another round?"

"The fire slowed them down, Kapitän, but tubes three and five are almost ready," answered Dengler.

"Let me know the second they are."

"Yes, Sir!"

Alarm lights flashed throughout U-4713 as crews welded hull breeches, dried electrical connections and tended to their wounded. In the Control Room Captain Zoeller considered what might be his final move.

*****

Chesapeake Bay
Confederate States of America
11:50 p.m. August 23, 1864

As the CSS Virginia steamed out of the channel on a direct route toward the anomaly in the night sky, Captain Brown scanned the Bay for anything.

"We're going to find out what the hell that things is, and, God willing, stop it once and for all," said Brown to his First Officer. "Who's out here with us in this fight?"

"Four ships altogether, Sir. Us, the David, the Albemarle, and the Charleston."

"Signal them to stay in formation behind us,"

"Aye, aye, Sir!" The officer relayed the orders to the rear of the ship, where flares and signal lights would communicate the order to stay in a wedge formation, with the Virginia taking lead. The four ships, all with their full

Chapter 43

With H5 giving them a needed break, Captain Zoeller and his First Watch Officer stood outside on the deck of U-4713, scanning the channel and Bay for any signs of the Eldridge. With her engines running, recharging the batteries, crews made emergency repairs wherever they were needed.

When the sky flashed black and gray it seemed to Captain Zoeller that he saw the Eldridge fade in and out, like a ghost leaving translucent images of itself as it hovered along the surface of the water.

"Did you see that, Dengler?" he asked of his First Watch officer, pointing to a place, more or less, where they'd last seen the Eldridge.

"I did, Sir. But I don't know exactly what I saw," he answered. They both scanned the sea waiting for the ship to again show herself in apparition.

"Helmsman!" yelled Zoeller through the open hatch, down into the control room. "Turn us around, 180 degrees."

The U-boat Captain put the binoculars back to his eyes.

"Whatever clever cloaking technology Einstein and the American's are employing, it still needs work."

"Ja," agreed Dengler, just as the Eldridge came back into view. This time the image solidified, and both Zoeller and Dengler noted that the seas had calmed completely. From a gaping hole in the side of Eldridge, smoke and steam bellowed out into the sky. "She's hit, but not from us." The comment wasn't meant to, but it stung. Zoeller let it go. "Und what's that, Sir? There's another ship. There, by her port side, low in the water."

"It appears to be a submersible," said the Captain. "It's covered in metal. Iron perhaps. It's not one of ours."

"The American's are dropping what look like mortars over the side!" said Dengler. "By hand! They're firing upon that vessel!"

"The enemy of my enemy is my friend!" said Zoeller, enthusiastically. "Let's come to her aid, shall we? Helmsman, position us five degrees starboard. Tubes three and five at the ready?"

"Yes, Sir!" answered Dengler.

"Whoever you are little ship, I will do my best not to sink you in the process." As U-4713 completed its 180-degree turn, a Junior Officer climbed up through the hatch, and handed the Captain a firing solution. He looked it over, and nodded. The torpedoes were programmed correctly.

"On my mark…steady…steady…" U-4713 turned enough to still have a good shot at the Eldridge without hitting the unknown ship. A moment more and they'd found the optimum position.

"Versenken! (sink!) "Fire! Fire!"

Two deadly torpedoes, the last two working in U-4713's arsenal were away. Every German officer in the control room had his eyes glued to the water, though the sky flashed around them and it was difficult to see. Two trails of bubbles gave no doubt that the weapons were moving ever closer to their target. In calm seas the torpedoes stayed true to their intended course, moving swiftly and surely.

Zoeller and Dengler both looked at their watches. Thirty five seconds and they'd know if the firing solutions were correct.

Unable at the moment to do much else, every able-bodied man aboard the CSS Virginia took up arms, mostly Enfield muzzle-loaded rifles, in an attempt to pick off the American sailors on the deck of the Eldridge. They were meeting with some success, especially against the unprotected crew attempting to hand launch ordnance over the side of the ship to the surface of the sea. This bought them enough crucial time to regroup and remount working cannons, replacing the damaged weapons on the side of the ship facing the enemy.

"Admiral, I think I see another ship. It's low in the water, perhaps a submersible," said Captain Powell.

"The David?" asked Admiral Brown hopefully. "About damned time."

Captain Powell gestured in the direction he'd been looking and signaled to the Admiral, who fixed his gaze through the spyglass toward the open sea.

"No, not the David. I can just make out the insignia," said Admiral Brown, but I don't recognize it. It's not one of ours. Do you know it?"

"I do not, Sir."

While the Officers of the Virginia gazed at the odd ship, unaware that two torpedoes were headed in their general direction, the small arms battle raged on. Unseen just under the surface of the water, two German torpedoes raced toward the Eldridge though the electric motor in one of the torpedoes had been damaged in the fire and was slowing. The first moved at its intended speed, 30 knots, which was six times faster than the Eldridge was sailing. When the first of the two weapons hit the right rudder of the Eldridge, the explosion sent seawater 200 feet in the air nearly blowing Rollins and Jack from their precarious, makeshift harnesses. When the fireball blew up and out of the sea the heat threatened to incinerate both men. Had they not been drenched in seawater, they might have burned to death.

The explosion knocked out propulsion on the starboard side of the ship, twisting the recently replaced drive shafts and destroying one of the two Diesel engines. Seawater poured into the compartment and only three of the four engineers escaped before the watertight hatch was sealed. But still the Eldridge limped on using the undamaged portside engine, trying unsuccessfully to distance itself from the CSS Virginia, which seemed to be attached at the hip.

Spitting water from his mouth, bitter from the explosive chemical residue, Jack cried out, as he regained consciousness.

"Hang on my friend!" yelled Rollins, encouraged that the winch had pulled them near to the top of the gunwale just before the torpedo hit. A few more feet and they were home free, but the crews needed to restart the finicky winch.

Henry and Jack watched as new depth charges rolled off the back, splashing into the sea underneath them. If the U-boat decided to suddenly dive, they'd have plenty to make them wish they hadn't.

When the second torpedo slowed, veering to the left toward the Virginia, the Admiral and Captain caught sight of it, and intuitively knew the menacing weapon, whether intended or not, was headed for them. Though they knew nothing of self-propelled underwater rockets, and they couldn't know there was enough iron on board the Virginia to trigger the magnetic detonator, they sensed they were under attack. The errant torpedo slowed further, zipped past the Virginia un-triggered, headed due west, toward land.

Both Admiral Brown and Captain Powell looked at one another and, without saying as much, realized they'd dodged a bullet, and a big one at that. They had felt and seen the results of detonation from the first torpedo against the Eldridge, but could only guess at exactly what had happened.

The ships had all repositioned themselves just enough so that the Virginia had two remaining guns that could be maneuvered into firing range. By orders of the Admiral, what was left of the artillery crews targeted the strange metal sea snake that had just fired an underwater rocket at them.

The chaotic battle in the mouth of the Chesapeake Bay between the U.S. Navy, the Confederate Navy, and the Nazi Kriegsmarine was nearing its conclusion, with no clear advantage given to any of the combatants. All three ships, badly damaged, were still a threat to each other, but all were running out of options. One more serious hit to the Eldridge and she'd go down quickly, the Virginia was already nearly lost, its pumps barely able to keep up with the volume of water coming in, and the fire-damaged and crippled U-4713 was limping along, out of working standard torpedoes, had no deck mounted machine gun, and was out of time.

*****

Norfolk Navy Yard
Confederate States of America
12:20 a.m. August 21, 1943

"This is something else, huh?" asked Special Agent Cornell of his partner, who nodded silently in agreement. "Who would go and break a bank window in a government building? Who would risk a hanging for that?"

"Dunno," answered his less than helpful partner, Special Agent Travers.

"Maybe I'm too caught up in this Rollins and Hickok thing," said Cornell, "and don't ask me how, but I think that Rollins broad and those other two bastards are behind this."

He kicked his foot through the remnants of shattered glass on the sidewalk in front of the Confederate Navy building and National Bank of the Confederacy. Most of the glass had gone inside, but the window was so large that some of it ended up on the sidewalk. The alarms had been silenced and a crew was already boarding up the broken window. A dozen additional agents combed through the interior first-floor of the bank, quickly finding the rock that had done the damage. Some 50 additional military personnel filled the area, with more pouring in by the minute.

"Well, they must need money by now," said Travers. "So why not a bank? Makes sense."

"Okay, sure they need money, but you don't hit a closed bank in the middle of the night. Everything's locked up tight. No, this was something else."

"Maybe it was some kid looking for kicks?"

"Maybe. But I don't think so." The agent turned left, then right, looking down any of the poorly lit streets he could see. He turned all the way around and looked toward the Park, noting the park bench and thick row of trees behind it. Something caught his eye, and he motioned for his partner to follow.

When they reached the park bench, some 25-feet from the bank building, he picked up a folded piece of paper.

"Hmm," he said satisfied, turning to his partner, showing him the printed likenesses of Henry and Margaret Rollins,' along with that of "Wild Bill" Hitch Hickok. When he picked up a women's lavender-colored handkerchief, still damp, presumably from tears, he was as certain and self-satisfied as he'd ever been in his law enforcement career.

"She's nearby. Come on." The Special Agents left on foot, Margaret's hanky folded in Cornell's pocket.

"Come on boys! Help me, here. Up and over!" When the Eldridge's assistant engineer called for help to swing the winch arm holding the two waterlogged men, he had trouble finding anyone who wasn't in the midst of some equally urgent crisis.

Smoke billowed out of two serious wounds, one amidships, halfway between the waterline and the top of the gunwale, and the other, even more serious, below the waterline near the rudder, where the breech flooded half of the engine room. The fact that the Eldridge was slowly sinking was something no one wanted to contemplate.

Still hugging her side, the Confederate ironclad CSS Virginia, had been trading nonstop small arms fire with the men above them. The thick iron sheathing on the top of the Virginia was proving durable, but there were so many open cannon and gun ports, that American sharpshooters were able to get some rounds inside the vessel. The close proximity prevented the Virginia from firing her cannons at the Eldridge. The blowback would do as much damage to them as to her enemy. For the moment they were safer right where they were.

Behind them U-4713, still able to somehow launch torpedoes, had Captain Hammond worried. General chaos, and missing gunners meant no one was firing cannons at the German. Still with no reliable on-board or long distance communication he was unable to do his job. From the bridge, he looked over the port side of his heavily damaged ship. When he saw Confederate sailors attempting to swing ladders up the side of his ship, like a band of crazed buccaneers, he cursed one name.

"Einstein!"

"Pardon, Captain?" asked Lieutenant Commander Atkins.

"Nothing. Just thinking out loud. What's our status?"

"Best I can tell, we've got a few holes to plug up, though those bastards keep sniping at us when they catch a glimpse of welding or movement near the largest breech. But for now we're pumping water okay, we've got one screw down, and another giving us limited propulsion. All of our weapons are good..."

"Then why in hell aren't we firing upon the two enemy ships close enough to piss on? I want these ships sunk now, Mr. Atkins, before they do the same to us!"

"We were about to launch another round of Hedgehogs at the U-boat, Sir, when the torpedo struck, and shook everything to hell back there. We're preparing to try again. We're trying to figure how to hand launch mortars at the ship on our side. We have to be careful, though, because they're so close. The first time we tried, we blew a hole in the top of their boat, but popped some of our own rivets below the waterline. Plus they're firing at us with...I don't even want to say it...muskets, Sir. We've seen 'em reloading by hand. They're actually pouring black powder down the barrel, and hand-stuffing bullets. We're firing back, but they're damn good shots. We've lost 11 crewmen to those guys. Sir, where the hell are we?"

Hammond shook his head. He had only the wildest suspicions, but couldn't bring himself to seriously consider them.

With no answer Atkins looked out of the window across the Bay. "About the only good news is the water is dead calm."

"Yes, I noticed that myself," said Hammond. "Thank God, because those swells would swamp us in a second in the shape we're in."

"Oh, and we're just now pulling in the two men we'd spotted overboard."

"Check them for weapons, and have them brought straight to the bridge."

"Aye, Aye, Sir."

Normally the electric winch would have been manually swung left and right, by at least two crewmen. By himself, with the dead weight of Henry and Jack hanging from its far end, the not-so-large lone crewman was having difficulty getting them close enough to the ship to be safely lowered to the deck.

"Please hurry!" pleaded Rollins, who was high enough over the gunwales to see solid footing on the deck. Around him smoke, confusion and the sound of small arms fire ricocheting off every metal surface was unnerving.

With limited propulsion and compensated steering, the Eldridge was having trouble navigating and making the turn Captain Hammond wanted, but Henry could clearly still see the not so distant lights of the port. As he focused his eyes, trying to stay calm, he noticed the lights glowing, flickering a smoky, yellow color. His heart sank as he realized they were not electric, but were likely kerosene or gas lanterns. That had to mean one thing. The nearby Norfolk Navy Yard was circa mid-1860s, not in the timeline where he'd last spotted Margaret. He put it out of his mind when another crewman finally came to help with the winch.

"It's jammed," the crewman yelled to the operator. The shockwave sent through the stern of the ship from the torpedo hit bent and twisted the base of the winch to the point where it could not be swiveled; it was stuck where it was. Though the rope was fully retrieved, the extended winch pointed straight off the back of the ship, some 20 feet out beyond the gunwale, with Henry and Jack hanging over the open sea.

Jack, having been secured to the first life ring, was about two feet higher than Henry in the rig. Two more crewmen arrived to help, and seeing the problem, had attached a cable to the bulkhead, making a crudely fashioned breeches buoy. With instruction from the crewmen, Henry helped secure Jack, who was still light-headed and offered no real assistance. After some difficulty, the crewmen were successful in hoisting Jack's nearly lifeless body on board. When Jack finally was lowered to the deck of the Eldridge, he was fully unconscious. It was only then that Henry saw the blood. Near Jack's waist, the top of his pants and lower part of his shirt were soaked in red. He was still breathing, but he'd taken a bullet, or been impaled by something; Henry couldn't tell.

"Get that man to sickbay!" yelled a crewman, seeing what Henry had seen.

"Oh, Lord, please, not again…" Henry whispered a prayer as memories of losing Hitch flooded his brain. "Please, not like this." He watched medics load Jack onto a stretcher and disappear into internal gangways, while they re-rigged the Breeches Buoy for the last stage of his rescue.

Captain Hammond, temporarily out on the deck just outside the bridge, surveyed the bedlam with his binoculars. When he focused on the rescue underway at the stern of his ship, he did a double-take.

"Henry?" he asked aloud. "Oh my God! Henry Rollins?" He smiled as shock and delight flooded his senses at the mystery and the miracle. "I'll be damned if it isn't Doc Rollins."

"Who, Sir?" asked Lieutenant Atkins.

"Just someone I thought I'd never see again," said Hammond. "You've got the Conn. I'll be right back."

Chapter 44

Jurisdictional Waters, Chesapeake Bay
Confederate States of America
12:42 a.m. August 21, 1864

The CSS Virginia was hugging the Eldridge so closely by design, that the two ships of almost the same length, continually banged against each other's hull. Admiral Brown realized that the great monster's cannons couldn't be fired at such a low angle, nor could its mounted guns, the very same guns that had wreaked havoc both on land and sea just 10 days earlier. In a stalemate of sorts, the two ships slowly moved in the water, generally eastward toward land.

"I'll ask again. Just where is my fleet, Captain Powell?" Admiral Brown, was as angry as he was mystified. The three additional ships that set sail to take on the Gosport Ghost ship were nowhere to be seen. The damaged steel sea serpent, slithering along just behind them, was the only other ship in the Bay.

"Are we able to fire upon the lesser metal beast out there, yet?" asked Admiral Brown.

"Yes, Sir. Just awaiting your command."

"Fire at will."

The Captain relayed the orders to the artillery officer who had been sighting the U-boat and making adjustments to the 9,000-lb Dahlgren smoothbore cannon. His four cannoneers, set at the four corners of an imaginary box around the weapon, were at the ready. The gunner shouted the commands.

"Load!" One of the cannoneers wore a strap of leather across his thumb. He tended the vent, to keep errant sparks from prematurely igniting the black powder. A sheepskin-covered ramrod, soaked in water, cleaned the tube. The charge of powder was placed in the tube and the rammer seated it. The shell, a 78-lb bomb with a fuse that could burn underwater, was loaded in last. The cannoneer removed his thumb from the vent hole and primed the weapon with a priming wire. The gunner eyeballed his target, U-4713, estimated at 366 yards away—the cannon could have fired a shell accurately up to two miles.

"Ready!" The friction primer, attached to a leather lanyard, was placed into the vent. When the gunner yelled "Fire!" the cannoneer pulled the lanyard firmly, setting off the friction primer, igniting the powder, which sent the projectile out of the muzzle at 1,054 feet per second.

Less than one second later the shell sailed over its target, missing the U-boat by 20 feet. Nearly all the crew on the deck of the Eldridge saw the shot, including Hammond, who quietly appreciated the help. The German officers on the bridge of U-4713 also saw the shot.

"Can we dive yet Mr. Dengler?" asked Captain Zoeller nervously.

"Engineering says all the breeches are welded shut—all that they know about," answered the officer. "But we have no more operational ordnance, and just seven percent batteries."

"We will have nothing at all if one of those shells finds us. Alarm! Fill the ballasts! Planesman! Dive! Dive! Dive!"

Alarm bells sounded as U-4713 prepared once again to submerge.

*****

Not quite yet aboard the Eldridge, Henry Rollins retrieved the Breeches Buoy and began the process of sliding into it. He halted momentarily when he heard his name.

"Rollins?! Rollins!"

Henry looked up and saw Captain Marcus Hammond, running down the deck.

"Hello Captain! Fine mess we're in, eh?" The two men stole a moment in the midst of battle to smile.

"Where's the other man?" yelled Hammond. "There were two of you!"

"His name is Jack!" answered Rollins, tangled in the harness. "Your medics took him below. He's injured, Captain, possibly lost blood. Please take good care of him."

Hammond ducked low as a fresh round of musket fire rattled off the side of the ship just over his head. The sharpshooters, scrambling among the wreckage on the deck of U-4713, had gone below decks, but those on the Virginia wouldn't let up taking pot shots at the Eldridge. Moments later the U-boat slipped beneath the surface before the Virginia could re-aim and fire again.

Captain Hammond gazed at the oddly flashing sky around them and shook his head.

"You and Einstein!" yelled Hammond, arms stretched wide, gesturing to the highly improbable battle and strange geophysical anomalies they were all experiencing.

"Don't blame me," said Rollins, "I was just along for the ride." Finally touching the deck, Rollins closed his eyes, relieved to have something solid under his feet, even if it was this 'damned boat,' as he told Hammond. He reveled in the irony of being back on the very same ship that had gotten him into so much trouble less than two weeks earlier. Captain Hammond helped him out of the harness and the two men quickly moved to the starboard side of the ship, away from the Virginia and its musket fire.

Hammond ordered a plate of food and a quart of drinking water for Rollins, as the men hurried to the bridge. "You're headed toward port, Captain," said Rollins, "but you should know we're not in 1943 or in any version of U.S. waters or U.S. territory that you'll recognize."

Hammond smiled, then chose his words carefully. "I think that the fact that we're engaged with a Civil War ironclad clued me into that possibility, but I still don't believe it."

"I fully sympathize, Captain," said Rollins. "I'm just glad to have someone I know share in the insanity."

As they climbed the exterior stairs to the bridge, Rollins continued.

"Rather than make for port, and a less than warm welcome, I think you— make that 'we'—should try to return home," said Rollins.

"I agree," answered the Captain, "but how do you propose we do that?"

"Watch the sky, follow the flashes and the wind. I believe that's where you came from and to where we need to return."

Hammond shook his head at Rollins' suggestion. "I saw my ship return in Philadelphia. I don't want any part of that. It wouldn't survive the stress—not now, not in the shape it's in."

"You certainly don't want any part of being stuck in the Confederate States of America in the 1860s, either, do you? Plus, I believe the stresses from the first trip were because of the electromagnetic additions to your ship, and that the vortex we created was mechanical, something we forced upon the natural universe."

"We? You mean Einstein," said Hammond.

"Well, technically, yes. Project *Canned Heat* had some problems, but what we've discovered is…well it changes how we must view the universe. Anyway, the vortex is different now, it doesn't require ships wrapped in cable and giant generators. It's…gentler actually, though potentially unstable. It could close at any minute, maybe permanently, and that would be the end of that. If we're successful in finding our way through, I don't think we'll transport back to Philadelphia, but stay in the Chesapeake Bay, just a different version than the one we're in now. I've been running this through in my head—the equations— so I could be off, but I think we'll go back to just where and when you were before you met the ironclad. In other words, Captain…home."

"And back into the middle of a raging hurricane with massive hull breeches, and a U-boat on our tail that we can't seem to bloody sink? And what about that floating tin can attached at our hip? Does she come too?"

Rollins was silent. It was a distinct possibility.

"There's one more thing," said Rollins. "I've been in Virginia ever since I left Philadelphia, and I think I was briefly in 1864 with that suicidal Nazi, but then came back to 1943. This is not the same Virginia and 1943 we know. For starters, in this world kiss the United States of America goodbye. Apparently the South won the Civil War, and the Nation split in two. As a result 1943 Virginia, and presumably the rest of the world, has become a very different and very unpleasant place."

Hammond could say nothing. He wanted to doubt Dr. Rollins, to laugh him off as a lunatic, but the circumstances of Einstein's experimental project, *Canned Heat*, and his proximity to musket fire and an 80-year-old Civil War ironclad gave him pause to believe the tale.

"We don't have a lot of good options, I'll grant you that, Captain," continued Rollins. "But assuming we survive this….this battle, or whatever it is, and choosing from among all the bad options, being stuck here is at the bottom of my wish list."

*****

In the murky depths at the mouth of the Chesapeake Bay, U-4713 had recovered some stability but was far from fully operational.

"We have just enough compressed air to blow the ballasts one time, Sir," said Dengler, reporting in from the U-boat's engineering team. "Everything except emergency lights are off. Running the engines for that short time did not help us much."

All non-essential electronics had been shut down in an attempt to conserve what little power remained in the batteries. The men, dripping from sweat in the hot, stagnant air, spoke, bathed in a dim red light. No longer fighting strong currents, the ship had some maneuverability, and its sonar was working, teasing them with its information.

"She's dead ahead, 1,200 feet, Kapitän," said the sonar operator.

Captain Zoeller clenched his fists in anger. "She's just sitting there in still water! Taunting us." He wiped his brow with his shirtsleeve, and turned toward his First Watch officer. "Dengler, we had 19 torpedoes in perfect working order two hours ago. Are you going to tell me we have none left? We've only fired four. By my math that leaves 15, plus the one special ordnance in the aft tube."

"Except for the special, which appears to be okay, all the rest were destroyed in the fire and explosion, Sir. We're lucky the whole ship didn't go up."

Almost more than anything else, Captain Walther Zoeller hated unnecessary commentary from his subordinates. Under different circumstances he would have berated the junior officer.

"Tell engineering and the gunners to take apart the damaged torpedoes and make me one that works. How hard can that be? I'm only asking for one—two would be better—but I'll settle for one."

"Can't we launch the special, Sir?" asked Dengler, daring the Captain's wrath.

Zoeller smiled at the thought. "Not and live to tell the tale. No, the G7e-UP1 has a very specific mission and target package. If we get out of this mess…I owe Adams that much. Get me one working torpedo, Dengler. Now!"

"Yes, Kapitän!" the First watch officer disappeared out of the control room back into the bowels of the ravaged ship.

*****

On board the Eldridge, Captain Hammond and a few officers assessed the situation afresh. Henry Rollins, inhaling a plate of lukewarm chipped beef and gravy, was treated as a civilian asset, and a very special guest, one with unique insight into their predicament.

"Uh, Doc. You can take off your life vest, you know?"

"Nope. I hate boats, and I can't swim," he answered between bites.

"Suit yourself. By the way, can't you just wave your magic wand, or snap your magic fingers and get us the hell out of here?" asked Hammond.

"It could be almost that easy," answered Rollins. "I think finding our way back to, and through the portal, is our only real hope."

"One day you'll explain to me just what that is, but for now how do you propose we do that with Admiral Antebellum out there, and the Nazis lying in wait?"

"It might be a long shot, Captain," said Rollins, "but what about trying negotiations? That ship looks worse off than we are. And we're not technically at war with the Confederate States of America, at least not any more. Presumably, they would like to see us out of their waters. Let's tell them we're leaving."

"Can you get us home, Doc?"

"It's all I've been working on for 10 days. Can't promise, but with what I've seen here today, anything's possible."

"We're down our starboard engine, and trying to do anything with that iron mess on our side means trouble," said Hammond. "If we separate from her it's all about who fires their cannons first. We're stuck like this. If they get as little

296

as 20 feet away they might risk firing; they'd be far enough away to do us damage and not suffer much blowback. They'd sink us with one more shot."

"We can't fire at them?" asked Rollins.

"Not until they're far enough away, maybe 30 feet or so, once our gunners' sights cleared our decks. We're in some damned, mutually-assured, destructive position at the moment." Hammond gazed out toward the flickering lights of the wharf. "I don't know, maybe it's worth a try. I wonder why they came at us, guns blazing, in the first place?"

"I think I know the answer to that," said Rollins. "The not so friendly German I shared my first trip with was a little trigger-happy. You must have noticed how much ordnance was missing when the ship returned to Philadelphia. He fired on, and almost sunk, that very same ship, and he shot up their land defenses pretty well, too."

"Oh yes, we met the German. He fired on us back in Philly before we killed him. I guess if he was shooting at them it might tend to piss them off," said Hammond. Straight and resolute, he stood up and spoke to his officers. "Okay, then. Let's give ship-to-ship communication a try."

An officer retrieved a battery-powered megaphone from a storage unit and handed it to the captain. Three officers, Hammond and Rollins left the bridge on the far side of the ship, to avoid Confederate sharpshooters. A medic rushed up to them before they rounded the bulkhead.

"Sir, the man you asked about is stable. We dug a bullet out of his abdomen, but it didn't hit any organs or bone that we know about. We've got him sedated—we think he'll make it."

"Thank you," said Hammond, who watched Rollins close his eyes and whisper thanks of his own. "What's it like in sickbay?"

"You don't want to know, Sir. I should be getting back."

"Dismissed," The medic took off running back to help treat the dozens of wounded and dying men stacked on cots throughout the lower decks. "I guess your young friend will survive, Doc, if any of us survive. This is one helluva mess."

Positioned away from potential musket fire, but close enough to be heard, Captain Hammond powered up the bullhorn and put it to his mouth. He spoke to his own crew first.

"This is the Captain speaking! Cease fire! All Eldridge crew! Cease Fire!" Slowly the pops from rifles lessened, as the order was relayed to the crew alongside of the ship taking pot shots. Then Hammond turned his attention to the Virginia. "Captain of the ironclad! I wish to parley, discuss a truce! We are not your enemy! Please identify yourself!!"

One by one the men aboard the Virginia halted their musket fire, and for the first time in an hour all was quiet. Surrounded by three officers, the white-bearded Admiral Brown appeared on the damaged deck with a large, copper megaphone.

"Not our enemy?" asked the Admiral, whose voice was loud and clear from the highly efficient nearly three-foot long, metal funnel he held to his mouth. The Admiral sounded incensed, but, due to the dire condition of his ship, felt forced into this brief ceasefire. "You are in our sovereign waters. How do you explain your actions of last week and of an hour ago?"

"With whom do I have the honor of speaking?" asked Hammond.

"This is Admiral Josiah Brown of the Confederate States Navy, acting commander of the CSS Virginia, which you engaged less than two weeks ago. Your attempt to reinstitute a blockade of this port will be unsuccessful."

"Good evening, Admiral. This is Captain Marcus Hammond of the USS Eldridge. We have no interest in a blockade, and we did not engage you in a previous battle, though we know why you would assume so. We'd been hijacked and commandeered by a lone, mutual enemy, who is now dead, though his compatriots are out there lurking in the water somewhere. We are sorry for any damage perpetrated against you and your Navy, and your Nation from last week, but any hostilities did not originate under orders from my government or from me. As for earlier today, you rammed us and fired first."

The Admiral and his officers spoke quietly for a moment. He placed the large megaphone back to his mouth. "You expect us to believe a lone pirate hijacked your mighty ship and fired its weapons alone?"

"Actually, yes," answered Hammond. "Please don't let that get out. It's rather embarrassing."

"And pray, good sir, what about the submersible?" asked the Admiral.

"Our mutual enemy!" yelled Captain Hammond. "She's still out there, by the way, and would be happy to sink either or both of us. I have highly sophisticated weaponry aboard to finish her off, but cannot do so while engaged with you, Sir."

The Admiral, insulted by the implication that his ship was incapable of slaying the metal sea snake, spoke with anger. "You fly the federal flag of the United States of America, and yet claim to be not mine enemy? Do you take me for a fool? We could finish you off this second and take down the slithering beast as well."

"But not without sinking yourself, Sir," answered Hammond without hesitation. "In this still water, we can see that you're sitting lower than you were just five minutes ago."

"As are you, good, Sir. My engineers tell me that in 20 minutes the water will begin rushing into this gaping wound in your hull, and your ship, too, will unceremoniously sink to the seabed."

"Then are we at an impasse?" asked Hammond. "Destined to both sink, neither of us the victor, leaving your port vulnerable to the submarine, who, I promise you is preparing to again strike?"

The Admiral and his officers once again spoke among themselves before turning back to the Eldridge.

"We admit to being in awe of, and without understanding of, your technology, weaponry, or sorcery—or whatever combination you wield—nor do we know anything substantial of your origin, but we are prepared to hear you further. Know this, too, Sir. Though we may not fully appreciate your tactical advantages, we know that you bleed, the same as us, and that it is only by our good grace that you are not already sunk."

Hammond didn't fall for the saber rattling and left his adversary with his final threats and his bravado intact.

"We start with an unconditional, mutual cease-fire," said Hammond. "We separate, and we both focus on making whatever emergency repairs are necessary to halt the deterioration of our situations. You may return to port, unaccosted, and we will…we will leave your sovereign waters, vowing never to return, and perhaps be given the opportunity to lure the submersible with us and finish that in which we are accidentally engaged."

Again the Admiral conferred with his officers before speaking. "Your hostility is no accident, Sir, and you have somehow hidden the rest of my fleet. What know you of their fate?"

"We know nothing of your fleet, only that which sits before us," answered Hammond truthfully. "We wish you no harm, only to leave in peace."

"We agree to your terms," continued Admiral Brown, "but we will not hobble back to port, as you would wish. We will remain here guarding our hard fought freedom, 100 yards away from you, with all of our guns trained on your hull at the waterline."

"Fair enough, Sir," said Hammond. "We are in agreement." He pulled the megaphone from his mouth, and turned toward Rollins and his officers. "I wish the Nazis were that easy to deal with."

"All things considered, they do seem a rather reasonable, friendly bunch," said Rollins.

"They didn't call it the Civil War for nothing, I guess," said Captain Hammond, head still spinning with the reality of where he was, and with whom he was talking. He led his officers back to the bridge. "Let's see if we can't save this ship, finish off the U-boat, and get back home."

"Your lips to God's ears, Captain," said Rollins, who had the sudden, chilling realization that Margaret may not be home at all. He'd last seen her on the wharf in whatever twisted universe had the Confederate States of America governing in 1943.

"By the way, I met your wife, Doc. She came to Philadelphia after you, ahh… disappeared. She didn't take kindly to all the Navy's 'hush-hush.'" Henry smiled and imagined her shaking things up, traveling to Philadelphia on her own, seeking out Captain Hammond, and probably even Einstein himself. "She's crazy about you."

Rollins thought about mentioning the fact that he'd just seen her 30 minutes earlier, but thought better of it, the comment requiring too many difficult explanations. Rollins began to mentally take stock; *Captain Hammond wants to return with the Eldridge and his crew to his 1943 home universe, yet here we are in the1860s. Margaret is, or was, in an alternate 1943, from which Jack and I just left...* trying to envision the jigsaw puzzle pieces troubled him, his logical, organized mind unable to reconcile much of what had happened, and what was still happening. All that was clear were his desires to hold Margaret close and kiss her hard. He didn't really care where they were, as long as they were together; of this he had complete clarity.

"I'm crazy about her, too," he said, finally.

Chapter 45

Norfolk, Virginia
Confederate States of America
12:58 a.m. August 22, 1943

"I have to think he'll try to return to where he last saw us," said Margaret, still sitting quietly in the shadows on the edge of the wharf. Hank stayed silent on the subject. "With all these fishing boats, it could start to get busy; I think it's risky just sitting here." Annoyed that the entire Southern law enforcement and military complex had apparently been mobilized to find them, she reached in her purse for another look at the wanted flyer. It wasn't to be found, nor the handkerchief into which she'd shed so many tears.

"Maybe the Park, Hank? It's quiet and dark there. But how will Henry find us? How will we find Henry?"

The two made their way down the derelict wharf, then along a darkened alley, passing the Rum Runner's Tap House, and 15 minutes later to the far side of the Stephen Mallory Memorial Gardens. The large park was some five acres, stretching from the beach road on the easternmost side, toward town and the government buildings on the northwest side. Not knowing what else to do, they sat on a bench, deep under the shadows of a towering pine. Hank sniffed the air and tugged at the leash.

"No, Hank. Stay," said Margaret. Hank whimpered and pulled again. "What's wrong with you?" She felt guilty that he hadn't been fed or had water in hours. She was in need herself, but too frightened to venture into a city that was out for her blood. When Hank pulled at the leash again, she gave in and stood as he pulled her with him behind the bench, well under the large tree. Hank, wagging his tail, turned triumphantly with something hanging from his mouth.

"Drop it, Hank," said Margaret disgusted with whatever old rag the dog may have dug up. When Hank complied, and dropped the item, Margaret looked closely. A single blue argyle sock, rich with Henry Rollins' scent, lay at her feet. She recognized it immediately, and though in shock at seeing it, she couldn't help embracing the bittersweet memory that flooded her thoughts. It wasn't too many days earlier that Henry had stumbled down the stairs in their Princeton apartment, wearing mismatched socks. She picked it up, clutched it in her hands and closed her eyes.

Nearly one mile across the massive park, two men, equally as intent on finding Henry Rollins as were Margaret and Hank, began their search anew.

"We'll canvas the Park, first," said Agent Cornell. "I wish we could find those other clowns to help us." His partner crushed out a cigarette and the men walked through the ivy-covered gate of the Stephen Mallory Memorial Gardens, flashlights in hand, looking for something, anything.

*****

With fully functional sonar and weak but operational propulsion, U-4713 moved slowly and easily underwater with the Eldridge and Virginia clearly indicated 1,100 yards to their east/southeast. Conserving what little power remained, the U-boat circled slowly, attempting to position itself perpendicular to the American ship, to set up a preferred broadside torpedo hit. When the green-yellow blobs of light on the sonar screen began to separate into two distinct images, the operator spoke up.

"Sir, the two ships appear to be moving away from one another."

Captain Zoeller looked over the man's shoulder and confirmed what he was seeing. At periscope depth, Zoeller then peered through the exceptional German optics and could see for himself that the two ships were indeed pulling away from one another. "Yes, it certainly does appear that way. We need to strike soon, if we hope to get both of them. Where the hell is Dengler?"

As if on cue, First Watch Officer Dengler, beaming with pride, arrived through the hatch. "Sir, we've got two working torpedoes, loaded in tubes three and five. You've got your two shots!"

Zoeller would not offer any praise, or offer Dengler the satisfaction of a job well done. The U-boat captain was still annoyed that it took an order from him for his crew to do what should have come as second nature.

"It's about time, Dengler. I want those men put on disciplinary review and their rations cut."

"But Sir..."

"Are you questioning my orders, Dengler? Surely you're not?"

"No, Sir," said Dengler. "I'll make it so immediately." Dengler began to step back through the hatch, but turned and spoke to the Captain. "Sir, two of the four Mechaniker torpedomen are already dead, shall I have the two still living bound and tied to their bunks?"

Zoeller didn't answer. "Oh, but that would leave no one to launch, would it Sir?"

Zoeller recognized the impudence and grabbed Dengler by the shirt collar, putting his hand around the smaller man's throat. "Perhaps I'll bind you, you ignorant fool!" He eased his hand away and shoved Dengler against the bulkhead before continuing his tirade. "I can't take the time to think for every crewman aboard this ship, Dengler. I'm trying to save our asses. I'm sorry if you think me harsh. Perhaps you'd be happier with us crumpled like a sardine tin at the bottom of the ocean floor?"

"No, Sir!" answered Dengler, gaining his composure and standing at attention. "Awaiting your new orders, Sir."

"At this point I don't give a damn what you do," said Zoeller coldly. "Just get out of my sight. Make yourself useful somewhere, if you can manage."

Zoeller turned his attention to the sonar and panel of instrument gauges. He could see that they were moving slowly and that the Eldridge was changing course. If his calculations were correct, and the ship's course and positioning held true, then they were less than three minutes from firing range. Zoeller ordered the crew to work up the final firing solution as he watched the Eldridge swing wide, back toward the center of the channel.

*****

"She's at firing range, Captain," said XO Atkins, peering out of the portside window on the bridge of the Eldridge.

"The "she" to which you are referring, Atkins, is the CSS Virginia, an ironclad circa 1864," said Hammond with a professorial air. He'd been listening to murmurings among the crew about their strange adversary, and the anomalies in the weather. He had decided to debrief the entire crew when the emergency was over, but thought he'd begin with his Executive Officer, one small piece of information at a time. "Keep your fingers crossed and pray that her good officers and crew stay true to their word. Are the cannons and the 50-cals manned and at the ready."

"Yes, Sir!" answered Atkins. "And they know it aboard the Virginia. They've been watching us same as we're watching them."

"Okay. Let's make sure we've got every available man working on the repair crews. Nothing much can be done about the starboard engine and screw, but we need to keep working on those breeches. We need 'em watertight if we ever hope to make it home."

"Sir, about that," said Atkins, "this new course we're on has us moving away from the Navy Yard, and back out into the open channel. Begging your pardon but isn't home our safest, nearest port, which is 15 minutes away, due west, in the Norfolk Naval Base?"

Hammond sighed. "No, not at the moment." He muscled his brain around the twisted reality into which they'd been thrown. "We're not where, or even when, you think we are. Home is back through that goddamned storm, I'm afraid."

A sudden squawk of static and electrical pops coming from the onboard communications speaker caught them all by surprise. It was the first time in hours the radio had shown any signs of life.

"Come…Bridge, come in Bridge!"

Hammond rushed to the receiver and picked up the handheld mic. "Hammond here. This is the Bridge."

"Sir…think…spotted…U… Yes! We…a confirmed periscope…15 degrees south and 1,100 yards east of us!"

"Dump remaining depth charges, train the .50-cals and cannons on her! Fire! Fire!"

The dark sky lit up with fiery orange flashes as the Eldridge threw everything it had at the U-boat. The firepower unleashed was awe-inspiring and formidable. Admiral Brown saw the ship was firing upon the sea snake and couldn't help but to be impressed and envious.

The Confederate Admiral also spotted the U-boat's periscope spying on them just out of the water, and though he'd never before seen one as elaborate, he had an idea that it belonged to the slithering metal sea serpent. He ordered his forward mounted cannons trained to the same spot targeted by the Eldridge, and 30-seconds later a volley of Confederate shells sailed through the air mixing with the tracer shells from the Eldridge.

For the first, perhaps only, time in the history of any universe, the United States of America and the Confederate States of America fought a common enemy together, and U-4713 was the unlucky target, but she wouldn't go down easily.

"Launch torpedoes three and five!" yelled Capitan Zoeller. "Hard to starboard, full speed! Alarm! Dive! Dive!"

Even as U-4713 began to slowly respond to the dive order, shells from the .50-cal machine guns strafed the water, and top of the conning tower just a few feet below the surface.

Dengler appeared through the hatch. "Sir, the power is gone. Batteries are at three percent and the props are not responding. We're dead in the water."

Zoeller clenched his fists so tightly that his knuckles turned white. "Did you launch my torpedoes?" he asked, attempting to maintain his composure.

"Yes, Sir. Torpedoes three and five are away!" Dengler looked at his watch and was marking time before impact.

Zoeller closed his eyes and smiled. Within moments they were out of periscope depth, and safely below the surface, away from the onslaught of enemy fire. All Zoeller and his officers could do was watch the sonar and listen. The U-boat went silent. The radio operator pressed his headphones into his ears, and through the hydrophone heard the telltale splash of depth charges, one of the most feared sounds for a U-boat crew.

"Sir," he said. "I've counted five splashes. Five depth charges are in the water."

The screen in front of the navigator flickered and dimmed in the low power, as did the emergency lights.

"Do we have enough compressed air left to blow the ballasts and surface?" asked Zoller.

"Yes, Sir," answered Dengler.

"Helmsman, are we able to turn?"

"Nein. We're drifting on whatever forward momentum we had, around three to four knots, straight ahead," answered the helmsman.

"And straight into the American depth charges," said Zoeller soberly. "If we surface they'll blow us out of the water with their cannons, if we stay submerged we die in the wake of their depth charges."

An eerie quiet crept through the cabin as fear grew. U-boats came by their "Iron Coffin" nickname honestly. They waited to hear or see if either of their two torpedoes would find a target. Only the sonar would give them any clue.

The crew on the Eldridge set the depth charges to detonate at 15 meters, 45 meters, and 90 meters. The first three barrels in the water were still sinking, the last two, closest to the surface, blew first, shaking the U-boat, further rattling the nerves of the crew inside. Dengler looked at his watch, back-timing against his launch order, the firing solution, and the distance between the ships.

"Fifteen seconds to target...ten...five...." The German officers all watched the sonar screen, which went suddenly cold and lifeless.

*****

Slow to maneuver, and some 30 yards away from the Eldridge, the CSS Virginia, down to one boiler, honored her ceasefire agreement. Repair crews had set about patching the holes below the water line, while manually operated bilge pumps, finally, began making headway in the race against the incoming seawater.

Unknown to both the Virginia and the Eldridge, two Nazi torpedoes launched by a highly efficient and accurate German crew were en route. The first, launched from tube three, had a magnetic detonator which picked up the massive iron signature from the Virginia's sheathing and behaved as it was intended. Without warning the explosion ripped the front third of the Virginia from the rest of the ship killing 75 men instantly. With the crumpled mass of wood and iron ripped in two, what was left of the mighty CSS Virginia sank within 15 seconds, the iron plating ensuring a rapid trip to the seafloor.

The concussion from the explosion rocked the Eldridge, and in the chaos no one saw the second torpedo sail straight ahead toward the center of the channel.

When another American depth charge detonated, this one even closer than the last, it rattled the U-boat so hard, it threatened to break the submersible apart. The concussion began to spin the ship underwater, changing its trajectory. When partially restored emergency power sent just enough juice throughout U-4713's navigational instruments, and the sonar came back to life, the officers cheered at what they could see. The obvious wreckage of a massive ship breaking apart, represented by scattered pulses of green light, assured them of a hit. They didn't need to witness the hit through a periscope to know they'd sunk a ship. But which one? There were two with which to contend.

Captain Zoeller and U-4713 had sunk 200 ships since deployment and knew how to read a sonar screen. The Captain opened his pen knife and scratched one more notch in the gray paint on the outer periscope sheath.

"Dengler, damage report."

Before Officer Dengler had a chance to leave the control room, cries were heard from throughout the ship.

"Sir, we need to surface, now!" screamed a German engineer from two decks below, his pleas coming loud and clear through the mechanical voice tube. "That last depth charge, water pressure, new breeches," he continued, "we can't keep up!"

"Confirmed, Sir," said the planesman who monitored the depth gauges. "We're sinking fast."

"Blasen die Vorschaltgerate!" ordered Zoeller. Within seconds compressed air forced seawater out of the ballast tanks allowing the still dead-in-the-water ship to surface in a last hope to save the crew.

"Gott verdammt Americans."

*****

Aboard the Eldridge, officers and enlisted all scrambled from the close call and eyewitness destruction just off their port side. They watched in horror as the ironclad sank in a matter of seconds. The crew immediately launched four lifeboats to look for survivors. Of the Virginia's full complement of 321 officers and crew, only seven were pulled from the sea and saved. Most were killed by the blast, the rest never had a chance to escape as the massive, iron-plated structure drowned them and dragged their bodies to the seabed. The only survivors were the men lucky enough to be on the deck making repairs. They were launched out into the sea like human cannonballs and later rescued.

The ship that had first been the USS Merrimack, before being scuttled by the retreating Union Navy, had been salvaged by the CSN, then retrofitted to become the CSS Virginia. The CSN would sing songs about the Virginia, marking the day she and her crew gave their lives. The most famous naval tune of the CSN was "The Ol' Virginny."

She sailed with pride for the Yanks and the Rebs,
She fought the good fight 'til the end.
Ol' Virginny met a foe cold and sleek,
and went to her grave in the Chesapeake.

There was no time to sing songs aboard the Eldridge. U-4713 emerged from the deep, even as debris from the Virginia's destruction still floated down from the sky. The Eldridge's gunners, immediately alerted, were seconds away from finishing the job both they and the Virginia started, but the 'hold your fire' order coming from the now working ship's P.A., stopped them. When they saw unarmed German flag bearers make their way to the deck, they knew why—surrender.

Chapter 46

U-4713 slowly came to a full stop and dropped anchor. Out of ordnance, except for unfired nuclear G7e-UP1, and out of options, Zoeller waved the black flag of surrender thus ending the great naval battle of the Chesapeake. Officially the battle was never confirmed nor denied. The only record of it exists locked away in a dusty file, in a forgotten room, in a quiet building somewhere in Arlington County, Virginia.

Manned with an armed contingent, the same U.S. Navy lifeboats that ferried the last Confederate survivors out of the water, turned around to meet U-4713.

First Watch Officer Dengler, and three other high-ranking officers were the first in the group of German prisoners taken to the Eldridge.

Zoeller remained on the deck of the U-boat overseeing the transfer of his crew, who, in his last move as Captain, had become P.O.W.s. It turned his stomach to know how close they'd been to victory, and to think that now in the waning years of the war, his service would be reduced to one more statistic, one more U-boat surrender.

"The hell it will," he thought, changing his mind. "I will not rot in some Myrtle Beach P.O.W. camp with the sand fleas and the fat, drunk American tourists singing on the beach." Momentarily out of view of the American guards, he slipped below deck and moved to the back of his ship, the rear torpedo room where he found Luca Adams' charred and lifeless body in the rising water and debris.

The nuclear-tipped torpedo had its timer hatch open, waiting to be set. Adams never had the chance, but Zoeller did. The standard issue timer was one with which Zoeller was well acquainted; all U-boat Captains were trained in the arming of ordnance. He set it for 25 minutes, and sealed the watertight cover.

The sea was winning its battle with the U-boat, causing it to seriously list. On his way back to the hatch near the conning tower, Zoeller met American guards and technicians onboard his ship. They surprised one another, and the meeting was awkward. Zoeller watched the American sailors as they ripped radios from their housings, discovered hidden code machines, looked for evidence of scuttling, and attempted to strip any other potentially useful technology from the ship before it sank.

Escorted topside, Zoeller's heart sank. When the American flag was hoisted aboard his surrendered ship, and photographers went below decks to document damage, it was all he could do to keep his poise. *Not yet, not yet.*

Captain Hammond was in a quandary. The capture of a U-boat and its full crew was a monumental achievement, but this U-boat was sinking, and his own ship was not much better off. With only one engine and one propeller working he couldn't tow it, and even if he could, to where would he tow it?

"Rollins, I say again, this is one helluva mess you and Einstein got me in."

"I don't know why you keep blaming me," said Rollins, knowing the Captain was only half serious, the half that referred to Einstein. "I've told you what I think the best option is. Head for the center of the channel, where this whole mess started. Sink the damned U-boat if it's in the way."

"It's sinking all on its own, Doc. But we could give the boys a little target practice."

Hammond gave the order to clear the U-boat of all American and German personnel, and to bring the U-boat captain to the bridge.

Zoeller looked at his wristwatch, and noted four minutes had elapsed since he's set the timer. He carefully checked his side arms. He carried two HSc Mauser pistols high on either hip, though it was customary to only carry one. He left one pistol in its leather holster, but had removed the other, hiding it behind his back, in the waistband of his pants hidden by his jacket.

Eight minutes later, Captain Walther Zoeller, the last to transfer from the deck of doomed Nazi U-boat, stood handcuffed on the bridge of the Eldridge, with three armed guards surrounding him. One of the guards presented Captain Hammond with Zoeller's sidearm, a treasure that is traditionally saved for the victorious captain to take as a trophy.

Hammond was unimpressed with the weapon. He'd seen plenty of Mausers, they'd been the most used Nazi sidearm for years. He looked Zoeller in the eye, still not knowing to whom he was speaking. He motioned for the guard to un-handcuff the prisoner, also customary between naval captains.

"I am Captain Marcus Hammond, and you are aboard the USS Eldridge. To whom do I have the pleasure?"

Zoeller never looked him in the eye. "Kapitän Walther Zoeller, U-4713."

A chill ran through Hammond when he heard the captain's name. A Captain Zoellner, with a name too close to the man standing before him, had been infamous for his brutal, deadly attacks on the Allies, his shooting of unarmed prisoners, and his unwillingness to pull combatant survivors from the sea. At that moment, with the uttering of his name, all protocol and conventions of war were on the verge of collapse.

"My brother died aboard the tanker *Charles Grant* off the Florida Keys in 1942," said Hammond. Sunk by a German U-boat said to be under the command of a Captain Zoellner. But that's not you, right Captain Zoeller?"

"Never heard of this Zoellner," said the Nazi, with a sneer. "Und I've sunk so many ships, who can keep track? One tanker off the Florida Keys is just like another. Who can really keep up? You Americans keep building them, we keep sinking them."

Hammond wanted to knock the German's teeth out, but thought of something far more deserving.

"Come with me, Captain," said Hammond, gesturing to the guards, who grabbed both of Zoeller's arms. The two captains, XO Atkins, the guards and Henry Rollins all left the bridge following Captain Hammond to the gunwales closest to the turret housing the large cannons near the rear of the Eldridge.

In the still night, U-4713 sat on the surface of the water, listing noticeably to her port side. A towrope, slack between ships, kept the damaged vessel from floating away. The men looked at its cold steel, all lost in thought of what horrific atrocities this one ship, let alone hundreds more just like it, had perpetrated against convoys loaded with food, troops, medicine, and even civilians headed for England.

Behind them the sky flashed, and they turned, fearing the storm had returned. It had not, but a rolling fog, appearing out of nowhere, now accompanied the extraordinary and odd flickering lights in the sky. They returned their gaze to U-4713.

"Atkins, perhaps you'd give the order?"

"With pleasure, Sir!"

"Gunners! Please dispatch the piece of German crap fouling up our lovely view of the Bay."

"Yes, Sir!" they answered in unison, making final trajectory adjustments before signaling 'At the ready.'

"Fire at will!"

The first rounds of the cannons book-ended a volley from every gunner fortunate enough to have the U-boat in its sights. The large cannons, the .50-cal machine guns all fired nonstop for 90 seconds until one well-placed cannon shell found its way into the bowels of the Nazi ship and its forward-most stockpile of damaged torpedoes. The resulting spectacle and fireworks display had almost every able-bodied American on board the Eldridge cheering, as the U-boat's own ordnance destroyed what was left of it from the inside out.

The ship sank unceremoniously as Captain Zoeller smirked, watched and braced for something extraordinary that would not materialize. Certain that the timer on the nuclear ordnance had failed, he hung his head in final defeat.

*****

With the CSS Virginia and U-4713 both removed from the equation, Captain Hammond worked toward preparing his ship. With one misfiring diesel engine, and multiple hull breeches, he hoped to sail through the anomaly, and into a version of 1943 that made some sense. While repairs were ongoing, Henry Rollins went below decks to find Jack and check in on him.

The severe damage, mostly at the hand of the Virginia, rendered parts of the ship's interior impassable. A makeshift morgue housed 32 souls entombed in body bags. With steady seas for the past hour, the crew's seasickness was mostly behind them. The worst affected that had surrendered to nausea and vomiting were weak, but back in action. Medics, and those deputized as medics, tended to some 50 injured crewmen, who were scattered near the sickbay. Walking among the cots, Rollins spotted Jack who was just sitting up, trying to get comfortable.

"Hey, Jack," said Rollins, cheerfully. "You're looking pretty well."

Still in pain, Jack forced a smile and nodded. "I've been better, but they tell me I'll live."

"That's the spirit," said Rollins, who pulled up a rolling medical stool to sit beside the bed. They sat in silence for a moment. "It's a lot to take in," said Rollins, finally.

"Yeah. I'm not sure what to think. My head is all messed up. It's good to see you, though. I see you're still wearing your life vest?"

"I hate boats and I can't swim."

"Seems like you spend a lot of time on the water."

"Ironic, isn't it?"

"I keep thinking I've lost it. Seeing you, at least I know all my memories aren't just some craziness," said Jack. "We met near Rum Runner's Tap House, right?"

"Yes, we did," said Rollins. "And you broke a bank window in a federal building, I stole a boat, which later exploded, we jumped into the sea, got in the middle of a nasty three-way sea battle, and traversed at least two universes and about 80 years. So what's not to understand?"

"At least I'm not alone in my madness," said Jack.

Rollins smiled. "Nope, I'm in it with you." He hesitated before speaking again. "Jack, I don't know if I can get you back home. Hell, I don't know if I can get myself back home. I think at this point we go where this ship and the universe takes us, and I have a feeling it may be to a place you won't easily recognize. I've already told you that where I'm from there is no CSA—the Yankees won the Civil War, and we're all one big happy dysfunctional family, more or less."

"I still can't hardly believe that," said Jack, wincing from a shooting pain. "No borders?"

311

"No borders," said Rollins. "The southerners are kind of pissed off still, but they're mostly over it. If we go back to my home, you may never see your family again."

"You promise?" asked Jack. "You think I have any interest in hanging out by Rum Runners with my ol' man? I'm leaving nothing behind. All this…" Jack looked around the room. "…this bullet to my gut, everything…it's an improvement over what I had. Thank you, even if it was all accidental, I wouldn't be here without you, and here, in the middle of this crazy shit, is better than my best day back home."

Rollins fought tears at hearing Jack's heartfelt sentiments, and found himself alleviated of much of the guilt he'd been feeling. "That's good to hear, my friend. We're not out of this yet, but I'm keeping my fingers crossed."

A medic came by to change Jack's bandage, and Rollins excused himself just as the ship jerked forward, starting the short journey to the center of the channel, where the flashing anomaly in the sky called out as a beacon.

"Jack, I can feel we're underway. Hang tight. It could get bumpy."

"See you, Henry," he said wincing, as the medic tended to his fresh stitches.

As Rollins made his way back to the bridge, he heard yelling near a heavily guarded gangway. With barely enough room for his own crew, some of the U-boat prisoners grumbled about food, water, and toilets. The German officers had it a little better, though not much. Zoeller, Dengler and four others shared a cabin designed for one man. Zoeller banged on the door, screaming at the guard.

"This is against the Geneva Convention! I demand to see the Captain!"

Rollins stood back and watched as the two guards unlocked the door, and ushered Captain Zoeller out on to the gangway. Rollins followed them toward the front of the ship, where they were stopped from using the interior gangway to the bridge. Repair crews had the floor ripped out as they tended to the ship's electrical systems. This forced the prisoner, his two guards, and Rollins up, though a hatch, and to the deck outside.

Rollins noticed that the air was heavier, thicker, and smelled differently, pungent with sweet ozone, like that just before a thunderstorm. As they neared the anomaly, the ship's P.A. crackled to life.

"Attention! This is the Captain. All Crew. Man stations below decks. All crew below decks. Prepare for the possibility of bad weather. Batten all hatches, secure loose items."

The guards, who wanted to return Zoeller to his provisional cell, argued with their prisoner who insisted on continuing to the bridge. Halfway between the two points, the guards relented and picked up their pace. The flashes, presumably light energy passing through the vortex, lit up the fog in increasingly bright, but silent flashes. The deck was eerily quiet, with most all crew activity having ceased. As they walked toward the bridge, Rollins watched Zoeller and the two guards suddenly slow. He hadn't noticed the Nazi Captain limping earlier, but now, whether real or faked, Zoeller slowed his walk to a shuffle, complaining of a sprained ankle.

Just a few paces behind them, Rollins watched the suddenly able bodied prisoner, as if in slow motion, retrieve the hidden Mauser side arm from the back of his waistband and fire a bullet into the neck of the unsuspecting guard to his right. With blinding speed he pistol-whipped the second guard, knocking him nearly unconscious where he fell to his knees before he'd even had a chance to react. Zoeller fired a second shot through the back of the guard's head, killing him.

When Zoeller and Rollins locked eyes, the Nazi raised his arm to fire his weapon a third time. A blinding flash and a sudden, dramatic upheaval of the ship, as if being lifted on the back of great whale, saved Rollins from Zoeller's bullet, which whizzed by his head. Both men were thrown into the air and catapulted off the surface of the deck, as the sky around them flashed and sizzled. The ship, and anything not tied down, returned to the surface of the sea with a great crash and hard starboard roll. Rollins stumbled sideways into the gunwale and grasped at the air just before going over the side and crashing headfirst into the sea.

The impact, made worse by the bulky life jacket, nearly separated his left shoulder and knocked the breath from his lungs. He struggled in pain to find the surface and air to breathe. When he surfaced and opened his eyes, he saw the Eldridge for a moment before it disappeared, faded into nothing, and left his plane of existence. Alone, floating on an empty sea, he scanned the horizon looking for something that might give him a clue as to where he was.

He never saw the orange nuclear fireball or the 40-million gallons of water displaced when an underwater detonation rocked the mouth of the Chesapeake Bay in a universe he'd just left.

Chapter 47

Norfolk, Virginia
Stephen Mallory Memorial Gardens
Confederate States of America
1:44 a.m. August 21, 1943

Margaret was awakened from her sleep by a quiet, but deadly-serious, growl coming from Hank. He tugged hard at the leash firmly wrapped around her hand.

"What is it now, Hank," she said, sitting up slowly, rubbing her eyes. Hank was motionless, except for the menacing curl of lips as he bared his teeth and continued to growl. She followed his gaze and saw what had him so agitated; light beams from two flashlights danced in the bushes just a hundred yards away.

"Good boy, Hank. Time to go," she said, adrenaline flowing, rendering her suddenly wide-awake. Hank didn't want to turn from the lights, but reluctantly followed her lead up and away from whoever was lurking in the Park.

The noise from the blast, even though a mile away, echoed throughout that part of the city, and even through the heavily wooded Park. Margaret turned just in time to see the sky flash and knew that whatever it was, it came from near the wharf.

The light from the two flashlights, stopped and turned suddenly back toward the disturbance. The two agents looked at one another, and turned to immediately investigate, thinking the explosion was possibly related to their search. They temporarily gave up their investigation of the Stephen Mallory Memorial Gardens and ran back toward the wharf.

No one, not even Henry Rollins, who was now floating in the same waters, had seen the Nazi torpedo. It was the last of two fired by U-4713. The first destroyed the Virginia, while the second failed to detonate when it crossed underneath the hull of the Eldridge. It had missed its target, having been launched on one side of the wormhole, and spat out the other, after having bounced around a skewed timeline, traveling 80 years from 1864 to 1943. When it hit the concrete breakwater, the detonation lit up the sky, sent chunks of mortar and earth 200 feet into the air, and carved out a divot 20-feet deep, taking out half the frontage road that serviced the wharf.

Rollins saw the explosion before he heard it. Though he had trouble understanding its origins or implications, an ear-to-ear smile covered his face as the light from the fireball lit up something with which he was quite familiar. He clearly saw the very same wharf from where he'd stolen the *Almost Home*, where he'd set out with his young accomplice, Jack, and from where he'd last seen Margaret. He may not have made it home, but he was one long swim closer to Margaret, if she was still there.

*****

Though positioned away from the bulk of the Confederate fleet, an explosion of the magnitude caused by an errant Nazi torpedo, especially with all the heightened security, set the C.S.N. and all available law enforcement into a frenzy, for a second time in the same evening.

"We're under attack," said Admiral Josiah Brown III, talking to the Navy commander on the phone. "Someone has launched a missile, or a torpedo of some sort, straight into port. I want all ships and crew that aren't already on high alert, to get to ready status immediately, and I want eight gunships out there now patrolling the channel. I think she's back."

"Who's back?" asked the commander on the other end of the line.

"It's got to be the Gosport Ghost…well you already know what I think. Eyewitnesses on the wharf saw the underwater rocket coming in just under the surface. This thing was launched from out there somewhere. Find out how and from whom."

Two C.B.I. Special agents arrived on the scene about the same time as C.S.N. and local fire personnel.

"Who's got jurisdiction out here, anyway?" asked the Special Agent of his partner.

"We do," answered Special Agent Cornell. "We answer to the goddamn President of the Confederacy. But we can leave this to the locals and the Navy; we're not going to find anything here."

"Not the doing of the Hickok-Rollins gang?"

"Oh, this is from them alright, but they're on the move. Let's go. We gotta lock down the city."

"Maybe we're safer in the car, Hank?" asked Margaret, trying to remember exactly how to find their Marathon parked on a side street. "We have plenty of gas, and at least we'd have a chance to make a getaway—we already know how good I am at that." Hank looked up at her and wagged his tail. She ruffled his neck fur and smiled. "Yes, I know, thanks to you. But on foot we're too vulnerable."

Hank seemed to agree and the two wound their way out of the Park, through the back streets of Norfolk, back, they hoped, toward their car.

Margaret found her mind wandering through the rolling hills of Maryland, and their little home in the country, but was shaken from the daydream.

"No! I'm not ready to leave here," she said. "Something's telling me that it absolutely was Henry that we saw out there on that boat, and that he knows we're trying to find him. Here. Not in Sugarland, not through some wormhole. Here."

Getting to shore was Henry Rollins' highest priority. With a severely aching left shoulder and waterlogged clothing, the going was slow, but methodical. On his back he'd kick with his arms at his side for a minute or two, stop for a rest, and turn to make certain he was still on course. When he saw the flashing lights from military and civilian authorities growing at the site of the detonation, he picked up his pace. When he saw searchlights combing the water, headed in his direction, he doubled his efforts.

With the channel in the middle, and the wharf to his left, he thought he'd better adjust his aim and shoot for the backside of the wharf near its end. In the dim light and from his low position in the water, he could just make out a rocky outcropping in front of tidal flats just before empty beach; but time was running short.

"Kick, Henry," he said to himself with a newfound energy. He added his arms into the mix, which no longer ached, thanks to stress hormones and the fear of being captured again. "I know they'll blame me," he said in a conversation with himself, looking up at the night sky. "Everybody blames me for everything, so why not? Kick, damn you!"

When exhaustion and muscle burn finally forced him to rest, he could see that he'd made good progress, but was still 150 yards from the end of the wharf. An armada of C.S.N. ships slowly moved out from the port and toward the channel and open water of the Bay.

"This time they sent the whole Navy," he said. When a beam from a searchlight nearly caught him in the face it ended his rest. "Kick, Henry!"

Most of the civilian and commercial neighborhoods of Norfolk were quiet. Businesses had all closed, except for a few random bars, which never closed. All the Navy men and a smaller contingent of Confederate Army and Marines were at their posts or in their ships preparing for a battle and a war Admiral Brown was certain was imminent.

After walking for 10 minutes, and after a few dead ends, at the end of a long two blocks Margaret spotted her Marathon. She'd seen others along the way, not surprising, as the Marathon was the only brand of car officially allowed in the C.S.A. They varied in color and style, but all were very similar, all were Marathons, but only hers had the badly rumpled fender she could identify.

"There," she said, checking over her shoulder, watching for lawmen or anyone at all. "Let's go."

Before she could go more than 10 steps, Hank spotted a leaking fire hydrant that had created a freshwater puddle with his name on it. After he'd consumed what seemed like gallons of water, he finally agreed to move on. Exposed on the streets, it seemed to her to take forever to make any progress. They traversed the first block without any problems, and she dared to hope they were home free.

"Excuse me! Ma'am!" came a man's voice from behind her. Margaret slowed, but didn't turn. "Ma'am. Stop. We need to talk to you."

She took a deep breath, and, in her head, practiced a southern sounding 'Hi, how you?' before smiling and turning to greet two men in ill-fitting suit jackets.

"I'm sorry, fellas." She oozed charm using a fake southern drawl and even less sincere, but believable, smile. Hank growled. "Stop that, Lee," she said, swatting Hank playfully on the nose. "This is Lee, named for Robert E." The men didn't bother flashing their badges, but she knew they were detectives.

"Where are you headed alone this time of night?" asked one of the men.

"Lee and I are headed home. I work for the Navy, a secretary, and picked up my dog from a friend. There's my car." She turned and pointed a half-block away toward her Marathon. "There's certainly been a lot of fuss tonight, but no one will tell me what's going on."

Not looking for a woman with a dog, or a car, the agents didn't even bother referring to their sketches each carried in a breast pocket. She'd snowed them perfectly.

"Nothing to worry about, Ma'am," said the agent. "Be careful and get straight home. You're right about there being a lot going on."

"Anything to worry about?" asked Margaret, fishing for information.

"Not for as pretty a lady as you," said the younger detective, taking a few steps closer. He stroked her arm, and then her cheek. He took her hand in his, ignoring her wedding band.

Margaret batted her eyelashes and looked demure, but Hank was not so good an actor, growling and barking at the detective who was much too close.

"Hank!" she scolded, pulling back on the leash. The two detectives shared a glance.

"Didn't you say his name was Lee?" said the older of the two.

Without a hint of being flustered Margaret answered. "Hank Lee, is his full and proper name. My Daddy was Hank, so he goes by both."

"And what was your name, young Lady?" asked the most interested of the plainclothesmen.

"I'm Dolores. Dolores Jackson, great, great grandniece of President Andrew Jackson. Truth be told, I think that's how I got my job at the Navy Department."

"And where's Mr. Jackson tonight?"

"He's a Navy man—a sailor. Just loves the water. He's out there right now, in fact." Her fake smile disappeared for a moment as the reality of her fabrication struck close to home. She fought back a tear, and wished she'd come up with some other tale instead, though the real emotion further sold her story.

"Come on, we gotta move," said the older officer. "Have a nice evening, Ma'am. Sorry to have bothered you." The two men watched as Margaret smiled, and she and Hank turned toward her car.

"Come on, Lee," said Margaret, pulling Hank hard, as he refused to respond to his new name. He nearly broke his neck looking behind him, watching the detectives as they walked away.

*****

The nearest boat, a small fast cruiser, scoured the water with a powerful searchlight. With the incoming tide working to his advantage, Henry Rollins made it around the end of the wharf seconds before the lights would have spotted him.

Hiding and resting behind a large rock jetty breakwater, Henry spied the armada of ships all entering the channel. He knew just what they were looking for, even if they did not. When he'd caught his breath he continued floating and paddling until he saw a spot on the slippery rocks he thought he might be able to traverse. Getting over the rocks was easy compared to navigating the mud of the tidal flats. He was less than 25 yards from the beach, but pulling himself through the putty-like, stinking mud was the hardest physical challenge he'd yet faced.

Losing one shoe in the process, he eventually found firmer footing, just as a new set of potential tribulations became evident; batteries of cannons and artillery officers stationed 20 feet apart, for a quarter-mile. He ditched his life jacket, and looked at the shoreline, sensing 'deja vu.'

"My God," he said. "I was just here."

Just past the rocks and the row of artillery was the very beach upon which Henry Rollins first came ashore days earlier as his nightmare first began. With the dunes acting as cover, Henry crawled on this belly to avoid being detected. At one point he could hear men talking. They sounded as if they were 10 feet away. By belly crawling south along the beach he cleared the potential threats to remaining undiscovered. He snuck up over the dunes, and across the road to the Stephen Mallory Memorial Gardens.

"This is all way too creepy," said Rollins, as he found the very same bench and tree line near which he'd spent his first night in this variant of home, an alternate universe he was beginning to despise.

"No wonder my poor Margaret nearly went mad," he thought. It pained him to think of her ordeal a year earlier and her travels to this place that was just enough the same, and yet, so different that it induced a constant state of unease and disconnection.

"And she came back here to look for me. My dear Margaret, where are you?"

*****

With Hank as co-pilot, Margaret wheeled the big car out of its parking place and out into the street, but she didn't move forward.

"Where now, Hank?" she said, really expecting the dog to give her an answer. She spoke aloud, considering all the possibilities.

"Let's assume that was for sure Henry aboard that boat. Maybe he's made it home? The boat disappeared with him on it, and we've seen no sign of him since. Maybe we should go back to Maryland, travel through that awful…whatever it is…and try to find Henry back home?" She looked at Hank, who twitched his eyebrows, and licked his lips.

"Or maybe he's still here?"

Whether an actual answer, or coincidence of timing, Hank barked loudly, startling Margaret.

"Okay, then. We keep looking here a while longer. But the longer we stay the more likely we'll get caught. So, where to?" Hank looked nervous like he had to pee. "Back to the Park? Near the wharf?" Hank barked again, and Margaret took it as a sign to go back to the places they knew he'd been. "We'll start there."

In less than five minutes Margaret and Hank had covered the 10 blocks to the southernmost edge of the Park. She found a particularly dark alley in which to stash the Marathon, and Hank was eager to get back out and relieve himself on the nearest tree.

Focused on peeing, Hank almost missed the faint scent of something familiar, something important. He walked slowly from the tree, punched his snout high into the air, but then lost it.

"Come on, Hank. Let's head back toward the water. Finding Henry is all that matters."

Covered in wet, sticky mud, sand had adhered to Henry Rollins like cupcake sprinkles on icing. Limping, with only one shoe on, he looked more like a creature from one of his beloved horror films, than he did a Princeton University PhD. Without going back to the ocean and risking detection, he had no hope of immediately rinsing off. He sat down on the bench, and took off his remaining shoe and sock. He wanted to laugh at the ridiculousness of it all, but couldn't muster the strength. Exhausted he simply laid the one sock over the back of the bench, then laid on his side, closed his eyes, and went fast to sleep.

The loud crack of thunder that came a moment later didn't move him. He'd heard it, but it just didn't matter.

Not so far away, someone else heard the thunder, too.

"Oh great, here comes the rain," said Margaret, feeling the humid breeze and cooler air come upon them. She looked at Hank. "Maybe we should go back to the car?" The two were well into the Park when the first clap of thunder surprised them. Hank shivered, never a fan of storms or loud noises. Margaret sensed this and leaned over to comfort him.

"You brave boy," she said, as he did his best to shake his fear. They continued on another 20 yards, Hank staying close enough to touch her legs as she tried to walk. When the first light raindrop hit her face, they stopped.

"Okay, time to go." They turned to walk back toward the Park exit nearest the alley when a fresh breeze hit them both from behind. Hank stopped, almost tripping Margaret in the process. "What now, crazy dog?"

It was in the air again. A weak, but familiar, odor caught Hank's attention, and he intuitively knew the unique scent meant something important to his master, his rescuer and best friend. He would do anything for her, so he barked again, and sniffed the air to be certain. The scent was stronger now, a delectable combination of rotting fish, mud, and dirty feet.

A second clap of thunder accompanied the arrival of a steady, light rain. Unable to sleep, and unable to ignore the weather, Henry sensed an opportunity to clean himself. When he finally sat upright, he heard a dog's bark from somewhere in the distance, but paid little attention. When he stood in the soft, mothering rain, he leaned back and let it wash his face and hair. The gentle breeze that had been blowing through the Park picked up Henry's scent, sending a certain Golden Retriever on a course straight for him.

"Hank!" yelled Margaret as he'd managed to again break free from her grip on the leash.

Henry heard a voice, but it was far away. He took off his shirt to better cleanse the mud and sand from his body. The rain was cool, refreshing, cleansing and he thanked the heavens for this one small comfort.

When he heard the voice again, it was masked by the dog's bark, which had grown much closer. When the big animal arrived at the bench, a leash in tow, Henry turned to look at him.

"You lost, boy?" Henry smiled and squatted to the dog's level, holding out his hands. At first Hank was nervous about getting any closer to the stranger. The dog looked for his master, but she was nowhere to be seen. When thunder and lightning crashed again the dog curled his body, tucked his tail underneath him, and walked sideways like a horseshoe crab to Henry's outstretched arms.

The friendly dog licked water from the face of the stranger who was showing him kindness in the midst of the storm. He knew the man's scent, and now his taste.

"Hank! Where are you?"

The voice was much closer now, and this time Henry heard it clearly. Overcome with emotion, fearing it was a hallucination, he was immobilized. He tried to speak, but no words would come. Hank barked again, and Henry finally whispered, answering the call.

"I'm here."

When Margaret Rollins, now soaked to the skin, emerged through the bushes to see her husband and her dog, she fell to her knees, sobbing.

"Margaret…" Henry wanted to yell it out loud, but could still only whisper her name. A second later he ran to the woman, helped her to her feet and they embraced and cried, trying to converse, but neither making any sense. Their attempts became so comical, they both spontaneously laughed, before hugging and kissing passionately. Hank, ever the willing voyeur, wagged his tail.

Chapter 48

When the reunited couple finally calmed enough to speak to one another intelligibly, Margaret formally introduced Henry to the new family pet, Hank, who was already far more than that to both of them.

"Henry, you're filthy, and smell like old fish," laughed Margaret, still wiping away tears.

"Maggs, you should have seen me," he said. "I think I spent most of my time in the water! I still can't swim! And I still hate boats!" They laughed, hugged, cried and kissed again.

She informed him of their 'Wanted' status, something he knew all too well, and of a special surprise.

"Henry," she said looking him in the eye, with the hint of a smile that comes only from someone bearing a secret. "I have a car. It's gassed up and a three minute walk from here."

The rain let up to a light drizzle and then stopped. "My God, Margaret. How? You never cease to amaze me."

"I'll tell you later," she said. "We have to move."

Henry grabbed his still wet shirt and followed barefoot as she and Hank led him toward this most welcome piece of news.

Before exiting the Park, Henry slipped his wet shirt on, and they stopped at the curb as Margaret checked for pedestrian or vehicular traffic. Seeing none, she motioned to Henry to come quickly and the three of them ran to the alley. Just as they loaded themselves into the big car a voice stopped them cold. Two men, pistols drawn, emerged from the shadows.

"Good evening Ma'am, Sir. Please step from the vehicle, hands in the air."

With the weight of the world suddenly upon them, they moved from the highest of highs to the lowest of lows.

"I'm sorry, Henry," said Margaret softly. "They must have followed me."

"I love you, Margaret," said Henry. Even as their worst fears unfolded, he smiled at the woman who'd done so much, risked everything, and harnessed the power of the universe itself to mount a rescue.

"Margaret?" asked the younger agent. "You lied to us, said your name was Delores."

"No law against lying to a creep that accosts an obviously married woman," said Margaret, all pretense of Southern sweetness removed.

"There is a law against lying to the Police," said the older of the two detectives. "Do you have any idea how many people want you in custody? I'll admit you had us fooled for a minute, Margaret Rollins, but when we looked at the flyer again, we made you. And Henry Rollins, you will hang for what you've done. Hell, you'll probably both hang."

"My only crime was breaking a public telephone," answered Rollins.

"Then your jailbreak, murder of a railroad worker in Emporia, and the strong likelihood that you're involved with reunification groups, not to mention the recent Yankee aggression here in our waters."

"I murdered no one!" protested Henry. "It was that fat sheriff from Southwood, and there is no Yankee aggression. Whatever was happening out in the Bay is all over. We're just trying to get home."

Margaret stepped forward.

"Officers," she said calmly, "we know we are on your wanted lists, but do we look like dangerous criminals? Do we act like it? We are an ordinary man and woman, at the wrong place at the wrong time. If you could see it in your hearts to turn the other way, we could make it very profitable for you."

The agents shared a look of disbelief.

"I am in possession of a large sum of money," she continued, "which I would give to you just for pretending that you never saw us."

"Are you attempting to bribe us?" asked the incredulous older detective.

"Yes," answered Margaret matter-of-factly, with nothing to lose.

"Why wouldn't we just keep your cash, if it really exists, and turn you in to the Feds and collect our reward?"

"Because you'd never find the money," said Margaret, "and even if you did, before they tried to hang us, we would tell your superiors that you'd each taken a bribe and kept a large some of undeclared cash. They'd watch you like hawks and question every new pair of shoes you bought for yourselves, or your children, for the rest of your lives."

The two detectives looked at one another, before the older one spoke.

"Suppose we do look the other way, how much are we talking?"

"$25,000 tax-free cash," said Margaret. Henry looked at her in disbelief, not imagining for a moment she had that kind of money.

"Okay, you give us the money, then we shoot you dead. We still collect the reward, we're rich, *and* we're national heroes," said the older man.

"You won't find the big money," said Margaret, "and true, you could settle for $10,000 reward money, for which you will be taxed heavily…but why not make it easy on everybody, and take nearly three times that much? You'll never find the money without our help."

A C.S.A. military vehicle its siren blaring whizzed by, but didn't see them in the darkened alley. "We're all running out of time," Margaret continued. "My way is quick, easy, painless. No one needs to know anything."

Henry, following Margaret's lead added his piece.

"On top of all that, all we really want to do is make it home," he said, "and never set foot in your country again. We're not your enemies, we've done nothing wrong, and your nation is under no military threat that we know of. This is the right move, Officers."

"I think Travers and Cornell might feel differently," said the senior agent to his partner. In the silence the two detectives shared an uneasy glance at one another.

"We'd need your guns," Henry added, "to ensure that you don't get trigger happy and change your minds after we give you the money."

The older detective laughed. "Don't piss on my leg and tell me it's raining. If you think we're giving up our guns, you're quite mistaken."

"How about the bullets, then?" asked Margaret, offering an alternative. "You produce your weapons, empty the chamber, give us the bullets, we give you the cash, and we part company. You won't shoot us, because you can't, and you still have your guns, and, incidentally, a lot of money that nobody needs to know about."

"How do we know you're not bluffing?" said the younger agent.

"Henry, please open the glove compartment."

"Slowly!" yelled the younger agent, pointing his gun at Henry's back.

Henry leaned into the car, used the ignition key to unlock the small glove compartment and for the first time realized Margaret wasn't bluffing. He pulled out two stacks of bills totaling $5,000.

"Give the nice men $5,000 just as a gesture of our good will," said Margaret. "With the rest we'll lead you to, you'll have $30,000. Not a bad day's work."

Henry handed the cash to the detectives who both quickly inspected the bills, putting the bundles inside their jackets. The $30,000 represented two years' salary for each of them, just for turning a blind eye. They looked at one another, and weighing their options, the older agent decided for them both.

"Deal."

The officers emptied their weapons and handed Margaret the bullets. She insisted they open their jackets to prove they had complied and weren't hiding additional weapons or cartridges.

"We'll leave the car doors open," said Margaret, "but we want to take our seats and leave right away after the transaction." The detectives looked nervous, but nodded as the couple took their seats, hands still in the air.

"Do you see that bad fender?" asked Margaret. The detectives nodded. "Peel back the loose metal." They did so with some difficulty, and discovered a small tightly wrapped canvas bag. After opening it and examining the contents, their eyes grew wide. They counted 20 bundles each with 25 $50 bills. Satisfied, the detectives each began daydreaming of the ways they might spend the windfall.

With Margaret behind the wheel, Henry took over the co-pilot's spot, while Hank paced nervously in back. Daring not to speak, she started the car, and pulled out into the street just as the rain returned.

"Rum Runner's?" said the younger detective, smiling. "We should celebrate."

They both knew most of dockers who hung out there, and who could supply them with women and whatever else money could buy. He pulled one of the stacks from his inside breast pocket, and then one of the $50s. They both reveled in their good fortune, ignoring the light rain.

Replacing the bill in his pants pocket, the young agent saw that his fingertips were smudged and blackened. Horrified, he pulled the waterlogged, and now obviously, worthless bill back out of his pocket. The streaked face of President Andrew Jackson, distorted and grotesque, smiled and teased them.

As the rain picked up they realized, too late, they were not wealthy at all, and had just let the real money drive away. Too embarrassed at having been outwitted, not to mention committing a capital crime, they decided not to call it in.

Special Agents Travers and Cornell, on the street less than five blocks away, would never know how close they came to capturing the C.B.I.'s 'most wanted.'

*****

Safely out of the city center Margaret and Henry were not much closer to being home. No longer detained, at least they were distancing themselves from the military complex that made up most of the Waterfront district. Margaret had a lot to tell her husband: there were conversations with Einstein to recount, her trip to Philadelphia, Baltimore, and Sugarland. She told him about finding the car in the barn, the boys in the tunnel and their stacks of counterfeit cash, and most importantly, all about her traveling companion.

"I named him in your honor, Henry," said Margaret, beaming with love and pride in the animal that had truly done most of the heavy lifting.

"Meet Hank. We're so lucky to have found him."

THE END

<u>Epilogue</u>

Following Dr. Henry Rollins' advice, Captain Hammond piloted the crippled Eldridge, along with its crew and prisoners, through the anomaly, sending them through the Multiverse, out of 1864 back to 1943, into the waning hurricane. Navy personnel in Norfolk were surprised, but glad to see them. Hammond and his crew missed experiencing the underwater detonation of the nuclear tipped torpedo a universe away, and no record of it was ever discovered.

U-boat Captain Walther Zoeller was quickly recaptured hiding on board the Eldridge, and, much to his dismay, sent to the Myrtle Beach P.O.W. Camp where he endured hard labor, before facing war crimes charges in Nuremburg, Germany, and his eventual execution.

Consulting maps, Henry and Margaret, with Hank ever by their sides, made their way back to the farmhouse at the border and its black market tunnel, miraculously avoiding roadblocks along the way. The Dietz boy's father apologized for his son's driving, and for the 'bad batch of bills,' which pleased the couple to no end. Dietz told them to keep the car, and so they made their way through the tunnel, into the Federated States of America, and to their second home in Sugarland to regroup.

Nonstop since their reuniting, and over the following hours, days, and weeks leading to years and decades, Henry and Margaret would remember new bits and pieces of their remarkable journeys, and share them with one another as if they'd just happened. Margaret was saddened to learn early on about Wild Bill "Hitch" Hickok and wished she could have known him and personally thanked him for his selflessness, courage and sacrifice.

In 1963, at teacher's conference held in Richmond, Virginia, in their home world, Margaret met a man, a history teacher named William Hickok. He was tall, funny and kind, and bore a striking resemblance to a man she'd seen on a Wanted Poster decades earlier. They shared a lunch between sessions, and Margaret was certain this was Hitch, though she never told her husband of the meeting. The memory was too traumatic for Henry, and the truth could never be revealed to the living Hickok, so she stored it away, and was glad to have bought his lunch and to have met the man, or at least one version of the man, who'd saved her husband. Hickok looked confused at her tearful thank you and goodbye at the end of the conference. She called him "Hitch," and he smiled. He told her that his friends in high school used to call him by that nickname, and they parted company.

Margaret and Henry found ways to smuggle money—legitimate C.S.A. currency—into Ophelia's household, and help make her family's and community's lives richer and more comfortable. When they got word to Ophelia about Sheriff Overstreet's true character, the strong, smart woman immediately stopped her courtship with him, throwing herself instead into her new passion, a church-based organization she founded with her daughters and named 'The New Underground Railroad.'

Henry missed Princeton, his job, and the excitement of life on campus. He tried every day for a full year to use Margaret's portal in the den, but was unsuccessful, though she could still travel at will. Since his new, apparently permanent second home world had little use for a Theoretical Physicist, he immersed himself in home study, with Margaret as his dutiful research assistant. They never tired of the mission to understand the complexities of spacetime and the Multiverse.

Some years later after the *Canned Heat* incident, called 'Project Rainbow' by some, and the "Philadelphia Experiment" by others, Henry and Margaret sought to clear their names and expunge any lingering records in the C.S.A. They were still on Confederate Bureau of Investigation's Most Wanted lists, and behind the scenes the C.S.A. had been quietly urging the Federated States to consider extradition. The Rollins put an end to all such activity by paying off both governments.

"It was really quite simple," Margaret would later explain to a small, select group of fellow travelers. "With access to the mining maps and all the geological records of home, which were far superior to what was available here, we started by sending the C.S.A. to one of the richest undiscovered gold deposits in the Eastern half of the continent, which happened to be in Cabarrus Country, North Carolina. There had been gold discovered there earlier, but we knew, after a little research, exactly where to find a few undiscovered treasures in our second home world, including a 20-lb gold nugget. Needless to say they were pleased. When we offered to do it again, and since Henry hadn't been associated with Navies firing on their ships in three decades, they agreed to clear our names, officially, in 1974. We've enjoyed a mutually beneficial relationship ever since."

Though neither Jack nor Henry ever saw one another again, they stayed in touch for the first few years, with Margaret running between them as intermediary. Jack, too, attempted to travel through the portal that seemed only to work for Margaret, but was unsuccessful. Through Margaret, the men tried to remain close, but Jack was quiet and had difficulty adjusting.

As a young man, Jack had joined the U.S. Navy shortly after the USS Eldridge pulled into Norfolk, bruised and battle-scared. He'd shared with Captain Hammond that he had nowhere to go, no family, no identification and no job. Hammond pulled strings, assisted in getting him citizenship, and a place aboard the Eldridge, serving under him for three years. After the War, Hammond was promoted. Jack left the Navy, moved to Maine, married and became a lobsterman, aboard a boat he had custom built and named the *Almost Home 2*. Years later Margaret tried to locate him, but he had vanished.

Henry Rollins and Doctor Einstein corresponded regularly for years before Einstein's death in 1955. Margaret, Einstein and Helen Dukas met for coffee in Einstein's Princeton garden the third Saturday of every month for 12 years

Margaret once asked Einstein how 'time travel' could be possible.

"Ve are all time travelers, my Dear," he answered. "Every time we remember a loved one, or revisit a special memory, we travel back to zhat time und place. Und our hopes und dreams for za future, ve travel forward to greet zem, too. How ist vhat you und Henry experienced all zhat different?"

Margaret and Henry's lives were filled with rich friendships, and a deep love for one another and for all of humanity, wherever it might be in the cosmos.

By the new millennium, both Henry and Margaret were in their early 80s, but through good genes and the miraculously restorative power of time jumping, they both appeared and acted 15 years younger. They settled into a pleasant life in the rural countryside of northern Maryland.

Henry rode his bicycle to town, and walked it up the steeper hills only after he turned 90. Hank lived a long and happy life and was buried under a big tree by the barn. He was the first, and in many ways, the favorite of many family dogs.

Margaret retired from teaching and volunteered her time in the Library of Congress, located in Washington, D.C., in their second home world. Henry was thrilled with her access to the massive library. She complained more than a few times that it seemed like all she did was transport books back and forth for him.

Henry wrote several books under a pen name that few would ever read. He puttered in the garden and around the house, when he wasn't arguing with an obnoxious young radio DJ who'd stumbled through a wormhole of his own, and tried to befriend the couple. Henry spent a good deal of his time studying and attempting to teach theoretical physics to students in college math clubs, but few paid him much serious attention.

On July 3, 2013, Margaret, arriving home through her portal, tossed the current issue of the *USA Today* newspaper in Henry's lap. It was one of his favorite ways of keeping up with the goings on of a place he still considered home, even though it remained a universe away and a place he himself couldn't visit. When he read the headline, he called Margaret back into the living room.

"Did you see this?" he asked.

"No, I haven't had time to really look at it," she answered, pushing thick, white hair from her forehead. "Why?"

"Remember back in the 1960s, and at the Centennial memorial of the Civil War, how I got it in my head that I'd figure out where the timeline skewed, and how the South won in this universe?"

"Yes, Henry, how could I forget? You were obsessed, having me check out every Civil War book in the library. It wasn't just the Civil War. You and I cross-referenced every disappearance in our world from 1864 forward, and don't get me started on the Bermuda Triangle fiasco."

"Yes, yes, I know all that, my dear. But this could be about the "three.""

She smiled. "You haven't mentioned the "three" in a long time." Henry discovered from transcripts of Civil War soldier's diaries corroborating stories about "three strange Reb soldiers," and how they found themselves at the detonation of Indian Cave during the Battle of Gettysburg. She glanced at the newspaper headline that read:

Gettysburg's Civil War Reenactment Turns Deadly. Three Civil War Reenactors Missing.

Two days later Margaret returned home from a day at the Library of Congress with a smile on her face as big as the moon. She awakened Henry, who was napping in his favorite chair.

"Henry, you'll never guess who showed up at the library today…"

www.ingramcontent.com/pod-product-compliance
Lightning Source LLC
Chambersburg PA
CBHW022206030726
47494CB00021B/1739